THE DOCKSIDE MURDERS

A JOHN GRANVILLE & EMILY TURNER HISTORICAL MYSTERY

SHARON ROWSE

ThreeCedarsPress

THE DOCKSIDE MURDERS

A John Granville & Emily Turner Historical Mystery

By Sharon Rowse

Published by Three Cedars Press
www.threecedarspress.com

ISBN: 9781988037417

The John Granville & Emily Turner Historical Mystery Series: (in order)

The Silk Train Murder

The Lost Mine Murders

The Missing Heir Murders

The Terminal City Murders

The Cannery Row Murders

The Hidden City Murders

The Dockside Murders

The Barbara O'Grady Series: (in order)

Death of a Secret

Death of a Threat

Death of a Promise

Death of a Shadow

Death of a Lie

Death of a Dream

1

Monday, September 17, 1900

As the early morning sun streamed into his office, John Lansdowne Granville stared at the quote that had arrived in the morning mail. Under an elaborate gold embossed letterhead was a neat column of figures, carefully inked, which added up to a sum that made him choke. And they were looking for his approval.

When he'd asked his fiancée, Emily Turner, to consult her friend Clara about the furnishings for their new house, he hadn't anticipated receiving a bill like this one. Or that the main rooms would require work done first. Probably he should have.

He considered the figures more carefully. How had they chosen so many furnishings so quickly? Then he realized these were just for the parlor. Surely that couldn't be right?

He reread the list, picturing each item of furniture, comparing it against what he remembered of the furnishings in his mother's elegant parlor. They matched. Apparently this was what it took to furnish a parlor.

Shaking his head, he looked at the total again. No wonder his father had always refused to discuss what he considered "household expenses."

And no wonder his mother had hired a decorator to design and furnish whatever room she decreed needed updates, if it took this many decisions to furnish one room. He could have encouraged Emily to do the same.

But no, he'd suggested she ask Clara Miles to help. He'd thought the two of them would enjoy furnishing and decorating an entire house. Which they were. He wasn't so sure about himself.

Especially since he was living in the resulting chaos.

What he needed, he thought with a grin, was a challenging case. One that would engage most of Emily's attention, and possibly Clara's as well, since the two of them worked well together. Life at Granville & Scott Investigations had been more than a little dull since he and Emily had finished two big cases a week ago.

There had been the usual small requests—a cheating husband here, a missing relative there—but nothing major. With that in mind, he glanced through the other correspondence on his desk. Not an intriguing new case in the lot.

He could always talk to Emily about hiring a decorator—one who would slow down the process, as well as taking his preferences as well as hers into account. Unlike Clara, who had excellent taste, but strong opinions.

Except that Emily did seem to be enjoying herself. Decorating her future home made a total change for her after the difficult murder case she'd solved in Victoria. And the house would be hers, too. After their wedding.

Emily was still talking about moving up their wedding date to next spring—which couldn't come soon enough for him. If the house was completely furnished and ready for her, perhaps she'd consider an even earlier date?

He frowned at the stack of mail in front of him. Maybe the afternoon mail would hold a more promising case. In the meantime, how much trouble could furniture shopping get Clara and Emily—and therefore himself—into, anyway?

The ringing of the telephone on his desk was a welcome interruption. "Granville."

"Benton here. I need to talk to you and your partner."

Well, it was a distraction. If not quite the kind he'd had in mind. "When and where?"

"My office. As soon as you can get here."

He considered telling the gangster he was unavailable for the next hour, just to make a point. Then he reconsidered.

Benton was often a good source of information, and never boring. Besides, there might yet be an interesting case involved.

"We'll be there," he said. "And this is regarding?"

"Your big fish. The one you missed on your last case."

And on that frustrating note, Benton hung up, leaving Granville listening to the buzz of an empty line.

And fuming.

GRANVILLE STRODE out of his own impressively furnished office, down a gleaming corridor and turned into Scott's equally impressively furnished one. Where he sat down and stared across the polished mahogany desktop at his partner.

Who grinned. "It's pretty early for thunderclouds. What's the matter? Your new office too lonely?"

"Hardly. Benton just telephoned."

"Benton? Called you? That can't be good."

"It isn't," he said, and relayed their conversation.

"Wait a minute. He said we missed the bad guy?" Scott said, looking like he'd unexpectedly bitten into a pickle. His partner was not a fan of pickles.

"He did."

"And just what does he mean by that?"

Granville pictured their lawyer, Josiah Randall, beaten and left for dead. And the complex tangle of legal and financial issues that they'd uncovered in finding his attackers. None of which answered Scott's question.

"It's Benton," he said.

"Yeah." Scott glowered at his desk, adjusting the ink pot and the pen-wipe on the leather blotter. "I thought our big fish turned out to be a very small fish."

"He did," Granville said, starting to see the humor in it. "Though I'm not sure the fellow is even big enough to qualify as a fish. Perhaps a minnow."

Scott grinned. "That's a point. I'm not sure anyone knows what he is," he said, sitting back in his chair, and slinging his feet in their worn boots up on the polished desk. "Other than useless."

"At least the case is closed. We won't have to spend any more time on him. Or on a mythical big fish," Granville said. Then he frowned.

Scott looked at him hard. "Wait a minute. I know that look. You're not lettin' Benton get to you?"

"No. But for Benton to say what he did, it's possible there's something else going on. Something bigger than our last case."

"Like what?"

"Last time we talked to him, Benton was talking about the fellow we were looking for being invisible. And he said something about rumors regarding goods flowing through the docks. Which he wouldn't clarify."

"Smuggling?"

"Probably. It didn't help our case any, though. Now he's bringing it up again. Why?"

"He likes messing with us."

"True. But not enough to call out of the blue."

"So why, then?"

"There must be something going on that impacts Benton directly."

"You're thinking Benton knows stuff he hasn't bothered to share," Scott said slowly. "Could be. But I still think he's just messing with us. Either way—what are we going to do about him?"

"We're going to meet with him. And find out what he wants from us this time."

"You're serious about this. You really think we didn't solve Randall's case?"

"No, we solved that case just fine."

"Then why are you going on about Benton?"

"Because his question got me thinking. What if the frauds Randall was exposing in court somehow connect to a larger scheme involving imports into Vancouver? One that's starting to impact Benton? The last thing this town needs is another Benton-level gangster."

His partner scowled at him. "You're telling me you think there really is a big fish still out there? Or should that be a bigger fish?"

Granville let out a crack of laughter. "Definitely a bigger fish. An invisible one. But one that had nothing to do with the attack on Randall."

Scott rolled his eyes.

"But I think we've spent enough time talking about fish, don't you?"

"I'd be happy never to think about another fish," Scott said flatly. "So who is this guy? If he even exists."

Working in the salmon canneries on a previous case had definitely left a mark on his partner. Scott still couldn't stand to order fish, not even when it was freshly caught and fried in butter.

"If Benton is right about this invisible schemer—someone we caught no trace of? Someone even Benton doesn't have a name for?" Granville said. "He'd have to be someone who operates entirely through manipulating others—pulling their strings, if you will. And very smoothly. Even Benton's strings, from the sounds of it."

He paused, glanced at Scott. "Like a puppet master."

Scott guffawed. "A puppet master? Well, it's better than a fish, I guess. But where are you getting all this from? We didn't leave any loose ends."

"No, we didn't," Granville said slowly, tapping the fingers of one hand on Scott's desk as he thought about it. "None that affected Randall, anyway. Except we never uncovered any connection between our case and Benton's interests. And there had to be one."

"Why d'you think that?"

"Because Benton isn't letting this go. And he's trying to irritate me into taking the case. It almost worked, too."

"But the trial was just last week, and there wasn't any puppet master in sight there," Scott said.

"Are you sure? I didn't pay much attention to the spectators in that court. Did you?"

"Nope. But even if I had, it wouldn't have mattered. Not if you're right, and this is someone we don't know about," Scott said.

"True. But it would be interesting to know who was there. This wasn't a murder trial, so it didn't draw a lot of spectators. I might ask Andrew Draper. He pays attention to these things."

"Draper? From the *News Advertiser*? I guess if you're a business reporter, you need to pay attention to the money guys," Scott said. "But I still don't get it. How did you get from Benton's taunt about missing the big fish to imagining a puppet master on a closed case?"

He grinned. "Maybe I think we need a new case. Let's go see what Benton has to say."

"It still sounds to me like Benton's trying to sell you fool's gold," Scott muttered as he followed him out the door.

2

As they climbed the plain wooden steps leading from the run-down warehouse to Benton's elaborate offices, Granville noted again the contrast between the gangster's violent world and the beauty he chose to surround himself with when he could. It made him unpredictable, which was a very real part of his power. Well, that and his utter ruthlessness.

Which had never stopped Granville in his dealings with Benton.

"I didn't appreciate your last comment on the telephone," he told Benton when they were eventually ushered into the gangster's presence.

The deference Benton's henchmen showed the fellow had always amused Granville, but he hid his smile. For the moment, he preferred that Benton think he was angry with him.

"I didn't think you would. But you're here, aren't you?" the gangster said, lighting up a fresh cigar.

And pointedly not offering them one, he noted. Benton never acted without a plan. Often a devious one.

That strategic mind was one thing Granville appreciated about him, no matter what he thought of his morals. It made Benton a worthy opponent, and a valuable ally.

When he wasn't trying to get them killed.

He considered Benton's expression for a moment, debating his next words. On some level, this was a game, if a risky one. It might be entertaining to see what Benton was up to this time. And which role the fellow intended to play today.

"So why are we here?" Scott growled before Granville could speak.

His partner didn't have much patience for Benton's schemes. The fact that Scott's sister was Benton's paramour likely had something to do with that.

"I want to hire you," Benton said. "To see if you can catch that big fish that didn't take your bait the first time."

Scott glared at him. "You want to hire me?"

Granville bit back a smile. His partner obviously hadn't expected that.

But Benton's easy use of the fishing term had surprised Granville. Eyeing the gangster's dapper attire, he couldn't imagine the fellow with a rod and reel, sport fishing. Much less out on the open ocean in one of those small, patched together fishing boats that tied up everywhere along the Cannery Row. It made him wonder if at some point in his unknown history, Benton had been a fisherman.

And how he'd ended up here.

Benton calmly met Scott's angry gaze. "I want to hire both of you."

"You mean you want to hire our firm," Granville said. "To do what, exactly?"

"To identify your big fish," Benton said, deadpan. Then apparently unable to resist the dig—or possibly because he knew what their reaction would be—he added, "Since you've missed him entirely so far."

"We closed that case," Scott said. "Besides, why should you care?"

"Whoever he is, he's become an annoyance," Benton said. "And I don't want to waste my men's time."

Another dig. Benton was definitely trying to manipulate them into taking this case. He must want the big fish—whoever he was—dealt with very badly. Why?

"I thought this fellow was beneath your notice. Small potatoes, I believe you called him?" Granville said.

"He's become greedy," Benton said. "And he's beginning to get in my way."

"Which sounds like he's your big fish, not ours. So why do you want him?"

"That's my business."

It seemed he'd hit a nerve. He eyed Benton's inflexible countenance and considered poking at him a bit further, but this wasn't the time. He'd made his point. "Then you don't know who this supposed big fish is?"

"I do not," Benton said.

"But you're sure he exists."

"Yes."

"This is the fellow you talked about on the last case. Said he was keeping a close eye on goods coming through the port. Particularly the import laws that were affected by Randall's cases." He paused, stared at the gangster. "The one we never found even a rumor of."

"That's the one," Benton said, meeting his eyes without a blink.

"And now you want us to find this invisible man."

"Yes."

"You called this guy a thief," Scott said. "Said he'd likely become a threat to you one day."

Granville was watching Benton as closely as Scott spoke. "You know more than that, don't you? And you knew it all along?"

"I did."

"And you chose not to fill us in?" Scott asked with a scowl.

"He wasn't Randall's attacker," Benton said. "And he didn't hire that attacker."

It was a typical Benton answer. And an accurate one, strictly speaking. It just wasn't very helpful.

No surprise there.

"But you still don't know his name?" he asked.

"He's hidden himself well."

"And now you want us to find him for you?" Granville said.

"That's it." Benton reclined back at his ease in the deep leather desk chair and drew deeply on his cigar.

"Before we even consider it, you'll need to tell us everything you know about this big fish. And what you plan to do to him when we find him."

"I'll go you one better," Benton said, blowing out a cloud of smoke. "I'll hire you specifically to clear him out of town. By any means you choose."

Which gave them the option of using legal means, Granville noted. Good. It meant they could accept the case.

"Is that the favor we owe you?" he asked.

"This? Hardly. But I pay a great deal better than that half-dead lawyer who hired you last time," Benton added, a dangerous glint in his eyes. And he named a sum that made even Granville's eyes widen.

"You'd do well to agree," Benton said.

A big fish that even Benton couldn't identify? The idea intrigued him enough that Granville was prepared to take the case for that reason alone. Though Scott might still take some convincing.

But the implied threat in Benton's last statement had Granville raising one eyebrow. "Oh?"

Scott looked from his face to Benton's and back again. Then he abruptly rose to his full height, looming over both of them, and thumped both fists on Benton's desk. Which had them staring at him instead of each other.

"For Pete's sake, cut it out," Scott said. "This is no time for a pissing match. You both know you're going to agree to it, no matter what anyone else—including me—thinks about it. So just get on with it."

Benton gave him an outraged stare.

For a moment Granville thought he was going to shoot Scott, just on principle. Then he'd have to take Benton out before he could get a shot off.

Instead, Benton started to laugh. "Not a chess player, I take it," the gangster wheezed out between gusts of laughter.

"Not exactly," Granville said dryly.

"Stupid waste of time," Scott muttered. "Give me cards any day."

Which set Benton off again.

"We make a good team though," Granville said. "And in this case, he's right."

"Even a broken clock is right twice a day," Benton said, but the usual acid was missing from his tone. "Deal?"

"Deal."

Scott just rolled his eyes as they shook hands.

"You sure you know what you're doing on this?" Scott asked the minute they left the warehouse. "I don't trust Benton's motives."

"You never do," Granville said, watching his footing on the uneven cobblestones. There were no sidewalks here, not even rough lengths of log.

"That's 'cause they're never trustworthy."

"True. Then why are you so worried this time?"

"Why? Because Benton just hired us. On some case that he says is connected to our big fish. Our non-existent big fish. The one we spent the last few weeks proving doesn't exist."

"We're not looking for *our* big fish. We're looking for Benton's big fish."

Scott glared at him. "Yeah. Your invisible puppet master. Good luck with that one."

"Look, Benton wouldn't be hiring us to find someone who doesn't exist. Much less give us *carte blanche* to deal with them our way, instead of his."

"Huh. It doesn't sound much like Benton, at that," Scott said as they turned onto Water Street. "Which just means he's up to something. And is dumping his problem on us."

"We're between cases," Granville said mildly.

"As if that answers anything." Scott shot him an annoyed look. "You were all hot under the collar about Benton saying we failed at this whole big fish thing half an hour ago. Now you're calling it just another case. What gives?"

"I've been thinking."

"That's not good."

"Very funny. I am still—let's call it curious—to look deeper into the possibility of a puppet master. One we might have missed."

"Curious?" Scott said. "I can think of a few better things to call it."

Granville ignored him. "If the puppet master actually exists, taking on Benton's case serves our ends as well as his. And we'll be well paid into the bargain."

"Uh huh."

"Plus Benton finally has to brief us on what he knows. He'll be sending over the documents he's amassed on his big fish later today."

"Sure he will. You really think he'll send everything?"

"Hardly. This is Benton we're talking about. But for whatever reason, he wants this fellow dealt with."

"Yeah. And us to take care of it. I don't trust him."

"Fine. That makes two of us. It doesn't matter. If the puppet master really does exist, we need to find him anyway."

"Why?"

Now Scott was just being ornery. And Emily needed to be part of this conversation.

"We need to include Emily in this discussion," he said. "Since it might overlap with her closed case, too."

"Because her bad guy did some work with our bad guys?"

"That's it."

"You're not saying Emily's case isn't closed?"

"Not at all. That killer is in jail, too. But if there's any connection between both our closed cases and this invisible puppet master Benton just hired us to deal with? Then I think Emily's perspective will be invaluable."

"I still think we'll regret taking Benton's case. But talking to Emily's a good idea. Maybe she can talk some sense into you."

THEY TRACKED Emily down at the office. She and Miss Kent were chatting with Miss Rizzo—who was still presiding over the reception desk. Granville had thought the latter was due to leave them and start back to her typewriting course again this week. Obviously not.

He considered asking what the plan was for the reception position, then decided he'd leave it to Emily to raise the subject. And wondered if he should be dismayed by how intrigued he was to learn the thought process behind her recommendation.

Growing up with sisters, he'd thought he understood how the female mind worked. Apparently that was only true in London society and English country homes.

Emily and her two classmates—as well as her friend Clara—were a continuing education in female society on this not quite civilized coast. He wondered sometimes if it was the colonial mindset, or if it was something about Emily herself, and the friends she gathered around her. Perhaps a little of each.

He found it refreshing how far Emily was from the rigid strictures of the upper-class world he'd known in England. Occasionally horrifying, but refreshing all the same. Life with her would never be dull.

3

Emily watched Granville and Scott walk into the office, looking so serious that she was worried. Had something gone wrong?

Scott caught her eye, and winked. "Benton," he said.

Oh. Usually the gangster seemed to amuse Granville, but he was a dangerous man, and one to be treated warily. "What's going on?" she asked.

"Let's talk about it in my office," Granville said.

Which meant he wasn't ready to discuss it with the rest of the team. That couldn't be good. She wondered what new adventure they were about to embark on. And found she was more than ready for a new challenge.

Helping Granville furnish his—no, their—new home was interesting, but it wasn't the same as a new case.

"Clara isn't with you this morning?" he asked her as he stepped back so she could precede him into the office.

"No, we're meeting later. She's gone to find fabric swatches," she said, wondering what the total lack of expression on Granville's face meant.

She trusted Clara's judgement, but her friend's enthusiasm for shopping could be a bit much. Especially if it meant that Granville would be living in the midst of a decorating upheaval for the next few months. She imagined that had to be difficult. She'd find it so, and she wondered how he felt now that the plans for his home's decor were unfolding. There hadn't really been a chance to ask him.

Maybe she'd have a talk with Clara about the proposed time frame for furnishing Granville's home. Even though it was also her home-to-be—which she still found a bit unsettling—she wasn't the one having to live through the chaos.

And so far, she and Clara had only tackled the parlor.

Still, as Emily seated herself at the small table at the far end of Granville's office, she glanced around her with pleasure. She'd spent so much time and thought over the layout of their new offices. And even more time on the furnishings that would work best for each of them, while still giving the right impression to potential clients. Until now, she hadn't been sure if everything would really work. But it did.

Once Granville and Scott had sat down, Emily looked from one serious expression to the other and back again, and all thought of decor fled. "What couldn't you tell me in front of the others?"

The partners exchanged glances.

"We've each solved our recent cases," Granville said. "Yours in Victoria, mine here. And all the bad guys are in jail. But both cases still had a few questions remaining. Loose ends we might never be able to tie up."

Not all of the bad guys were in jail. Emily's mind went immediately to the look on poor Betsy's face when she'd found the girl lying dead of a knife wound. She still had some unanswered questions about that day.

Betsy's killer was in jail, and the second man—the informant—had made a deal with the prosecutor. But there had been a third man —a hired thief—who worked with the killer. He hadn't been involved in Betsy's death, but he'd been there. He knew what *really* happened that day. All of it.

And she hadn't been able to find him. Not even his name. That still rankled.

Was Granville saying she might be able to fix that?

As her fiancé explained Benton's issue with what the gangster insisted on calling their big fish, and his own theory as to how it fit with their closed cases, Emily could barely sit still. He was saying that!

She forced herself to listen with focused attention. She didn't want to miss a single detail. It all made so much sense.

"Is this big fish of Mr. Benton's in the importing business, then?" she asked.

"He's someone with a connection to the docks and importing, at least," Granville said. "Benton still hasn't given us much information, though I'm hoping the files he's sending over will help us there."

"Don't hold your breath," Scott muttered.

Granville shot him a grin, then turned back to her. "If there's another player who had some peripheral involvement in both our completed cases, this opportunity is too good to miss. Which is why we've taken on Benton's case."

"Those cases are closed. Finished," Scott said forcefully. "And that's what makes this whole mess such a bad idea. Not to mention, we'd be working for Benton. You see that, Emily, don't you? Can you talk some sense into this hard-head?"

"But this is fascinating," Emily said to both of them. Then, to Granville, "You remember the third man, the hired thief I couldn't find on my case?"

"Of course. He's the one who wasn't involved in the actual murder."

"It still bothers me not to know who he is. Or who hired him. If there is a big fish still out there…"

"Granville insists on calling him the puppet master," Scott put in.

"Because he works behind the scenes? And we don't see him, or even know he's there," Emily said, and smiled at both of them. "Oh, I like that."

Scott rolled his eyes.

"And this puppet master may well be the one who hired your third man," Granville said. "Are the Victoria police still ignoring their witnesses about the third man?"

"Yes. Their case is closed."

"And rightly so," Scott said. "Your case should be too."

"It is," she told him. "Just not all of it."

She grinned at his answering scowl, and turned back to Granville. "This puppet master. Wong Sun probably knows who he is."

"And Benton may suspect it. And the likelihood of either of them telling us is, sadly, minimal," Granville said.

"But he's in Vancouver?" Emily asked

Granville glanced at Scott, then back. "That's an excellent question. We think so."

"Then that might be part of why I couldn't learn anything about the third man. Maybe he was also from Vancouver, hired here, and sent to Victoria just for Theft. Mr. Ying and Mr. Lau might not even have known his name. They talked about recognizing 'violent men' like him."

Granville was nodding. "That makes sense. And the puppet master…"

"Should have some of the answers I need," Emily said.

"If he even exists. And if we can find him," Scott put in.

"Are there other loose ends from your case?" Granville asked her.

"Your *closed* case," Scott said.

"It's just I never got a chance to find out what the third man knows. Or how he and the man who hired him are connected to everything else. I know we don't always get all the answers on a case, but I still want to know."

She glanced over at Scott. "I'm sorry, Scott."

Scott rolled his eyes. "I should have known. There's a reason you two are engaged. You're perfect for each other."

Emily had to laugh. "That's good to hear. Even if you don't mean it as a compliment."

Scott groaned.

Emily grinned at his expression, and turned to Granville. "So what now?"

"Now we have some work to do," he said with an answering grin.

JUST THEN THERE was a soft knock on the door.

"Come in," Granville said.

Laura Kent's face appeared. "You have a delivery from Mr. Benton," she said.

Emily frowned a little. Why did she get the strong impression that Laura was holding back giggles?

Laura stepped back as Trent staggered through the doorway with an armload of files. Emily had to fight back a giggle or two of her own at the martyred expression on his face.

Formerly Granville and Scott's apprentice, Trent Davis was now their assistant. In his eyes, that meant he was now a detective in training. And he clearly felt his new status was not being taken seriously enough.

"Remember, this was your idea," Scott told Granville as Trent dumped the files on his desk. "Don't come complaining to me when your eyes are burning after a few hours of trying to read that lot."

"At least Benton was prompt in sending these," Granville said. "Though knowing Benton, that's probably a bad sign, in itself."

At that, Emily couldn't help herself. As Trent followed Laura back out the door, she started to laugh. Granville winked at her.

"We needed a new case anyway," he said. "But speaking of burning eyes, since Benton's concerns seems to center on the docks and be tied to the importing business, why don't we get Mac and Miss Kent to go through these. They can also take another look at any of the companies that our various lawyers dealt with, and pull out the ones that are involved in importing."

Scott rolled his eyes. "That figures. Which lawyers d'you mean? Just the crooked ones?"

"All of the ones we looked at in the last case."

"We're looking for patterns, then?" Emily asked.

"We are indeed," Granville said. "As well as any connections or overlap between the various companies and their businesses."

"Good thing you're planning to bring in Mac and Miss Kent,

then," Scott said. "I don't know I could stand to spend any more time on those files. And the two of them seem to like this stuff."

"Someone has to," Granville said, sharing a smile with Emily. "Besides, it frees Scott and I to ask a few questions."

"Draper?" Scott asked.

Granville nodded. "And Clay Daniels, too."

"I understand talking to Officer Daniels," Emily said. "But Mr. Draper is a business reporter, isn't he? Do you think he might know about the smuggling?"

"That's actually a good angle," Granville said. "We'll have to ask him if he's heard anything. But it was Randall's trial I wanted to ask him about." And he explained his thinking.

"Oh, that's good," she said. "A business reporter would be paying attention to who might be interested in that kind of trial. But wouldn't Mr. O'Hearn be the one to ask about smuggling rumors? He's been promoted to the crime beat for the *World*."

"Good point. Scott and I will track O'Hearn down and see if he's heard anything new. Then we'll head down to the docks. See if we can pick up any rumors there."

"I'm still not in favor of this case," Scott said, but his thick eyebrows were no longer drawn together. "Just so you know."

"It beats going through these files," Granville told his partner with a grin.

"Wait. You're going to talk to all these sources, and you aren't including me in your plans? I thought I was part of this firm," Emily said, just to unsettle both of them.

"You want to go with us to the docks, too?" Scott said, frowning again. "The kind of dives we'll be going to are no place for a lady."

Accurately reading her expression, he turned red, and looked hurriedly to Granville for help.

"Where we'll be going, we need to fit in. I won't be wearing this suit," her fiancé said smoothly, smoothing the lapel of his hand-tailored linen jacket. "Not if I want anyone to talk to me. You wouldn't be comfortable wearing the kind of risqué outfit that you'd need to fit in."

She wouldn't? Emily gave him a slow smile.

It sounded like quite an adventure to her. She'd be safe enough with the two of them, after all. Even if she wasn't quite sure where she'd find an outfit like that, she'd love to try one on. And she'd bet *she* could get an informant to talk, in that kind of outfit.

From the look on his face, Granville realized he'd made a misstep. Emily bit back a gleeful smile. She wasn't entirely serious—the extra freedom society granted to an engaged woman didn't stretch quite that far—but she didn't plan to tell him that.

He recovered quickly, though. "I thought perhaps you and Clara would rather talk to other sources first. The two of you will have a perspective we haven't even thought of."

It was a good answer, but it wasn't going to get him off the hook. Not that easily. "You're right," she said. "Perhaps Clara can join the three of us."

And nearly laughed aloud at his expression, which would have spoiled the whole effect.

Besides, she was starting to wonder why she couldn't be included in this expedition of theirs.

Just then there was another quick rap at the door, and Laura stuck her head in. "I'm sorry to disturb you again," she said. "But Emily, your mother wants to talk to you. She says it's urgent."

So much for working on the new case. While Granville and Scott headed off to see what they could dig up on their puppet master, she had to face *that* conversation with Mama. The one about her wedding. The one she'd travelled to Victoria last month to avoid.

And it wasn't a conversation she could have over the telephone.

***

TWENTY MINUTES LATER, Emily sat uneasily on the edge of the Queen Anne armchair in Mama's crowded parlor. Between dread of the upcoming confrontation, and the chair—which she was convinced was stuffed with the original horsehair, and was like sitting on a log—she probably looked nearly as uncomfortable as she felt.

Mama didn't seem to notice. Which was most unusual. Mama

always noticed Emily's posture, and was quick to correct any short-comings.

She considered her petite mother more closely. Mama was wearing a very becoming morning gown, but she also wore what Emily and her sisters privately called "Mama's General face".

Mama's maternal great-grandfather—who lived to a great age—had been a somewhat famous General who had served in the Napoleonic wars. He'd had no sons or grandsons to follow the family military tradition. It was Emily's firm conviction that Mama had spent too much time with that very opinionated old gentleman as an impressionable child.

The odd thing was, Mama seemed to be at a loss for words. That never happened. Could this be about something other than her wedding plans, after all?

"Your message said you needed to talk to me urgently," Emily prompted her. "Is something wrong?"

"Not at all. In fact quite the opposite. Your sister Jane is engaged," Mama said, beaming.

"How lovely for her," Emily said, meaning it. She might find her eldest sister annoyingly rigid, and dull as dishwater to boot, but she was family. And Jane had always wanted to be married, and to have a home and family of her own.

"But when did this happen? And to whom is she engaged? I didn't know Jane was even seeing anyone in particular."

"Mr. Cyrus Bray is her fiancé. He is fairly new to town, and began to show a decided interest in your sister while you were in Victoria. He very properly asked your papa's permission several days ago, and proposed to Jane just this morning."

"This morning? How exciting. But where is she? I must wish her well," Emily said. "She must be over the moon."

"I asked to speak with you first," Mama said. "Jane's engagement changes things. Which will impact you."

Judging by the look on Mama's face, she was not going to like what came next. Emily braced herself.

"By rights, as the eldest, Jane should be married first," Mama said. "And Mr. Bray is not the sort to wait for his bride. Which does not mean a hurried wedding; he will expect all the fanfare possible. And since, like your Mr. Granville, he has no family here, all of that will fall to me."

"Go on."

"I cannot plan two weddings at the same time," Mama said. "I am sorry, Emily. I'm afraid we will have to postpone your wedding to Mr. Granville. Possibly for another year. Or two."

For a moment, all Emily could think of was the overwhelming relief she felt. She wouldn't have to deal with wedding details at all for at least another year.

No endless discussions about the number of bridesmaids she'd need, and who they'd be. No lectures on how vital it was not to offend anyone by not including their daughter in the wedding party. No more decisions about silk tulle versus lace for a headdress. Or what music would be played in the church. Not that she minded discussing music, it was the endless arguments she hated. Mama's taste in music was so completely different from her own.

Then she thought of Granville's desire that they marry even sooner than planned. She pictured his face as she told him this latest news, and her heart sank.

"I really am sorry," Mama was saying. "But the time will pass quickly, you'll see. Now, let me bring Jane in, and you can congratulate her."

Emily stared after her, wishing she could go and hide in her room for the rest of the day. Instead, she had to find the words to congratulate her sister. When all she could think was how she'd break this news to Granville.

4

When Emily got back to the office, Granville and Scott were still out on their interviews. Good. She wasn't ready to talk to Granville about Jane's engagement, not yet. She'd said all the right things, congratulated her sister… Even asked all the right questions about the new fiancé.

All the while feeling like she was going to be sick.

Wait an additional year to marry Granville?

Ask him to wait three years for her? Or more?

She just couldn't. Not either one. But she couldn't see a way out of it.

Not unless she was really serious about eloping with him.

Which sounded madly romantic, and was probably mostly uncomfortable—sneaking out of the house in the dead of night, and fleeing town ahead of pursuit. Both things she'd do without hesitation during an investigation. Or to save Granville, as she'd done when she'd gone to Chinatown that night.

But eloping?

She was still underage. Was there anywhere they *could* be married without her parent's consent? She'd have to find out. Maybe Clara would know.

She couldn't talk to Granville, not yet. Her feelings were too confused. But she could talk to Clara.

Who would be horrified at the very idea of an elopement. But possibly more horrified at the idea of her losing Granville. Which was the fear she didn't want to admit, even to herself. Three years was a long time to ask any man to wait. Four years was even worse.

But there was something else that was bothering her. Something fleeting in Mama's expression. And something in the way Jane had talked about her newly beloved.

Who was this Cyrus Bray that her sister was suddenly engaged to? The one Mama had called "not the type of man to wait."

He hadn't been in town long. Just long enough to sweep Jane—of all people—off her feet. But where was he from? Who were his people?

All questions she'd never thought mattered. But perhaps she'd been wrong. At least this once. When it came to her sister's new fiancé, she needed exactly those answers.

Clara would know.

Clara's parents lived in a house on a large, well-landscaped lot, set back from the street and am looking out over the ocean. Only a few blocks from Emily's family home, the style was very similar, with its steeply pitched roof, Tudor siding and a monkey puzzle tree near the front carriageway.

Emily followed her friend's tightly corseted figure down the long hallway to the second parlor. The house felt quiet after the hubbub that had surrounded Cecily's wedding, though she could hear a low hum of female voices coming from the morning room. She wondered who was visiting.

The smaller of the family's two parlors was deserted at this hour. The maid had been in, though, she noted. The mahogany dressers gleamed with polish in the sunlight filtering through the lace drapes, and each of the heavily embroidered cushions on the two sofas and the loveseat were plumped up and sitting absolutely straight.

"Emily, I'm so happy you called. All anyone wants to talk about is every detail of the wedding and Cecily's honeymoon, and I'm sick of it." Closing the leaded glass double doors behind her, Clara turned to face her. "Now, what is so important the we needed complete privacy?"

Quickly Emily filled Clara in on her own sister's news and wedding plans.

"Jane is engaged?" Clara said. "And to Mr. Bray? When did all this happen?"

"That's what I wanted to know," she said. "I was only away for a little over two weeks, and I've never even heard of the man. Even during the five days I was back in town for your sister's wedding, no one so much as hinted that he was courting Jane."

Clara nodded. "I was caught up in Cecily's wedding details, but even so. If there had been any rumors of a pending engagement, or if he'd been showing a marked interest in her—I would have heard."

"And you haven't heard anything?"

"Nothing," Clara. "Not one single hint."

"*You* not hearing the latest gossip? I didn't think that was possible," Emily said teasingly.

Clara seemed not to notice. "Nor did I. Which is most odd. When is her engagement to be announced?"

"I don't know. He just asked her today. Though Papa knew. And had approved the match."

"So I imagine the notice will go in the papers tomorrow. Or perhaps the following day. She did say yes, I assume?"

Emily grinned. "Of course."

"Of course she did. And when is the wedding?"

"Two years from now."

"So they're going for a formal affair," Clara said. "Which isn't surprising."

"Do you know anything about him? This Mr. Bray?"

"Not a great deal, I'm afraid. He's one of the newer businessmen to arrival in town, but Papa has mentioned him approvingly several times, so he seems to be fitting in," Clara said.

Then she gave Emily a searching look. "But why do you say it like that? Is something wrong? Other than the seemingly secretive and rushed nature of this romance, I mean."

Emily's eyes widened a little. "You don't think she's in trouble, do you? Jane?"

"Is it possible?"

"There hasn't been time to be sure. Unless she was compromised and someone found out, and they had no choice about marrying. But... Jane? I didn't think she approved of men enough to lose her head like that."

"I didn't think she much approved of anyone," Clara said on a giggle. "And I doubt she found herself in a compromising position. No rumors, remember?"

"Of course."

"But you haven't answered my question."

"I was hoping you'd forget about it," Emily said. "Because all I have is a feeling that something isn't quite right. Mama was— holding back something, I think, when she told me the news. And Jane seemed even more critical than usual."

"No outpourings of wedding nonsense, then?"

"Some. But I'd have expected Jane to be over the moon. Though Mama *was* quick to point out that as the eldest of the three of us, Jane would require a very formal wedding. Her groom-to-be would expect it."

Clara tilted her head to one side. "Your mama isn't holding to that outworn rule, the one that says the eldest daughter has to marry first, is she?"

"I'm afraid so."

"And what, exactly, does that mean for you and Mr. Granville?"

"We'll have to wait."

Clara's blue eyes grew wide and her generous lips set firmly. "But that means... You'll have to delay your own wedding plans by another *year*?"

"I'm afraid so," Emily said. "And Mama said a year at best, too."

"So three, or even four years before you can marry? But that isn't fair!"

"I know. I'm glad to avoid all the details Mama's been pestering me with, but Clara! I'm so afraid Granville won't wait for me that long. I'm not sure I can wait, either."

Clara reached over and patted her hand. "Don't be silly. Of course he'll wait for you. But still… there must be another way."

"Now that Granville has the house, he's been talking about moving up our wedding date. And I was beginning to like the idea. I even planned to talk to Mama about whether a wedding next spring would be possible. And now this! Three or four *years*? I'd rather elope."

To Emily's surprise, Clara nodded, not looking in the least shocked. "It's a reasonable solution to an impossible situation. If you really think your Mama will hold firmly to her timeframe."

"You know how she is. Once she's made up her mind, nothing short of a volcano exploding will move her."

"I think one of my mother's cousin's daughters eloped a few years ago. I shall have to find out more," Clara said. "If you're really serious, that is?"

"I think I might be," Emily said softly. "Unless…"

"Unless?"

"Unless there really is something wrong with Jane's engagement," she said in a rush. "Mama can have some very fixed notions, but she isn't often completely unreasonable. And asking Granville and I to wait four years…"

"That isn't reasonable," Clara agreed, her head tilted to one side as she stared at Emily. "You think she's uneasy about this Mr. Bray, and using your wedding date as a way to get you to look into him, do you?"

"How did you know? That's exactly what I'm wondering," Emily said. "Her mind works that way—when I was younger, it used to take me months sometimes to figure out what she was really up to."

"Then this should be amusing," Clara said gleefully.

"But what if I'm wrong? I don't want to be the one to destroy my sister's engagement, her chance of happiness. Just because I'm afraid of losing Granville."

"You don't want to see her married to a bounder, either," Clara said briskly. "Come, you know your father is wealthy. Your sister's dowry must be substantial. And we know too little of this man."

"So what are you suggesting?" Emily asked. Half hoping and half fearing her answer.

"You're the one who wants to be a detective. And you just solved a murder case, didn't you? So, you investigate."

"But he's my sister's fiancé. How can I ask prying questions about him?"

Her friend gave her a shrewd look. "How can you not?"

Clara knew her too well.

Time for a change of subject. "Then we'll investigate Mr. Bray," Emily said briskly. "You'll help?"

"Of course. I am clearly behind on my gossip, in any case."

"Thank you. And I think we should start by talking to Tim O'Hearn."

Clara gave her an uneasy look. "Are you matchmaking?"

Actually she hadn't thought of it. But now that Clara mentioned it, it was a good idea. "Why? Do I need to?"

"I don't know what you mean," Clara said.

"Oh yes, you do. You just don't want to admit it. Which means things aren't going well between the two of you."

"There's nothing to go well," Clara said, looking away. "Papa would never approve. Tim's not the son of some lord like your Mr. Granville."

Emily ignored that comment as the trap it was. "Don't you miss him?"

"I miss being involved in investigations. I thought I'd suffocate on all the details for my sister's wedding," Clara said, to Emily's astonishment. "But that that's all I miss."

That would do for now. "Good. Then we have two investigations to work on. And Mr. O'Hearn would be a good person for us to start with on both of them."

"Two? Mr. Bray and who else?"

Emily filled her in on the discussion she'd had earlier with Granville and Scott. "So we're looking into the puppet master," she finished.

"Let me see if I have this straight," Clara said. "This puppet master. He's the one you think might have hired the thief—the third man you couldn't find on your Victoria case. I know that didn't sit well with you. And this new case gives you an excuse to keep looking for him, doesn't it?"

"It might," Emily said carefully. "Though sometimes there are loose threads after a case is closed. I just have to accept that. The man who killed poor Betsy is in jail, after all."

Clara gave her a shrewd look. "And have you accepted that?"

"Well…" She hadn't realized that Clara had understood exactly how hard it had been for her, not tying up every single threat on her first solo case. Though she should have known—it was Clara, after all.

"That's what I thought," Clara said.

"It can't hurt to ask a few questions."

"You always say that," her friend said. "And then you drag me along with you."

"You said you missed investigating."

"I do miss it. But this is two new cases you want to work on," Clara said. "And we're still working on the decor for Mr. Granville's house. Which I'm enjoying. We can't work on that and *two* new investigations."

"Of course we can."

"But it will take much longer to finish decorating the house," Clara protested.

"Unless we can prove there is something wrong with Mr. Bray, we have at least three years to finish that decorating project," Emily said, that reality hitting her all at once.

Clara gave her a weighing look, then nodded. "Fine. When do we start?"

"Now would be best," Emily said.

She didn't want to go back to the office today. She still wasn't ready to face Granville with the news about their wedding.

5

Granville tracked Andrew Draper down at the Terminal City Club. Since today's business was confidential, he sent a message to the reporter to join him and Scott—whom he'd signed in as a guest—in the wood paneled comfort of the cigar-scented smoking room. Which was currently empty except for the two of them.

As the dapper reporter joined them, he looked from one to the other and smiled. "You have a new case, don't you? And you want my help," he said as he sat down in the black leather club chair facing theirs.

"We have. And we do," Granville said. "Except this time, we can't tell you much. Not yet, anyway."

"Now you have my attention," Draper said. "Not least because I did so well out of your last case."

"I saw the headlines. Congratulations," he said. "It was a good story."

"Thank you. I had good material to work with, thanks to you two." Draper leaned forward, his intent gaze going from him to Scott and back again. "If this case is going to be even half as good, then I'm interested."

"It may be nothing," he began.

"Probably is nothing," Scott said.

Granville ignored the remark. "But if this case turns out to be something, it may make an even better story than the last one," he told the reporter.

"Same terms as before, then?"

He nodded. "It will be a shared exclusive, though. We'll be bringing in O'Hearn as well, as we did on the salmon cannery case. Is that going to be an issue?"

"Not at all. We worked well together on that story. He's still green, but he's sharp, and getting better by the story. And those headlines didn't hurt either of us," he added with a smile.

"I'll also need your word that you won't print anything until the case is done."

"You have it. And I'm in. What did you need to know?"

"The names of anyone you noticed in the gallery during the Peabody vs. Randall trial."

"Now I'm intrigued," Draper said, fingering his luxuriant mustache. "You want to know everyone who was there?"

"No, I'm primarily interested in anyone you might have paid particular attention to. In your official capacity."

"So. You're looking at business men, or at least anyone connected to money and business," Draper said. "And ones who attended the Peabody vs. Randall trial. Now why?"

"Never mind why," Scott said. "Who'd you take notice of? If anyone."

"It would help to know what direction you're looking in, at least," Draper countered.

Scott frowned at him.

Granville hid a grin to see his partner getting drawn into the case, despite his protests. "We're not sure ourselves," he said. "So we're reluctant to be too specific this early in the case."

"We need to cast a wide net," Scott put in with a grin of his own. "To catch a bigger fish, you see."

Granville rolled his eyes at Scott's less than subtle humor. "What I can tell you," he said to the reporter. "Is that we think there's a connection to goods imported through the port. Though it may be a well-hidden one."

"Then you are likely looking for the man funding the operation, and not the man running it?" Draper said.

"That's one possibility. But probably not the only one."

"Good enough," Draper said. "For now, at least. I'll have to consult my notes, and then I can give you a list."

"Does anyone spring to mind? Perhaps someone you took particular note of at the time?" Granville asked.

Their puppet master wouldn't have missed that trial. And surely Draper would have noted him? Though he suspected it was equally possible that the puppet master was someone that even Draper would have overlooked entirely.

Draper nodded slowly. "It was not a well-attended trial, as you'll recall. So there were several men I was surprised to see in attendance."

"Such as?"

Draper gave him three names, which Granville took note of. "Why those three?"

"All of them run successful businesses. I couldn't see how that trial would be of interest to them," Draper said. "But all of them have some connection to the importing business. Does that help?"

"It might," Granville said. A thought struck him. "Was there anyone attending in a social rather than a business context? Perhaps in a group? Or with his wife?"

"No one who stood out. I'd have to check my notes, but I do believe there were one or two others that might apply to," Draper said. Then he gave Granville a significant look. "Including Mr. Bray."

"And who is Mr. Bray?" he asked.

Draper looked surprised. "You don't know?"

"Never heard of the fellow. Why?"

"Because I have it on good authority that he just became affianced to your own fiancée's sister."

Granville thought back to the day of the trial. Emily hadn't so much as mentioned the fellow being there. Or even greeted him. Nor had she said a word about her sister dating anyone.

Something strange was going on there. Was it possible she hadn't known about the relationship?

"Just how good is your informant?" he asked Draper.

"The notice will be in tomorrow's paper," the reporter said. "I've seen it."

Granville pictured Jane Turner's tight lips and the arrogant tilt of Miriam's chin, and wondered which sister was engaged. He wanted to ask if the announcement could be a hoax, but he'd already said too much.

"I'll get back to you with those names," Draper said, after an assessing look at him.

"We'll look forward to it," Granville said.

He needed to talk to Emily.

But first he wanted to talk to Daniels about smuggling. And O'Hearn as well.

SINCE THE OFFICES of the *World* were on their way to the police station, Granville decided to stop there first. A harried looking reporter told them Tim O'Hearn was out for the afternoon. "Probably chasing another headline," he said bitterly.

Granville considered leaving a note, but doubted this fellow would deliver it. He'd call O'Hearn later.

"On to police headquarters?" he asked Scott, who nodded.

Clay Daniels wasn't in, either, but the officer behind the desk recognized them. "He'll likely want to talk to you," he said. "You can find him walking his beat. This time o'day," he glanced at the large clock on the far wall, "you can find him down the docks. Try along Alexander near the Ironworks."

Granville thanked him and they headed out.

They finally found Daniels in full uniform further out along the docks, near the Hastings Mill. The salty ocean air was sharp with the scent of fresh cut timber, and there were several ships docked waiting for the piles of lumber to be loaded.

The policeman smiled to see them. "You two bringing me more work?"

"Not yet," Granville said. "Actually, we might save you some. For now, at least."

"So you want information, then," Daniels concluded with a nod. "What is it this time?"

"Smuggling," Scott said. "Especially down here."

"Smuggling," Daniels repeated thoughtfully. "Things seem pretty quiet. There's not much going on, as far as I know. What were you expecting?"

"Not here," Granville said. "You eaten luncheon yet?"

"At this hour? Of course."

"Then can we buy you a cup of coffee?"

"I wouldn't say no."

"Where's good?"

"I'm done here anyway. Come on." With a grin, Daniels beckoned them to follow, and headed back along Alexander Street.

He led them into one of the nondescript taverns that lined the waterfront and sat down at a table at the back. This place was just as grimy, just as smoky and smelled as strongly of stale beer as any of them. Granville didn't have much hope for the coffee, but since he was here for the information, he didn't much care.

The coffee surprised him. And their guide's grin grew wider as Granville drank another mouthful, just to be sure he wasn't imagining the first.

"That's why I come here," Daniels said. "The cook here used to work on one of those tramp steamers. He picked up some tricks. His coffee is the best of 'em. He won't tell me what he puts in it, but it somehow turns burnt tavern coffee into something different."

"He certainly does. What's the name of this place?" Granville asked.

"The Docksider."

"Not very imaginative," Scott said.

"Try the coffee," he said.

"I'm not as fond of coffee as you are," Scott said, lifting his cup.

Granville watched with amusement at the look of shock on his partner's face as that slightly spicy, slightly sweet flavor hit his taste buds. "Told you."

"I could drink this stuff," his partner said.

"Good. Because we'll be back here." He turned back to Daniels. "Any of the food good here?"

"It doesn't match the coffee," Daniels said. "But it's a cut above the usual fare. Especially any dish from the Far East. In fact, if you don't recognize a dish, it's probably going to be good."

"You sure you're not hungry? Since we're here."

"Well. I could use a bowl of noodles. The beef ones."

Scott gave him a skeptical look. "In this weather?"

The police officer laughed. "Try it. You'll see."

Granville signaled the bartender, who doubled as a waiter, and held up three fingers. "What he orders."

Daniels rattled off something incomprehensible. The bartender grinned, and yelled something into the kitchen.

"Good enough. And thanks for the tip," Granville said. "Now, about that smuggling."

"What are you looking into?"

"At the moment we're chasing rumors."

"You are? That's not your usual style," Daniels considered him for a moment. "So this isn't something you're talking to me about officially?"

"No. It's a long way from that."

"And your client?"

"Confidential."

"Your sources?"

"Also confidential. But several have solid connections, if sometimes questionable reliability."

"So what do you want from me?" Daniels asked.

"I'm looking for what seem to be unconnected pieces," he said. "Rumors, petty thefts, burglaries, physical attacks. Anything that's been happening in this part of town. And especially if some of it is concentrated in one area. Or if it's increasing."

"You're talking about pockets of crime?" Daniels said.

"That's it." It was a good description—one he'd have to remember.

"So what's behind your interest in these particular pockets? You must suspect an organization of some kind."

Which is why Granville appreciated working with Daniels. "There may well be one, but it's a person I'm looking for. Let me tell you the story of a puppet master."

"A puppet master?"

"He operates behind the scenes, manipulating others, and orchestrating a theft here, maybe a beating there. Providing money, or men, or a plan. Whatever is needed. And does so anonymously." Granville paused as three bowls of noodles were slapped onto the table, along with a small bottle of some kind of red sauce with Asian characters on the grimy label.

"Hot sauce," Daniels said, grabbing the bottle and giving it several hard shakes above the bowl.

He was used to spicy curries, but something about the size of the bottle made Granville wary. He shook one drop of the stuff into his bowl, stirred, and spooned up a mouthful.

And had a second to taste chilis with an unfamiliar spice—then he thought his mouth was going to scorch.

Scott had been reaching for the hot sauce, but glanced at Granville's face, and moved his hand back. Daniels grinned a little, and spooned up another mouthful of his noodles, which he ate with evident enjoyment.

Cautiously, Granville stirred his noodles even more thoroughly, and tried another mouthful. Not bad. In fact, it was very tasty. Next time he'd leave off the hot sauce. Although it did seem to counteract the heat of the room. And on a cold, wet day? Then that burn might be very welcome.

"You were talking about a puppet master, I believe?" Daniels said. "If this guy's invisible, how do you know he even exists?"

"I don't," Granville said. "I've been told he does, but that information may be unreliable, since I haven't yet worked out the informant's motives."

Scott paused in demolishing his noodles long enough to snort derisively at that. "His motives? His own interests."

"Exactly," Granville said. "And we don't know what his interests are, in this case. Only what he says they are."

"And what does he say they are?" Daniels asked.

"Stopping the puppet master from treading on his own turf."

"Which would be smuggling?"

"It's one possibility. Importing, anyway."

"Legally?"

"That would be the question."

There was a little silence.

"So you're fishing in the dark, basically," Daniels said.

"We are."

"And you're hoping I'll know something that will help?"

"No," Granville said. "We're alerting you to something that, if it does exist, is spreading like some unknown disease through this area. And could be just as deadly."

White lines appeared around Daniel's mouth. "I'm just one officer. And you know about the ongoing investigation into our Chief. Credibility is not exactly the police force's strong point at the moment. What are you hoping I can do?"

"You're the one who's here. You're walking this beat every day. If this puppet master and his schemes are real—and I'm increasingly inclined to believe they are," Granville said. "Then you're uniquely positioned to spot his tracks—those pockets, if you will—and to see hints of the larger plan behind it all."

"Whatever that plan may be?" Daniels said.

"It will be about profit," Granville said. "It always is."

6

E mily found the familiar decor at Stroh's Teashop comforting at a time like this. She'd even been able to request her favorite table—the one in a back corner with a large palm giving them some measure of privacy from the interest and gossip of the other patrons. And Clara was always happy to come here for the pastries, especially their afternoon tea with scones.

Emily paid no attention to the tinkling of the bell over the door, until the murmur of voices spiked louder, a ripple of sound moving towards their table. "I think your friend is here."

Clara set down her teacup carefully in its dainty saucer. "He's as much your friend as mine."

"Not by his choice, though," Emily countered, and looked up to greet the young reporter.

He was probably only five years younger than Granville—and nearly the same number older than her—but Tim O'Hearn always seemed more like her contemporary than Granville's.

Though as she watched him walk towards their table, red hair flaming and his eyes fixed on Clara's profile, she noted changes since she'd last seen him. His face seemed a bit more angular, his expression a little less open. Suddenly he seemed older, more confident.

She wondered if working with Mr. Draper on reporting the Sinclair case had anything to do with that. Or was it his feelings for Clara that were maturing him so quickly?

She darted a quick glance at her friend, but Clara's face—with her gaze fixed on her half-empty teacup—was unreadable.

Once O'Hearn was seated and his tea poured, Emily nodded to their waitress, who brought out the three-tiered cake stand that held dainty sandwiches, scones and slices of cake. She was pleased to see Clara's glee at the tray of imported Devon cream and thick strawberry preserves.

To Emily's amusement, O'Hearn reacted to this female ritual with easy acceptance, though the dainty ham and melon quarter sandwich with the crusts cut off looked ridiculous in his large hand. She glanced over at Clara to share the joke, but Clara was too busily ignoring the reporter to notice. Perhaps a little matchmaking was needed here.

But not until after she'd learned what she needed for their cases, Emily decided, leaning forward a little. "Mr. O'Hearn..." she began.

"It's Tim, remember," he said with his easy smile. "Surely it hasn't been that long since I've seen you?"

Not measured in weeks, perhaps. But he'd changed a good deal in that time. She wondered again what had happened, to put that look in his eye and have Clara ignoring him so industriously.

"It feels longer," she said diplomatically.

He nodded. "I've heard rumors of your involvement in a murder case in Victoria. You'll have to tell me more."

Emily didn't know whether to be proud or horrified. "You can't print anything."

Her parents would never recover from what they'd see as the shame of it, she thought. To have their unmarried daughter investigating murders? Unthinkable.

Though getting her name in print for her involvement in a murder case might convince both of them that she and Granville needed to wed as quickly as possible. Then she'd be Emily Granville —Mrs. John Granville, officially—and his name was already well-known for investigations. Her lips quirked at the thought.

This just might be the threat that would convince her mother to change the plans for her wedding. If she needed it.

Tim was looking at her with some concern. "Of course not. I'd never print anything about either of you," and he glanced at Clara before looking back at Emily.

"Unless we wanted you to, of course," Emily said.

O'Hearn—Tim—studied her face. "Yes. Then I would be more than happy to write any story you chose to tell me."

He really must love Clara, to make such a sweeping promise. "That is very generous of you," Emily said.

"What's wrong?" he asked in sudden concern, looking from one to the other of them.

Clara gave Emily a little nudge, and she nodded, though she glanced around her to make sure none of the other tables were close enough to overhear their conversation.

"This has to remain confidential, but my sister Jane has recently become engaged," she said. "To a Mr. Cyrus Bray."

"Then congratulations are in order," Tim said. "Or are they?"

Emily exchanged glances with Clara. This was much harder than she'd thought. Telling a reporter about her family's concerns, even if it was Tim, felt like a betrayal of sorts.

"Well, that is the problem," Emily said. "I don't know. My sister hasn't known him long, and this engagement seems very sudden. I haven't even met him yet, so perhaps I'm just being overly cautious."

"No, you're not," Clara said. "You are very good at understanding people, and the way your mother talked about Mr. Bray worried you."

So did what Jane had said, but Emily appreciated Clara's tact in not mentioning that. What if they uncovered nothing and Jane married the man after all? Having a reporter—even this one—know that her sister had once had doubts about her future husband? That would be unfair.

"And you wondered if I had heard anything about the man?" Tim said diplomatically.

"Yes," she said.

"Nothing untoward. He's been in town for only a few months now, but he seems to have established himself pretty quickly."

"He has money, then?"

"From what little I know, he does. Which doesn't mean he isn't a fortune hunter, though. If that's what you're worried about."

It was one of the things, but Emily wasn't about to share that. "What does he do, exactly? I gather it's something financial?" was all she said.

He gave her a sharp look, but accepted the change of subject. "Not exactly. Or at least not entirely. He imports goods, mostly from the Far East, I think. He seems to have some connections in Hong Kong. I'd have to ask around to learn more."

Emily and Clara exchanged glances, and Emily shook her head. It couldn't be.

"What aren't you telling me?" Tim asked.

"Have a little more tea," Clara said, reaching for the teapot. "And perhaps a scone? This could take some time."

"What will?" Tim asked, accepting a scone. "There's more here than just your sister's engagement involved, isn't there?"

"I'm sure the two aren't related," Emily said, nodding her thanks to Clara as she refreshed her tea. They couldn't be. Could they? "Mr. Bray and our newest case, I mean."

"You have a new case?" Tim asked.

"Well, our firm has a new case," Emily said. "Granville hasn't talked to you yet?"

"No. Why?"

"There might be a story in it—at very least a business story. I know he had some questions for Mr. Draper, and he was planning to talk to you, as well."

"But do you think there's a story there?" he asked.

Emily considered his question for a moment, running quickly through what little they knew about the case so far.

Her third man wasn't likely to be much of a story, was he? She might want answers, but no one else would care.

And from what Granville had told her, the puppet master had

little if any connection to the attack on Mr. Randall. So that wasn't a story.

Mr. Benton was focusing on imports, though. Which might be a story. And Mr. Benton's interest in the puppet master meant whatever he was involved in, it was probably illegal.

What if the puppet master was hiding his identity because he was posing as a legitimate businessman, though? That kind of scandal could be a big story.

And what about the imports themselves? Selling and collecting chinoiserie imported from the Far East had come up several times in her Victoria case. And it had been a minor connection to Granville's case, too. Though it hadn't been helpful in solving either case. But still.

What if chinoiserie was the connection between their two cases and this puppet master? Maybe they should be focusing their search for him on people involved in those imports?

She couldn't wait to talk to Granville about it. That just might be the piece they'd been missing. And she hadn't even considered the possibility until Tim had mentioned that Mr. Bray imported goods from the Far East. Now she couldn't believe she hadn't thought of it sooner.

Too bad she couldn't tell Tim any of this. Not yet.

"If there is story, it will likely involve goods coming through the port," she said carefully.

"Smuggling?" he asked.

That seemed to be the first thing people thought of, she noted. Which was interesting in itself. "It's a good possibility. Though probably not the only one. What have you heard?"

"A few rumors here and there. Nothing substantial. Certainly not enough for a major story," he said. "Are you sure about this?"

"No, that's just the problem. At the moment there's no more than rumors, with a single confirmation from a connected but unreliable source," Emily said. Hiding a grin at her impromptu description of Mr. Benton, which struck her as quite apt.

"Let me look into it, and get back to you," he said. "You're sure there's nothing else?"

"Well, it's only a theory at the moment... But the smuggling might be connected to imports of chinoiserie," she said.

"Which explains your reaction when I told you Bray was involved in importing from the Far East," the reporter said. "Since imports from those countries are often chinoiserie."

"But they could also be tea, or silk. Or even opium," Clara said.

"They could," Emily said. "I confess it was the chinoiserie connection I thought of first. Though Mr. Bray has only been in town for a short time, and I think the case we're working now has been going on much longer than that. It's probably just a coincidence."

"Doesn't mean he isn't involved," Tim said, seemingly unwilling to let go of that angle.

"Since he's engaged to my sister now, I hesitate to think so badly of him," Emily said, stretching the truth a little. She just didn't want Tim to narrow his research into her sister's fiancé too quickly.

Clara gave her a sideways glance. Emily gave her a half smile, and her friend nodded at her. She understood.

"I don't trust coincidences," Tim said.

"I don't either, but easy answers are a lazy man's choice," Clara said.

Tim frowned. "Are you calling me lazy?"

"Should I be?" Clara said. "Success takes hard work. In any venture."

While Tim stared at her friend, Emily looked away and sipped her tea. Whatever was going on between the two of them, she could tell they were having more than one conversation. Including a non-verbal one. And they'd have to work it out between themselves.

Though she had a few questions to ask her friend. Later.

"More tea, Clara? Tim?" Emily said when it was clear neither of them was going to say another word.

Clara glanced the tiny pendant watch she wore pinned to her blouse. "It's late. I really should be getting home," she said. "Are you coming with me, Emily?"

"Yes. I hadn't realized it was so late. But thank you for joining us for tea, Tim. And you'll be in touch with the results of your research?"

"Once I've had time to do a thorough job of it," Tim said, with an unreadable look at Clara, who was gathering up her things. "I'll send you a note."

"Thank you," Emily said, rising and shaking his hand. "I appreciate it more than I can tell you. And I'm sure you'll be hearing from Granville in the next day or two, as well."

She turned to her friend. "Are you ready?"

"Yes, I am. Good afternoon, Tim," Clara said, with exquisite politeness.

"Good afternoon, ladies," Tim said, equally politely, standing as they rose.

Emily rolled her eyes at the two of them.

7

Tuesday, September 18, 1900

The following morning, Granville arrived in his office early, fleeing the continuing chaos of his home. The builders had already arrived and begun to set up—to "get ahead of the heat," the contractor had told him. The main floor of the house was now a warren of ladders and protective cloths and a few walls now sported holes he didn't want to think about. He'd had to pick his way carefully through the mess just to get to the front door.

Work hadn't even begun yet, and already plaster dust and the sharp smell of solvents permeated everything. He could only imagine how thick it would be by evening.

Perhaps he should remove to a hotel for a few weeks? But it was his house, dammit. He wouldn't be driven out by a few inconveniences. And every day they worked brought closer the day the house would be ready for its new mistress.

Then there'd be nothing impeding his marriage to Emily.

He wondered how the discussion with her mother had gone yesterday. Emily had seemed almost ready to move the wedding date forward, even as close as the coming spring. Had she raised that possibility with her mother?

Then there was the matter of her sister Jane's engagement to Mr. Bray, the fellow who had been at the Randall vs. Peabody trial. Draper had been right—the engagement notice was in this morning's paper. And Emily hadn't come back to the office yesterday.

At the time he'd thought nothing of it, but now he wondered if she might be avoiding him. Something to do with her sister's marriage, perhaps? Or their own?

He wouldn't ask her. Emily would tell him when she was ready. Adding more pressure to a situation she was already finding difficult wouldn't help.

With a grimace, he turned his attention to the stack of files on his desk. Benton's files. Such as they were.

Miss Kent and Mac hadn't had time to start on them—they were taking care of the paperwork for a surveillance case he and Scott had just wrapped up. So he'd spent a little time flipping through them. And found them as much of a waste of time as the expedition to the docks. Which had netted them exactly nothing.

At least Draper and Daniels had been somewhat helpful.

Finally he'd put the whole stack of files aside for this morning.

The files didn't look any better now. Most of them seemed to contain a collection of shipping schedules, train schedules and calendars with cryptic notations. Plus the occasional memo with half the information blacked out. There was nothing to identify the shippers, the cargoes, or the destinations.

What were they supposed to do with these?

Scott's arrival was a welcome distraction. The big man subsided into the larger of Granville's guest chairs and considered him across the desk.

"What's biting you?" he asked.

"No good morning?"

"Judgin' by your expression, this isn't one." Scott's eyes shifted to the stack of files Granville had shoved aside. "Still nothing?"

"Not a thing. And it seems deliberate. I don't get what Benton is up to."

"He hates sharing information."

"He hired us."

"Yup. And he's going to make us work for it."

"Oh no, he isn't," Granville said, standing. "You with me?"

"Oh, this isn't going to go well," Scott said, still seated. "What happened to being reasonable?"

"I warned him," Granville said, grabbing his revolver from the desk drawer and heading for the door.

As Granville came to a halt in front of a solid brick house with a red-painted door, Scott gave him a quizzical look. "I thought you were planning on challenging Benton. What are we doin' at my sister's place?"

"You'll see," Granville said as he reached for the elaborate brass door knocker and gave three quick raps. Then he paused and listened for any sign of life within. It was early. Probably he should have waited for a more acceptable time for a morning call.

But he'd had his fill of waiting for Benton to be reasonable. Frances Scott was a much better option. Either she'd be royally angry with him for his impertinence coming to her home, especially this early. Or she'd find the standoff between himself and Benton amusing. Either way, he'd probably learn something.

He was betting on the whole situation amusing her, but he probably should have at least waited for a more reasonable hour. Especially if there were still tensions between Benton and his lady over the Scott's younger sister.

"I hope you're not implying that you expect to find Benton here? At this hour? You're insulting Frances!" Scott muttered.

The door swung silently inwards and a heavily muscled, black clad man stood there. "May I help you?" he asked.

Well, he certainly sounded like a butler, Granville thought with an inward grin. Even if he didn't look much like one. He wondered where Benton had found the fellow.

"John Granville and Sam Scott to see Miss Frances Scott," he said. "Is she in?"

The unlikely butler gave him a withering look. "I shall inquire," he said, and shut the door in their faces.

Beside him, Scott had started laughing. "I thought demanding to see Benton at this hour was dumb. But demanding to see Frances? Just when I think you've gotten over your fits of stupidity, you do something even worse."

"Thanks a lot."

"Any time."

Behind them the door creaked open. "The lady will see you," the butler said, and led the way into a very formal parlor.

Granville was surprised to see that none of the furnishings or the few decorations bore any trace of their owner's flamboyant personality. In addition to being Benton's lady love, Frances Scott was a very popular fan dancer in the main room at the Carlton.

"Frances isn't happy with us," Scott said, glancing around. "Not if she's banishing us here."

"It feels about as welcoming as Skagway in midwinter," Granville said.

"I think that's kinda the point."

"I don't suppose we'll be offered coffee."

"I doubt it," Scott said with a wide grin.

"And he'd be right," said an acerbic voice from the doorway. "Just what are you two doing here at this hour?"

Granville looked up to see Frances Scott, wearing a brocaded wrapper and glaring at him with those magnificent eyes. "We're working a case for Benton," he said.

"Is that supposed to be an explanation?" she snapped. "He isn't here."

She didn't even bother pretending that the gangster was never there. It was one of the things he admired about Scott's sister—she didn't play games. And she didn't apologize for who and what she was. Instead, she virtually dared anyone to judge her for it.

In some ways, she and Emily were a lot alike.

A thought that would probably horrify most of Vancouver society

—such as it was. The exception would be the two ladies themselves. Frances would be amused, and Emily? Emily would be pleased—she liked Frances, and admired her fiery nature.

There were a lot of reasons he loved her.

"Benton isn't likely to tell us what we need to know. I'm hoping you will," he said.

Frances gave him a hard look. "That will get you invited in. But this had better be good."

"It is," he said, thinking fast. "It will be even better if you were to offer us coffee."

"It's a good thing Scott is with you," she said, nodding to the butler who was hovering in the doorway. She turned and led the way into a small room that was bright with the early morning light.

Once they were all seated in comfortable armchairs facing a small fireplace, he leaned forward. "What do you know about Benton's big fish?" he asked her.

She frowned at him, and shook her head with a confused expression. He grinned. "Nice try. Neither of us are going to believe you don't know practically everything about Benton's business."

She slid her gaze to Scott, who nodded with an answering grin.

"Oh, very well. But shouldn't it be *your* big fish?" Frances said, giving Granville a frosty look. "And why are you asking me?"

"Because you'll tell us."

"And why would I do that?"

"Because whoever this is, he's a threat to Benton. Not to us. And as such he's threatening this lifestyle you've built." He paused, glancing around the cozy room, then back at her. "And you aren't bound by Benton's rules."

She smiled at that. "Very well argued. Ask your questions, then. I might choose to answer a few of them."

It was Scott who spoke up. "We know too little about this big fish, and the information Benton's sent us isn't much help. Granville here is calling the fellow a puppet master, because from the little Benton told us, the guy seems to operate behind the scenes, getting other people to do his dirty work. Which'll make him very hard to find. Anything you can tell us might give us some idea where to start looking."

Frances cocked her head to one side, looking from Scott to Granville and back again. "Tell me what you do know."

Scott looked over at him, and he nodded.

"We believe that the puppet master and Benton have business interests in common, and that the former's expansion has recently become a threat of some kind to the latter," Granville said. "We believe that these business interests have to do with shipping, and goods coming in through the docks, and perhaps being sent on by rail."

"And the information Benton gave you?"

"Is essentially a collection of shipping schedules, train schedules and calendars with cryptic notations."

"And what connects these documents?"

"Nothing I've been able to find, with the limited information I have. Though I have people digging into it further," Granville said. He'd left the files on Miss Kent's desk, with a note.

A small smile tugged at the corners of her mouth. "I begin to see why you're frustrated. But surely you didn't expect Benton to give you easy answers. Even if he had any."

"Of course not. That's why we came here."

At that she laughed, a delighted chuckle. "You have a very interesting way of winning an argument."

"Thank you. I try."

"I'm afraid I can't give you much help, either," she said. "I don't think Benton himself knows who this puppet master is—which is a good name for him, by the way. He does indeed seem to operate behind the scenes."

She paused, and played with the sash of her robe, seemingly thinking. "In fact, I'm not sure if Benton actually knows he exists, so much as seeing the results of his actions means someone like him must exist. If that makes any sense?"

"It does. Unfortunately. If Benton really doesn't know much more than he's told us, then this case is going to be twice as difficult as I'd anticipated."

Scott gave him a look that clearly said, "I told you so." Seeing it, Frances gave another chortle.

"These actions that alerted Benton to the existence of this puppet master. Can you give us any details?"

"I'm sorry, I don't know them."

He gave her a considering look. Was she lying? In the end it didn't matter—she clearly wasn't going to tell them anything.

"But one thing I can tell you," Frances said. "You're right about it centering around importing. And around the docks."

"Thank you, that's a help. We've already begun to look there, but we'll keep that focus. And perhaps sharper eyes than mine with find some connections in Benton's files."

Frances rolled her eyes. "Don't hold your breath. I've seen his ideas of organization," she said.

8

Emily felt nervous about going into the office, which was ridiculous. She couldn't avoid Granville forever. And surely he'd understand about the wedding dates. Wouldn't he?

In any case, she'd been nervous for nothing—Marie Rizzo, their temporary receptionist, quickly told her that Mr. Granville and Mr. Scott were out of the office.

"He's left word that he'd like everyone to gather in the meeting room at ten," Marie said. "Except myself, of course. It's a good thing I'm here to deal with any calls, since there seem to be a lot of these meetings."

Which was true. Emily suspected the information shared at these meetings were one of the reasons everyone seemed to work so well together. Which, from her limited understanding, was not usual. Though she'd never worked anywhere else, so she couldn't compare. But it worked here.

She also suspected that Marie was hinting that she'd be open to a job here. And perhaps even that the firm would benefit from such a move. Which Emily agreed with.

From what she'd seen, Marie was doing an excellent job on reception. They needed to hire her before someone else did. She wasn't sure Granville was convinced though. And it had seemed too soon to ask what he thought of Marie's work.

The list of things she wanted to discuss with Granville—at an appropriate time—was getting uncomfortably long.

TEN O'CLOCK CAME TOO SOON.

But Granville and Scott weren't back yet, so Emily relaxed a little. She looked around the long table at the familiar faces, and felt very glad to be back in Vancouver. She'd never forget her first real case—but this was where she belonged. She'd missed working with her friends.

And long-distance telephone conversations with Granville were just not the same. Especially not when both the local and long-distance switchboard operators were able to listen in if they chose to.

A commotion at the door distracted her, and her nervousness returned as Granville and Scott walked into the room.

It was ridiculous to be nervous around Granville, of all people, Emily chided herself as she watched him stride to the head of the table, while Scott took the seat on his right. Was that a new suit Granville was wearing? The perfectly tailored cut certainly looked good on him.

"Thank you all for making the time to meet this morning," Granville said as he sat down. The familiarity of his voice immediately calmed Emily. She was being a goose.

Just stop it, she berated herself. And forced herself to focus on what he was saying.

"As of yesterday, we have a new case," Granville said. "And Scott and I wanted to brief everyone as quickly as possible. Benton has hired us to find an invisible man, and run him out of town. By any means we deem necessary."

"*Benton* hired us?" Trent said. "And we took the case? Why?"

"Because with that mandate, we can work within the law. And because this invisible man may have a connection to the two cases we just closed," Granville said. And he proceeded to explain about the puppet master.

As he did so, Emily watched the faces around the table. Trent looked skeptical, Mr. Mackenzie looked interested. And Laura looked oddly satisfied.

Which intrigued her. Laura had a gift for seeing patterns where others saw only random chaos. Her friend's expression told Emily that she wasn't the only one who'd been bothered by those loose threads her Victoria case had left. And maybe a few from the Randall case, too.

Did that look on Laura's face mean she had some ideas where they could begin? If so, she'd have to pry it out of her later. Laura didn't yet feel confident about expressing her opinions until they were asked for. And why should she, when she was still—officially—their receptionist?

Emily made a mental note to talk to Granville about that, too.

"We've made a little progress on the case since we took it on yesterday morning," Granville was telling everyone, and Emily focused on his words. "Scott and I have met with Draper and Daniels and enlisted their help. And we've asked a few questions at the docks. We do have confirmation that Benton believes that this case centers around importing. And around the docks."

"Confirmation?" Trent said with a wink. "You mean Miss Frances told you that, don't you?"

"Of course," Granville said, grinning at his apprentice. Then he sobered quickly. "This isn't going to be an easy case. It's slow going, and the puppet master is very well-hidden. We're going to need everyone's help."

"I'm in," Trent said immediately.

"We've closed out all of the urgent files," Miss Kent said. "What can we do?"

"Those files Benton sent over yesterday," Granville said. "I can't find any logic to them, if it even exists. Would you and Mac go through them and see if you can find anything?"

"We can do that," Miss Kent said after a quick glance at Mac, who nodded. "What are we looking for?"

"Patterns. Anything related to importing, and especially if it also involves any of the players from our last cases—both the attack on Randall and the murder in Victoria—could be important. Which is why I asked Draper if he'd noted anyone at the Randall vs. Peabody trial he hadn't expected to be there. He gave me these."

Granville passed a handwritten list of three names to Emily on his left, and she looked at the names with interest, then passed the list on.

"See if you and Mac can find anything that connects these names to either case or to the files," Granville said to Miss Kent. "Look particularly at any importing companies. Or connections to them."

Laura nodded, and jotted it down. Emily was impressed to see the speed with which her friend was using shorthand.

"With any luck, we should have something for you tomorrow," Laura said.

"Thank you. We can use any information you can dig out," Granville said. "Other than these names, Scott and I didn't learn much that was new yesterday. We didn't hear even a whisper of trouble on the docks. Though we haven't yet had a chance to talk to O'Hearn."

"Clara and I had tea with Tim O'Hearn yesterday afternoon," Emily said. "I told him we had a case, and that it seemed to be connected to imported goods coming through the docks. He mentioned having heard a few rumors, and has promised to look into it and let us know what he finds."

"Which explains why Scott and I couldn't find him." Her fiancé smiled at her. "You just saved us some time."

"Good. But I might have a theory about the imports. As I was telling Tim about our new case, it occurred to me…," she paused and glanced around the table, before looking back at Granville. "Could imports of chinoiserie be the common link between the puppet master and our two closed cases? Maybe that's where this new investigation should start."

"It's an excellent idea," Granville said. "Miss Kent, would you also see if you can find any connection to imports from the Far East in Benton's files or involving these three names?" and he tapped the handwritten list of names that Scott had handed back to him.

"You might add Cyrus Bray's name to that list," Emily said, working hard to keep her tone neutral. "Tim told Clara and I that Mr. Bray specializes in importing goods from the Far East. I'm sure there's nothing in it, but just to be thorough."

"You know Mr. Bray?" Miss Kent asked.

"He has just become engaged to my eldest sister," Emily said.

"Draper mentioned he was at the Randall vs. Peabody trial, too," Granville said.

She hadn't known that. What had Mr. Bray been doing there? she wondered, watching Granville. And what was her own fiancé thinking of this sudden engagement? His face gave nothing away.

"My sister's engagement was just announced this morning. I haven't yet met Mr. Bray," she said.

He gave a little nod, as if he'd been wondering about that, and Laura looked up from her notes and gave her a funny look. Her sister's sudden engagement probably seemed odd to all of them.

It seemed even more odd to Emily. Especially when she hadn't known about Mr. Bray at all. An oddity she was determined to get to the bottom of.

Her gaze focused on Laura, who had been flipping through her stenographer's notebook, and who was now reading something on the page she'd stopped at.

"Did you find something, Laura?" she asked.

Laura looked up and blushed a little when she found all eyes fixed on her.

"What about Mr. Sikes?" she said. "He was the loser in Randall's first big case about import fraud. The one that started all the trouble. Could there be some connection between Mr. Sikes and the puppet master?"

"Excellent idea, Miss Kent," Granville said with a nod. "Perhaps if we use Sikes's name, we can shake something loose down at the docks. Have another look at that file, would you? And see if it ties in any way to the files Benton sent."

Emily noted Trent's face light up at the mention of a return visit to the docks, but Granville's plan had made a connection for her, too.

"Wait just a minute," she said. "If chinoiserie is the connection to the puppet master, then…"

"Then what?" Trent asked, practically bouncing off his chair.

She held up a hand while she thought. What had Papa said this morning? "The bulk of those goods must come in on the *Empress* liners, since they are the largest steamships making a regular run between here and the Far East. And none of that line were in port yesterday, when you were asking questions."

"So if there are rumors, they might be loudest when the goods are being unloaded," Granville said. "That makes sense."

"The *Empress of China* is scheduled to arrive today," she said. "Papa mentioned it at breakfast."

"Then I think we need to head back to the docks later this evening, and try our luck again. Scott, are you in?"

"Course," the big man said.

"Me too," Trent said.

"I'm afraid I need you elsewhere tonight," Granville said.

Trent's face fell. "Doin' what?"

"I'll fill you in later," he said.

Emily was amused to see Trent's face set in stubborn lines, but impressed he just gave a brief nod. She was pretty sure Granville was hiding a grin, and wondered what he was up to now.

9

When the meeting ended, another urgent message from her mother sent Emily straight home. Instead of focusing on the new case, she found herself being dragged into a yet another discussion of her sister's wedding.

She'd thought planning the details for her own marriage was tedious. This was six times worse, because Jane was even more fixated on every detail than Mama had been.

She'd attempted to tell her mother that she had work to do, but Mama had refused to listen. Emily's only consolation was that she could use the time to find out more about her sister's fiancé. Including where and how Jane had met him.

As she stitched yet another painfully slow stitch for Jane's trousseau, trying to keep her stitches even, Emily wondered if Mama had been scheming to give her the opportunity to question Jane about the fellow. It would be just like her to do that.

"This is beautiful, Jane," she said as she stitched.

It really was. The pale pink silk of the delicate blouse looked like the inside of a sea shell. It wasn't a color she'd pictured Jane wearing in a thousand years.

And normally she wouldn't have commented on the colors Jane

wore. But there was no surer way to get her talking. "Is this for your honeymoon trip?"

"Yes," Jane said, beaming. "He's taking me to New York. And I'll need stylish outfits—we're going to 'hit all the high spots' as he says. We'll be on the train for several days."

"It sounds wonderful," Emily said. And it really did.

She'd love to go on a trip like that. If she were going with Granville, that is. Did Jane feel that way about Mr. Bray? Or was it the romance of the travel and a honeymoon in New York City that had her beaming?

"I know. It's the kind of honeymoon every girl dreams of," Jane said, jerking Emily out of her reflections. And her big sister gave her a superior look.

Emily swallowed the retort she wanted to make. She wasn't here to bicker with her sister.

"You never did tell me," she said, trying to sound eager. "How did the two of you meet?" Pretending she was Clara, who could never hear too much gossip.

"It was so romantic," Jane gushed, sounding like she was channeling Clara herself. "He really swept me off my feet."

He had? And her pragmatic sister was happy to have been swept off her feet? That made no sense. Maybe Jane really was head over heels in love. Or she was pretending hard to be.

And Emily wasn't sure which it was.

"Tell me," she prompted.

Jane was happy to. "It was at the Miller's ball. Mrs. Miller introduced us, and he—Mr. Bray—asked me to waltz, twice in a row. Then he spent the next set procuring refreshments for me. He didn't look at anyone else."

Emily made a mental note to ask Mrs. Miller at the first opportunity how that introduction had come about. Or better yet, she'd ask Clara to do so. No one would wonder at that question from her very social friend. "And then what happened?"

"He called the next afternoon. With flowers. And then he took a party of us on a drive through Stanley Park the following day. And then…"

Emily tried very hard to look interested as Jane ran through her activities of the last two weeks. It sounded like her would-be brother-in-law had followed all the rules for a successful courtship. He'd just crammed it all into two weeks, which was suspiciously fast.

Perhaps he really had fallen for Jane at first glance. It was possible, wasn't it?

Or perhaps he had a more mercenary motive. Emily glanced at her mother, who hadn't said a single word through Jane's stream of words. Which was most unlike both of them.

No, something was off here. It was a good thing she'd already decided to look into Mr. Bray.

"And what does Mr. Bray do?" she asked at the first opportunity. "I gather he's in business?"

"Yes," Jane said. "He runs a very successful importing firm. He's originally from the East Coast—he's American, you know—and has family in Boston. And you know I've always liked Americans."

"How interesting," Emily said. "How did he come to choose Vancouver?"

"He says he's expanding his trade with the Far East, particularly China and Japan, so it was either here or Seattle. You know how I love chinoiserie. And then he knew Mr. Miller, so that 'tipped the balance,' as he puts it. And he chose to settle here," Jane said rapidly. "Luckily for me."

"Congratulations, again," Emily said, busily making mental notes while setting another careful stitch. "He sounds perfect for you."

Too perfect, in fact.

She glanced again at her mother, who was wearing her imperturbable face. She wondered what lay behind that serene expression. She couldn't shake the feeling that her mother had engineered this meeting—and put Jane's delicate blouse at risk—to give Emily the information she'd need to investigate her sister's fiancé. And probably so she could intervene if she thought Emily was missing the point.

Mama's unusual silence meant that this stitching session was unfolding as she'd planned, and that Emily was asking the right questions. And it probably also confirmed that her mother indeed wanted her to investigate Jane's fiancé. Though she'd never actually say so.

Somehow, having that confirmation was even more unsettling than just suspecting what Mama was up to.

At least when she told Granville about their delayed wedding plans, she'd be able to assure him that the supposed delay wasn't real. It was all for show.

Wasn't it?

Over an hour later, Emily had finally escaped the sewing session. She and Clara were seated at their favorite quiet table beneath the palm tree at Stroh's, sharing a pot of tea and a plate of pastries.

"So it was Mrs. Miller that introduced your sister and her fiancé?" Clara said thoughtfully. She reached for a sweet roll sprinkled with crushed walnuts and took a thoughtful bite. "I was at that ball, and I don't remember the two of them dancing two waltzes, let alone two waltzes in a row."

"Are you saying it didn't happen?" Emily asked.

"Your mother didn't contradict Jane's version?"

"She never said a word."

"Hmmm. I'm not saying that it didn't happen…"

"Yes, you are. You just don't need words to do so."

Clara smiled. "I'm glad you recognize that. I'm not sure if Jane is hiding something, or if it's those 'rosy clouds of love' the greeting cards would have us believe in."

"Clara, what's wrong? I've never heard you so cynical."

"It isn't cynical if it's true."

Emily didn't respond, just looked at her friend. Who looked away. And didn't say a word.

It had to be Tim O'Hearn, Emily decided. But she'd change the subject, for now. And see if she couldn't throw the two of them together during this investigation.

"Which do you think Jane is doing?" she asked Clara instead.

"I don't know enough to even speculate. Not yet. But someone will have noticed them. I just have to find out who."

"Could you start with Mrs. Miller?" Emily asked.

"Because she introduced him?"

"Yes. And because Mr. Bray and Mr. Miller are in business together. At least according to Jane."

"And you'd like to know more," Clara said with a quick nod. "Mrs. Miller has her weekly 'at-home' this afternoon. And the announcement of your sister's engagement is sure to be discussed. Why don't you join me, and we'll see what we can learn."

"Thank you," Emily said with a smile. Normally she found the ritual of the 'at-home' tedious beyond anything—a roomful of ladies dressed to impress, all gathered for the pleasure of hours spent sipping tea and discussing the latest gossip. This was different. "I'd be pleased to join you."

MRS. MILLER'S front parlor was a revelation. And not the good kind, from Emily's perspective. Over-decorated, with small ornaments everywhere and so many patterns it almost made Emily feel a little dizzy. The room was hot, and overcrowded, which didn't help matters.

"Have a look at the chandelier," Clara said in an undertone as they waited for their hostess to greet them. "Something like that might work in your new home. What do you think?"

"Granville's home," Emily corrected her automatically, glancing at the intricately wrought light fixture.

It wasn't too hideous. Or it wouldn't be except for the tiny burgundy silk shades around every electric candle, which clashed with the crimson of what had to be insanely expensive handmade silk flowers draped across the mantlepiece. "It might be quite nice. Without all the fripperies."

Clara smiled, and turned to greet their hostess, quickly introducing Emily.

"It is a pleasure indeed to meet you," Mrs. Miller gushed. "Especially today. Why, it was only weeks ago that I introduced your sister to Mr. Bray, and here they are officially engaged. It is such a romance."

So much for Emily's concerns about how to introduce the subject of that fateful meeting. "Yes, Jane was just telling me about how they met. She credits their engagement to that meeting, and to you, you know."

"Does she indeed?" Mrs. Miller said. "Well, I confess that I thought they might suit. And when Mr. Bray asked for an introduction, I was only too happy to arrange it. I wish all my introductions were that successful."

"Our hostess is quite the matchmaker," Clara said to Emily, as Mrs. Miller beamed. "This is the third engagement she has been responsible for."

Emily wasn't sure that was a compliment, regardless of how that lady saw it. "Was Mr. Bray equally smitten? Was that why he asked for the introduction?" she asked.

She tried to gush as though it was the most romantic thing she'd ever heard, but was afraid she hadn't pulled it off. She'd never had it in her to gush.

From the look Clara sent her way, she still didn't.

Mrs. Miller didn't seem to have noticed, though—she'd given a little sigh. Presumably at the romance of it all. Their hostess didn't seem the most perceptive of women. Which was lucky, in this case.

"He didn't say," Mrs. Miller said. "But then, he didn't really have to. He'd had his eye on her from the moment she entered the ballroom with your parents. And he watched her everywhere she went. I'd been keeping an eye on him, you see, because he's new to town, and so eligible."

Emily looked at her hostess. Did the woman not understand what she'd just said?

Mr. Bray had known exactly who Jane was, and he'd been following her around the room. Before they'd even met. To her mind, that was creepy.

Of course, she also thought Mrs. Miller's attempts at matchmaking were creepy, but that was probably a flaw in her, not her hostess. Emily glanced over at her friend, who was watching both of them with a small polite half-smile on her face. Oh no. She knew that expression.

Clara would be happy to tell her later about her social flaws. No matter. This was more important.

"Jane tells me your husband and her new fiancé are in business together. Does Mr. Miller know you were keeping an eye on Mr. Bray?" Emily said, trying to sound as open and naive as possible, as if this was a perfectly natural question. Which it wasn't.

"I wouldn't tell just anyone, but since it's your sister he's engaged to..." Mrs. Miller leaned a little closer, lowered her voice. "My husband asked me to help him, if I could. Mr. Bray needed a wife."

Needed. Not wanted. Needed. And wasn't that interesting?

"It's so kind of your husband to be concerned for his partner," Emily said, trying very hard to keep a straight face. And not to look at Clara.

"Oh, they're not partners," Mrs. Miller said. "Not yet, at least. Just friendly colleagues."

Did Mr. Miller know how dangerous his wife's lack of discretion could be to his plans?

She could see it all now. Mr. Miller was determined to impress Mr. Bray. Perhaps even to help him make the right connections. And Mr. Bray?

She'd thought he might be after Jane's dowry. And he probably was. But now she was wondering if he was even more interested in Papa's influence. Papa knew all kinds of people because of his position with the Canadian Pacific Railroad, with their network of railroads that crisscrossed the continent.

What exactly was Mr. Bray up to? And how big a role did Mr. Miller play in his plans? She gave their hostess a considering look.

She wasn't likely to get those answers here.

"Where is Mr. Bray from, do you know?" she asked instead. "Jane mentioned he was new to town."

"Boston, I believe. Though he doesn't have that odd accent. But he's been quite involved in shipping to England and the continent. And now he's solidifying his connections with the Far East."

Mr. Miller was either as foolish as his wife, or he was quite besotted with her. Possibly both. She wondered just how solid those connections were. And what Mr. Bray was really up to.

Whatever it was, he wasn't going to use her sister to get there.

No matter how she annoyed she sometimes felt with Jane, she was family. Nobody got to play games with her family.

10

It was early evening by the time he and Scott reached the docks. While tiny in comparison to the London dockyards Granville was familiar with, Vancouver's busy harbor stretched along the water all the way from Heatley Street on the east side to Thurlow Street on the west. Railroad tracks ran between the docks and the city, with the impressive bulk of the Canadian Pacific Railroad Station anchoring them on one end and the busy lumberyards of the Hastings Sawmill on the other. The wharves themselves were built out on long poles that elevated them over the waters of Burrard Inlet.

The CPR station was busy with trains arriving and leaving, but from inside the station, Granville could easily see across the tracks to where the wharves lay, dark and quiet. Which wasn't unusual at this time of day, unless a steamliner or a cargo ship had arrived late. Then the wharves would be a hive of activity, and the lights would burn all night.

Tonight wasn't one of those nights, though there were several ships docked, and several more anchored in the harbor. No matter. If there was information to be had, Granville knew exactly where to find it.

He and Scott turned their steps east towards the taverns favored by the longshoremen who worked the docks. They automatically turned into the Beaver Tavern, the lowest and grimiest of the lot. Granville liked it for its unrepentant lack of pretense. And they served half-decent whiskey, despite the low price. It was also the best place for gossip from the docks.

People minded their own business here, but underhanded deals and backroom agreements were standard fare. If there were rumors around the Empress liners, this was the place to find them.

And if Miss Kent was correct in suggesting that Sikes's dealings were part of some larger scheme, this was the place to start digging.

The place was crowded, thick with smoke and the smell of spilled beer and sweat. The sawdust underfoot could probably have used changing several days ago, but loud laughter and the swell of conversation made up for it. Granville was always glad to have Scott, with his bulk and his ready fists, at his back when he came here.

Granville headed straight for the bar, Scott right behind him. "Two whiskeys," he shouted over the din, and held up two fingers.

The shifty eyed bartender gave him a dirty look, just like he'd done the first time Granville had been here. Nearly a year ago, now. It was hard to believe so little time had passed, given all the changes in his life. A job, a fiancée, new friends and a new business.

Two half-full glasses slid down the bar, and Granville caught them with the ease of long practice, handing the second one to Scott. His gaze swept the room, then he spotted a table that wasn't completely full. And since he didn't know anyone here, it didn't much matter whom they talked to. Nodding to Scott, he led the way.

There were three men already standing around the battered table, half-empty mugs in front of them. From their faded overalls and their sweat drenched denim shirts, they'd obviously just finished a full shift.

"Which ships unloaded today?" Granville asked the fellow standing beside him. Stocky, with dark eyes and hair, and the muscles and battered hands of someone who worked hard for a living.

The fellow gave him a flat look. "Who wants to know?"

Granville shrugged. Even without his tailored suit, his voice, with its overtones of upper-class English schooling, gave him away every time.

"The one who's buying your next round," he said.

Money might not buy everything, but a few rounds of beer often worked magic. If these men took against you, though, you were done.

"Why?"

Granville liked this fellow. Most didn't look beyond the free beer.

"My partner and I are investigators," he said, and indicated Scott with a nod, "Our client is having problems with someone who imports goods from the Far East and is illegally undermining his own trade."

Which was close enough to the truth. Then he waited with some curiosity to see how the fellow would respond.

"Big money hurting small money, is it?"

"Something like that," Granville said.

The fellow snorted. "Good enough. But it's two rounds. For the table."

"We'll make it three," Granville said. "What can you tell me?"

"The *Empress of China* is in. We unloaded her today. She'll be loading and sailing tomorrow."

He'd thought he recognized the white sides of the sleek steam-liner gleaming through the gathering dusk. Undoubtedly the Silk Train had loaded and was already on its way, racing the clock and the thieves across the continent to the silk mills of New York.

"What was she carrying?" he asked.

"Mostly silk, tea, and china," the fellow said.

Which was normal for all three of the *Empress* liners. "Anything unusual?" Granville asked.

The fellow drained his mug and thumped it back on the table. Obviously it was time for the next round.

Granville glanced across at Scott, who was deep in conversation with the man beside him. No help there.

"I'll be back in a moment," he said, hoping his informant would still be there when he returned, and waded his way through the crush of bodies to the bar. When he returned with six mugs of beer, he caught everyone's attention.

"So, you were saying?" Granville said as he placed one of the mugs in front of his new friend.

"There was just one odd thing," the fellow said, and drained half of the new mug.

Rolling his eyes, Granville slid a second full mug in front of him.

The fellow grinned, showing sharp white teeth and winked at him. "That's more like it. Anyway, I don't much notice what I'm unloading. One bale looks a lot like another. But we had a few small orders, with a bunch of different buyers, all heading for one warehouse."

"And that's unusual?"

"Yeah. It's cheaper to combine small orders, since they're all going to the same place anyway. Might not be crooked, though."

"But you think it is."

The fellow shrugged. "Lot of money comes through this port. Easy enough to ignore the rules, pay people to look the other way."

"How would that work?"

"Don't ask me. I just see the shipments come and go. Most of it is big crates—could hold anything—because it's the cheapest way. After a while you start to spot the stuff that's different."

"And you begin to wonder why," Granville said.

On its own, the discrepancy didn't sound like much. It could mean anything, or nothing. But Granville had a feeling what he was being told was important.

"Do you remember any of the buyer's names on those orders?" he asked.

"Nah."

"The name Sikes mean anything to you?"

His informant frowned, and finished off his beer. "Rings a bell. I couldn't swear to it, though. We were moving pretty fast. I just caught that there were different names."

"Did you catch the address of this warehouse?" Granville asked.

"Part of it. On Water Street. 100? 110? Something like that. In the hundreds, anyhow."

That might help. Granville thanked the man, finished his whiskey, and fetched the next round for them before collecting Scott.

"You have any luck?" he asked his partner as they exited.

"Not sure how much help it is. But it seems there've been rumors of more stuff sliding past customs than usual," Scott said. "You?"

"A warehouse we need to check out. Or maybe a block of warehouses. But it'll have to wait 'til full dark. Less chance of running into someone then."

"What about a night watchman?"

Granville shrugged. "If they have one, we'll just have to avoid him."

Hiring a night watchman could draw attention to an otherwise unremarkable warehouse. And it was hard to find one who would overlook criminal activity, and yet not steal from his employer. From the little he'd learned of their puppet master, Granville suspected the fellow would take the risk of leaving the warehouse unguarded.

"This might be the first real lead we've had on this one," Scott said. "Think we're starting to make progress on figuring out who Benton's playing pissing games with?"

Granville could only hope so. But he wasn't feeling optimistic quite yet. "I think we're getting closer. But this case isn't exactly starting off well. I'm not ready to call any of it progress yet."

Scott chuckled. "Well, you can be the cautious one. We've got some rumors and a warehouse to check out. That's good enough for me."

Unfortunately they also had a nameless puppet master with an unknown agenda lurking in the shadows. One whom Benton appeared to be wary of.

No, it wasn't time to celebrate yet.

Dusk had fallen and the shadows were spreading as Granville and Scott strolled along Water Street towards Abbott. It was still light enough to see into shop windows and read the signs, but details were blurring in the hot, smoky air. Which was perfect for this little excursion.

Granville was fascinated by the diversity in the establishments along here. A barber shop was next to a corn merchant, who shared a wall with a tea importer. Further down the street was a livery stable, two Chinese laundries, a cigar factory, a specialist in tents and sails, two warehouses and the Vancouver Box factory.

He nudged Scott with an elbow. "My money's on one of those two warehouses."

"Seems reasonable. What's the address?"

"My informant couldn't remember. But he was sure it's on this block."

"So which one are you bettin' on?" Scott asked as they strolled closer.

Granville looked from one to the other. Both buildings were solid brick, and well maintained. After the fire of '86 that had leveled the downtown, most of the building done in the city was brick. Each warehouse bore a small, discreet sign. One read 'Wm. K. Clark & Co., Commission Merchants', the other 'McIver & Allan, Commission Merchants'.

"It could be either of these," he said. "Except from what I saw in Randall's file on Sikes, a commission merchant is the opposite of what I'd expected."

"And what's a commission merchant when he's home?" Scott asked.

"They take in a variety of goods, then sell them on behalf of others, for a small percentage of the sale. A commission," Granville said.

"And what was different on the Sikes case?"

"Sikes did something similar, but on a much smaller scale."

"What does that mean?"

"Sikes imported goods for a variety of small shop owners, taking his commission up front. Then the shop owner delivered the order to his own customer, who has already paid for it."

"So where's the illegal part?"

"It's in the profit," Granville said.

"Naturally," Scott said with a grin. "But how, exactly?"

"Sikes sold directly to his customers, and cheated them on the order. But it was small money. Not likely to be worth our puppet master's involvement."

"You do know you haven't explained anything yet, right?"

"In Sikes's case, the customer paid quite a bit more than the goods he received were worth," Granville said, his tone deliberately patient. Just to irritate Scott. "Sikes would underbid on his commission, to secure the deal. And then inflate everything else. So he earned extra money. Unfairly so."

Scott rolled his eyes. "Yeah. I figured that part out. What's the rest of it?"

"You mean where would the puppet master fit in?"

"Exactly."

He had to grin. "You've got me. That's the part that eludes me."

"Eludes, is it? You mean that fancy Cambridge education of yours isn't helping you sort this one out?"

"Oxford," Granville said automatically. "And no, it isn't. But I'm hoping this warehouse will tell us something. Since an operation of this size?" He nodded towards the nearer of the two buildings. "Might just be worth a puppet master's time."

And before Scott could extend the joke, he added, "And I don't know which warehouse. So we'll probably have to break into both of them."

He should probably worry when Scott just nodded and looked pleased, Granville thought. Except that he felt the same way. The prospect of a bit of action was a welcome one.

Probably something else that should worry him more than it did.

But from what Benton so carefully hadn't said, he suspected this puppet master might not stop at profiteering. The fellow needed to be caught, and taken off the streets. A little breaking and entering was nothing against murder.

And it felt good to be doing something. Illegal or not.

THE LOCK on the back door of the first warehouse was badly rusted, and looked older than the building itself. This far from the light cast by street lamps out front, it would soon be too dark to see much. Granville lit a lucifer that he drew from a box in his pocket, and Scott leaned closer to get a better look.

With a grunt, the big man shook his head. "Too rusty to get open without a key. Too solid to break without a lot of noise," Scott said.

Granville nodded, and stepped back, scanning the brick walls for other entrances. There were few windows looking out on the alley, but there was a set of stairs descending to what might be a basement of some sort. Which was unusual this close to the water. He wondered what they did about flooding,

Pointing out the stairwell to Scott, Granville headed down, with Scott immediately behind him. The stairs led to a low, narrow door. Scott nodded when he saw the small lock on this one, and pulled out the two flexible pieces of wire he often carried.

Granville lit a second lucifer and held the tiny flame high as Scott crouched over the lock. Within seconds Scott let out a pleased grunt, and stood back, the open lock dangling from his fingers.

"Nicely done," Granville said, and pushed the door inwards.

Utter blackness greeted them. Granville drew a lantern from the bag he carried, holding it low so it wouldn't reflect back into the alley behind them. It lit on the first try, and he bent his head to step through the low door.

The first thing he saw was boxes and crates of all sizes and shapes piled in uneven stacks reaching almost to the low ceilings. Raising the lantern higher, he could see a maze of uneven paths through the stacks. There seemed to be no order to it all, and no logical direction to take.

He began to wind his way towards the front of the building, stopping now and again to peer closer at the shipping labels.

"What kind of an idiot organizes a warehouse like this one?" Scott muttered from behind him. "How do they ever find anything?"

"I think that's rather the point," Granville said.

"What d'you mean? What point?"

"It wouldn't be easy for anyone not familiar with the place to find anything in here. Especially if they were in a hurry. Or it was after hours, and dark."

"You mean if they were breaking in? Like us?" Scott said.

Granville laughed softly. "I noticed that each stack seems to be for a different recipient. And most of them seem to be for shops rather than individuals."

"Pass me that lantern, will ya?" Scott said.

When Granville complied, his partner lifted the light and peered closer at several stacks in turn.

"Looks like you're right," he said after several moments. "Which fits with that theory you were building."

"Even if it doesn't help to explain it," Granville said wryly. "Any ideas what's going on here?"

"Nope," Scott said, handing back the lantern. "Except I can only see one stack per buyer here. Wouldn't stuff be stacked together?"

"I think we can assume it's organized like this for a reason. It's up to us to figure out what they're trying to hide."

Scott glanced around him. "Maybe this company really does import goods for this many small businesses?" And he waved his arm in a rough circle to indicate the endless stacks that surrounded them.

"I suppose anything is possible," Granville said. "There could be a legitimate reason why having so many customers works for them. But it would suggest their potential profit isn't much bigger than Sikes's."

"Not much room for a puppet master to make money, then."

"No."

"Unless inflate the charges for shipping to cover it? Or they're using several fake names for each customer," Scott added with a frown.

"Now that would be truly devious," Granville said. "I rather like the idea. Though it doesn't get us much closer to understanding what's really going on. Let's keep looking, shall we?"

"Yeah. Why don't you read out the customer names. I'll write 'em down," Scott said. "Then maybe we can see where we are."

"And while we're at it, can you note what country they're shipped from?" Granville said.

"What for?"

"Just putting things together," Granville said.

"Can do," Scott said, well used to how reliable Granville's instincts could be. Though neither of them would ever label them instincts, of course. Not out loud.

An hour later, dusty and frustrated, Granville called a halt. "This doesn't seem to be getting us very far. Is there a pattern to where these shipments are originating?"

Scott flipped back through the pages of scribbled notes. "They're all from China or Japan."

"All of them?"

"Yup."

That was interesting. Not useful yet, but interesting. "And have any of those buyer's names repeated?"

Scott flipped through the pages again, more slowly this time. "Nope."

"I didn't think so," Granville said.

"But we've only covered about a quarter of this place."

"If that," Granville said. "If we kept going, we'd be here until daybreak."

"So? We might as well do the job right while we're here."

"Except the information we already have fits the pattern we're looking for. And the longer we're here, the more likely we are to be caught."

Scott grimaced. "You really think they're paying someone to keep an eye on this place?"

"No. But they could have someone that checks all their buildings once a night. And our lantern light could be enough to give us away, if someone was looking hard enough."

"If it helps us solve this, it's worth the risk," Scott said doggedly.

"We still don't know that this is the right warehouse," Granville said.

"So what d'you suggest?"

"Let's check out the other warehouse. And tomorrow, we'll ask

Miss Kent to compare the names you've got there to the city direc-tory. That'll tell us if some of these companies actually exist. And what kind of merchandise they carry."

"We could just break into some of these boxes, see what's inside," Scott said.

"Too risky. And I'd rather not alert our puppet master we're onto him until we know what we're working with. Right now, we're just firing random shots, and hoping to hit something."

Scott grinned. "Sometimes that's all it takes to scare off a predator."

"Mostly the four-legged ones," Granville said with a straight face. "And I doubt that approach would scare off this bad guy. More likely to make us targets."

"You've got a point," Scott said when he stopped laughing. "Okay, let's go have a look at that other warehouse."

Unfortunately, the second warehouse, while better organized, was filled with floor to rafters with large, sealed crates.

"This doesn't tell us anything," Scott complained once they got inside.

"Too soon to say," Granville said absently, lifting his lantern higher. "Why don't we start on a list of where these came from, and who they're going to. Then see what that tells us."

It told them next to nothing. Unlike the first address, all of the crates were addressed to McIver & Allan. Each crate had a packing slip still attached, though, and those told them a great deal.

"It's all furniture," Scott said in a disgusted tone.

"I see that," Granville said. "And it all comes from either the United States or Eastern Canada. Which eliminates them from our search. This isn't our puppet master."

"Unless someone got clever, and they're hiding other stuff in these crates," Scott said.

"Which wouldn't match the information we received earlier," Granville said.

"We've been lied to before."

"True enough. Let's see what else is here," Granville said. "At least if it's all crates this size, it shouldn't take too long."

Scott grumbled a bit, but they worked their way through most of the warehouse in short order. It was all large crates. And the packing slips all confirmed the contents as furniture, their origin as either the US or Canada.

"We need to break one of these open," Scott said. "Just to be sure."

"You're right," Granville said. "But it's too soon. And too hard to cover up the damage."

"So what then?"

"We follow up on the leads we found tonight. For a start, Mac can dig into the reputation and financials of both these firms for us. He might find enough to eliminate one of them."

"So if McIver & Allan's money all comes from furniture..." Scott said.

"Then there's no need to raise suspicions by breaking open crates," Granville finished for him with a grin. "And quite frankly, I've had enough of warehouses. Time to work on our strategy over a whiskey or two."

"Good plan," Scott said.

11

Wednesday, September 19, 1900

On Wednesday morning, Granville escaped his house ahead of the builders, ate a quick breakfast at Mary's, and took a brisk walk. He zig-zagged along residential streets overlooking the harbor, then took Georgia Street, which was quiet except for the occasional delivery wagon. It was too early for the tram, though he planned to take it back to the office later. For now, he needed to stretch his legs and think.

When he reached the Stanley Park gateway, a wooden arch spelling out the park's name in letters shaped from branches, he paused and checked his pocket watch. Plenty of time. Stepping onto the sturdy wooden footbridge—wide enough for ten people to walk abreast, and more than fifty feet long—he walked swiftly towards the thick forest on the other side.

His footsteps echoed hollowly on the thick planks of the bridge. He savored the experience of walking less than six feet above the waves of Burrard Inlet, as he did every time he crossed here. At the far end of the bridge, he turned left onto the path that wound along the shore.

It was still early, the air cool and the park quiet. Though horse-drawn wagons full of tourists and sightseers would throng the path later in the day. For now, he had to himself the vista of forest on one side and rocky ocean shores on the other. After the expedition to the docks last night, it was just what he'd needed.

He drew in a deep lungful of fresh air, laden with the scent of salt and the kelp that had floated ashore overnight. Then he lengthened his stride and turned his mind to the problem of the puppet master. Something wasn't adding up.

The one thing Benton had told them was to look into shipping and the docks. And they'd finally had a little luck with their expedition last night. So what had it gained them?

Other than more questions.

The small shipments that had come in on the *Empress of China*, the two importing companies that might or might not be involved? They seemed too small to matter against Benton's criminal empire. If this was the extent of the puppet master's world, why would Benton care?

The more he dug into this case, the less sense it made.

Which meant he was missing something. Benton would have a reason, and likely a devious one. That's how the fellow was made.

So why had he hired Granville & Scott Investigations?

The gangster probably had half the town afraid of him, and the other half either worked for him or owed him money or favors. He had his own army of thugs, and with the amount of money he undoubtedly made from his various illegal enterprises, he could hire more anytime he needed them. So why set them on this puppet master? And with so little useful information?

Smuggling was the first thing that came to mind, and Emily's comment about the links to chinoiserie was insightful. But did it help them?

His stride lengthened as he considered the implications. Certainly Benton was involved in smuggling, likely on a variety of fronts. And there were plenty of other smugglers in town, most of whom Benton either used or ignored. So what made this one different?

Whatever the puppet master was up to, it had to be lucrative to make him a threat to Benton. Or he had to be causing the gangster problems in some other way.

A flash of light caught Granville's attention, and he looked up to see he'd already reached the lighthouse at Prospect Point. There was no fog this morning, but the lighthouse served to warn any ship against venturing too close to shore. The rocky narrows were dangerous, and he'd heard the tales about more than a few deadly wrecks over the last dozen years.

He stopped for a moment to appreciate the view. The sea was calm this morning, but small waves crashed against the rocks of the point. The currents were tricky here.

A steamliner began to round the point. She was black-hulled with a clipper bow, a smaller vessel than the all-white *Empress* line. Like the *Empress of China* and her sister ships, this was a combination ship, with three tall masts in addition to her smokestack. Unlike the *China*, instead of double smokestacks, this ship sported only a single tall smokestack. Which was currently belching out thick black smoke.

Combination ships were built for long ocean voyages. Just how many oceangoing vessels docked in Vancouver on a regular basis? And of those, how many were from the Far East?

As he watched the steamliner make her determined way towards the harbor, he wondered where this one was coming from, and what goods she carried.

The puppet master would know.

The sudden thought drove everything else from Granville's mind.

If they were looking at some kind of smuggling ring, something big enough to threaten Benton, would it be limited to the Far East? Emily was probably right about the connection to chinoiserie. But it was too early in this investigation to limit their thinking to one region of the world. Or one steamship line.

He needed to know more about all the shipping lines that used this port. Emily's father would know, or be able to point him in the right direction.

And it was time to draw on the Pinkerton's resources, which was one of the benefits of their affiliate status with that international firm.

———

BY THE TIME Granville walked back to the park entrance and caught a tram to the office, Scott had arrived. They sat in Granville's office and compared notes from the previous evening while they updated the case file. Then Granville filled him in on what he'd seen in the park.

"We need to think bigger if we're going to find this puppet master," he finished.

"Sounds like she's a tricky one. The color runs deeper than what showed at first," Scott said with a grin, alluding to following a narrow seam of gold and finding it led to a rich strike.

"It would be good if this led to riches. Right now it feels more like one of those treacherous seams that entices you to dig deeper and deeper yet. And then vanishes without a trace."

"Well, we've had some experience with those, anyway," Scott said. "So where d'you want to start?"

"I think we need to brief everyone else on what we know so far..." he began, when there was a rap on the door.

Emily poked her head in. "Oh, good morning. I'm sorry to interrupt," she said, looking flustered. "I didn't realize you were both here."

Which wasn't like her.

"Come in," he was quick to say. "Is everything all right?"

"Of course," she said. "I was just wondering how it went? Your visit to the docks last night, I mean?"

"We were just talking about calling a meeting, and bringing everyone in."

"Oh, good. Somehow it feels like this case is moving very quickly, and in too many directions."

"Getting away from us?" Scott said with a grin.

"Something like that. Maybe I'm just feeling unsettled after all that time I spent on my Victoria case."

"Not at all. I was just telling Scott that I think this case might prove to be much more complex than anything we've seen yet."

"Especially with Benton involved," Scott said.

Emily nodded. "That makes sense. And it will be even more important we pool our information."

"Indeed," Granville said. "Miss Rizzo can cover reception."

He glanced at Emily to see her reaction, wondering if she'd say anything.

She didn't.

He was beginning to appreciate the wisdom of having both Miss Kent and Trent free to attend meetings whenever necessary, though. Which seemed to mean promoting Miss Kent and hiring a permanent receptionist. And the way this case was evolving, they'd need the help sooner than later.

He wondered if Miss Rizzo would consider not returning to the typing school, and accept a permanent position here instead. He'd been impressed by how well she interacted with every client, and the way her attitude reflected on his agency. It was worth considering.

ONCE EVERYONE WAS SEATED around the conference table, Granville began. "This puppet master case is showing signs of being much larger and more complex than we'd at first considered. Sharing information will be critical. Any updates for us on Benton's files, Miss Kent? Mac?"

Miss Kent glanced at Mac, then began. "We do," she said. "The files Mr. Benton sent over are a mess, as you already know. He seems to have been tracking every ship that uses our harbor and had an international port as their point of origin."

"Not just ships from the Far East, then?" Granville asked her.

"No, though most of them are, of course," she said.

"The CPR doesn't advertise Vancouver as 'The Gateway to the Pacific Rim' for nothing," Mac said with a grin.

It made sense. But he still wasn't ready to narrow his focus. "Go on."

"There are schedules for ground transport—mostly railway schedules—that would connect with each ship's docking," Miss Kent said.

"Which again suggests smuggling," Granville said. "But still doesn't confirm anything. Go on."

"There are a few names listed, here and there, but nothing that connects to the last cases, or to the list that Mr. Draper gave you."

"Anything else catch your eye?"

She shook her head. "The various schedules suggest the beginning of a pattern, and that whatever this is concentrates on shipping from the Far East. But those alone aren't enough to help much. We'd need more information."

"Mac? Anything on the financial end?"

"Not in those files," their accountant said. "Did you and Scott find anything last night?"

"We have a bit more information," Granville said. And he filled them in on the previous night's expedition to the docks and to the two warehouses, though he kept his thoughts about what might be involved to himself for the moment.

"And you think all of this is related?" Miss Kent asked him.

"I'm hoping it is," Granville said.

"How can we help?" Mac asked.

"We need a lead," Granville told them all bluntly. "Something that will give us a direction in finding whoever is behind this. I'm hoping that you and Mis Kent can dig it out for us."

"What do you need us to do?" Miss Kent asked him.

"We need you to find out everything you can about the owners of those two warehouses," he said. "And Mac can dig into the reputation and financials of both firms."

She nodded, her pencil flying over the pages of her ever-present stenographic notebook. "Anything else?"

"I'm afraid so," Scott said, handing over his own notes. "These chicken scratches represent the firms William Clark & Company is doing business with. It would help to know who owns them, and what kind of business they're in."

"That's easy," Miss Kent said. "They should all be in the directory."

"But there's pages of them," Scott said. "And my scrawl isn't exactly easy to read."

Miss Kent just smiled. "Leave it to me," she said.

"Thank you both," he said. "Emily? Trent? Anything to add?"

"Nothing to report," Trent said bitterly. "Watching out for Miss Frances wasn't nearly as helpful as me going to the docks with you would have been."

"But we needed to be sure that Benton wasn't being subtle and arranging meetings from Frances's home," Granville said. "And you've proven that."

Trent looked doubtful, and Emily smiled at him.

"I have nothing to report, either," she said. "Clara and I have begun searching for social rumors, but it may take some time."

His plan was working, then. Granville sincerely hoped that meant a respite for him on the infernal redecorating chaos that his home had become.

"Thank you all," Granville said. "This is a good start. Unless something comes up, let's meet again tomorrow morning. Same time. Emily, do you have lunch plans?"

"No, I don't. Why?"

"I thought we might take your father out for luncheon."

She frowned at him. "What are you up to now?"

He just grinned and taking her hand, pressed a kiss into the palm. "I have a few questions he might be able to help with."

She gave him a speculative look, and her eyes started to sparkle. "Shipping?"

"Something like that. Well?"

"Of course. I'd love it."

"Good. Noon, then?"

"Perfect. That gives me time to take care of a few things."

As she left his office he thought she looked less burdened than she had earlier. Which was a relief.

She'd tell him about whatever was bothering her when she was ready—though if he had to guess, it was something to do with her sister's engagement. But it was hard to see her so worried and do nothing to help.

12

Leaving Granville's office, Emily felt much better at the thought of spending a little time pursuing this case together. It gave her something to think about other than Jane's inconvenient engagement. And her questionable fiancé.

She'd finally met him at dinner the previous evening. Cyrus Bray was a suave, polished man in his mid-thirties, with a well-cut suit and pomaded hair. He looked vaguely familiar, though she couldn't think from where. He seemed to her a little too slick, his eyes too knowing. And his dark good looks made Jane's angular features look harsher than ever, though the beginning of jowls suggested he'd run to fat in a few years.

There was something obnoxious about his attitude, too. He was too ingratiating with her parents, while carrying himself as if he felt superior to all of them. It wasn't a pleasant combination.

Recalling Jane's anticipation of her honeymoon worried Emily. The thought of spending that much time with Mr. Bray—and the intimacies such a man might expect—turned her own stomach. She was afraid Jane was in for a difficult, maybe even an unpleasant marriage.

If they went through with it.

Which they wouldn't, if she had anything to say about it.

Still, it worried her. What if she couldn't find anything serious enough to change Jane's mind?

Lunch with Papa and Granville talking about shipping lines and smuggling would be a welcome distraction. But first, she needed to talk with Laura.

She turned her feet towards Laura's desk, and found her poring over Benton's files. She was running a finger down a handwritten list from the file, and making shorthand notes in her notebook.

"It's impressive," Emily said, stopping beside her friend's desk. "The way you can make sense of someone else's chaos."

Laura started, and looked up. "Emily. I didn't even hear you. I was trying to sort out this file."

Emily considered what she could see of the file. "You went through this file already, didn't you?"

Laura nodded. "Guilty. I can't help thinking I must have missed something."

"A missing thread from one of the cases we just finished, perhaps?"

"Yes, something like that."

"I'm so glad to hear you say that."

Laura gave her a shrewd look. "You're bothered by it too, aren't you?"

"Yes, but it was my case," Emily said. "You have a better sense of patterns when they are buried in too much information than I do. Or any of us does. So if you think we've missed something, then we have. It's that simple."

"I think your expectations of what I can do are too high."

"And I think you undervalue yourself," Emily said with a smile. "Which your supposed position as our receptionist doesn't help."

"I don't mind."

"Well, you should. You're doing far more for this firm now than what you were hired to do. And that needs to be recognized."

"I've had two pay raises already. That's more than fair," Laura protested.

"Is it?" Emily shook her head. "If you were our analyst, rather than our receptionist, would you have said something more in the meeting we just had?"

"No, of course not," Laura said. Then as Emily continued to look at her, she dropped her gaze. "Well, perhaps…"

"Perhaps nothing. It matters."

"Mr. Granville always asks my opinion. And listens when I have something to say. He's a good man, Emily."

"I know he is. I'm very lucky."

"You are," Laura said.

"But that doesn't change the fact that you need to be recognized for the quality of work you are doing."

"But…"

"Never mind," Emily said, seeing that Laura was starting to look upset. "I'll speak with Granville. He won't hesitate to make changes, once he's aware of the situation."

"But I don't want him to think I'm complaining."

"Why not?" she asked, feeling fierce. Then as Laura's face tightened, she backed off. "Never mind, he won't. This won't be a problem—just leave it to me. But in the meantime, what were you not quite ready to say in the meeting? Was it to do with what isn't in the files, by any chance?"

At that Laura smiled. "You're good at this. Yes, that's exactly it. See, I've been looking at how these are put together…"

Emily dragged a spare chair towards the desk, sat down and leaned forward as Laura began to explain what had caught her attention.

* * *

AT QUARTER TO TWELVE, Emily looked up to find Granville watching the two of them with a grin.

"What are you finding so amusing?"

"Nothing at all. Are you ready?"

The grin didn't change. She eyed him skeptically but decided not to argue, fun though it would be. Not when she still hadn't told him about Mama's demand that they postpone their wedding.

The thought was an uncomfortable one. "Yes, let's go," she said quickly.

They met Papa at Garrity's Steakhouse. It was a good choice. Papa tended to stick with his club, but he appreciated a good steak, and a change of venue would be good for him. Plus she felt less on exhibit here than she did at the Vancouver Club, with its separate entrance and rigidly restricted access for women.

"Good to see you, Granville," Papa said, standing as they approached the upholstered booth where he'd been seated. The two men shook hands, and Papa gave her a peck on the cheek as she arranged her full skirts carefully on the seat opposite them.

"And you, sir," Granville said.

"You'll have to come for dinner one evening soon," Papa said as he accepted a menu from the waiter. "Have you met Bray yet? No? We'll have to change that. My eldest, Jane, and he have just become engaged. Capital fellow. Emily will have told you. I'll have my wife set something up."

Emily shifted uncomfortably under the quick look Granville sent her. She hadn't mentioned her impressions of Mr. Bray, either. It really was time to talk to him about the whole situation. She couldn't just keep putting it off.

Especially not when it was clear he and Mr. Bray would be meeting soon. Unless she could talk Mama out of issuing the invitation?

She dismissed that thought immediately. It would raise too many questions, and that would never do. Not in a society as small and as closed as theirs. Any aberration was cause for gossip, as she knew all too well.

Not that she usually cared.

Once the orders were placed—all three ordered steak with all the trimmings—Papa looked from her to Granville and back. "Well then. Why are we meeting here today? No problems with your engagement are there?"

"Of course not," Granville was quick to say. "It's simply that some questions regarding international shipping came up on a case, and it seemed a good opportunity to invite you for luncheon."

Papa looked from her to Granville and back, as if questioning her involvement in a case, but thankfully he didn't address it. "Shipping, is it?" he said. "What d'you want to know?"

"Anything you can tell us about the various lines that use the port here, and what their routes are," Granville said. "Beginning with one particular ship."

When he described the ship he'd seen that morning, Papa smiled. "That's an easy one. She's the *R.M.S. Aorangi*, out of Australia."

"R.M.S.? The Royal Mail Service? The *British* Royal Mail Service?"

Papa nodded. "She was put on this route last year. Carries the mail as well as passengers from Sydney to Vancouver, by way of New Zealand, several Pacific Islands, and sometimes even Yokohama."

"How many passengers can she carry, do you know?" Granville asked.

"Of course I know. She's the competition, after all," Papa said with a genial smile that telegraphed how little he felt the mighty *Empresses* had to fear from the little *Aorangi*. "She has one hundred First Class and fifty Second Class berths."

"And she handles goods as well?"

"Yes, on a limited basis."

Emily exchanged glances with Granville. What were the implications for their case?

"How many other lines carry goods into Vancouver?" he asked. "Even on a limited basis?"

Just then the waiter brought their orders, and Papa liberally applied Worcestershire sauce to his steak. Emily was amused—and relieved—to note that her steak was less than half the size of the men's, which covered most of their plates. She couldn't imagine eating that much meat. But she'd certainly enjoy hers.

As they ate, Papa talked. His knowledge of the shipping lanes proved to be enormous. "It's my business, after all," he said when Granville expressed his appreciation of that fact. And proceeded to explain in detail just which lines carried goods here, and from where.

Not surprisingly, the bulk of the traffic came directly from the far east. By and large, now that the railroad lines were through, it was cheaper to ship goods cross-country than it was to ship them all the way around Cape Horn.

Emily enjoyed her meal and listened carefully. Papa would be offended if either of them took notes, so she and Granville would have to compare their memories of all of this information when they got back to the office.

It might be a good chance to talk to him about Jane's new fiancé, as well. And the impact on their own wedding. Suddenly her steak seemed much less appetizing.

———

EMILY AND GRANVILLE were back in his office by half past one. Once they'd compared notes on the various shipping lines and vessels Papa had shared with them, and assembled a list of them, Emily drew in a deep breath.

"There's something I need to talk to you about," she said.

"I had noticed you seemed concerned about something."

Of course he had. She nodded. "It's about Jane's engagement," she said. And couldn't find the words that came next.

"Go on," he said.

"Mr. Bray… well, I don't like him," she said in a rush. And berated herself for a coward.

"I wondered if that might be the case."

"However did you know? Do you know him? I know you told Papa you hadn't met, but I thought perhaps in passing?"

"No. I hadn't even heard his name before I learned of his engagement to your sister."

"Oh." Now what?

"And you don't like him because…" he prompted her.

"He's slimy, and full of himself, and I think he might only be interested in Jane's dowry. Or worse."

"Worse?"

"The shipping. Papa's position and connections. Mr. Bray imports goods from the Far East," she said.

"Yes, so you mentioned. Is that what you and Clara have been looking into?"

"However did you know that?" she demanded.

"I didn't. I guessed. I have come to know you rather well, you know," he said with a smile.

She smiled back, but it felt like an effort, and she was afraid it showed. Which it must have, because he looked concerned.

"What's really going on, Emily?"

She swallowed again, and felt like an idiot. "Well…"

This time there was no prompting. He just let the silence build.

She felt more and more tense. This was utterly ridiculous, she berated herself. This was Granville, after all. Not some very proper suitor she barely knew.

"Jane is the eldest, you see, and Mr. Bray wants to get married with all the pomp possible and Mama says our wedding has to be postponed until after theirs. At least three years. And maybe even four," she said in a rush, trying to get the words out before she could get nervous again.

He said nothing for a moment, and she felt like someone had died.

Then he grinned. "And to top it off, all this is caused by a fellow you don't even like. Is your mother really that traditional?"

Emily felt a weight roll off of her, and smiled back, feeling more than a little foolish. "Not at all. I suspect she doesn't care for Mr. Bray either, and is hoping I'll look into him, if only to keep our wedding on track. Or maybe she's hoping you will do so."

His grin widened. "I had no idea your mother was so devious."

She laughed at that. "You did so. You had her pegged from the moment you met her, and you've been buttering her up ever since. I've decided that you know far too much about women for any man."

"Does that mean you're not going to investigate Bray, so our wedding will be delayed?"

"I am going to run that man out of town," Emily said decidedly. "For causing all this trouble, if nothing else."

And it was Granville's turn to laugh.

1 3

When his telephone rang just after three, Granville was still replaying his conversation with Emily. He wasn't happy about any talk of postponing their wedding, though he suspected that between Emily and her mother, Jane's engagement wasn't likely to last long. He almost felt sorry for Cyrus Bray, bounder though he might be. The fellow had no idea what he was in for.

He was more concerned that Emily had hesitated to tell him what was happening, though. Surely by now she should be comfortable turning to him when something went wrong?

The telephone rang and he reached for the handset. "Granville."

"It's Carver," the lawyer said. "I have something for you on the matter we recently discussed."

It took him a moment to make the connection. They hadn't brought Robert Carver in on this new case, but they had hired him for the Randall case and the hunt for the no-so-big fish. Carver must be referring to that. What angle was he exploring now?

"Go on," he said.

"It's best we do this in person. And bring Scott."

Which meant Carver thought they both needed to be armed. And careful. Who was after them now?

"We'll be there shortly," he said, and replaced the handset. The situation with Emily —and getting information from Pinkerton's— would have to wait.

He checked that he had his knife and drew his gun out of the drawer, holstering it. Then he strolled into Scott's office. "Carver wants to see us."

"Now?"

"Yes."

"He have news?"

"He says so. Bring your gun."

"Like that, is it?" Scott grabbed his own weapons, checked they were loaded, and followed him out of the office.

———

As they strolled into Carver's well-furnished outer office, Granville was amused to see that it was no longer deserted. Or dusty. In addition to the neatly suited young man behind the clerk's desk, Carver must have hired someone to clean the premises.

Both were good signs that the lawyer was back on his feet, and taking his profession seriously again. It was good to see.

The clerk stood up. "Mr. Granville? Mr. Scott?"

At their nods, he said, "Mr. Carver wanted to see you right away," and ushered them into the familiar office.

"Granville. Scott. Good to see you both," Carver said, rising and coming around his desk to shake hands. "Have a seat."

"What do you have for us?" Granville asked.

"Not what you're expecting, I'm afraid," Carver said. "Were you down on the docks last night?"

That was a surprise. How had the fellow heard? "We were. You have good informants."

"Connections," Carver said with a small smile. "Also, I still have a few grateful clients. Which is useful, in this town. And I heard you spent some time at the Beaver Tavern."

"We did," he said. "And this concerns you how?"

"It concerns me because the man you were seen talking to was murdered last night."

"What?" Granville said. "When?"

Out of the corner of his eye, he could see Scott's hand move so it was resting on his gun.

"Sometime early this morning, I hear," Carver said, ignoring Scott's implied threat. "Most likely on his way home from the tavern. His body was found in an alley off of Alexander."

"Who did it?" Scott growled.

"Don't know. The killer wasn't seen, and no one's talking," Carver said.

"But you think he was killed because he was seen talking to me?" Granville asked.

"That's what I hear," Carver said.

Was this the puppet master's work? If so, it was the first indication they'd had that the fellow could be lethal. Though given Benton's concerns, that probably shouldn't have been a surprise.

It also suggested the puppet master was now aware that he and Scott were investigating him. If he hadn't been before.

No wonder Carver had asked him to bring Scott to the meeting. "Do you think this is related to the Randall case?"

The lawyer looked from him to Scott and back. "You mean you don't?"

"Not directly," he said. "We have a new case, though, which may well be related. If this one ends up in court, we'll be working with Randall. But I think we'd best hire you as well."

"If this is linked in any way to the last case, I'll consider myself still hired," Carver said. "Then anything you tell me will be protected by solicitor-client privilege."

"That's more than fair. Just be sure to bill us for your hours," he said, and filled Carver in on their hunt for the puppet master.

"Interesting. This is definitely connected to your previous case, legally speaking," was Carver's verdict.

"You think the puppet master is really that worried about what we might dig out?" Scott asked the lawyer.

Carver frowned. "If the fellow behind this is your puppet master,

I've heard a rumor or two that he's made talking about his business a killing offense."

"Which could explain why we haven't been able to unearth any rumors about him at all," Granville said. "I'm impressed that your connections are talking."

Carver nodded.

"This guy's not going to be so invisible if he's started killing people," Scott said.

"He hasn't," Granville said. "This puppet master wouldn't consider getting his own hands dirty. He'll have hired someone to take care of such details for him."

"I agree," Carver said. "But he wouldn't hesitate to have you both killed if he decides you're a threat."

He could try. "I think it's time Scott and I had another chat with Officer Daniels," Granville said. "Thanks for the information, Carver. And if you hear anything else related to our puppet master, please let me know."

"I'll do that. Watch your backs."

"Always do," he said with a grin.

THEY WERE IN LUCK. It appeared Officer Daniels had been assigned to the murder of the dockworker that had talked to Granville the previous night. But that was where their luck ran out.

They tracked the policeman down on at the murder site, in a grubby, refuse strewn alley behind a warehouse. It reeked of stale piss and spilled blood, but other than the smell and a large bloodstain on the packed dirt, there was nothing to show a man had died here.

Granville looked at the size of the bloodstain. "I gather he was stabbed?"

"Mmmm. His throat was slit," Daniels said, his eyes scanning the alley as he spoke. "Quickly and efficiently done, too. There's no sign of a struggle."

Granville glanced around him. Daniels was right. Even on this hard-packed dirt, something would still show if the dead man had fought back. Probably he'd been taken by surprise. Followed from the tavern, then?

It was an unsettling possibility. Especially if Carver was right that the dead man had been killed for talking to them.

Whoever had killed him, he'd been patient. Waited for his moment. And he probably worked for the puppet master.

He needed to find that killer. And fast.

Before the puppet master decided to turn the killer on them.

"Is this related to the matter you told me about yesterday?" Daniels asked.

The officer's eyes lit up and he took hurried notes when Granville explained his meeting with the victim the previous evening.

"You say he gave you information on some suspicious shipments coming through the harbor," Daniels said. "What exactly did he tell you?"

Granville filled him in on the conversation.

"And you think this relates to this invisible gangster you think might be operating behind the scenes?"

"I'm not sure he's a gangster," Granville said. "Not exactly. It's beginning to look as if all of this centers on shipping and importing. We've found nothing to suggest he's involved in the usual vices."

"No gambling, drugs or prostitution?" Daniels said.

"No. Just importing. And murder," Scott said, glancing at the blood on the pavement.

"Interesting. So what's his deal?" the officer asked.

"I haven't been able to work that out yet," Granville said. "Too little to go on."

"What about the warehouse this poor fellow told you about. Down on Water Street, you said?"

"He couldn't remember the exact address, and there are two on that block that might fit. William K. Clark, and McIver & Allan, both listed as commission merchants. Do either of those names mean anything to you?"

"No," Daniels said slowly. "They're both legitimate businesses, as far as I know. But I'll ask around. If there is a connection, I want to know what it is."

"Just be careful," Granville said. "Whoever's behind this apparently doesn't like to be talked about."

"And he's lethal," Scott said. "Or at least the killer he hires is."

Daniels smiled a thin smile. "Sounds like both of them need to be taken off the streets."

"Agreed," Granville said. "Is there anything else you can you tell us about this killer?"

"Not much, I'm afraid," Daniels said. "I'm hopeful the coroner can give us a few details about the knife, but even that won't help much at this stage. He's used to killing, though. This was an efficient murder. There was only one stab wound, and no hesitation marks."

"And the victim?"

"A dockworker, exactly as you said. So far all I've learned is that he gambled heavily, though not where. This could be a debt gone bad."

"Except there was no struggle," Granville said, glancing at the dirt around the body. "You'd expect an exchange of words, some shoving and pushing. I don't see any signs of either."

"Not if the killer is an enforcer of some kind," Daniels said. "Then this is the scene I'd expect to find if this murder was about a gambling debt. And not your smuggler, or whatever he is."

Granville nodded. "Anything else?"

"No, but if I come across something that might help you, I'm willing to share information. If you are."

"Of course," Granville said, and the two men shook on it.

14

On their way back to the office, both men were quiet. Granville wasn't sure what Scott was thinking. But for himself, he was running through everything they'd learned so far, looking for connections that would make sense of it.

If he'd been right in his suggestion to Daniels, the puppet master —the scheming mind behind it all—wasn't a typical gangster. So what was he?

Benton, ruthless gangster though he was, didn't seem to know much about this fellow, either. And he'd been concerned enough to hire their firm to find the fellow. He'd also given them free rein in how they chose to do that.

Very unlike Benton's usual style.

The few facts they had about the business itself all seemed to hinge on the sales of imported merchandise. And this murder had just confirmed they were on the right track.

But what kind of merchandise? And why?

Whatever it was, there had to be money in it. A lot of money. Nothing else made sense.

His question from that morning came back to him—if they were looking at some kind of smuggling ring, just how large was it?

How much money were they talking about?

Enough that this puppet master was prepared to be ruthless in disposing of anyone he perceived as an obstacle to whatever scheme he'd concocted. And he'd hired a cold-blooded killer to ensure that.

But nothing they'd found so far pointed to anything that looked particularly lucrative.

Meanwhile, they had to brief the team on the murder, and what it might mean for each of them.

Twenty minutes later, everyone was gathered in the meeting room.

"There's been a murder," Granville told them bluntly, looking around the table at their concerned faces. "The fellow I talked with last night was knifed in an alley off of Alexander early this morning."

And he quickly briefed them on the status of the murder investigation and their meeting with Daniels.

"You think it's the puppet master?" Trent asked.

He nodded. "We have to assume so. I don't think this threat will touch any of you, but I'll ask all of you to be vigilant as long as we're working this case."

"Are you in danger?" Emily asked.

"His hired killer hasn't tried to kill us yet," Granville said. "But Scott and I suspect he's been following us. I think we have to assume we're all in danger."

"Thank you for not hiding that from us," Emily said.

"You all needed to know," he said bluntly.

"This is serious," Scott said. "None of us should go out alone. Trent, Mac, you both own guns?"

Both men nodded.

"Then carry them," he said.

"I agree," Granville said. "And ladies, any time you leave the office, for whatever reason, if one of us isn't free to accompany you, then call a hackney, and charge it to the office. I don't want you walking anywhere alone."

"What if it's just a block or two, to pick up a sandwich?" Emily asked.

"Even then," he said. "Or better yet, order your lunch delivered and bill it to the office. In fact, having things delivered should be our first option. And only if there are two people in the office."

"I agree. No one should be in the office alone, either," Scott said. "Not until this is done. And there should be someone with a gun in the office at all times."

"But how will that work? We have to be able to go out and investigate," Trent protested.

"We'll make it work because we must," Granville said. "And I'm counting on each of you to make sure it does. Protecting the team comes first."

Trent nodded, looking suddenly proud.

"We'll need to work out a schedule amongst ourselves," Granville said. "Emily, can you talk to Miss Rizzo about this? She's the one who knows where each of us is, so she's the logical person to keep the master schedule. Each of us will have to work with that."

Emily nodded. "Of course. But she's only here for another week."

"It's time to change that. In recognition that Miss Kent's new role as our investigative analyst has now become full time, Scott and I have agreed that we need to hire a permanent receptionist. I plan to speak with Miss Rizzo about accepting that position, if none of you have concerns about her in that role. Are there any concerns?"

No one had any, though he noted Miss Kent looked a bit overwhelmed. Probably he should have spoken with her first. Emily looked pleased, though, so he couldn't have blundered too badly.

He was enjoying working with a team, but it did complicate things.

"We shouldn't travel to the office alone, either," Mac said. "I can walk Miss Kent home. And Miss Rizzo, too, if she accepts the position." He turned to Miss Kent. "And back again in the morning, if you're agreeable?"

She nodded. "I'm not worried, but I'd be glad of the company. And two pairs of eyes might see things that one misses."

"Good," Granville said. "I'll make sure Emily gets home safely." He glanced at her, pleased to see her fierce look in return.

"Trent and I can travel together," Scott said.

"Or with anyone else who needs it," Trent added, and Scott nodded.

"We don't know how long this case will last, so we'll all have to be flexible," Granville said. "And please tell Scott or myself if any of you see anything that worries you."

***

GRANVILLE AND SCOTT went back to his office, where he used his private line and dialed the number he'd been given any time he needed this kind of assistance from Pinkerton's.

"Research," said a brisk male voice over a line remarkably free of crackling.

"We're looking for information on the ownership and any possible criminal links on three firms," Granville said after he identified himself. "William K. Clark & Company, McIver and Allan, and Vancouver Box, all located in Vancouver, Canada."

"Just a moment." There was silence on the line except for a faint buzz, then the voice came back. "We have no files on any of the three."

"Thank you. I appreciate your effort."

"Welcome." And the line disconnected with a click. Leaving him exchanging glances with Scott.

"Nothing, I take it?" his partner asked.

"No."

"Not a lot of help when there's a killer out there," Scott said.

"Perhaps Mac and Miss Kent will find some answers for us on the warehouses we broke into. Since no one else seems to."

"They're probably still digging, too."

"Or trying to read your handwriting," he said with a grin.

Ten minutes later there was a rap on the door and Miss Kent's head appeared in the opening. "Do you and Mr. Scott have a moment for Mac and I?" she asked. "We think we have some information on those two warehouses that might be useful."

Perfect timing. "Of course. Come in."

Once the four of them were seated around the small table at the far end of the office, Miss Kent opened her stenographer's notebook.

"I'm not sure how helpful any of this is," she said. "But McIver & Allan is owned by Jasper McIver and Donald Allan. They are primarily furniture wholesalers, though they will also special-order unusual items for large customers."

"All of which sound innocuous enough," Granville said.

"It sounds boring, is what is sounds," Scott said. "But given the way this case is going, I like boring."

"So we might be able to ignore that firm," Granville said, "If the financials back up what Miss Kent has found. Mac?"

The red-headed accountant placed a stack of papers on the table, and slapped a hand on top of it. "I spent most of the morning with the Registrar of Companies. It took me two hours just to collect this information," he said. "And another two to review it."

Scott rolled his eyes.

"However, I can just sum it up for you, if you'd like?"

"Please," Granville said.

"Boring," Mac said, grinning at Scott. "This firm is boring, from start to finish. Everything is straightforward, clearly laid out. If they're hiding so much as overcharging on a wash stand, I'll eat my hat."

"Which would be a shame," he said with a grin. "It sounds like we're agreed that McIver & Allan is not the firm we're looking for, then. What can you tell us about William K. Clark & Company? Miss Kent?"

"He doesn't exist," she said. "William K. Clark, I mean. Not in any of the records I could get hold of, anyway. The firm is owned by one Philip Abernathy, who does exist—at least on paper. But there's no sign of the man himself. No address other than the firm itself, no phone number, nothing. I've begun calling him the invisible man."

The same thing Benton had called the puppet master. "Interesting," Granville said.

"And I'll tell you what else is interesting," she said, leaning forward and tapping the table in front of her. "Philip Abernathy may or may not actually exist, but in addition to this warehouse, he also owns the Vancouver Box Company. At least on paper."

"So what do those two companies with their invisible owner do?" Scott asked her.

"Well, Vancouver Box is the simplest. They make boxes. All sizes and shapes of boxes, for firms like Clark & Company and McIver & Allan."

"Anything to add, Mac?" Granville asked.

"The financials look pretty straightforward, too," Mac said. "On the surface, anyway. Except..."

"Except?" he said.

"Clark & Company seem to do quite a few small special-orders. Which must be costing them a pretty penny, given the shipping costs. Vancouver Box does the shipping for those orders," Miss Kent said.

"In addition to making the boxes?" Granville asked.

"Yes. Which struck me as odd," Mac said.

"I wonder what they're up to," Granville said. "Can the two of you look into where these special shipments are going, please? As well as any information you can get your hands on about what exactly is in these shipments. And who the clients are."

Both of them nodded. Miss Kent's pencil was flying across the pages of her notebook. Good. It meant every detail would be accurate.

"Have a deeper look at Vancouver Box, too, while you're at it," Granville said. "Which brings us back to the more interesting company. Tell me more about Clark & Company"

Miss Kent looked across the desk at Mac, who nodded and gave her a reassuring smile. She drew in a deep breath.

"I think they're crooked. Really crooked."

Granville smiled. "I certainly hope so. It would mean we've found the first solid lead on our puppet master. Even if he's hiding behind a slew of fake names. But I need details, Miss Kent. What makes you think they're crooked?"

She smiled back. "The few details I do have. Clark & Company specialize in imports from the Far East. From what I can find, it is mainly porcelain and lacquer ware, with some textiles. They advertise that they'll do those special-orders, too."

"That explains the crates from China and Japan," Scott said.

She nodded. "All of that stuff is really popular right now. And you have to have connections, if you're going to import it directly. Those firms Clark & Company is doing business with? Most of them are small local merchants who sell a variety of goods."

"Probably they're happy to order from Clark & Company. Unless they're being swindled," Granville said.

"Like Mr. Randall's client was by Mr. Sikes?" Miss Kent said.

"Exactly. Is there any sign that's happening?"

"I don't have access to that information," she said.

"But the financials suggest the opposite," Mac said. "They seem to be losing money on those imports. And I've done work with a few of the smaller merchants Clark & Company deal with. They carry what they call 'exotics', the kind of stuff they'd get from Clark & Company, because it's expected. But they don't make much profit on it, either."

"So Clark & Company might be taking losses on a number of small accounts. Which would be tedious to keep track of, as well as bad for business," Granville said. "What else have you found?"

"Buried in the list Mr. Scott made of firms Clark & Company had shipments for, there were perhaps half a dozen that were in the name of the store manager rather than the owner," Miss Kent said. "When I finally tracked the ownership down, all of the stores were owned by the same man."

"Our invisible Mr. Abernathy?" Scott asked.

She laughed. "No. That would be too obvious. They're owned by an equally invisible Mr. Barnabas Jones."

Neither Abernathy nor Jones were on Draper's list of unexpected attendees at Randall's trial, either. "That's impressive work, Miss Kent," Granville said.

"Thank you, sir."

"No 'sirs' required here, remember? You're a valued member of our firm."

She flushed with pride. "Thank you. I'll remember."

"And in the list of firms Clark & Company deal with, is there any connection to other cities?" Granville asked her.

"Clark & Company seem to ship all over North America. At least a third of their business is in Vancouver, though. No other city stands out so far," Miss Kent said. "But I'll keep looking."

"Thank you," Granville said, and turned to Mac. "Anything odd about Mr. Jones's stores?"

"Not much yet," he said. "But I'll keep looking, too."

"What about the profits on these orders for Mr. Jones's stores?"

"There are none," Mac said. "They've declared a loss for the last several years."

"What?"

Mac nodded. "According to their filings on record."

Granville sat back. "That makes no sense. Whatever is going on, someone has to be taking in a decent profit to make all this subterfuge worthwhile."

He thought for a moment, and turned to Mac. "Have you been able to find any detail on these firms this Jones supposedly owns?"

"Not yet," Mac said.

"It might be interesting to do so," Granville said. "And is there any way of getting more information on the real ownership of all these companies? If we assume neither Abernathy nor Jones actually exist? Then someone must have set them up."

"Miss Kent and I can dig deeper," Mac said. "But we'll undoubtedly need a lawyer's help. Any chance we can work with Carver again? He was good with similar material on our last case."

"I've already talked to him about it. And it might be helpful to include Randall in the discussions as well, since the original case against Sikes was his," Granville said, handing over Randall's card. "I'll let both know to expect your call. Ask both lawyers to draw up contracts for this case and I'll review them."

Mac nodded and pocketed the card.

"Meanwhile, Scott and I will keep looking into the attacks, see if we can track down the puppet master from that end."

"We'll check back later today," Scott said.

"And be careful," Granville said. "The fellow we're after is ruthless. I don't want him focused on either of you. In fact, for now, don't mention Abernathy or Jones to the team. Not until we know more."

Mac and Miss Kent nodded, though he noted the latter looked worried. Still, the fewer people asking obvious questions about the puppet master's business, the better.

It was bad enough that the puppet master was probably having him and Scott followed. He would not make a target out of anyone else.

15

Thursday, September 20, 1900

By Thursday morning, the office felt a little more normal, but to Emily's mind, it was still too quiet. She found it unnerving.

Granville's warnings about the killer the day before had been a hard thing for everyone to hear. And probably a harder thing for him to tell them. But his determination to keep them all safe had been apparent. They'd all heard the promise in his words, seen it in his eyes.

After the meeting, though, it had felt as if no one wanted to so much as make a noise that might draw attention to them. What, did they think that a killer lurked outside, waiting and listening for an opportunity to 'take them out', as the penny dreadfuls would have it? She smiled to herself at the notion of Mac reading a penny dreadful.

When nothing had dangerous or threatening happened for the rest of the day, everyone began to relax a little. She considered that a good thing. It was one thing to take reasonable precautions. It was another to let a possibly groundless fear get in the way of their investigations.

Granville and Scott might be targets, and even Trent if he were with them—neither of which she could think about for very long without that numbing fear spreading through her again. And needing to remind herself all over again that all three of them were dangerous in their own way.

They were also smart enough to take this threat seriously.

But as for the rest of the team? Not even the most ruthless gangster would go after them, surely? After all, she was no threat to a gangster. Nor was Laura, or Mac.

Oh, they'd be careful, all of them. She'd make sure of that. But they had a job to do. Besides, the only real solution to this threat was to see the puppet master behind bars. Then the problem would be permanently solved.

Stepping into the office this morning and finding that uneasy atmosphere back was unexpected. She didn't like it. And she for one wasn't about to stay cowering in the office in fear. Not when she had a potentially criminal would-be brother-in-law to investigate.

But first she needed to talk to Granville. She'd been thinking about his safety precautions. And how effective her aunt's small revolver had proven on her last case. If Granville felt Trent and Mac needed to carry a gun, then shouldn't she do so as well?

It was something to think about.

***

HALF AN HOUR later Granville and Scott returned from wherever they'd gone, and Emily took hold of her courage in both hands, and followed Granville into his office.

"I did get in touch with Pinkerton's yesterday," Granville said with a smile when he looked up and saw her.

"Oh, good," Emily said. "What were they able to tell you?"

"Not much, I'm afraid. There's no sign of any of the companies being involved with criminal activity of any sort. At least not in the States."

"What about here?"

"They don't have a lot of information on Vancouver crime, yet.

Apparently that's what they gain from our affiliation with them," he said. "The fellow I spoke with was very insistent that we share any criminal activity we uncover in this case."

"Oh," she said. "Well, I guess that makes sense. But what do we gain then? Aside from referrals, like the Cannery Row case."

"Pinkerton's has extensive sources in the States and England," he said. "So if we need to trace someone's criminal activity in either country, they'll be happy to help."

"You mean someone like Mr. Bray?" Emily said with sudden interest. "If I'm right about him being a schemer, that is. He's from New England somewhere. Could you find out what Pinkerton's might know about him?"

"I could," Granville said. "His interests certainly seem to overlap with this case."

She considered that. "Maybe hold off on calling them until I get a little more information on him. And what he's up to. We should be able to ask better questions then."

"Just be careful," he said.

She frowned at the implication. "I'm not afraid of Mr. Bray."

"No. But you wouldn't want him to know you're investigating him too soon."

For a moment she felt irritated. "I know what I'm doing." She'd just solved her first case, after all. "You worry too much."

"You don't think that's a fiancé's privilege?"

"No. I don't. I get quite enough of that from my parents," she said, no longer in the mood to discuss the possibility of buying a gun with him.

"What about a husband's privilege?"

She glared at him. "Only if you want our marriage postponed for the next ten years."

Then something in his expression gave him away. She tilted her head a little and stared at him for a moment. "Oh. You're teasing me."

At which he grinned. "Guilty."

"Fine. Just you wait."

His grin widened.

"I am careful, you know," she told him.

Or at least she tried to be. Most of the time, anyway.

AN HOUR later Emily was waiting in the hired hackney outside Clara's home for her friend to join her. She had to smile. It was a glorious blue and gold afternoon. The air was slightly crisp and there wasn't a cloud in the sky. It felt like she was miles away from the oppressive feeling of the office, instead of a few blocks.

It was probably a good thing that Clara hadn't been at yesterday's meeting, she decided. There was no need for both of them to worry needlessly about a killer who had no interest in them. Then too, Clara might have some scruples about safety, and she didn't want to waste time arguing with her. They were hardly likely to be a target.

Even if for some reason someone had followed her—which wasn't likely—they would be safe enough. The puppet master wouldn't expect trouble from anything women shopping and gossiping might discover. Or from her sisterly interest in Mr. Bray.

Clara's flurried entry into the hack distracted her from that thought.

"Emily! What was so urgent that you had to drag me away?" Clara said, dropping into the seat opposite.

"Are you complaining about investigating? Is there something you'd rather be doing, then?"

Clara frowned at her. "Well, no. Thanks to you, I escaped another session of post-wedding frenzy. I think I was about to become responsible for writing thank you notes for Cecily's signature. Our writing is very alike, you see, so…"

Her voice trailed off, and she gave a melodramatic shudder. "Can you imagine spending an afternoon like today going through all those gifts and writing someone else's thank you notes?"

Emily gave her a thoughtful look. "You weren't really complaining. And now you're not really upset at the idea of re-examining the gifts in detail. So. What are you trying to hide from me?"

"Me? Hide from…" Clara stopped in the midst of giving her an offended look, and dropped her hands in her lap. "You know me too well."

Emily smiled at that, and gave the driver the signal to go. She'd already given him the address.

"I think we know each other too well," she said. "So what is really wrong?"

"I have some information, and you're not going to like it," her friend said in a lowered voice.

"Information? On what?"

"On Mr. Bray. And Jane," Clara said.

"Bad news about Mr. Bray can only be good news for me," Emily said. "What is it?"

"Not this time," Clara said darkly, then met Emily's gaze. "Oh all right. No dramatics." Again she paused.

"Out with it, Clara."

"There are rumors all over town that Mr. Bray… that he and Jane… well, that they were seen in a compromising position," Clara said in a low tone. And looked away, as if she didn't want to see Emily's reaction.

Or maybe she was being delicate, and giving her a chance to recover? Which Emily considered beyond foolish. "Jane? In a compromising position? I don't believe it," she said flatly.

"I'm sorry, but it's true. They'll have to marry now, no matter what you find out about him."

"Utter nonsense," Emily said firmly, and Clara gave her a skeptical look. "Well, it is."

"It isn't, I'm afraid. You'll just have to accept it."

"Jane doesn't have it in her. She'd find being compromised far too uncomfortable," Emily said bluntly. "I'm a little worried how she'll deal with a honeymoon, quite frankly. She doesn't seem to have thought past white satin and lace."

"You never know about someone. She might be willing, now that she's engaged," Clara said, giving her a significant look. "And it's one way to be sure of a fellow."

Emily glared at her friend. "I can't believe you still think that way. In this day and age!"

"You mean if you and Mr. Granville had to wait four years to marry, you wouldn't do something drastic, just to be sure of him?"

Emily blinked at Clara, stunned. Maybe her friend didn't know her as well as she'd thought. "I probably would do something drastic, as you put it," she said after a moment. "But not for that reason. And I'd hardly call it drastic."

Clara blushed a little, surprising Emily again. "Then why?"

"Because he's Granville, of course. Haven't you seen him in a tuxedo?"

"I had no idea…" Clara said, then floundered to a stop.

Emily grinned. She hadn't either, not really. Not until her mother's edict had made a four-year delay a possibility, and she'd really thought about what that meant. "You mean you've never had those thoughts about Tim O'Hearn?"

"I've told you, we're not involved. Certainly not like that," Clara said, but she went beet red. Which didn't suit her delicate blonde complexion.

Emily took pity on her, and changed the subject. "I still don't believe it about Jane, though. Where did you hear this rumor, anyway?"

"Well, I was at Mrs. Smythe's 'at-home'. Her oldest daughter whispered it to me."

"You know Mrs. Smythe is the worst gossip," Emily said. "And she's especially fond of sharing bad news. She and Mama have been cordial enemies for years."

"Well, yes. But then I heard the same thing at Mrs. Reed's. And when I had tea with the Younger girls."

Emily considered that for a moment. "That's pretty quick-spreading gossip for an engagement that was only announced the day before yesterday."

"If you ever listened to it, you'd know how fast gossip can spread," said Clara tartly.

"What if it isn't real?" Emily said.

"Emily… really. You're going to have to accept this."

"No, I'm not. Think for a moment, Clara. If a false rumor is being spread, who would benefit from it?"

"Well, Mrs. Smythe always likes to be first… Wait a minute. You're thinking Mr. Bray is the one who gains the most, aren't you?"

"If he is a schemer with his eye on Jane's dowry and my father's connections, then yes," Emily said. "And he might benefit from a hasty marriage, too, no matter what he told Mama."

Clara was nodding. "It makes sense. Though I've never heard of such a thing."

"You're not saying you believe that every piece of gossip is true?"

"Hardly. But it's mostly harmless."

"No, it isn't. Gossip destroys people, if it's used maliciously or as part of a scheme. And how do you know that other hasty marriages didn't have someone scheming behind them?"

"Other than the bride—or her mother—making sure of her groom, you mean?"

"Really, Clara. How often do you believe that's really true?"

Clara looked taken aback, then thoughtful. "Well, I don't really know. It's the common assumption, I suppose…"

"More gossip?"

Clara looked even more thoughtful, then began to look intrigued. The hack came to a halt, and she looked around. "Where are we?"

"It seemed a good time to visit your Grandmama. If anyone will know the source of a tasty rumor, it will be her."

"You only think that because she likes you," Clara said as she followed Emily up a walkway bordered by neatly tended shrubbery, leading up to a finely appointed mansion.

"You're not her granddaughter. If you were, then you'd know that *never* is the best time to visit her," Clara muttered as the crushed seashells the path was made from crunched underfoot. "And you didn't even know about the rumor when you gave that driver the address."

Emily just smiled as the butler opened the door.

16

After a day that left them with more questions than answers, Granville and Scott spent half the night down on the docks, looking for anything that might lead them to the informant's killer.

And found nothing.

No one had heard anything. Or seen anything. No one knew of a hired killer who was deadly with a knife. And no one was willing to talk to them about shipping irregularities. Or anything else.

Even after the murder that morning. Which could only mean that the puppet master had cowed them into silence.

How was that even possible?

As the stars began to fade toward morning, Granville and Scott sauntered out of yet another bar and onto the misty streets, through which the streetlights beamed dimly.

"The more we dig into this case, the more it seems we're missing something," Granville said as they strolled. "This is all too elaborate, for something that doesn't seem to be making anyone much money. Yet the setup, and the fear the puppet master has engendered— there's a lot of money at stake somewhere. Where is it?"

"We need to find the motherlode," Scott said softly. For all the big man's seemingly carefree saunter, Granville noted that his eyes were alert and scanning the streets for any movement.

"Or the local equivalent of it, anyway," Granville said wryly.

"Is this just the puppet master we're dealing with?" Scott asked. "Or is there someone else at play here too?"

"Other than the hired killer, you mean? I doubt it. Once we've dealt with the puppet master, we can circle back and make sure of it, though."

"I look forward to that," Scott said with a grin.

"I'm sure you do," Granville said with a straight face, and Scott's grin widened.

"So how exactly do we find him? This puppet master?" Scott asked.

"Obviously not by asking questions. The trouble is, we've been marked. And we're going to be useless as investigators until we do something about this tail we seem to have acquired."

"You see him?"

"No. But he's there." The itching between his shoulder blades had told Granville that they'd been followed from the moment they hit the docks.

"Yeah. I know," Scott said with a scowl.

"And it seems we'll need him out of the way before we can really start digging into this," Granville said.

"I've been watching for him," Scott said, scowling. "And I haven't seen even a shadow moving."

"Likewise," Granville said. "Either we're imagining it…"

"Which we aren't. So this guy's really good," Scott said. "You figure it's this assassin?"

"I do. And I'd say it's time we laid a trap for him. You game?"

"Oh yeah," Scott said. "What d'you have in mind?"

He grinned at his friend. "Remember those claim-jumpers in the Klondike?"

"The ones who wouldn't give up?" Scott started to smile, and it spread into a broad grin. "That'd work. Where should we ambush them?"

"I was thinking about the Carlton."

"My sister's place? You wouldn't. Benton will kill us."

"Oh, I don't know. And I'd been meaning to talk to him anyway."

"We'll be lucky if talk's all we get," Scott muttered as he matched Granville stride for stride as they headed towards the club.

———

As the final wail of a trumpet and a storm of applause ushered Miss Frances Scott—in her alter ego as fan dancer Franny from Frisco—off the stage, Granville's gaze swept the exuberant crowd in the bar at the Carlton. Franny's shows were always well-attended, but tonight seemed particularly crowded. Which suited his purposes very well indeed.

"Our pursuer shouldn't stand out here," he said.

"Maybe he'll let down his guard," Scott said.

"Hardly. But Benton's men are here, and they keep a sharp eye on anyone who goes near Frances."

Scott looked at him, and a grin started to curl his lips. "You wouldn't."

"Watch me."

Suiting action to purpose, Granville began to wend his way through the horde of hollering men towards the back of the stage. He'd been wanting to have a little chat with Scott's sister anyway, and now seemed like the perfect time.

Though he doubted Benton would think so.

Their pursuer might not be too happy about it either.

"I hope you know what you're doing," Scott muttered from behind him.

"Probably not. But I'm doing it anyway," Granville said.

"And you don't want Emily in the middle of this mess. I get it," Scott said into his ear as the pressure of the crowd around them pushed them into one another. "But have you thought about what Benton's reaction is going to be?"

He was counting on it. "Of course," he said, just to irritate Scott.

They'd never see eye to eye on the subject of Benton. Part of it was due to the role Scott's sister played in Benton's life, and Scott's reaction to it. Part of it was that for whatever reason, Benton seemed to like Granville, and gave him latitude he'd never allow others.

Granville just hoped that extended to helping him scrape off this watcher who seemed to be stuck to them.

Benton would never have agreed to help if Granville had simply asked him, but when it came to Frances, the fellow was as protective as a grizzly. The analogy had him grinning.

Then they were through the hidden doors at the back of the bar and winding their way up the narrow stairs to the second floor and Frances's private dressing room. Granville still hadn't caught sight of anyone following them, and the music mingled with the buzz of voices was too loud to hear anything.

He knew someone was there, though. He could almost feel the press of eyes on his back. It was unsettling, like an itch you couldn't reach.

He turned down the hallway towards Frances's room, Scott on his heels. Turning another corner, he quickly stopped out of sight of whoever was behind them.

As Scott came around the corner behind him, Granville hauled his friend into place beside him, with a muttered, "Quiet now," in his ear.

They waited.

Nothing.

Then a thin, wiry man clad in dark grey whispered around the corner. He paused, black eyes startled, when he saw the two of them watching him.

Then the man in grey moved backwards faster than Granville had ever seen anyone move, whisking himself back around the corner.

And straight into the arms of two of Benton's largest thugs.

Granville was already in motion, and right behind their watcher.

"Careful, he's fast. And he's got a knife," he yelled to Benton's men.

The warning came too late. One of the two was already bleeding from what would have been a fatal neck wound if he hadn't swerved just a hair in time. The other was trying to block the thin man from sliding along the wall to escape. It was a losing battle.

Taking in the situation in a split second, Granville launched himself towards their watcher with all the frustration and protective instincts he possessed.

He nearly missed.

The fellow was that fast.

But Benton's men were experienced too, and the uninjured fellow got in a hit that the man in gray couldn't entirely dodge. It slowed him just enough that Granville was able to grab an ankle. And hold on.

Then Scott's bulk was landing on both of them, and the gray man didn't stand a chance.

Granville couldn't move, either, but he didn't care. He tightened his grip on the fellow's ankle, just in case.

AN HOUR LATER, all five of them stood in Benton's office, facing Benton. Who was glowering at them from the other side of the desk.

The gray-clad man was hog-tied hand and foot—the second of Benton's men had proved very handy with a rope—and Benton's injured man had been roughly bandaged and was no longer dripping blood everywhere. That was Scott's doing. He'd become quite skilled at treating injuries on the Klondike goldfields.

Benton was eyeing all five of them as if wondering which one of them he was going to kill first. They couldn't have that.

Granville stepped forward. "I should explain," he said.

"You'd better," Benton said. "If you think you can explain your decision to bring your troubles to my lady's door."

Benton was in full protective mode, and looking to make someone pay.

Interesting. Granville had a moment of fellow feeling. Then he focused on what he needed to do to protect his own lady.

Which meant taking the puppet master down. Along with his pet assassin.

"Scott and I were being followed as we tracked down the puppet master—your big fish," he said bluntly. "And there's been at least one death in our wake. There's no guarantee that anyone we talk to will be safe. And that includes your lady."

Benton made a sound halfway between a snort and a growl.

Granville kept talking. "We'd never have gone into the Carlton, let alone gone backstage towards her dressing room, if we hadn't known you had good people watching out for her."

He met Benton's angry gaze with his own purposeful look.

"Scott and I would have made sure that this fellow," and Granville gave the gray-clad man a contemptuous look. "Never got near Frances. But without the help of your men, I don't think we'd have caught him. And he needed to be caught."

Benton didn't look appeased. Not a surprise.

"We all need answers," Granville told him. "But first, you and I need to talk. Is there somewhere safe you can stash him until we're ready to question him?"

Benton didn't answer, just nodded at his two henchmen, who promptly left the room, with the much shorter killer dangling helpless between them.

And looking about as harmless as a cobra.

"So talk," Benton growled.

Scott frowned at Granville.

Who gave them both a hard look. "Whoever is behind these killings, we need to know who he is. And shut him down."

"I don't know who he is," Benton said.

Granville watched the gangster's face closely. He seemed to be telling the truth. "But you do know considerably more than you were willing to tell us the last time we spoke."

"Perhaps," Benton said, watching him just as closely. "I know a great many things I choose not to share."

There was a warning note in the gangster's voice.

Granville ignored it. "People who have helped me are dead thanks to this fellow. And still others—possibly including both your lady and my own—are at risk. I don't care who the puppet master is. He has to be stopped."

"I agree," Benton said.

The unexpected statement nearly derailed Granville's argument. There was something here he was missing, and it was probably important. Whatever it was, he needed to know. Now.

"You know who he is," he said.

"No," Benton said harshly. "I don't."

"But you knew he was lethal."

It wasn't a question, but Benton gave a brief dip of his head.

"So why haven't you done something about him before now?" Granville said.

"I did. I hired you two. Remember?"

"Yes. Two days ago. Why not before then?"

Benton's face was expressionless. "He wasn't threatening any of my businesses. And I found him diverting."

"Diverting?" Scott burst out. "You found a cold-blooded killer diverting?"

"He wasn't killing anyone at first," was the answer. "Just an unprincipled businessman who was somehow keeping his identity and the extent of his dealings secret from me."

Watching the glint in Benton's eye, Granville suddenly had his answer. "It was a game of wits," he said. "The fellow amused you."

"He did."

Scott was scowling, but Granville was too busy putting the pieces together to be annoyed. Perhaps that was why Benton tolerated him —they had the same need to solve complex questions and figure out what was really going on in any situation.

"Which is why you told us so little about him, as well," Granville said, watching Benton's eyes. "We were your next move in the game against this puppet master. And you wanted to see what we could learn of him on our own."

The gangster's eyes flickered, and he nodded once.

"This isn't a game," Scott said, glaring at both of them.

"No. It isn't," Granville told him. "Which is why he hired us in the first place."

Benton's calm expression revealed nothing.

No matter. Granville had his missing piece.

One of them, anyway.

"So what changed?" he asked Benton. "The dockworker who was killed? The puppet master's assassin daring to come here, so close to Frances? Or something else?"

The gangster's face still gave nothing away, but a slight clenching of his hand on the last statement did. There had been something else, then.

Something had changed in the game between Benton and the puppet master. What?

Whatever it was, Benton was unlikely to tell them. But it had to be important. He'd work it out.

Perhaps the puppet master had finally overstepped himself, and moved onto Benton's patch? That was worth exploring. But in the meantime…

"I need everything you know about this fellow if I'm to stop him," Granville said. "Even the rumors. And I'll need your help in getting answers out of the chap we caught tonight."

"Deal," Benton said. "Now, let's see what this assassin can tell us." And he called for his henchmen to bring the fellow back into the room.

———

DESPITE THEIR BEST EFFORTS, and even under Benton's form of persuasion, the killer stoically refused to tell them anything. Not the identity of the puppet master. Not why he'd killed the dockworker. Not even why he'd been tasked with watching them.

And he gave them only one name—Philip Abernathy.

The fellow Miss Kent had already told them about. The invisible man, she'd called him. One who didn't seem to exist, except on paper.

The gray man claimed it was the only name he knew.

"How d'you contact him, then?" Scott demanded.

"Post office box. We use it as a dead drop," the fellow said.

It made sense. And gave them exactly nothing to go on. Unless that name was an alias for the puppet master himself.

With that possibility firmly in mind, Granville had made sure that they had all the details on where this box was, and the number.

Then he had the satisfaction of calling Officer Daniels, and seeing him arrest the gray man for the dockworker's murder.

"At least that's the watcher out of our way," Scott said as they headed for the nearest bar. "We've seen the last of him."

"I hope so," Granville said.

"Ah, you're too cynical," was his partner's reply.

"Perhaps," Granville said. Hoping Scott was right. But he couldn't shake the feeling that everything about their dealings with the assassin had been too easy.

They were still missing something.

And he didn't like the feeling.

17

Friday, September 21, 1900

On Friday morning, Granville's uneasiness from the night before persisted, waking him from half-remembered dreams. The painters arrived early, and the air was thick with the reek of paint thinner and oil paint, though the actual painting hadn't yet begun. He was in no mood for dealing with any of it, and had fled to the office even earlier than usual, still uneasy.

Reviewing the thin case file proved to be no help, and he couldn't face spending the day behind a desk. As soon as Scott came in, he left a note for Miss Rizzo, and they headed down the stairs and turned towards the docks.

"We're missing something," he told his partner as they walked. "With the assassin in jail, we've an opportunity to see if the lack of that threat loosens anyone's lips."

Scott just nodded, and matched his stride to Granville's.

Two hours later, they'd worked from one end of the docks to the other and drunk far too much bad coffee. To Granville's intense frustration, they'd made little progress with the case.

"Maybe no one's heard he's in jail yet," Scott said.

"Or they don't trust that he'll stay there," he said. "Let's try the Post Office. They should be open by now."

"You want to see if they have anything on Abernathy?"

"Exactly," Granville said, draining his coffee and leaving a coin under the cup.

Unfortunately, the clerk at the Post Office was no help either. Frustrating as that was, it wasn't much of a surprise. But someone must know who the puppet master was, and Granville was determined to find him.

"Think it's worth trying the assassin again?" Scott asked as they pushed through the heavy glass doors of the Post Office and out into the bright sunshine. "He might have something to say after a night coolin' his heels."

Granville shielded his eyes from the glare, and glanced around him. "Might as well," he said.

Just then a hail from behind them had Granville's hand falling to the gun at his hip, concealed under the summer-weight jacket he wore.

"Wait up," came Trent's breathless voice.

He looked over his shoulder at their windblown assistant, and grinned. "Did you run all the way from the office?"

"Yeah. So?"

"Why are you dashing about in this heat?"

"I've got an urgent message for you," Trent said. "From Officer Daniels."

The uneasiness Granville had been feeling suddenly crystallized. "Go on."

"You know that assassin you arrested last night?"

"What about him?" Scott asked.

"He's out," Trent said flatly.

"Of jail?" Scott said. "Already?"

"He escaped? How?" Granville demanded, hearing the harshness in his voice and not caring. Not when the assassin was free.

"Dunno," Trent said. "All Daniels said was to let you know right away. Oh, and something about own rec... reckoning?"

"Recognizance," Granville said automatically, focused on what that information meant.

They'd let a killer go free.

Someone had pull. And probably a judge on his payroll. Presumably the puppet master.

But this was a murder charge. How had he pulled this off at all, never mind so fast?

Scott was muttering darkly about crooked cops and judges who could be bought.

Granville was wondering whether the assassin's orders included leaving town immediately. Or if he and Scott were now the fellow's primary assignment.

His jaw tightened and his eyes quartered the street, searching for any sign of the killer.

One part of his mind noted Scott doing the same. Most of his focus was on finding the assassin. And neutralizing that threat—permanently this time.

"We need to get back to the office," he said. "Now."

SINCE MISS KENT and Mac were out, Granville gathered the others into the front office and briefed them on the events of the previous evening, and what they'd learned about the puppet master's hired killer. Including that the fellow had named Abernathy as the man who'd hired him.

Then he told them the killer was no longer in jail.

"So he's escaped?" Emily said.

"Been released," Granville said.

"I don't understand," Emily said. "How is that possible, if he killed that poor man?"

"We'll be looking into that," Granville said. "But I suspect the answer is that there were no witnesses."

"Or none who didn't suffer a sudden lapse of memory," Scott said.

Granville nodded. "Exactly. For him to have been released so quickly, a number of bribes must have been paid. Plus any evidence the police had either vanished, or wasn't found sufficiently compelling."

"Then you're still in danger?" Emily asked.

"I think we have to assume we all are," Granville said. "This assassin hasn't tried to kill us yet. But he has been following us."

Emily's eyes narrowed a little. "You're taking every precaution."

"Of course." He looked from her to Miss Rizzo to Trent. "As I trust are all of you. We can none of us take our own safety for granted. Trent, I assume you were armed when you left the office to look for us?"

The lad nodded, touching a hand to his hip beneath light cloth coat he wore.

"And is Mac armed?"

Miss Rizzo nodded. "He made sure I knew that, and where they were going," she said. "He's expected back by two."

"Good. Any other questions?"

"You mentioned that the assassin said he communicated with his boss through the post office," Emily said. "Does that mean he never met him?"

"I think it quite possible," Granville said. "Whether Abernathy is an alias for the puppet master or not, he seems to be an expert in remaining invisible. One way to ensure that is to work entirely through other people."

"Someone must know who he is," Emily said. "I assume you started with the post office box this morning."

She really had come to know him. "We did."

"And no one at the Post Office remembered Abernathy?" she asked.

"I'm afraid not," Granville said.

"Too bad. That would have made our life easier. But he must have filled out a form to rent the box in the first place?"

Granville nodded. "He did. All it took was Scott's best smile," he began—at which his partner made a face.

It broke the tension, and made Emily laugh. Which pleased him, and probably Scott too.

"Just a smile?" she teased Scott, who gave her a very fake scowl and grumbled something.

"That plus a substantial bribe got us a look at the form," Granville finished. And deliberately let the silence stretch.

"So what did it say?" Trent demanded.

He grinned at the lad's impatience. "Box 377 was rented several years ago by Philip Abernathy," he said.

"And the address?" Scott asked.

"Care of Vancouver Box Company."

"That's it?"

"I'm afraid so," he said.

"Figures," Trent said.

"The Post Office doesn't require more," Granville told him.

"Which is a pity," Emily added. "How are we supposed to find this invisible man now?"

As if on cue, they could all hear the telephone on his desk begin to ring.

AND SUDDENLY EMILY'S day was looking brighter. She and Granville were headed for Chinatown.

As she stepped up into the carriage Granville had hired to take them to there, she checked out the plush leather upholstery and satin lined walls. It even had small gas lanterns you could light after dark.

"This is very nice," she told him. "But we aren't going that far, especially since the carriage won't even get us past the entrance to Chinatown. I thought hiring transport was only supposed to be if one of us was traveling alone. Couldn't we just take the streetcar, then walk a few blocks?"

"We're safer traveling this way," he said. "Especially from a killer who prefers to use a knife or a garrote. He's fast, and he's silent. And it's hard to see him coming."

She swallowed hard. Granville's words made sense, in a gruesome kind of way. And she'd had some experience with being knifed on a previous case. That had only been a glancing blow, but it wasn't an experience she wanted to repeat. Especially when the knife wielder was a professional killer, like this assassin was.

She gave him a sideways glance. "And if it was just you in danger? Would you still have hired the carriage?"

He just smiled.

"What if I had a gun," she asked. "Would that change anything?"

"Guns are illegal in town," he said. "And dangerous in the hands of amateurs."

"Then how can you ask Mac to carry one? He's a bookkeeper."

"Ask him sometime about his experiences in Oregon. He not only owns a gun, he's a crack shot."

"Oh. So that justifies breaking the law?"

"No. Being targeted by a killer does. I have no confidence in our city police being able to protect us against an assassin they couldn't even keep in jail."

She gave him a sideways look. "Does that logic justify my wanting a pistol of my own?"

He grinned. It wasn't the first time she'd mentioned the idea.

It wasn't that she was looking for permission, exactly. More like trying out the idea. She could see all the advantages of having her own pistol, but somehow… She hadn't quite been ready to take that step.

"You tell me," he said.

Clever of him.

"A small pistol would be very useful. But they aren't legal here. And the idea of shooting someone, even to bring a killer to justice…" She shook her head.

"It's different if they're trying to shoot you," he said. "But shooting someone isn't about justice."

"I know. But it would make it easier to arrest someone. It might have been useful today, for instance."

"Perhaps. But what's really dangerous is to carry a gun unless you know how to shoot. And are prepared to use it if you need to," he said.

"I could use it to threaten them."

"No. You have to be mentally ready to kill someone if you have to."

"I don't think I could," she said.

"Then you don't want a gun."

"Perhaps not," she said, considering it. "My aunt carries hers everywhere. I just can't imagine going to a dinner, or a tea party, with a gun in my bag. I might like to learn how to shoot, though."

"When this case is over, I'll take you to a gun range, and show you how," he promised.

"Thank you," she said. "I'll hold you to that."

He grinned at her. "I know you will."

As the carriage neared Chinatown, Emily could feel her anticipation building. And the fear built along with it. What would they find waiting for them?

"I'm still surprised that Wong Sun actually telephoned you," she said, partly to distract herself. "And asking to meet with us? It's most unlike him. What do you think he wants?"

"I agree that it's out of character," Granville said. "And I suspect it may be something to do with the puppet master."

"You think Wong Sun knows about him?"

"I think his sources of information are excellent," he said.

Emily considered that, and wondered just how much of what went on in her own family's home Bertie as their house boy knew about. And how much he might tell his uncle.

Multiply that by everywhere the Chinese in the city worked or provided laundry or delivery services, and how easily Wong Sun seemed to command attention from his own people... Granville was probably understating the matter.

"Are you concerned it will be dangerous for us?" she asked.

"No. He invited us. And besides, he seems to like you."

That was true enough, though she didn't understand why Wong Sun should do so. Despite his education at several excellent British schools in Hong Kong—or perhaps because of it—the old man seemed to avoid anyone who wasn't Chinese. Which was probably not surprising given the attitude of most of society towards Orientals from any land.

"I'm glad Bertie will be waiting to guide us, though," she said.

It would be good to see a familiar face. And they'd have no chance of getting through the locked gates and maze of interconnecting passageways on their own.

Then the carriage was rolling to a stop and Granville was taking her arm as the driver let down the steps for them, and there was no more time to think.

Granville and Emily followed Bertie as he guided them quickly and efficiently through the maze of streets and stairways that took them to Wong Sun's home. He noted that Bertie had little to say, and seemed slightly uneasy. There was clearly no point in asking Bertie why Wong Sun invited them today.

They'd have to wait, and see. He tucked Emily's hand more firmly into the crook of his arm, and shifted the other arm so he could easily reach his gun.

Once they were inside the surprisingly large rooms, there was no sign of Wong Sun. Granville found himself observing the large, ornately carved pieces of furniture that he could just make out in the dim light with more interest than the last time he'd been here. The pieces were made of some dark wood, obviously Chinese, and felt very old.

He glanced around the room. The drapes, the hangings on the wall—all were clearly silk, all covered with authentic Chinese embroidery in traditional patterns. He had to grin.

He'd never thought he'd be grateful for his mother's Oriental phase, when she'd redone the dining room and the larger sitting room at home in authentic Chinese style. And she'd insisted on explaining every purchase, and the significance of every piece, right down to the embroidery on the wall hangings, to all of them. At length.

He hadn't realized how much he'd absorbed.

But now a single glance was enough to tell him that everything here was authentic. Much of it was antique. And all of it was expensive.

For the first time he wondered how all these heavy pieces had arrived here. They must have been shipped from China at some point, which would have been even more expensive. But here they were.

He knew many of the wealthier Chinese merchants imported goods, mostly for sale in Chinatown itself. Did Chinatown's merchants have the connections to bring in such valuable goods? Someone certainly did.

Looking at the exquisitely carved furnishings, he pictured the stacked boxes of imported goods and furniture in the two warehouses he and Scott had been rummaging through the other night. Most of them had come from the East, and probably at least a third from China. Perhaps more.

Just how extensive was the trade in Chinese goods? And who were the customers?

He mentally compared the shipping labels on all those boxes and the information Mac and Miss Kent had dug up about the anonymous owners. Could one or more of those well-hidden owners be Chinese? It seemed a logical possibility.

There might even be some connection between the puppet master and the merchants of Chinatown. Which could easily change the nature of this case.

It was worth looking into.

***

JUST THEN, there was a rustle in the curtains covering an interior doorway, and Wong Sun appeared wearing an elaborately embroidered silk tunic and dark trousers. He bowed slightly to Granville—

who immediately returned the gesture—then more deeply to Emily, who curtseyed and smiled at him.

Wong Sun's lips turned up slightly, and he looked back at Granville. "There is someone you need to meet," he said in a voice like a drift of dry autumn leaves. "He has information you will want to hear, but you must only speak in response to what he says. I'll need your word on it."

Information? He'd take anything he could get, and be grateful for it. "You have my word."

Wong Sun gave that tight smile of his, and nodded towards a doorway that disappeared into the gloom. A tall, very thin and wiry man stepped out into the light and moved towards them.

It was very clear in these surroundings that the fellow's slanting dark eyes marked him as Chinese, though his height suggested that he might be half-white.

He was also the assassin. The fellow they had arrested the night before, who'd been released just this morning. Granville's only link to the puppet master.

And he was here.

Granville's hand automatically went to his empty holster, before he remembered he'd had to surrender the weapon on entering Wong Sun's home. At least they hadn't found his dagger.

What was the puppet master's hired killer doing here? And what could the assassin need to tell them that would lead Wong Sun, of all people, to arrange a meeting?

He braced for a fight, silently cursing himself for not insisting that Scott join them on this visit. He'd been half expecting to see the assassin on the streets. Not here.

A half-glance told him Wong Sun's eyes were fixed on him. He had the uncomfortable feeling that the old man hadn't missed a single nuance of his expression.

"He is not a threat to you now. He leaves town tonight, and you will not see him again," came that papery voice. "But first, he has information for you."

Granville burned to ask the fellow a few pointed questions of his own, but he was bound by his own word.

He was acutely aware of Emily on his left. She was watching the fellow with her head tilted a little to one side, as if she was wondering something similar. She had a considering look in her eyes that he'd come to know very well.

Then the assassin cleared his throat and looked directly at Granville. "Ask your man what changed," he said in a lethally soft voice.

"My man?" he asked. "You mean Scott?"

The gray man gave him a narrow-eyed smile. "Not him. The one who hired you."

Benton. That figured. "Changed when?"

"Just before he hired you."

Granville thought fast. "Something changed then, between him and your employer. Did they have an agreement that one of them broke?"

"Perhaps. And perhaps the other sent a message."

Granville looked at the assassin in front of him, thought about everything he knew—and didn't know—about this case.

"Your employer—you named him Abernathy. Did he use you to deliver that message?" he asked, choosing his words carefully.

"He did."

Which suggested the puppet master had one of Benton's men killed. Which one?

He'd ask Benton, except that the gangster would see that as a weakness—on both their parts. He'd have to send Scott and Trent after rumors, instead.

"I see," he said. "And why did Abernathy decide to send this message?"

"Your man might have changed the original terms of their deal."

There had been a deal between the gangster and the puppet master, then. Granville wondered how that deal had been agreed to, if Benton had never met the puppet master—as he claimed. "And your employer didn't agree?"

"No. He did not."

"Why use you as the messenger?"

"He's found me effective before. When he felt my particular… skills were needed," was the dry response.

"And your attack on Scott and myself? Another message?"

"Of course."

Granville could feel the tension radiating from Emily as she stood silent by his side. He was sorry for it, but all his focus had to stay on the lethal killer in front of him. "And now? That message has been delivered."

"No. You're still alive. And after my arrest, I'm no longer invisible. No longer useful to him."

"He'll hire someone new, and send them after me. Us," Granville said.

"Yes. They won't be as good as me," the gray man said with no trace of pride. "But they won't stop, either."

"Thank you for the warning," he said.

"But what about you?" Emily said suddenly to the gray man, surprising all of them. "You know too much about your employer. Mr. Abernathy, wasn't it? Surely he can't afford to let you live."

The gray man gave her a look Granville couldn't read. "No," he said softly. "Abernathy will have me killed. If he can find me. I thank you for your concern."

"I'd rather you were in jail," she said bluntly. "But I'd not see you dead. And Mr. Abernathy deserves to be in jail, too, if he's paying you to kill."

"Abernathy is not his name," the gray man said. "And he has made very sure I cannot identify him. I suspect you know that."

Emily glanced at Granville, who nodded.

"I am here only to deliver a warning before I disappear," the ghost said to her. "But for your kindness, I will answer your questions about the murder you investigated in Victoria."

Granville looked from the gray man to Emily.

How could he know about that? Unless this killer was Emily's missing third man? The fellow who had been hired as a thief, and sent to Victoria.

Which meant that both the puppet master and his assassin had known who Emily was. And she'd been in more danger in Victoria than even his worst imaginings.

His hands clenched at his side, and he had to force himself not to reach for his hidden knife. Wong Sun had assured them of their safety, and that the assassin was leaving town. Just ahead of the puppet master, from the sounds of it.

He glared a warning at the gray man as his brain worked furiously. If the assassin was the puppet master's next target, that would explain why he was now willing to answer Emily's questions. But what did it mean for her?

He glanced at his fiancée. Her eyes were fixed on the assassin, but couldn't read her expression.

If the assassin was her missing third man? They'd been right about there being a connection between Emily's Victoria case and Abernathy. Or whatever the puppet master's real name was.

And Granville was bound by his own word not to ask a single question. It all rested on Emily now.

She took a step forward, her gaze intent on the assassin's face. No hesitation there, Granville noted, his hands still clenched at his side, his every sense alert for the slightest hint of threat towards her.

Emily considered the gaunt man in front of her. If he was talking about her Victoria case, he *had* to be the third man. And he fit what little description she had for the third man.

But what else was he?

She could tell from the way Bertie stood that he didn't like the man in gray—he kept darting glances between him and his uncle. And Granville had recognized him, too. She'd seen that right away.

But it was the mention of Abernathy that told her exactly who he was.

This was the killer Granville had arrested last night. The assassin who had been shadowing him and Scott.

Emily felt her knees shake under her at the realization, and only determination kept her upright. She would not give in to such a weakness. This conversation was too important.

She shot Granville a sideways look, trying not to be obvious about it. His face was inscrutable, as it often was when he was on a case. But she knew him well.

His taut alertness beside her told her he was ready to defend her at any moment. He knew the man in gray for the threat he was, even when he just standing there.

As did she.

Even before she knew who he was, she hadn't missed the coiled tension in the gray-clad man's bearing. He looked like the buzzing of electrical wires overhead sounded. Potentially lethal power, held ready to be unleashed at any moment.

And this deadly man was now willing to answer her questions about Betsy's death?

She took another step forward, her gaze intent on the face of the man in gray.

"You were there, weren't you?" she said. "When that young girl" —likely he hadn't even known Betsy's name—"was killed? And you saw it all."

"I was," the man in gray said, his tone level and his eyes flat. "And I did."

"Did you kill her?" she asked outright. He seemed to respect bluntness. And in his present circumstances, he had no reason to lie.

"I did not."

She swallowed hard and reached for her courage. "Yet the two Chinese men involved seemed afraid of you. Why, if you are not the killer?"

"I am not her killer," was the soft-voiced answer. "But they know who I am."

An assassin. "You live there, then?"

A silence. Then the man in gray said harshly, "I grew up there."

His face showed nothing, but his voice… Those must be painful memories. Which was the answer—and the proof—she'd needed.

Emily nodded once, and asked the most important question of all. "Did we—I mean, did the police—arrest the right person?"

A wry smile crossed his face. "Yes, you arrested the right man," he said very deliberately.

So he *was* the third man. She'd finally found him.

And he'd just confirmed she'd been right about what had happened there. Her Victoria case was truly closed. She had no more loose ends.

But they still had a puppet master to find.

She looked straight at the man in gray. "Who hired him, then? The killer we arrested?" she demanded

"No one hired him. It was his own hasty nature that ended with the little one's death. But he sometimes worked with the man who sent me to Victoria," he added reluctantly.

"He worked with Mr. Abernathy?"

"Yes."

"The collector did?"

"Yes."

How to make sense of that? Emily narrowed her eyes, watching the gray man's face closely. She had to figure out which questions *this* killer was willing to answer. And which answers would give them the leads they needed to find the puppet master.

"Why would the collector do so?"

A half-lift of one shoulder was the answer, and for a moment Emily was afraid that was the only answer she'd get. Then he said, "A matter of business."

"The same business that saw Mr. Abernathy sending you to Victoria?"

"Yes."

Not chinoiserie, then, but collectible pottery. How did that fit? As she considered the man in front of her, Emily thought about where they were meeting, and how elusive the puppet master seemed to be. Perhaps they'd all been looking in the wrong direction.

"Is your employer—Mr. Abernathy—connected to Chinatown?"

"Sometimes," was the man in gray's cautious answer, after yet another darting glance at Wong Sun.

"How?" Emily asked, glancing at Wong Sung, whose face showed nothing. No help there.

"Different things."

That wasn't helpful, either. She'd have to be more specific.

"Is Mr. Abernathy Chinese?" Emily asked. It made sense, and names could be misleading.

"No," he said.

That wasn't the answer she'd expected. Though as she examined the grey man more closely, she noted the blend of Chinese and

English in his features. Perhaps that gave him an ability to move between the two worlds that made him useful to his employer. Which didn't mean he'd be accepted by either world. Poor man.

Her flash of sympathy was cut short by something hard in his flat gaze, a reminder the man was an assassin. His job was killing other people. And he was good at it.

She fought back a shudder, and scrambled to keep the interrogation on track. "Why would the Chinese be willing to work with your Mr. Abernathy at all?" she asked, pleased to note her voice didn't quiver, not matter how unstable her knees felt at the moment.

"He is a good customer," the man in gray said.

He was? How interesting.

Emily nearly asked what the grey man's employer purchased, but thought better of it. She was unlikely to get an answer. And she didn't know how long the assassin—the hairs rose on her arm at the thought—would be willing to answer her questions.

She tilted her head a little as she considered him standing so still opposite her. "Does being a good customer entitle your Mr. Abernathy to ask for special treatment?"

A glance at Wong Sung, followed by the slightest of nods. "Sometimes."

"What kind of special treatment?" she asked.

"Information."

Emily wasn't sure where to go with this. It almost seemed like the next question should be Granville's. Just behind her Emily could feel Granville shifting his weight slightly, as if he wanted to speak. He must have thought so too.

The man in gray hadn't missed the movement, slight as it was. He turned his head towards Wong Sun in a very deliberate movement, and received a nod in return.

The assassin bowed deeply to Wong Sun, inclined his head towards Emily, and melted back into the space behind the curtain from which he'd appeared.

Apparently their conversation was over.

And she wasn't quite sure what to make of the information she'd been given, which seemed raise more questions than it answered.

The carriage ride back to the office was a silent one, with both Granville and Emily caught up in their own thoughts. Back in the office, and once again seated on either side of his desk, he looked across at Emily. He couldn't read her expression, and she wasn't meeting his eyes.

What was going on in that head of hers?

"Are you disappointed with what you heard?" he asked her.

"No. Or not exactly, anyway," Emily said, tracing some kind of pattern with her finger on the desktop.

Something was worrying her. He waited.

"But Granville, we have to find your puppet master," she burst out.

"I know," he said. "He needs to be stopped."

Emily looked up at him. "Especially with what the man in gray had to say. The one who works for Mr. Abernathy. He's your assassin, isn't he? The one who was released this morning?"

He wasn't surprised she'd figured it out. Just sorry she had to face the fellow. "Yes."

Emily nodded, then her eyes dropped back to the ever more elaborate patterns her finger was tracing. He'd never seen her like this before. What was she thinking?

He waited.

Finally Emily's hand stilled, and she carefully placed her hands in her lap and sat back. Her eyes met his. "This is all connected. If we can believe the man in gray, he's my third man."

"So he said."

Emily paused, straightened her spine. "And his boss—this 'Mr. Abernathy'—sent him to Victoria to steal pottery. And he also hires the gray man to kill people he finds troublesome. Right?"

He nodded, amused and impressed at once. Emily had put everything together as quickly as he had, even though she knew fewer of the details.

"Abernathy has to be the puppet master, doesn't he?" Emily asked. "Since the assassin—but I can't call him that."

He grinned. "I'd begun thinking of him as the gray man."

"Because he dresses in gray," Emily said. "Yes, I see. I was thinking about him the same way. There's something gray about his face, as well as his hair and clothing. And it fits. He moves rather like a shadow, did you notice?"

"Or a ghost," Granville said.

She smiled at him. "That's even more accurate. I like that. So, our ghost said it was Abernathy who hired him in both situations."

"Yes," Granville said. "Always assuming he's telling the truth…"

"Which he might not be," Emily said thoughtfully. "But he was deferring to Wong Sun on some of our questions. Did you see?"

"I did indeed," Granville said. "And I would give a great deal to know what lay behind that dynamic."

Emily nodded. "Wong Sun's actions suggested he also knows the truth, whatever it is, and he required the ghost to answer our questions honestly."

"Or not answer at all, in some cases."

"Yes." Emily paused, straightened her spine. "It seemed the ghost owes Wong Sun in some way. I wonder how?"

"I suspect he is going to help him disappear," Granville said.

"Since the puppet master would otherwise have him killed?" She nodded. "That makes an ugly kind of sense. It's awful, isn't it? But I suppose it fits his pattern."

"Pattern?"

"All of the puppet master's actions have been ruthless. Such a man wouldn't have much loyalty in him."

"No, he wouldn't," Granville said, impressed again by her quick mind. And her resilience in facing the reality of a ruthless killer.

"I still can't see why the puppet master would be involved in a Victoria pottery heist in the first place," Emily said.

"How valuable was this pottery collection?" Granville asked.

"Very," she said. "Though only to a collector. Granville, it was the ugliest pottery imaginable. All spiky bits everywhere. It's as if someone stuck a fistful of thistles onto teacups and plates and saucers, then turned them into clay."

He bit back a laugh at the face she was making. "I'm sure there is great artistry involved if they are that realistic."

"Thistles, Granville," she said. "Expensive thistles."

At which he did laugh.

Emily smiled back, green eyes dancing. "Though I really can't see why—or even how—your puppet master would be involved in such a small transaction."

Granville thought about all the shipments of goods imported from the East he and Scott had found in the warehouses on Water Street the other night.

"It's too bad it wasn't a collection of Chinese pottery that was stolen. Then everything would tie together nicely," he said with a straight face.

The notion drew a laugh from her.

"Then even the Chinatown connection would make sense," she said. "Because who would know better where to find sources for valuable Chinese pottery than the merchants of Chinatown? But no. I was stuck with a thistle collection."

He grinned, then took in the expression on her face. "What have you thought of?" he asked, watching her closely. Her approach to solving a case was so different from his.

"This Mr. Abernathy, who hired the ghost as both assassin and thief," she said. "*Is* he the puppet master?"

"He would be an excellent fit for the puppet master," Granville said. "Except..."

"Except?"

"Philip Abernathy doesn't seem to exist, except on paper."

Emily's eyes widened, and seemed to glow greener as the sun caught them. "You'd mentioned he was invisible, but not existing at all? How is that possible?" she asked.

Granville told her about the work Miss Kent had done, and the meager information she had been able to uncover about Abernathy.

"So," Emily said thoughtfully. "If Philip Abernathy is an alias... Is it possible the puppet master isn't English at all?"

"You think he might be Chinese?" he said.

"The ghost said he wasn't. But I don't know how much we can rely on his word—he could easily have lied," Emily said. "And the ghost himself is Chinese. Or at least half-Chinese. There seem to be links to everywhere. Is it possible?"

"Anything is possible," Granville said, considering it. "Whoever the puppet master is, he's done a good job of hiding his identity. But I doubt it. Chinese merchants are barely tolerated in Vancouver—I suspect that if the puppet master were Chinese, it would be too big a secret to keep hidden for this long."

"Too big a secret. I wonder..." Emily's eyes narrowed a little. "You mentioned that the ghost said he'd communicated with his boss through the post office. Does that mean he never met him?"

"I think it quite possible," Granville said. "And the ghost implied as much again today, when he said he couldn't help us identify him. Whether Abernathy exists as more than an alias for the puppet master or not, he seems to be an expert in remaining invisible. One way to ensure that is to work entirely through other people."

"Someone must know who he is," Emily said.

"It's a matter of finding that someone. Since we can't exactly question a man who exists only on paper."

Emily grinned. "It might be fun to try," she said.

He laughed. "And our investigation might indeed come to that. Though I hope we are better investigators than that."

"What about Mr. Benton?" she said suddenly. "He must know about Abernathy. Or have some idea who's behind him, at least. Even if he doesn't know who the puppet master is."

"It's a good question," he said. "It never made sense that Benton didn't know more about our puppet master than he told us. Or that he'd let the fellow move in on his territory, unchallenged."

Emily sat forward eagerly. "What did Mr. Benton gain out of what the puppet master was doing, then?"

He met her eyes and smiled. "I still don't know," he said. "There's money in this somewhere, you can count on it. Big money. We just haven't figured it out yet."

She made a face. "Why is it always money that makes people do awful things to others?"

"It isn't always money," he said. "Unfortunately. But in this case, it's the only thing that seems to fit."

She looked sad, and worried again. Granville didn't like to see her like that.

"Back to our hunt for the man who exists only on paper," he said. "Shall we bring in Miss Kent and Mac and find out what they've been able to learn about Abernathy?"

"What an excellent idea," Emily said with a quick smile. "Perhaps we can have tea, as well. And maybe a scone or two. All this hunting for killers seems to make me hungry."

If they made her smile like that, Granville decided he'd personally fetch all the scones she wanted.

2 1

W hile Granville arranged for Miss Rizzo to bring tea and scones into their meeting, Emily had hoped to have a quick word with Laura. She still hadn't had a chance to find out exactly what was going on between her friend and Mac. But everything was set up so quickly there was no time for a quiet word.

Perhaps that was just as well, she decided once Laura and Mac joined her and Granville around the meeting table in his office. At the moment, her friend clearly had other things on her mind.

The minute they were seated, Laura looked expectantly from Emily to Granville. "I understand you'd like an update. What information do you want first?"

"Whatever you think is most important," Granville said.

Laura and Mac exchanged glances.

"Go ahead," Mac said.

Laura beamed. "I think it's clear now that this is some kind of smuggling ring," she said with barely suppressed excitement.

"That's excellent work. But what makes you think so?" Granville said, looking from Laura to Mac.

"It's complicated," Laura said. "We were looking hard into Philip Abernathy and finding nothing that led directly to an actual person.

So we reviewed Mr. Randall's active cases, and noted he had several against Clark & Company. And I noticed that the small merchants who hired Mr. Randall to sue Clark & Company? They also used Vancouver Box to ship small orders of merchandise to the United States."

She paused and glanced around the table. "And they did so every time they received a shipment from Clark & Company. As did all of the outlets owned by Barnabas Jones. Which makes no sense."

Emily leaned forward. "Why not?" she asked.

"Because there's too little profit in it," Mac said.

"Why? What were they shipping?" she asked him.

"According to the customs forms, mostly small items of decorative china and pottery," Mac said. "Chinoiseries."

Just as she'd suspected. Emily's eyes met Granville's. He winked at her.

"There's a strong market for these decorative items, but the potential profit on such small shipments is too low to be worthwhile," Mac said. "Unless they charged a huge handling fee. Which they didn't."

"And the truly interesting thing?" Laura added. "The merchants Randall represented had all stated they only did business locally. We checked with a few of the other merchants, and none of them had any record of ever shipping those items through Vancouver Box."

"Which suggests that someone—presumably at Clark & Company—is using these merchants as a cover to ship items across the border on a regular basis," Granville said thoughtfully. "With very little profit showing on the books?"

"Yes," Mac said.

"What volume of shipments are we talking about?" Granville asked.

"A few parcels each from dozens of merchants," Mac said. "Every month."

"And the items that were being shipped always seemed to include a number of covered containers of different sizes and designs," Laura said.

Emily pictured what she'd seen in the shops in Victoria's Chinatown. "You mean fine porcelain items? Small boxes or jars with matching lids? I've seen them in blue and white as well as multi-colored ones."

"Just like those," Laura agreed.

"Those are popular items," Granville said absently, then looked a little embarrassed to find them all staring at him. "My mother is fond of the stuff," he said with a wry grin.

"All of those items could be ideal for hiding something small and valuable you were trying to smuggle across borders," Laura said.

"And Clark & Company could explain sending those small shipments on behalf of their customers as being good customer service," Mac said. "As long as no one checked with the customers. And with such small orders, why would they bother?"

"This all ties in with what little information we have. We'd need to find out exactly what they might be smuggling," Granville said. "And how."

Mac nodded, and Emily noted both he and Laura wrote that down.

"Meanwhile, I think we need to bring the rest of the team into the meeting," Granville said. "Scott and Trent need to know about what you've uncovered, and Emily and I need to brief all of you on our meeting in Chinatown."

"I think the two of them are back," Emily said. Scott and Trent had been investigating something down at the docks, but she'd heard voices in the outer office.

Granville nodded. He must have heard them too, which was why he was bringing the whole team in now.

"Why don't we move to the meeting room," he said. "I'll see about a fresh pot of tea. Do you and Mac need any help bringing in whatever files you'll need, Miss Kent?"

"No. In fact, if Mac can move the files?" Laura said, and Mac nodded. "Then I'll take care of the tea and advise Miss Rizzo about the meeting, if you'd like. And maybe check if there are more scones."

"Thank you," Granville said. "If you can make the arrangements with Miss Rizzo, I'll get us some scones from the bakery."

And he gave Emily a very private smile that made her knees wobble.

———

FIFTEEN MINUTES later they gathered in the meeting room. Emily smiled to see an entire plateful of fresh scones in the middle of the table, along with a large 'Brown Betty' earthenware teapot steaming gently beside it. Once everyone was comfortably seated, it didn't take long to brief them about what she and Granville had learned in Chinatown, and what Mac and Laura had found out.

Then Granville turned to Scott and Trent. "How did you two make out with your inquiries down on the docks?"

"It seems your ghost has indeed vanished," Scott said. "Rumor is he's left town."

"Which isn't surprising. It was pretty clear he didn't expect to live long if he stayed," Emily nodded.

"Not once the puppet master got his hands on him, anyway," Scott said.

Emily couldn't help wincing. Then she saw Granville noticing her reaction, and felt bad, especially when he shot a warning glance at Scott. Who looked a bit embarrassed.

"Funny thing is, no one would admit the assassin existed before, but now he's safely out of reach, everyone seems to know about him," Scott said, quickly changing the subject.

"Perhaps that's the secret to our puppet master's invisibility," Granville said. "He hired an assassin so deadly that people were too terrified to talk about either of them."

"I heard the ghost'd kill over the smallest thing," Trent said. "They say he was deadly. And ruthless. The slightest whisper against the puppet master was enough to get you killed."

"Hell, even mentioning the puppet master was enough," Scott said. "We heard a few rumors that the ghost took out one of Benton's best enforcers a while back. After that, no one would talk."

"Not even Benton," Granville said dryly. "Funny he never

mentioned that little detail. I take it people are talking about the fellow now?"

"The ghost, yes. The puppet master, no," Scott said.

"That means we don't have to be so careful, then," Trent said, cheerfully oblivious to the byplay.

"Not so fast," Scott said. "I'm guessing the puppet master will be looking for a new assassin pretty darned quick. It's why there isn't a lot of talk about him even now. They're afraid he'll just find another assassin, one even worse than the ghost."

"I'm guessing you're right," Granville said. "It might take him awhile to find another suitably lethal killer. But I'm not willing to risk any of our lives on that assumption. We keep our safety precautions in place until the puppet master is behind bars. Understood?"

Trent nodded. "Got it. So what about the search for this Abernathy character?"

"We haven't found anything solid on him. Or on Barnabas Jones, either," Laura said. And quickly explained to the others about the second man who also seemed to exist only on paper.

A detail Emily found fascinating. "These paper men. They have to be fakes, don't they?" she asked.

Laura smiled. "Probably. But we just don't know yet. And we can't prove any of it."

"Keep looking," Granville said. "And we have the list of intercontinental ships docking here that Mr. Turner sent us. Can you check these suspicious shipments against which ships were in port when these shipments came in? And which ships and ground transport left around the time the shipments were sent out as well? That may give us something, too."

Mac and Laura exchanged glances. Emily noted with interest how easily they came to a silent agreement.

"We'll do what we can," Laura said. "We may need Trent's help."

"The three of you can work that out," Granville said. "Is there any proof that would stand up in court for any of this?"

"I don't think we have anything much yet," Mac said. "But I'd like the two of us to work with Carver and Randall on exactly what proof we might need in court."

"They may also have advice on cutting through the paperwork Mr. Abernathy is hiding behind," Laura said.

"Yes. And that needs to be a priority," Granville said. "It's urgent we talk to Abernathy. If he exists." He glanced around the table. "The way I see it, we have three major issues when it comes to dealing with the puppet master once and for all."

He ticked them off on his fingers as he spoke. "First, we can be fairly sure he's making most of his money through smuggling, though we aren't sure what he's smuggling or how. Except that it seems at least some of it is hidden in oriental porcelain containers."

Second, it looks like at least a few of the puppet master's companies are committing fraud. But can we prove it?

And third, Philip Abernathy looks like a strong candidate to be the puppet master, but he may only be a paper front for the real puppet master to hide behind."

Granville paused, and his gaze swept the faces around the table. "Is there anything I'm missing? Anyone?"

One by one, they shook their heads.

"Nope, you're pretty clear," Trent said, apparently speaking for all of them. "So how do we go about it? Who does what first?"

"That's the easy part," Granville said. "First off, as I said earlier, finding Abernathy needs to be a priority. Or if he doesn't exist, then whoever is hiding behind that persona."

"How do we do that?" Trent asked.

"We keep digging into Abernathy," Granville said. "And I suspect we have a lot of digging to do."

"But what does that mean?" Trent asked.

"It means that if Abernathy isn't the puppet master, he'll still have a connection back to him. Somewhere. Even if Abernathy only exists on paper. And we have to find that connection," Granville said.

"Meanwhile, Scott, Trent and I will pay Benton a visit. We need a few answers there, too."

"And Clara and I have another ladies 'at-home' to attend," Emily said. "It might be interesting to see if anyone there has heard of Mr. Abernathy."

"Be careful what you ask," Trent cautioned her.

She gave him the look he deserved for that, noting with annoyance that Granville's shoulders were shaking slightly with silent laughter. Which wasn't helpful in the least.

"But about the information on that post office box…," Emily said to Granville. "You mentioned that the contract showed the date when the box was rented by Mr. Abernathy."

"Supposedly," Trent muttered and she shot him another look. He subsided.

"It did," Granville said, leaning forward in quick interest. "What are you thinking?"

"Since I'll be looking for gossip that might lead us to Mr. Abernathy, that contract date could tell us how long he's been in business. Even suggest how long he's been in town."

"Good idea," Granville said, flipping through his notebook. "Here it is. August of 1897. Just over three years ago."

"I think I have the incorporation date of the two companies as well, which might be useful too," Laura added, flipping through her own notebook. "Hmm. It looks like both Clark & Company and Vancouver Box were incorporated in October of 1897."

Which Emily found extremely interesting, since Mr. Bray wasn't even in Vancouver then. She smiled at her friend. "That's very useful. Thank you," she said.

"Do you have incorporation dates for Mr. Jones's companies as well?" Granville asked.

Laura shook her head. "No, but we can look into it. Since we're digging into him anyway."

"It might tell us something," Granville said. "But don't waste a lot of time on it."

"We won't," Laura said.

Emily was again fascinated by how easily Laura and Mac seemed to work together. Then another thought struck her.

"When you're looking into the companies, would there be a photograph in any of the documentation? Mr. Abernathy must have rented that box in person, and the clerk might recognize a photograph."

"It isn't a usual requirement," Laura said. "But a visiting card type of photograph might have been needed for publicity reasons. I'll look for anything that might be helpful."

"Thank you," Emily said.

"If that's all...?" Granville asked, looking around the table. When none of them had anything to add, he nodded briskly. "Why don't we all meet here on Monday morning, then, and see where we're at. Shall we say nine?"

Since that seemed to suit everyone, it was set.

Her mind churning with too many questions, Emily hurried back to her desk. She needed to get hold of Clara to confirm that she'd be accompanying her to Mrs. Hart's 'at-home'. The idea of braving that company without the armor of Clara's superior social élan gave her chills.

And she needed to let her friend know that they were no longer just looking into Mr. Bray's doings. Now they were searching for the elusive Mr. Abernathy.

And if that didn't intrigue Clara more than searching for yet another bonnet, she didn't know what would.

EMILY WAS REACHING for the telephone when Granville stuck his head around the door of her small office.

"Do you have a minute?" he said.

"Of course," she said. "Come in. What is it?"

She was probably trying to read his expression, he thought with an inward grin as he drew up the chair opposite her and sat down.

"Our earlier discussion was—unfinished, shall we say?" he said, watching her equally closely. "I wanted to follow up, and see what you thought now."

"Well, you said all along that we were dealing with a smuggling operation of some kind," Emily said with that contagious smile of hers. "And now with what Laura found... Is that big enough money to be the reason behind all this?"

"It could be, though we still don't know enough of what's going on to be sure. The details she uncovered should help us figure it out."

She frowned. "How?"

"The most profitable item to smuggle in shipments that small is drugs," he said.

"Opium again?"

"I suspect so."

"I thought Mr. Benton didn't deal in drugs?"

"He doesn't. But perhaps he doesn't mind if someone else does as long as he gets a cut of the profit."

"And was that what he was doing?" Emily asked. "Getting a cut of the profits, I mean?"

"That's one of the things Scott and I need to look into."

Emily thought about that for a moment. "If this case is about smuggling opium, where is it going?"

"Most likely to the United States, since it's legal right across Canada and heavily taxed across the border."

"Then where are they getting it from?" Emily asked. "The ghost made a point of mentioning Victoria's Chinatown. And he that Abernathy was considered a good customer there. Do you think the puppet master gets his opium from the factories there?"

"It seems inconvenient, when there are factories in right here in town."

"The ghost didn't mention Vancouver's Chinatown," Emily said. "And neither did Wong Sun."

"We didn't ask either of them about Vancouver's Chinatown, though."

"No, we didn't" she said. Then she met his eyes. "You're going to go back and ask him, aren't you?"

"Probably. After I talk to Benton. I might start by asking a few questions at the local opium factories, though."

"Won't that be dangerous?"

He shook his head. "Not since it's all legal here. There's no reason for my questions to be seen as dangerous."

He could see her mentally filing the information away. "Promise me you'll be careful what you ask, though?" was all she said.

He grinned. "Always."

Then his grin faded and he met her eyes. "As long as you promise the same. The puppet master is dangerous, and asking about his business can be lethal. You need to be very careful who you talk to about him, and how you ask."

"I know, and I'll be careful," she promised.

He could tell she meant it, which eased his concern for her a little.

2 2

The Harts lived in one of the newer mansions along Blue Blood Alley, that section of Seaton Street with the view straight out over the harbor to the mountains beyond. Mr. Hart was an executive at one of the banks, Emily thought, while Mrs. Hart was trying to become a society leader. From what Clara had told her in the few minutes it took the carriage to get here, Mrs. Hart's efforts weren't working terribly well.

As she descended the three shallow steps from the carriage, she accepted the assistance of the driver's upraised hand—more for show than any real need. The charade often irked her, but this time, it was part of her investigations. She found thinking of herself as being undercover made attending all these 'at-homes' a much more interesting exercise.

It was one of the things she'd learned from Clara's Grandmama. Among other nuggets of gossip that they were now following up, the venerable dowager had explained that one of the secrets of success in this tight, closed society was the ability to act a part.

It was the twinkle in the old lady's eyes even more than her words that had riveted Emily's attention. Anything that her new honorary Grandmama—for as soon as that lady understood why they were there, she'd quickly extended that honor to Emily—took that much delight in was something Emily wanted to know more about.

"No-one can live up to society's expectations," Grandmama had explained. "Not for long, anyway. It's too hard to be so perfect. And your every action is scrutinized, all the time. You must know what I mean?"

Emily thought of the delight her mother's arch-rival Mrs. Smythe enjoyed at every one of Emily's social blunders. And grimaced.

"I thought so," Grandmama said. "There's too much life in you to escape the worst of the gossips. And once you're married to that handsome young man of yours, it will be even worse."

Worse? That didn't even bear thinking about.

Though she'd happily scorned such gossip over the years, she had wondered how her more daring actions might affect Granville, once they were married…

"Then how do you cope?" Emily blurted out. "Let alone enjoy it, as you seem to have done."

"For some it comes naturally," was the answer. "Take Clara here —she has no difficulty adopting protective coloration. And she has damn fine taste in her choices, too. I like that new bonnet of yours, child."

At which Clara blushed, looking a bit overwhelmed.

Grandmama winked at Emily. "I believe she has something of me in her, though she's good at hiding it. She doesn't know I know, of course."

"I can hear you," Clara said, as if she hadn't just turned fiery red.

"But what about people like me?" Emily said. "None of this comes naturally. Mostly I don't care. I'm just as glad to be spared the nonsense. But sometimes…"

"Sometimes it would be useful, eh? Which is likely why you're here today."

Emily wondered if the look Clara shot her could actually burn. "Yes, it is," she said frankly. "I am looking into my sister's new fiancé. Who may be an underhanded schemer. And who also may be connected to a case Mr. Granville is working on. I need to know if you have any pointers. How you would handle it?"

"Ah, that's where the secret comes in," the elderly woman said with that wicked twinkle. "Some try to live as though society's rules are real. The problem is, then you have to be perfect. Always. Which isn't possible. And the smaller the society, the more perfect you have to be."

Emily thought about her elder sister. This explained so much. "So what is the alternative?" she asked.

"I always liked thinking of the rules as defining a role I played in social situations," Grandmama said. "One I could hide my real self behind. I found it amusing how easily fooled people are, and how much you can observe from behind that mask."

Emily could see the power in that, but she couldn't imagine spending her life playing a false role. But she and Granville likely wouldn't go into society all that often anyway, she'd consoled herself. They had an agency to run, and cases to solve.

Suddenly she realized that for her, joining the social whirl only seemed worthwhile when she was working a case. And then any mask she donned would simply mean she was working undercover.

Impulsively she stood and hugged the old lady's delicate, lace-covered shoulders, held ramrod straight against the back of the embroidered armchair she sat in.

Now it was time to put her new honorary Grandmama's words of wisdom to the test.

SHE AND CLARA followed the meandering path of carefully chosen river rock to the gracious steps leading to the gleaming white double doors of the Hart's massive Tudor style home. Emily raised her eyebrows at the size of the double turrets that looked as though they belonged on a different house.

"More money than style," she said softly to Clara.

Who choked, and threw her one of an admonishing look. "Not now, Emily!"

They were met at the top of the stairs by a stern-faced butler, stiffly correct in black and white. Probably rented for the occasion, Emily decided, wishing she could share the thought with Clara, but not willing to embarrass her friend further. It didn't sound as if Mr. Hart earned enough money to justify a full-time butler. As it was, the mortgage on this house had to be costing him a pretty penny, even at the ridiculously low rates available now.

Surrendering their light poplin wraps, they waited for the butler to announce them, then joined a dozen other ladies in Mrs. Hart's expansive morning room. The room with its butter yellow walls and large windows overlooking a large, landscaped garden at the rear of the house, was a pleasant one. She suspected that even in the gray, wet days of November it would seem so. But on a clear fall day like today, the room seemed flooded with sun.

She noted that the clear light wasn't exactly flattering to several of the ladies present. But it showed Mrs. Hart herself to excellent advantage. Which struck her as an interesting twist in the social game being played here. Though not a very strategic one, based on the explanation Grandmama had given.

Unless the woman actually wanted to offend half her guests.

It was certainly a possibility, she thought, watching their hostess make her graceful way to Clara's side. The woman was wearing a silk morning dress of a pale-yellow tone that looked radiant in this light. With her honey brown hair done up in a coronet that caught the light, she looked angelic.

Except the for malicious twist of her mouth as her gaze settled on Emily.

"Clara, my dear, welcome," Mrs. Hart said. "Do introduce me. I don't believe we've met, Mrs...?" And she held out a white gloved hand to Emily.

"Of course, Mrs. Hart," Clara said. "May I introduce Miss Emily Turner."

"Charmed," Mrs. Hart said, touching the very tips of her fingers to Emily's outstretched one.

It was a very subtle snub. Which made no sense. She'd never met the woman before. Why was she being snubbed?

"Your sister was just here," Mrs. Hart was saying. "Such a lovely girl. And quite the conquest she's made, with Mr. Bray. Now there is a gentleman."

There was something challenging in the look she gave Emily, as if daring her to question the statement. But why? What was she up to?

"Indeed," Emily said, deciding she didn't like this woman at all. But the woman's barely veiled animosity could prove useful. And she'd just introduced the topic Emily wanted to discuss.

"I just met Mr. Bray myself the other day," she said, as if conceding the point. "Have you known him long?"

"He hasn't been in town that long. But I met him soon after he arrived," Mrs. Hart said. "He was impressive from the start."

Were they talking about the same man? "He certainly seems to have swept my sister off her feet," Emily said, watching to see how her hostess would respond.

"With such a catch, I doubt that was hard," Mrs. Hart said with a sly look and a little laugh.

Now she was insulting Jane? What was wrong with this woman? Emily gave Clara a quick glance.

Her friend understood the request for help and quickly stepped in. "I see your 'at-home' has attracted the usual throng this afternoon," she said, glancing around the parlor. "Is there anyone I haven't met?"

"Oh, I doubt it, Miss Miles," Mrs. Hart said. "You are such a regular at my little entertainments."

Was that what was wrong with the woman? She was feeling slighted? Emily wondered. It seemed ridiculous, but what else explained her behavior?

Unless the silly woman was attracted to Mr. Bray, and annoyed at his engagement to her sister? Which would be no help it all when it came to unearthing dirt on Mr. Bray. It would also meant Emily couldn't ask about Mr. Abernathy, and expect to receive any kind of helpful answer. She'd have to stand quietly aside, and leave all of the questioning to Clara.

Which, given her newfound awareness of the possibilities of

working undercover in her social circles, was unexpectedly—and intensely—frustrating.

"I was surprised to hear of Mr. Bray's engagement," Clara said. "If there had been any indication his interest had veered in that direction, I would have expected to hear about it. But no. Not a word. You must have known, though? You always seem to know the latest gossip before everyone else."

"Well," Mrs. Hart said, feigning modesty with downcast eyes.

It looked utterly ridiculous, and not the least believable. Emily had to force herself not to shake her head at such a display.

"I might have heard the tiniest hint," Mrs. Hart said.

"I knew it," Clara said. "But tell me, what had you heard? And who was your informant?"

"Oh, I couldn't…" Mrs. Hart said, letting her voice tail off in a manner that made it very clear to Emily, at least, that she was dying to tell them all about it.

Emily opened her mouth to make a comment, and Clara gave her such a look that she shut it quickly without uttering a word. This was better left to the gossip professionals, no matter how galling it was to be silent now.

She needed any information she could get on Mr. Bray. And Clara was the woman for the job.

"Come now," Clara said, leaning a little closer. "I'll never tell a soul, I promise. And Emily doesn't care for gossip."

"Well, in that case," Mrs. Hart said, leaning a little closer to Clara. "I suppose it can't hurt, just this once…" She pitched her voice lower, but it was still perfectly audible to Emily.

"Mr. Bray intends to buy the company he is working for, and has been looking for investors. And Mr. Turner is interested," Mrs. Hart said with a breathless little laugh. "And of course his good opinion will influence a number of others."

Papa was considering financing an obvious schemer like Bray? Could he not see how grasping the man was?

Did Mama have any idea about this? But she must know some of it, Emily realized. Now those awkward meetings with her mother and Jane about their respective wedding plans began to make sense.

And how just much time did she have to expose Jane's fiancé before Papa signed something there would be no recovery from?

She'd have to find a way to get Mama alone, and ask her about this. They needed a plan. And she needed all the help she could get.

This couldn't be allowed to continue, not any of it. Even Jane didn't deserve this.

And Papa would sink all of them, if he really did invest with Mr. Bray.

Mrs. Hart was simpering and whispering something to Clara, as if she didn't think Emily had heard a thing. But the malicious little glances she was sending Emily's way told another story. She knew exactly what Emily had heard.

The woman was a menace.

A useful one, perhaps, given what she'd just learned about Mr. Bray. Assuming that Mrs. Hart's "gossip" contained at least a little truth, that is. Which remained to be seen.

But a menace all the same.

No wonder Grandmama had sent them here. It was proving most educational. And it was past time she learned more about the company Mr. Bray was working for. The one he intended to buy, apparently.

23

Saturday, September 22, 1900

On Saturday morning, Granville met Scott and Trent for breakfast at Mary's Cafe. Even if he'd wanted to, he couldn't have eaten at home. The noise and dust that the builders sent up was becoming less bearable each day. They seem to have finished the renovations in the front parlor—which at least had evenly plastered walls and new lighting fixtures now—and moved on to the dining room. But none of the rooms looked like much at the moment.

He still made a point of checking in with the contractor every morning. He'd learned long ago that even the hardest worker does better work if someone is paying attention to their results.

Walking into the normal chaos of the busy cafe was a relief, and Granville's stomach growled at the smell of coffee and frying bacon. When had he last eaten?

The other two arrived a few minutes after him, and luckily it didn't take long to place their orders. In the silence that followed their waitress's departure, Trent looked from Scott to Granville.

"So what are we gonna do about the smuggling?" he asked. "And why did we need to meet so early?"

"We need to find out exactly what is being shipped across the border that can be hidden in decorative containers and vases and is earning them so much money," Granville said.

Scott gave him a shrewd look. "You think it's drugs, don't you?"

Granville nodded. "Opium, at a guess. It's legal enough to ship the stuff across the border, but the customs duties are prohibitive."

"So dope smugglers can make a mint," Trent said.

"Yes. If they're good at it."

"If the puppet master is smuggling opium to the States, where's the stuff coming from?" Scott asked.

Granville had been turning over that very question in his mind since Emily had raised the question earlier. "If all the shipments were going to San Francisco, I might guess that it was coming straight off of the same *Empress* steamliner that the chinoiserie came in on," he said.

"But why..." Trent began.

"There are factories that can refine the raw opium in San Francisco," Scott said before he could finish the question. "They aren't so common elsewhere."

"But since what Mac and Miss Kent have uncovered so far suggests that they're selling right across the States, the drug being smuggled is probably not raw opium. It's likely processed in the factories here in town. Or through those in Victoria," Granville concluded.

"It would be ones in Vancouver, wouldn't it?" Trent said. "I mean, why would the puppet master bother with a factory in Victoria, when the same thing's available right here?"

"That's an excellent question," Granville said. "And normally I'd not even consider the Victoria factories. At least not at first."

"But...?"

"But in this case, we can't disregard it. There may be a connection between the puppet master—through his Abernathy front—and the Chinatown in Victoria. The ghost told us Abernathy is a customer there, a good one. Which could explain why he sent his half-Chinese killer to help steal the pottery in Emily's case."

"We only have the ghost's word that any of that is true," Scott protested. "And he's the puppet master's assassin."

"He was. He no longer is. And neither the ghost nor Wong Sun had any reason to lie to us."

"That you know of."

Granville shrugged. "We have too few facts in this case. And we're running out of time to solve this thing. I'm not willing to ignore information, no matter where it comes from."

"Does Miss Emily know people from her Victoria case? Maybe she could help," Trent said.

"No, she cannot," Granville said firmly. "It would put her in too much danger."

"But opium is legal," Trent protested.

"Yes. But smuggling is not. And given how complex these various organizations are, and how willing the puppet master is to kill, there's probably a lot of money at stake. Do you want someone to go after Emily?"

"No, 'course not," Trent said with a scowl. "But…why aren't we on our way over there? To Victoria, I mean. Investigating, instead of talking about it."

Granville would have liked nothing better. "Because Scott is right. We can't afford to waste time on assumptions. Those who act like fools, are rewarded like fools."

"So. What do we know about opium?" Scott said into the little silence that followed. And winked at Granville.

"Right," Granville said. "We need to look into where they're getting it from, as well as where it's going."

"You're thinking of tracking the drug forward from the factories?" Scott asked.

"Or backwards from the customer," Granville said. "But not yet. Between Vancouver and Victoria, there must be more than a dozen opium factories. We could waste quite a bit of time even finding them, never mind getting the answers we need. I think we need to start on the retail end."

"So we talk to the stores licensed to sell opium?" Scott said. "That makes sense."

"And maybe the unlicensed ones, too?" Trent said tentatively, still looking a little chagrined from his earlier *faux pas*.

"Which would be even harder to find. And likely even less willing to talk to us," Granville said, hiding a grin. He pushed back his chair and stood up. "Again, that would take too much time. No, we need to start at the top."

Scott groaned. "Not Benton again. He was barely civil yesterday. We come back again, he'll just set his henchmen on us."

He shrugged. "Benton's the one who chose to hire us. If he wants the puppet master dealt with, he'll answer our questions. And it would be useful to know if he's getting a cut of the puppet master's smuggling profits."

"So you're just going to ask him?" Scott said. "Can't you think of anyone safer to question?"

"Certainly. Abernathy. And Wong Sun," Granville said. "But Benton is first."

"You can't think of a better plan?"

"Nope," Granville said. "But I'm open to whatever nets us the puppet master. Unless you have a better idea?"

"You're going to get us all killed. You know that, don't you?" his partner groused as he rose to his feet and checked his that his revolver was fully loaded.

Granville chuckled. "No one's managed it yet. We're a pretty tough lot."

As the three of them finished their coffees and headed for the street, Granville mentally reviewed his conversation with Emily yesterday. Something was still nagging at him, leaving him uneasy. But he couldn't quite put his finger on it.

He ran through their conversation again, and it hit him. When Emily had pointed out that the ghost hadn't said anything about Vancouver's Chinatown, and wondered if the puppet master's connection was to Victoria's Chinatown, not here, it had made a lot of sense. But they only had the ghost's less than straightforward answers to go on. With no way to check them. And wasn't that convenient.

Leaving them relying too heavily on what the ghost had said. If the fellow had deliberately misled them, it could prove deadly for Emily.

He needed to deal with that possibility. Now.

"I've re-thought our plan," Granville said just as Scott paused inside the thick oak doors leading to the street. "We'll start with Chinatown first."

Trent turned to stare at Granville. "Not Bertie's uncle, again?"

The lad's concerned look would have amused Granville in other circumstances, but not today. "Not this time. I want to get a feel for how difficult it is to buy opium first."

Scott just shrugged, but Trent looked ready to argue with him. Granville didn't have time for it. He stepped around Trent, clapping Scott on the shoulder as they headed for the nearest electric streetcar stop.

Less than fifteen minutes later they were strolling along Dupont Street, considering the various shopfronts that lined the block. At a glance, the street held three groceries, two laundries and at least one tailor. They spoke with several grocers with no results. Now Granville had his eye on the large, elaborate storefront at the end of the block.

A wide variety of unusual foodstuffs hung in the window and more were set out in wooden boxes just inside the doors. Including a number of dried herbs and gnarled roots, which indicated this Chinese grocery was a pharmacy as well.

Making it the most likely candidate to have an opium license. Granville wasn't about to waste any more time on stores that didn't have one. Getting a straight answer as an Englishman in Chinatown was challenging enough without spending half their time in the wrong places.

It turned out he'd chosen well this time.

The shop did have a license to sell opium, and the shopkeeper seemed willing to answer a few questions. When he asked about buying in bulk, however, the shopkeeper was quick to explain that bulk orders must go direct to the factories. He seemed to suffer a sudden memory loss when Granville asked about the names and locations of these factories. Which wasn't exactly unexpected.

He was surprised he'd gained as much information as he had.

He took very polite leave of the fellow and strode towards the door. At least he now knew better than to waste further time talking directly with the shopkeepers.

"Granville, since you didn't get anywhere on the opium, why don't you ask him if he knows Abernathy," Trent said, putting a hand on his arm as he reached the door.

"If I thought Abernathy actually existed, I might attempt to do so," Granville said. "Or if I had a photograph of the fellow. Or even a sketch. Now, if you don't mind…"

Trent immediately dropped his hand, and Granville pulled open the door and exited. As he strode down the street, he heard in his head the incessant ticking of a clock, counting down the hours they might have left before the puppet master found a new and even deadlier assassin to send after all of them.

2 4

E mily glanced around the small milliner's shop that was Clara's current favorite place to spend time. Every shelf was covered with dainty confections in every shade, some covered with flowers, others with extravagant plumes or ribbons galore. It felt to her as if there was too little room to breathe, but Clara was in alt.

"Emily, this hat would complement my new fall coat, the blue one, don't you think?" Clara asked, twirling in front of the mirror.

Emily rolled her eyes, but considered the bonnet as requested. It was a golden brown that would indeed complement the coat and would suit her friend very well. "I think it would, but the one you tried on earlier, the other brown one with the hint of blue in the trim made more of a statement, I think," she said. "It depends if you want to be noticed, I suppose."

"Of course I do," Clara said, giving the other bonnet a considering look. "And I think you might be right."

Clara tried on the other bonnet again. She considered her own image, then looked past it to Emily's expression in the mirror. "I do like it, but are you sure you aren't just trying to get me to make a decision so we can follow your latest lead?"

Emily smiled. "Just because I'd rather be finished here doesn't mean I'd try to talk you into buying something that wasn't right for you. If you want something to wear with your new coat, that one is the most "you" of everything you've tried today."

Clara turned towards the milliner, who had been hovering in the background as she tried on hat after hat. "Well?" she asked. "What do you think?"

Emily knew this was the moment of truth. Not that it mattered to her, not as long as Clara made a decision and they could get on with their day. But she'd started to wonder recently whether, after so many shopping sessions with Clara over the last few years, she wasn't starting to develop a sense of style of her own. And she had to admit she was curious what the hat's creator would say.

"I think your friend is right," the milliner said. "You wear hats well, and you have a good eye. Which is why you're one of my favorite clients. Any of the hats you tried on today would suit you well. But there's something just a little more when you put on that particular hat. I think it would be a shame if you didn't buy it."

Clara looked surprised for just a moment, then nodded. "I'll take it."

As the milliner went into the back to wrap up her purchase for her, Clara shook her head. "I'm impressed."

"What? You think I can't recognize a stylish hat when I see one?" Emily said, teasing her.

"No. But I nearly missed this one, because you have to picture the total effect of the hat with the coat to see it. You've developed a real eye since you met Granville." She gave her friend a shrewd look. "Or perhaps it was always there, and you simply never cared enough to look."

Just then the milliner came out with the hat box, and Emily was relieved not to have to answer. She suspected her friend was right, but she wasn't ready to talk about it. It seemed she'd developed an interest in fashion, something she'd never had much time for, and she wasn't entirely sure that was a good thing.

"Since you're done with your shopping, let's follow up on what we learned yesterday. It's time to investigate a thief," Emily said briskly, and led the way out of the too small shop, with Clara hurrying after her.

"Thief?" Clara said. "What thief? Emily, wait. You didn't say anything about a thief."

"EMILY, what thief are you talking about?" Clara demanded when she finally caught up with her several doors down, just outside Stroh's teahouse.

"Weren't you listening when Mrs. Hart told us what my sister's fiancé is really up to?" Emily said.

"Mr. Bray? He's trying to buy the company he works for. He's also hoping to get your father to invest. And to persuade all of his friends to invest as well, I gather," Clara said in an annoyed tone. "Yes, I was listening. And I heard no mention of theft."

"What do you call it?" Emily said. "He's willing to steal Jane's good name in a fake engagement, and then use Papa's gullibility to get him and his friends to invest in some company that is likely a fraud too."

"You don't know any of that. His company could well turn out to be a gold mine."

"It could just as easily be a fraud," Emily said. "Are you willing to ignore what we've learned of Mr. Bray so far?"

"Emily, we've learned nothing," Clara said in exasperation.

"Exactly," Emily said with a nod. "And don't you find that a little strange? He's a new-comer, and he seems to have become a part of our usually closed little society very quickly. Everyone knows who he is and is happy to include him, but no one seems to know much about him. Including you. Don't you find that odd?"

Clara opened her mouth to say something—probably something cutting, Emily thought with an inward smile. But then she stopped and stared at Emily. "You know, I do. It's as though he's gained everyone's trust, but it isn't clear how."

"He's a crook, that's all. A confidence artist, if you will," Emily said decidedly. "And I'm going to prove it."

"How?"

"With your help," Emily said, grinning at her friend's look of consternation.

"I still don't see…" Clara began.

"Let's go in," Emily said, waving towards the teashop. "I'll buy the scones, and we can make our plans."

Her friend frowned at her, but nodded, as Emily had known she would. "Fine. But only if you order the expensive version with imported clotted cream and the berry preserves."

"Fine," Emily said, and led the way.

* * *

"I can't believe you talked me into this," Clara said as they strolled along the wide wooden sidewalks that ran along Hastings Street. "Or that Tim—I mean Mr. O'Hearn—went along with it. He has deadlines on a Saturday, you know."

"I know," Emily said. "And he knows there will be a story in it for him."

"What story?" Clara said. "All we have right now is a little gossip and no facts."

"Which is why we called Tim," Emily said. "We need to know more about Mr. Bray and this company of his. And reporters are the ones who excel in digging out facts."

"Yes, but he covers the crime beat, not the business one. He isn't going to know where to start."

"Yes he is," Emily said with a sideways glance. "He's bringing Mr. Draper along—you know, the business reporter for the *News Advertiser*. Who *will* know the facts. Or at least, how to dig them out."

"I don't believe it," Clara said. "First you waste Tim's time, and now you're dragging another reporter into this?"

"Mr. Draper was already a part of the puppet master case," Emily said. "Granville brought him in on Monday."

"Yes, but we're not investigating the puppet master. We're looking into your sister's fiancé. It's hardly the same thing."

"Are you sure about that?" Emily said. "We talked about the chinoiserie connection."

"I know what you think it means. But you're dragging me all over town, carrying a hatbox, I might add," and her friend lifted her arm, displaying the item in question for emphasis. "And you have no facts at all to back up any of this."

Emily glanced over at the brightly striped pink and white hatbox, tethered to the crook of Clara's arm by even brighter pink ribbons, and grinned. "Your hatbox provides us with an excellent disguise," she said. "No one would ever suspect we're looking into a confidence scam when you're carrying that."

Clara stopped and glared at Emily. "You…" she began, then took a second look at her hatbox. And burst into laughter.

"You're right," Clara said after her laughter had subsided. "And it will be your task to explain to these two reporters you've commandeered that I'm carrying it because we're in disguise."

And she started to laugh again.

Emily rolled her eyes. "I wish you'd take this seriously."

"I am," Clara said. "Which is why you need to explain the hatbox. Or stop at my house to drop it off first."

"It's in the wrong direction," Emily said. "And there's no time."

"Then if you expect us to be taken seriously, especially by this business reporter neither of us has ever met," Clara said. "Then you need to let them know we are serious. And the only way a hatbox like this one is serious is if it's part of a disguise."

Emily blinked at her friend. "You're right."

"Of course I am. And I'm right that we have too little information to be bringing reporters into this, too."

"Well, whether you are or not," Emily said. "It's too late in any case. Here they come."

Clara glanced at the bustling crowds around them, took in the 'G. Trorey, Jewelers' sign, then looked up at the four-sided iron clock they stood beside. Then she glared at Emily again. "You told them to meet us by the jewelry store clock?" she said. "Emily, that's such a cliché."

"Perhaps it is," Emily said. "But it fits well with the hatbox and our cover, don't you think?"

And with a smile she turned to greet the two reporters, inwardly gleeful at the flummoxed look on Clara's face. Now her friend would spend the next hour wondering if she'd planned to use the hatbox as a disguise all along.

She hadn't, but it was too good an idea not to use. And it tied in nicely with meeting here. It seemed shopping could be a useful pursuit, after all. She hid a grin at the thought.

"Miss Turner, well met," Tim O'Hearn was saying as he strode up. "Miss Miles." And he amused Emily further by adding an inclination of his head towards Clara that was almost a bow.

The tall, red-headed reporter was accompanied by a shorter, sturdier man with a groomed mustache and a very dapper look to him. Now Tim stepped back a little, and gestured towards the fellow. "May I present Mr. Draper. Draper, this is Miss Turner and Miss Miles."

"A pleasure," the shorter man said. "I gather you ladies might have some information on a story the two of us are working on. Might I have the honor of inviting you to tea?"

"I'm afraid we have just had tea," Emily said before Clara could agree. "But it's a lovely afternoon. I thought we might stroll for a bit. Since it is in character with our disguise as two ladies enjoying a pleasant afternoon of shopping. Hence the rather obvious hatbox." And she winked at Clara.

Tim grinned at both of them.

Clara just shook her head. "Somewhere we cannot be overheard would be lovely," she said.

"An excellent idea," Mr. Draper said, and offered an arm to each of them.

As they strolled along Hastings Street away from the business district, and towards the quiet streets and stately homes of Millionaire Row, Emily was pleased to note that Tim had been quick to take Clara's other arm. She definitely still had hopes for the two of them.

"I spoke with Mr. Granville earlier in the week," Mr. Draper said. "Your fiancé, I believe?"

At Emily's nod, he continued, "So I assume your information concerns this elusive puppet master he talked of?"

"Not directly," Emily was quick to say. "But then, with the puppet master, nothing seems to be direct. No, this concerns another importer, a Mr. Bray, and the company he works for."

"I see. And Mr. Bray is recently engaged to your sister, I believe?"

"He is. And he is becoming a firm fixture in our little world, for all that he is so new to town," she said.

Mr. Draper gave her a shrewd look. "We were all new here at some point," he said. "But I suspect that is not your concern, is it?"

"It's his importing company I'm most concerned about," she said bluntly. "From what I've heard, he intends to buy that company and expand it, and I'm suspicious of his intent. And his funding sources."

"What did I tell you?" Tim said to the other man over Clara's head. "It's never what you might expect with these two."

From Clara's expression and Tim's wince, Emily suspected her friend had just pinched him for that statement. Not that she blamed her.

Unlike Tim, Mr. Draper kept his expression professional. "You suspect some connection between Bray's company and this puppet master, then?" he asked her.

"Coincidences make me suspicious," Emily said. "Especially when it comes to the puppet master. Can you tell me what you know about Mr. Bray's company, Trans Pacific Trading?"

"Not a great deal," the reporter said. "As I'm assuming you already know, they import goods from those countries which are served by the shipping lines which dock in Vancouver."

He cast a quick sideways glance at her, and Emily gave a quick nod in agreement.

"The company has half a dozen employees and has only been in business here for three years, with Mr. Bray joining them eight months ago," Mr. Draper continued. "Most of the goods come from the Far East and are shipped across the continent by rail once they reach our shores,"

"Are these goods mostly for our Canadian and American markets, or are they then shipped on to England?" Clara asked.

Judging by their faces, her friend's question surprised the two reporters as much as it did her. Emily hid a smile at the same time she chided herself for allowing Clara's blonde curls and pretty smile —and that hatbox—to make her forget the sharp mind behind them.

When Clara took an interest in something, she never forgot the details. And something had snagged her interest about this case. Emily wondered what it was, even as she said, "Why do you ask, Clara?"

"If the company is less than legal," Clara said. "Then I'm assuming some of the distribution networks must be hidden and complex. A company that did illegal business beyond this continent would have to be bigger than one that did not."

Tim's grin widened as Clara spoke, but Emily was mostly watching Mr. Draper. Who looked absolutely astounded by the statement, even as he leaned forward a little to answer Clara.

"You're quite right about the complexities of an illegal network," he said. "Though the notion seems to be beyond the grasp of most of our local authorities. And your question is an excellent one— possibly the most important one at this stage of a story."

"Or an investigation," Emily put in.

Both Clara and Mr. Draper ignored her.

"Do you know yet what the answer is for this company?" Clara asked.

"I think so," Mr. Draper said. "From everything I've learned about them, they sell only into the Canadian and American markets. And their specialty is chinoiserie for the home market."

Clara nodded. "You mentioned a few days ago that you thought the importing from the Far East might be the connection to the puppet master, did you not Emily? Which is why you've been suspecting a connection between Bray and that case."

"It is," Emily said, surprised again. She hadn't realized her friend had been listening.

"It's would be good to have that confirmed," Clara said. The statement seemed to apply equally to all of them, but Emily was amused to see Mr. Draper stop in the middle of the sidewalk, pull out his reporter's notebook and jot something down.

Clara smiled, and turned to face Emily. "It seems to me that in our planning for Mr. Granville's dining room, it would be interesting to draw on that style of decorating, and incorporate a few key pieces of chinoiserie into the design. I think we'd benefit from a visit to Trans Pacific Trading, to see what lines they carry, don't you think?"

Then before Emily could respond, Clara looked back at Mr. Draper. "Do they sell directly to the public as well as wholesale, do you know?"

"I believe they do, though they may have a furnishings consultant who works on commission in dealing directly with the public," Mr. Draper said with a bemused look.

"Then maybe Mr. Granville might be convinced to hire this person?" Clara asked Emily. "On a consultation basis only, of course. And only for the duration of this investigation? Though of course we wouldn't tell them that last bit."

"Of course," Emily managed to say, fighting back the laughter that was threatening to overwhelm her.

With a satisfied nod, Clara turned back to Mr. Draper and Tim. "Then it sounds like we all have a place to begin. If we learn something about Trans Pacific Trading, or if either of you do so, perhaps we could meet again, and for tea this time. I believe it would be beneficial for this case, and for the story you're working on, to pool our knowledge. Don't you think?"

As both reporters nodded wordlessly, Clara turned back to Emily. "We have time this afternoon to make enquiries with Trans Pacific Trading. About Mr. Granville's decor needs."

"Good idea," Emily said. Adding with a smile for the other two, "I'm afraid that means we'll need to turn back, now, gentlemen."

"That's an excellent idea," Mr. Draper said as the four turned their steps back the way they had come. "In fact, we could accompany you to Trans Pacific Trading now. It's on Abbott Street, just up from the Union Steamship wharves. About seven blocks from the Trorey Clock. Which is not an area you ladies will want to spend too much time in, especially not after dark."

"We appreciate the offer," Emily said. "But we have hours yet before sundown. And I'm already concerned that my shopping there will alert Mr. Bray to our interest in him and his company. Having two reporters along…"

"Would not be a good idea," Tim said. "You're probably right. We'll need to keep our investigations quiet, too."

"Especially since the fellow is your brother-in-law to be," Mr. Draper added. "I wouldn't want to be responsible for a rift in your family."

"I appreciate that," Emily said. "But none of us can afford to underestimate the puppet master. It stands to reason that someone who is that subtle in their own dealings will be looking for any hint of subterfuge in those he deals with."

Tim's mobile face sobered immediately. "I hadn't considered that," he said.

"Emily and I have a legitimate reason to be there," Clara said. "And an even better reason to bring Mr. Granville along, should we find ourselves uncomfortable there. As long as there are no apparent connections between your stories and our visit, we should be fine."

"But we would appreciate your escort as far as Carrall Street," Emily said, mindful of her promise to Granville. "It's only a block from Abbott."

Which didn't take them long to reach.

"We will bid you ladies adieu here," Mr. Draper said as they reached the edge of the business district. "Despite the disguise provided by Miss Miles's hatbox"—and he tipped his own hat in that direction—"we wouldn't want someone taking note of the four of us. I look forward to our next conversation."

Carrall Street was an intriguing mixture of small offices, a restaurant or two, barber shops and several warehouses, including a spice importer. Suited and hatted men carrying briefcases walked briskly by them as Emily and Clara paused to assess which direction Trans Pacific Trading lay.

As they turned their steps towards the water, Emily drew in the aromas of fresh-ground coffee and cinnamon. Mingling with it, she could smell horse manure from the streets, tar from the docks and rusting steel from the railroads, all threaded through with the briny smell of the sea. She decided she might not want to be here after dark, unless perhaps she had a gun—and knew how to use it—though she still wasn't sure she ever wanted own a gun. Perhaps after dark it would be best if Granville was with her.

But in any case, she was glad she and Clara had decided to come here today. There was an energy and a purpose to this street, mingled with a shivery feeling of being close to exotic places she'd never been. Or even thought of going.

She drew in another lungful of air, catching a hint of some spicy scent she'd never smelled before. Where had that come from? And she wondered what Granville thought of traveling. Or specifically, of the two of them traveling together.

"We should talk about what we need to know. And how to ask it without raising their suspicions," Emily said to Clara as she spotted the weathered Trans Pacific Trading sign several buildings down. "It might help to know how large their business is."

"Just leave it to me," her friend said.

Emily wasn't at all sure that was a good plan, but this was no time to discuss it. Clara had stopped just outside the rough board structure to consider a small plate glass window that displayed several china pieces, including two vases of blue and white porcelain, with colorful silk unrolling behind them as a backdrop. Despite the location and the rough exterior of the building, they clearly employed someone who knew a bit about decorating a home.

"These aren't displayed well, but it's a start," Clara said, though she seemed to be talking mostly to herself.

The window display reminded Emily that she had already purchased a few items of chinoiserie, intending to include them in her future home.

"Did I ever show you the blue and white vases I purchased in Victoria?" she asked Clara. "Perhaps we could build on those."

Clara just smiled tolerantly and headed for the door.

Emily was growing more uneasy about this excursion by the minute, but short of creating a scene, there was little she could do now but follow her friend.

Once they were inside, the wooden crates stacked in haphazard rows in every direction emphasized that this was mostly an importing business, though she did see a long counter on the far wall, with glass fronted display cabinets beneath the countertop. A small selection of various china patterns were displayed there, and several bolts of colored silks were stacked against the wall behind the counter. The air smelled of dust and straw, with a hint of that earthy smell she associated with some of the cheaper silks.

She glanced around her, hoping not to see Mr. Bray. No one seemed to have noticed them yet. Clara, of course, had already spotted the display counter and was wending her way through the crates towards it. With an inward sigh, Emily followed her.

They reached their destination at the same time as an older man dressed in a rough blue overall, who looked surprised and a little worried to see two ladies making their careful way across the sawdust covered floor.

"Can I help you miss? Ma'am?" he asked.

Clara beamed at him. "We're looking for some decorative items for a house. Your things here, they are imported from China, are they not?"

"Some of 'em," was the cautious answer.

"Is there someone here who can show us what you have? Or even better, someone who can produce some assistance on which items would best suit our purpose, and how to display them?"

Emily was amused to see the look of relief crossing the man's face. "Oh, you want our decorating chap. Just wait here," he said, and disappeared behind the same narrow stack of crates he'd appeared from.

Clara looked around her, then met Emily's gaze. "This is… interesting. I don't think I've ever been to a wholesalers before."

"Neither have I," Emily said. And so far, it was a disappointment. There was nothing to see. And nothing that told her what might be going on here. All the crates had markings on them, and what she assumed were customs labels, but none of it told her anything.

"It seems we'll have to wait for this decorator," Clara said and moved closer to inspect the china on display. "I don't think any of these pieces will work. Emily, what do you think?"

Emily thought that the pieces she had purchased at a grocers in Victoria's Chinatown were much nicer than any of them. "Perhaps they have other, better pieces somewhere," she said diplomatically, not wanting to make enemies at this point.

"Indeed we do," came a voice from behind her, and she and Clara both jumped a little.

"Sorry, didn't mean to startle you," a man's voice said, as he came around a different stack of crates to face them. "It's the sawdust, you know. Muffles sound."

Emily nodded, relieved to see it wasn't Mr. Bray. This man was dark haired and complected, and very well groomed. He looked to be in his mid-twenties, and was wearing a tailored gray suit with an oriental pattern on the silk handkerchief tucked in one pocket. At least he looked like he understood decorating.

Clara smiled at him. "I can't wait to see what else you have," she said.

"If you can tell me a little of what you're looking for, I'll see if I can meet that expectation," he said, returning the smile.

As Clara talked about her plans for Granville's dining room, Emily fought to keep a straight face. One grandiose idea after another rolled from her lips, all based around an oriental theme, of course. By the time she was done, there would be a table for twenty, place settings to match, and every conceivable decorative item to fulfill the currently fashionable concept.

"I'm nearly sure the room isn't big enough to seat twenty," she said when Clara paused. "Though your concept sounds as if it would be spectacular."

Clara gave her an annoyed look. Apparently she wasn't planning on actually working with the fellow, but Emily figured that since they were spending time here anyway, they might as well see if they could get another room's decorations taken care of.

"Let me show you some of what we have," the young man was quick to say, and steered both of them towards a tall closed cabinet against the far wall. Flinging the double doors open, he said, "I'll show you some options for dining tables in a moment, but this should give you some ideas about what our various directions could be."

Emily stared at the riot of colors and patterns—many rich with gilt—and felt her head start to spin. Her earlier thought that she was developing some sense of style? What was she thinking? Seeing this abundance of choices made her want to go and investigate something immediately.

What a good thing they were here because of an investigation.

Emily glanced over at Clara, who was moving towards the

cabinet as if drawn by an irresistible force, her gaze locked on that chaos and a gleam in her eye. Oh no.

If she didn't intervene, Granville—and eventually Emily herself —would be living with a dining room far too ornate for either of their tastes. It didn't bear thinking about.

Staring from Clara's intent look to that cabinet of excess, Emily suddenly realized that since Granville had lived in rental accommodations since she'd met him, she didn't actually know his tastes, either. Except for in office furnishings.

She closed her eyes for a moment, as if that would make all of this go away. It didn't, of course.

She drew in a deep breath, ready to take control. But it was too late.

Clara had already turned to the salesman. "But this is perfect," she said. "I have a few ideas."

And before Emily could get in a word, her friend had engaged the decorator in a rapid-fire conversation that proposed and eliminated decorating ideas and stylistic touches that Emily had never heard of between one breath and the next. It was like a game of table tennis played by two experts, with the ball bouncing rapidly between them. All she could do was shake her head.

There was no stopping this now.

That was fine. She was here to investigate, so investigate she would. She'd deal with whatever design disaster ensued from this visit later. Preferably much later.

She looked at the contents of the cabinet with new eyes. If she didn't have to live with any of it, what could she learn about Trans Pacific Trading from their choice of merchandise? If this was representative, they carried a wide range of china styles and patterns, ranging from table settings to decorative vases and covered jars in a variety of sizes. Not unlike the merchandise Clark & Company imported, actually.

Were they competitors?

She moved closer to the cabinet to take a better look at those lidded jars, then carefully lifted a smaller, rounded one—in a rather attractive traditional blue and white pattern, she noticed—off the shelf. Made of fine, almost translucent porcelain, it was surprisingly light.

She lifted off the lid and peered inside. It was roomier than she'd expected. The shape was deceptive. Replacing the lid, she hefted it in her hand for a moment, her mind racing.

If Granville was right that Clark & Company were using similar items to smuggle drugs to the States, then was it possible that Trans Pacific Trading were doing the same? Just how similar were these two companies?

She took another look at the stacks of crates. How could she find out what was in them? If she grabbed that crowbar someone had left on a nearby crate and started trying to pry them open, as she wished she could, it would create the kind of scene she was trying to avoid. But she needed to get a better sense of what else this company imported.

Clara and the fellow Emily suspected was about to become Granville's new decorator—a Mr. Tremblay—were still talking intently. But while she was considering the china, they had been moving gradually along one wall towards the back of the warehouse.

Which might be more effective than prying open crates, she decided, not bothering to hide her grin as she followed them.

They paused in front of an elaborate dining table surrounded by eight carved chairs. It was beautiful, made of some deep red-brown wood with a subtle gleam. She thought it might be rosewood, but Clara would undoubtedly tell her what it was later.

Both the table and the chairs looked solid, the carving subtle but very well done. The curving lines of the legs appealed to her. Emily could actually see herself and Granville dining at such a table.

Meanwhile, the decorator was pulling out an extra leaf from inside the table to extend it and then another. Emily watched as a table which comfortably seated eight suddenly accommodated a dozen people, and then sixteen. To her surprise, Emily began to realize that this dining set might indeed work in Granville's house. Their house.

And it would look lovely with the blue and white vases she had already purchased. Perhaps Clara's instincts and sense of design might be right for them after all.

And her own detective instincts might be right too. Clark & Company also imported a little furniture, so it seemed they also had that in common with Trans Pacific Trading. Perhaps her theory wasn't as outlandish as it had first seemed.

Meanwhile, Clara and Mr. Tremblay were now moving further back into the warehouse. Here and there between the cases, she could now see the occasional piece of furniture unpacked and set up. The other two were headed towards a side cabinet which matched the table they'd just looked at. It too was beautiful.

And would probably cost Granville a pretty penny. Not that he would mind. If he liked the table, that is. One thing she did know was that he was willing to spend money on quality goods.

Which was a good thing, because Clara was now being shown a cabinet-style bar which matched the other pieces. And then a serving table.

Emily was impressed with the quality of what Trans Pacific carried. She was even more impressed with how similar the selections of chinoiserie were to those carried by Clark & Company. The more she considered the matter, the more she thought that the similarities between the two companies were significant.

She had no idea if the quality was similar, but perhaps it didn't matter. If Trans Pacific carried more expensive goods, perhaps that allowed them to reach a different set of customers for their goods, both legal and illegal? What she needed to know now was about Trans Pacific's distribution. Who were their customers, and how far did they ship?

As she thought about how best to find out, an image of Mr. Bray's smarmy face crept into her mind. Why did he want to purchase this company, and why now? If there was so much money to be made from smuggling, why would the current owner even sell?

And surely Papa would not invest in a company where the financial reports made no sense. Because if most of the money came from smuggling, the reports to investors would have to be mostly fiction. Wouldn't they?

What if Trans Pacific Trading was actually a legitimate company at the moment? And Mr. Bray had somehow uncovered the company's potential for making a lot of money through smuggling. Was that possible?

If the puppet master was involved, though? She'd suspected all along that Mr. Bray was the kind of man the puppet master would find useful.

If Granville was right about the opium smuggling… What if the puppet master had more opium available than Clark & Company could handle? He'd need another company able to take on part of the distribution. And given the similarities between the two companies, Trans Pacific Trading would probably be an easy choice.

If the management of Trans Pacific was crooked, and open to smuggling drugs, that is. If they were legitimate, though, it wouldn't work. Which might be—in the puppet master's eyes—a waste of an opportunity for everyone to make a lot of money.

Enter Mr. Bray.

It would explain why Mr. Bray wanted to buy the company. And his sudden interest in her sister, too. As well as their rapid engagement, if he'd decided Papa's influence was his best hope to raise the money he needed. Or maybe the puppet master had suggested it.

Emily gritted her teeth at the idea of either man using her family like that. One way or another, she and Granville needed to bring these two villains to justice.

It was time to talk to Mama.

26

Less than twenty minutes later, Granville had collected Scott and Trent and headed out. As they left the building and strode towards the rougher part of town, his eyes scanned the busy street, looking for anything out of place in the rush of carts and delivery wagons. His hands hung loose at his side, ready to reach for his gun.

The odds were good that the puppet master hadn't had time to hire another assassin yet. But then, the fellow seemed to specialize in convoluted plans. Who was to say he hadn't made plans to replace the ghost if the assassin was ever arrested? Or killed.

He glanced over at his colleagues, keeping pace beside him. Both were armed. And both were keeping a sharp eye out for another assassin.

The upper floors of some of the three- and four- story brick buildings they were walking by would make ideal spots from which to target them. And the alleys they passed were equally dangerous. Though it was unlikely a single man would take on all three of them at once.

Unless he had the perfect vantage point.

He angled his steps slightly so that all three of them were

walking too close to the buildings to allow for an easy shot from above.

"You really think this puppet master will send another assassin after us?" Trent asked suddenly.

"Most likely," he said. "Since he obviously knows we're investigating him. But finding a new assassin that deadly, and one the puppet master can control, may be a difficult proposition. Which should give us time to ask a few questions. Making this a good time to talk to Benton."

"You sure about that, Granville?" Scott asked. "Messing with Benton is a bad idea."

"We need to find the puppet master," he said. "And figure out whether Abernathy exists or no. Benton knows more than he's telling us."

"Nothing new there. Benton always knows more than he tells," Scott said. "It's annoying as hell, but knowing more than anyone else is part of his stock in trade. And it's made him one hell of a lot of money."

He grinned at the truth in that.

He and Scott had both learned the hard way never to ignore how strong the lure of easy profit could be. It still amazed him, the similarities between what some businessmen were prepared to do for profit, and how far some miners would go to take possession of a rich gold field. And so far, this case seemed to be all about someone's profit.

Starting with Benton's. The gangster had hired them to deal with a threat against his own profit, after all.

Or had he?

As they turned down Water Street, the buildings around them changed from red brick four story office blocks to lower wooden warehouses with rough-shingled walls, he speculated about Benton's motives. Just how big a role had the murder of his man played in the gangster's decision to finally deal with the puppet master?

At the top of the rough stairs, Benton's offices now included a waiting area with expensive leather armchairs that were just short of comfortable. Which was undoubtedly deliberate on the gangster's part. Intimidation sometimes took subtle forms, and Benton loved keeping people off balance.

When his burly henchmen finally showed them into the office itself, Benton didn't look surprised to see the three of them. Nor did he look offended, which surprised Granville. But he had kept them waiting for nearly a quarter of an hour. Perhaps he considered that enough of a win in their ongoing battle of wits.

"And what can I do for you gentlemen?" the gangster asked

"We have a few questions."

"Of course you do. So what are you waiting for? Sit."

Granville kept his expression neutral as they sat down in the row of upright chairs in front of that mammoth marble desk. It was all part of the game.

"What do you know about Philip Abernathy?" he began.

"The assassin named Abernathy as the fellow who hired him," Benton said. "Which means Abernathy could be your puppet master. The one I hired you to find. So why are you asking me?"

"Answer the question and I'll tell you."

Benton's thick brows drew together, but one corner of his mouth ticked up. "One of these days you'll go too far," he said.

"Probably," Granville said. "It's a good thing you find me amusing at the moment, then."

Benton considered the three of them in silence for a long moment, his hands steepled in front of him on his blue-veined marble desktop. Then he gave a slight nod.

"I believe that Abernathy runs several small businesses, though I've never met the man. His dealings are too small to interest me," Benton said dismissively. "I assume you've heard by now that the assassin we caught yesterday has left town?"

Granville nodded.

"I'm hearing rumors someone is searching for a new assassin," Benton said. "Presumably the puppet master."

"We've heard the same," Scott said.

"Making your efforts to take the assassin down a waste of time. So what else have you three done lately?" Benton challenged them.

"We've uncovered the fact that except for the few companies he owns on paper, Philip Abernathy doesn't seem to exist at all," Granville said.

"Then you know almost as much as I do about the man," Benton said.

"Almost?" Trent said.

Scott and Granville both glared at him.

"What?" Trent said, an aggrieved look on his face. "It's the obvious question."

"Your employers are worried I'll shoot you—or worse—for your impertinence," Benton said smoothly.

"What's worse than being shot?" Trent said.

"Shut up or you'll find out," Scott told him.

Trent opened his mouth to argue back, when Granville shot him a look that had him flinching a little.

He hid a smile. The kid was growing up fast, but he still didn't have much sense of self-preservation. They'd have to work on that.

Benton was scowling, but Granville didn't sense any heat behind it. He suspected that the kid amused him, too. But the gangster's tolerance was more limited than his interactions with Granville himself might suggest. And Trent had been pushing his luck.

"Do you know of anyone who has ever met Philip Abernathy?" Granville asked Benton.

"No," Benton said. "I've wondered if the name was a cover for your puppet master."

"Yet you never looked into it?"

"Wasn't worth the effort," Benton said. "Abernathy was operating in a limited sphere. And in any case, he wasn't interfering with my business. I saw no reason to mess with his."

The suspected puppet master hadn't been interfering with Benton's business? That wasn't what he'd implied before.

Granville considered Benton's mild expression while his mind rapidly rearranged everything he'd learned about the puppet master since this case started.

"So what you're saying is that the puppet master's business served as a convenient scapegoat for some of your more under-handed dealings," Granville said. "People were terrified enough of the assassin that they didn't ask too many questions. A situation you found advantageous."

"Well done. I knew you'd get there eventually," Benton said.

"As long as it wasn't too quickly," Granville said, watching the other man closely. "So what changed?"

"What makes you think something changed?" Benton countered.

"Your hints became a little more helpful," Granville said. "And, of course, you hired us to take out the puppet master. Making it fairly obvious."

Benton grinned at his sarcasm.

"Well, we're happy to take care of the puppet master in any case," Granville said. "Since you're paying us well. And the fellow has become a threat to people I care about. So any hints that might help us identify this villain would be useful."

"If I had anything that would help me find him, I wouldn't have needed to hire you, now would I?" Benton said.

Granville didn't entirely believe him, though he was certain Benton now wanted the puppet master—whoever he was—removed from the game. And given the games Benton liked to play, that was a good piece of information to have.

So Benton either had no information on Abernathy at all, or telling them what he did know would have revealed too much of his own business dealings, which he'd never do. Either way, they were on their own from here.

Especially if this ended up in court. Benton would never testify against the puppet master in a court of law.

After thanking Benton—and earning himself a hard look from the gangster, who wasn't entirely certain if Granville was being sarcastic. Which he was—they made their way downstairs.

27

Sunday, September 23, 1900

It was a brilliantly clear Sunday afternoon, with just a hint of autumn coolness in the air. After the church service he'd attended with the Turner family, Granville and Emily strolled through the quiet town to Garrity's Steakhouse. The waiter had recognized them, and was happy to meet Granville's request by seating them at an out of the way table.

It crossed his mind that today Emily should have been seated in the midst of the restaurant for all to see. She glowed in a flowing dress of what his expert eye suggested was hand-tailored Chinese silk, in a golden-green shade that flattered her green eyes and ivory complexion.

The increasing demands of this case meant that he hadn't seen her at all on Saturday, so he'd been glad of her request that they talk privately today. Though given the tension he'd felt when Emily was near her sister and future brother-in-law, he suspected she might have an ulterior motive. Which proved to be the case.

"Thank you so much for taking me out for luncheon today," she said, smiling across the table at him. "It was bad enough sitting with

Mr. Bray at church. I don't think I could have borne being polite to him over the soup."

"I'm always happy to be of service," he said. Emily made a face at him, after glancing around first to make sure no one was paying attention to them.

"Besides, I wanted to talk to you about him before you had to spend much time with him," she said. "I have a plan. And I was afraid I wouldn't get the chance to explain it."

"I'd rather talk to you than to him in any case," Granville said.

"Well, I wouldn't think much of your judgement if you didn't," she said tartly.

He winked at her. "I see your impressions of the fellow haven't improved with familiarity."

"I don't like him," Emily said. "And I don't trust him near any of my family. Not my sister. And especially not Papa."

He grinned at her tone, as she'd meant him to. Even though he knew she meant every word. "Your Papa? I sense a story there. Has Bray some connection to your father?"

She filled him in on what she'd learned during the last few days about Bray, and especially about his intent to buy Trans Pacific Trading. "And he's looking to do so with money from Papa and those Papa can influence," she said with some heat.

"Interesting. Why is Bray so intent on buying that particular company?"

"I think his interests are very much less than legal," she said with some heat, then glanced around her again. Leaving forward, she lowered her voice, and explained the similarities she and Clara had seen between Trans Pacific and Clark & Company.

"If the current owners of Trans Pacific are running a fully legitimate business, then a confidence man like Bray would see a lot of profit to be made in exploiting the potential illegal channels," she finished and sat back, watching him carefully.

Granville's mind worked quickly through the problems and opportunities such a move would create.

"He'd have to have at least two sets of books, as Mac suggests

Clark & Company do," he said. "And his investors would see very little of the real profits."

"Yes, that's what I think. You have to admit Mr. Bray makes a perfect villain for this kind of undertaking."

"He does indeed. So I take it you're planning to defeat his plans?" he said.

Emily smiled fiercely. "Yes, I am. I knew you would understand. And I'm looking forward to it, too."

She added a slather of butter to the crusty bread that came with the butternut squash soup they'd both ordered. The subtle hint of cloves mixed with the rich scent of butter had Granville's mouth watering.

Emily looked around carefully before leaning forward again. "Mr. Bray is far too new in town to be the puppet master," she said in a low voice. "And he's too obvious, if you know what I mean?"

"I do. Our puppet master is subtle," he said. "Not one to draw attention to himself, or to stand out in any way."

"That's it. And my sister's fiancé is all about his role as the most splendid being in the room."

He laughed, and raised his glass of wine to her. "You really don't like him at all, do you?"

"No. I told you. And I like him even less now I know he's probably using my sister to get Papa interested in his stupid company. Or at least what he hopes will become his company."

She took a sip of her own wine, and put the glass down with a thump. "But I think Mr. Bray might prove helpful."

"In his own destruction?"

"Why not?" Emily said. "He's involved with importing, and he's looking for money to take over Trans Pacific Trading. Plus he has no conscience and fewer morals. He'd be a useful tool for your puppet master—if he isn't involved with him already. Which I suspect he might be."

"Why is that?"

"Because Trans Pacific seems so remarkably similar to Clark & Company. And I doubt Mr. Bray's ability to so quickly identify a company so perfectly suited for his particular skills. Especially in the short time since he moved to town. Nor, I'd be willing to bet, is he smart enough to do so."

He gave her a sharp look. "You think that Trans Pacific might already be one of the puppet masters' allied companies?"

"I think they would be a perfect fit if they became one," Emily said. "That is, if Mr. Bray manages to buy them. The company, I mean."

"That could make sense," Granville said. "But it seems a stretch given the facts we have now."

"Not if I'm right about Mr. Bray," she said. "I wouldn't put anything beyond him."

"And I wouldn't put anything beyond the puppet master," he said. "If I'm right about him."

He looked across the table to see Emily beaming at him.

"If Scott were here, he'd say that's why we are so perfect for each other," she said.

He would, too, Granville thought and winked at Emily. "And he'd be right, too."

She surprised and amused him by winking back. "Don't I know it?" she said.

Suddenly her expression grew serious. "Mr. Bray really is a villain, Granville," she said. "And I can prove it, I know I can. With your help."

He rolled his eyes dramatically and was rewarded by her laugh. "I know that tone. Now what are you up to?"

"Well, Clara and I might have engaged a decorator on your behalf," she said, not quite meeting his eyes.

He stared at her for a moment, picturing the chaos Clara and Emily's idea of decorating had already caused in his life. Wasn't that enough?

But she would have a reason. She always did.

"A decorator?" he said. "Why is it I'm suspicious that this is no ordinary decorator?"

"Well, I'm not even sure he's a very good decorator," she confessed. "But he does work for Trans Pacific. His name is Mr. Tremblay."

"So you're sacrificing my, or rather our house to the hunt for the puppet master? That figures, as Scott would say."

"I knew you'd understand," she said with a grin. "And Clara will make sure to keep the fellow in line, after all."

Which wasn't especially reassuring. He tried not to think about what the house had looked like this morning, covered from the front door to the back entrance in white plaster dust. He'd left a trail of footsteps when he'd left home this morning.

"And who is going to keep Clara in line?" he asked her.

She just shook her head at him.

"What role did you want me to play in all of this?" he asked.

"You need to meet with Mr. Tremblay, the decorator, as well as Clara and myself, to discuss your needs for the dining room."

"The dining room," he said flatly. "That sounds like a room you might know more about than I do."

"And why would you think that?"

When she put it like that, she probably wouldn't. Her mama seemed less obsessed with decorating than his own had been. And less fond of discussing it at the dinner table too, probably. Though he wasn't about to admit that to her. Or to Clara.

It looked like he'd be meeting with this decorator. But if he'd learned anything about his fiancée since they'd become engaged, it was that Emily seldom had only one end in mind. He wondered exactly what they'd be learning from the fellow.

And what it would cost him.

"But I do have one other request," Emily said as she pushed her empty soup bowl a little away from her so that the waiter could replace it with the roast chicken she had ordered.

"Oh?" Granville said when the waiter had served his steak and was out of earshot. "And will I enjoy this request more than your last one?" he finished with a straight face.

"Well, I *hope* you might prefer dancing with me to discussing furnishings with a decorator," she said in a worried tone.

Which she immediately spoiled by giving him a conspiratorial grin.

"I can think of very few things I enjoy more," he said with an answering smile.

It was at once both the diplomatic thing to say, and the complete truth. And it pleased him that she had the confidence to make the request and expect that to be true. "I gather someone is holding a dance?"

"Oh, not just a dance," Emily said. "This is the Fifth Annual Black and White Ball. It's a fundraising event, held in honor of St. Paul's hospital, and it gives people a chance to put on their finest attire and really shine."

"I'm surprised this is the first I'm hearing of it, then," he said. "Will there still be tickets available?"

"We've been a little busy with some major cases over the last few months," Emily said. "But the tickets won't be a problem. Mama is one of the organizers, and she reserved them in our name quite some time ago."

"So this is not so much a request as it is a command performance?"

"We don't want to let Mama down," she said, casting him a mock-demure look from under her eyelashes.

"Certainly not if I want our marriage to occur in this decade," he agreed. "What a good thing I enjoy dancing with you."

"And I you," she said. "Besides, it's an excellent opportunity to hear the latest gossip." She paused to take a bite of her scalloped potatoes in creamed sauce.

"I've never heard you speak of gossip as a positive before."

"This case seems to have given me an appreciation for how useful a little society gossip can be to a detective. If you know how to listen," she said with a shark's smile. "And I find when it comes to Mr. Bray, I'm very motivated indeed."

He grinned at her intensity, glad it wasn't focused on him. This ball should prove more entertaining than he had anticipated.

2 8

Monday, September 24, 1900

It wasn't much past six when Granville got to the office on Monday morning. He hadn't even bothered with breakfast. Something about Friday's conversation with the ghost was still niggling at him, and he needed to take another look at his notes.

As he looked back flipped back through the notebook, Emily's comments about what the ghost had told them—and not told them—suddenly made a different kind of sense. He didn't have answers, not yet. But he would have.

He spent some time updating his case files, and even more time staring out the window at the as the sky gradually lightened, listening to the clatter and clang as the city gradually wakened. By the time Scott arrived an hour later, he had an answer. Or at least the beginnings of one.

"Let's go," he said, grabbing his suit jacket and hat from the coat tree. He was half-way out the door before his bewildered partner could catch up with him.

"Where are we off to at this hour?" Scott said. "Nothing's even open yet."

"The cafe is," Granville said. "I'm hungry."

His partner gave him an assessing look. "I can see that," he said.

Scott knew him well. He didn't ask a single question until they'd ordered, and their coffee and breakfasts were on the table. Then he gulped down some coffee and looked Granville straight in the eye. "So what's wrong?"

"What makes you think something is wrong?"

"I've seen you this focused before. Either something happened yesterday. Or you've decided we missed something on the puppet master case."

Granville took a bite of scrambled eggs so fresh he could still see the steam rising off of them. "Pass the salt, please," he said, just to annoy Scott.

It didn't work.

"So I'm right," his partner said with satisfaction as he handed over the salt shaker. "And you're not upset enough for there to be a problem with Emily. Which means it's something to do with the case. So spill it. I haven't got all day."

"I think we may have been wasting our time in Chinatown," Granville said slowly, spreading butter on a thick slice of toasted sourdough.

"What?" Scott said. He didn't look best pleased at the idea. "Where did you come up with that one. And why now?"

He grinned. "The one thing we did learn yesterday is that without a connection in Chinatown, it isn't easy for a white man to purchase opium in any quantity." Reaching for his coffee mug, he drained it and signaled for a refill.

"That's hardly new."

"True. But everything the ghost told us pointed to the puppet master—either directly or through Abernathy—having connections in Victoria's Chinatown. Not here."

Scott had put his fork down and was scowling at him. Not a good sign. "We already talked about that. So what?"

"Think about how little we've learned about the puppet master to date. Even Benton calls him the invisible man. The fellow has to have worked pretty hard to hide himself that well. Having key connections in another city probably help him bury his real identity," Granville said. "As well as what his various businesses are really up to."

"You're thinking that would make him more likely to buy his opium in Victoria, too? Since he already has those connections," Scott said.

"That's it."

"He could bring it across Georgia Straight on a dark night, get around any port security that way."

"Exactly," Granville said as he stirred cream into his coffee.

"But why would our slippery puppet master ever have worked with Emily's bad guy? The man collects china."

"Don't forget Miss Kent's theory that the opium is likely shipped across the border in items of Chinese porcelain."

"And Emily's collector knows a lot about chinoiserie," Scott said.

"Exactly," Granville said. "The puppet master might have had a use for someone with that expertise. Anything he ships over the border has to appear to be legitimate, in case it gets inspected by customs agents."

Scott was frowning. "It all fits."

"So you agree?"

"It fits everything we know about the puppet master," Scott said. "But at this point, we have a lot of theories. Not much proof. So now what?"

"Now we get back to hunting down the puppet master." Granville checked his pocket watch. "And we have just enough time for another cup of coffee before we meet with the team."

THEY MADE it back to the office just in time. Emily and Clara were chatting with Trent. Mac and Miss Kent were waiting in the conference room, and they had invited Robert Carver to join them. So there would be eight of them seated around the expansive table, and there was still plenty of room, he thought with a quick rush of pride in what they were building here.

Once everyone had moved to the meeting room and was seated, Granville looked around the table.

"Good morning to all of you," he said. "Carver, thank you for joining us. Would one of you like to brief us on your meeting?"

To Granville's surprise, it was Carver who answered. "You do seem to get involved in the most complicated cases, Granville. But your team is solid."

"Thank you. I concur," Granville said, though he noted the look that Miss Kent shot Carver. She didn't look happy. What was that about?

"I do have some information I'd like to pass on first," Carver said. "If I may?"

At Granville's nod, he continued "It seems that rumors are starting to spread about your puppet master. I'm not sure why the truth is coming out now."

"It might have something to do with the fact that the fellow's enforcer was arrested last week," Granville said easily. "The assassin was charged with murder, and has since fled town."

"What? How did that happen?" Carver said. He didn't seem to be expecting an answer.

Granville and Scott exchanged amused glances but neither of them mentioned their own role in the matter.

"One thing that is clear," Carver continued. "If we can tie a name to your puppet master, and connect him to the assassin, there's no doubt he'll serve some serious jail time, at the very least."

"And even more jail time if we can tie him to the smuggling," Mac added. "Carver's told us what we need to look for, and once we have a name, we should have enough evidence to go after him that way. If we have a good lawyer."

All eyes turned back to Carver, who shrugged. "If Randall is willing to work with me," he said. "He's the obvious choice for this, since it started with his cases. And he's still—much as it pains me to admit it—decidedly better in the courtroom when it comes to explaining complex business matters. I'm rather better at confusing them."

"The two of you proved an unbeatable combination our the last case. I see no reason we shouldn't take advantage of the same thing this time," Granville said. And paused for a beat, watching Carver.

The fellow was good. No expressions crossed his face, though this decision had to be important to him. The formerly disgraced lawyer still had a lot to prove.

As the silence stretched, Carver's shoulders fell just a hair, as if expecting a blow. If he hadn't been looking for it, Granville would have missed it. Carver would make a damned good poker player.

"Randall agrees with me," Granville said. "And I look forward to watching that trial unfold."

Carver smiled at that. "First you have to catch this puppet master of yours."

"I think we might have another connection that could lead us to him," Emily said. And proceeded to detail what she'd learned about Bray and Trans Pacific Trading.

Carver looked slightly surprised at her participation. Which was a major mark against the fellow. He might be a good lawyer and fighting back against some bad decisions he'd made in the past, but if he didn't respect Emily, then this was the last case this firm would work with him on, Granville decided.

Unless this was this the first time the lawyer had worked with Emily on a case?

And Carver was looking reluctantly impressed, so he might redeem himself. Granville just hoped the lawyer was a fast learner, or they wouldn't be working with him in future.

He turned back to the others. "Mac? Miss Kent? Any luck in making connections between the various ships in port and the shipments from any of the companies we suspect tie to the puppet master?"

"We're still searching," Mac said. "But we have verified the list of the various ships and the dates they arrived and departed. And we have some sense of their declared cargo. But so far, we haven't found any links with any of the companies we suspect are connected to the puppet master."

"Good work on the lists. I'd appreciate a copy of them," Granville said. "What about Abernathy? Or Barnabas Jones? Have we anything else that will help us find either of them?"

It was Miss Kent who answered. "No, I'm afraid we don't," she said, then shot another unreadable look at Carver. "Every record we've been able to find for the men leads to a dead end. The only addresses we've found either don't exist at all, lead to post office boxes or are in care of other companies located in either Britain or the United States, which we don't have records for. The same with phone numbers. I still don't believe either man actually exists."

"I'd have to concur," Carver said. "The public records are unusually convoluted, and very difficult to navigate. It feels deliberate to me. The end result is that, on the face of it, both Abernathy and Jones are legitimate. Legally, I'm not sure where you'd start to go after either of them. And it would take a long time."

Time they didn't have.

"All right," Granville said. "We'll keep looking into them, especially Abernathy, but let's be clear that our focus needs to be on the puppet master. And hunting down those facts that will put him away for life."

He looked around the table. "Mac, Miss Kent…"

"We'll stay on the financial end, see if we can dig deeper and find out who is really behind those companies," Mac said.

Miss Kent nodded.

"I can keep working with them," Carver said.

"Good," Granville said. "Scott, Trent and I will pay a visit to some of those companies, and see if we can shake anything loose. We meet back here at five."

"Don't forget that you have an appointment with Clara and I at Trans Pacific Trading this afternoon. You need to be there by three," Emily reminded him with a smile he suspected only he could decipher.

Thankfully. She was enjoying this far too much.

"Then I will meet you there," he said with a smile that made her blush.

ONCE THE MEETING ENDED, Granville grabbed his hat and jacket and headed for the stairs. Reaching the street, a combination of frustration with a case that wasn't moving fast enough and worry about the puppet master hiring a new assassin lengthened his gait. He was halfway along the block before the Scott and Trent caught up with him.

The fresh air and the movement had been enough to clear his head.

"Trent may have been right on Saturday that we could have asked about Abernathy in Chinatown," he said to Scott over his left shoulder, as Trent's anxious face popped up on his right side.

"Maybe," Trent muttered. "Not that the shopkeeper would've recognized the name, even if they'd met him. Haven't you noticed that the Chinese have as much trouble with our names as we do with theirs?"

Granville hadn't, but that didn't mean anything. He hadn't spent much time in Chinatown itself, and some people had more problem with accents than others.

"It was still a good suggestion," he said. "One we might explore later."

"Where are we going, anyway?" Scott asked.

The big man was walking on Granville's other side. He didn't look particularly worried.

"Miss Kent and Mac have been doing an excellent job delving into the paperwork behind these various businesses, but sometimes there's no substitute for paying a personal visit. We'd do better with a photograph of Abernathy, though."

"I thought Abernathy didn't exist, except on paper," Scott said.

"I'd be happier if we could prove that. What if we're wrong?"

"So we're going to pay a call on Philip Abernathy?" Trent asked.

Granville laughed. "He might not exist, remember?" he said. "No, we're going to see if we can acquire a photograph of the fellow."

"The one who doesn't exist? How?" Trent demanded.

"Scott and I are going to Clark & Company to enquire after Mr. Abernathy. You are going to visit Vancouver Box."

"Why don't I get to come with you?"

"Because as part of your new responsibilities, you're responsible for the frequent shipping a variety of often unwieldy packages out of the country," Granville said. "And for making sure it gets there in one piece."

"I'm responsible for… what? That makes no sense."

Granville ignored his protests. "It does when we're working with Pinkerton's. It's entirely possible that we might need to ship evidence on a case back east. Not that you'll tell that to the hard-working folk at Vancouver Box."

"But…"

"However, you are looking for a company with sufficient experience shipping valuable items that you can trust to hire for this kind of work," Granville finished.

"But why?"

Scott was laughing as he answered for Granville. "Because you need to convince your impossible boss that Vancouver Box is trustworthy. So you need to know everything about the company. Who owns it, who works there, what they do, what they charge —everything."

"Even photographs," Trent said, his eyes lighting up. "I get it. But if I say I work with a detective agency, won't they be suspicious?"

"Frequent shipping. Valuable items," Granville repeated. "Trust me. Unless you're dealing with Abernathy himself—which I expect is highly unlikely—they'll be too busy trying to sell their services to worry about what exactly your company does."

Trent sighed loudly. "Fine. Where is it?"

Granville consulted the slim notebook he carried in an inner pocket, and read out the address. "It's only a few blocks west of here."

"That's just down the block from Clark & Company," Trent said. "Aren't you going the same way?"

"I've changed my mind. I think we'll start by having a chat with Benton. We'll see you back at the office at five."

He clapped Trent on the back, ignoring both their apprentice's stunned expression and Scott's look of frustration, and turned his steps north towards Benton's offices. At this time of day, they might just catch him.

Benton wasn't in.

"That'll teach you not to call first," Scott said, but his expression was relieved. "So we might as well go talk to people at Clark & Company. What were you even planning on asking Benton, anyway?"

"I still want to know exactly how he was profiting from the puppet master's smuggling operation."

They were standing toe to toe on the sidewalk outside the warehouse that was also Benton's place of business. Scott was frowning at him, and Granville knew his own expression was far from friendly. But he also knew he was right.

"You're starting to grasp at straws," Scott said bluntly. "You're already playing a dangerous game with Benton, and you don't have enough proof to ask him that kind of question. He'll see through you, and you know it."

"I need to confront him, face to face," Granville said. "Right now, all I'm sure of is that he's still not being straight about any of this."

"It's Benton, you idiot," Scott said. "He's never straight about anything. And this is no place for us to be having this argument."

Scott was right about that. Fighting his temper and his need to make progress on this infuriating case, Granville checked his pocket watch. He had an hour and a half before he was to meet with Emily at three. It probably wasn't enough time to chase Benton down, at that.

"Fine," he said. "Clark & Company it is."

By half past four, Granville, Emily, Clara and Scott were gathered in Granville's office. Emily and Clara were each seated demurely in one of the upholstered visitor's chairs. Scott had swiped a straight legged chair from the meeting room and was leaning back in it, balancing on two legs with his feet on the desk. Granville was leaning back in his desk chair. He and Scott had half-full glasses of Scotch in their hands, while the ladies had requested glasses of water, which they were sipping with every evidence of enjoyment.

It had turned into a much hotter afternoon than predicted, feeling more like August than September. By the time he'd found the Trans Pacific warehouse at the bottom of Abbott Street, Granville had been wishing he weren't wearing a woolen suit, and was dreading spending the next hour or so in a stuffy warehouse.

He could only imagine how the ladies had felt, given the tight lacing their corsets required. He couldn't imagine being so restricted in this heat. Undoubtedly they found the cool water welcome. Though he'd noticed Emily giving his Scotch a long glance, and there was a gleam in her eye that had him wondering.

"Well, that was a waste of a visit," Scott was saying. "Clark &

Company didn't seem particularly excited about potential investors."

"Privately held company," Granville reminded him.

Scott grunted. "They didn't seem to know much about Abernathy. And they sure weren't willing to talk about him."

"There has to be a way to break this case open. All we need is an edge."

"Easy to say."

"True," Granville said, and took a deep swallow of Scotch. The burn felt good as it went down.

He could hear the frustration in his partner's voice and couldn't blame him. They seemed to be meeting nothing but stone walls at every turn. He was finding it hard enough not giving in to his own frustration.

Perhaps Trent was having more luck with Vancouver Box. Though he doubted it. The puppet master, whoever he was, ran a sophisticated operation. He'd found ways to seal off every avenue of enquiry. And where subtlety failed, the fellow had already proven himself ready to use intimidation and lethal force.

And he couldn't shake the feeling they were running out of time.

Scott looked from him to Emily, and then to Clara. "How did you make out with Trans Pacific Trading?"

Emily made a little choking sound, and Clara buried her face in the handkerchief she'd quickly pulled from her bag. He frowned at both of them as Scott let out a guffaw.

"Like that, is it?" his partner asked.

"I didn't expect to learn much from one meeting," Granville said.

"Especially a meeting with a decorator," Clara added with a sideways glance at Emily.

Her partner in crime grinned, then turned to Scott. "Really, it went very well. We even decided on the exact shade of pale bronze for the dining room walls. It seems Granville is very particular about paint colors."

Scott choked on his Scotch, then lost whatever sense he had, practically rolling on the floor with laughter.

Granville scowled at him, then looked across the mahogany

expanse of his desk to meet his fiancée's bright eyes. His earlier frustration had burned away in the shared laughter, and she knew it. "You do know you'll pay for this, don't you?"

"Of course. I'm looking forward to it," she said. "But…do you think Scott will recover in time for the team meeting?"

* * *

HE DID.

By five everyone except Trent had gathered in the meeting room. Glancing at the seven faces looking back at him, he was pleased to note that both Carver and Randall had been able to join them, as had Clara. No sooner had Miss Rizzo brought in the tea tray than Trent burst into the room. Their assistant fell into a seat beside Scott, apologizing all the while.

"But it was worth it," he said. "They don't get much custom at Vancouver Box—the office is smaller than this room. And the guy working there, George, was glad to talk. He isn't much older'n me, and he really liked the idea of being the one to get a new customer. Nearly fell over himself telling me about the company, and making all kinds of promises about what they could do for us. Just look."

And he spread a company brochure and a list of prices on the table in front of him, still talking. "When I asked about how long the company had been in business and about the owner, George was all apologetic that he didn't have answers for me. I asked about business cards, the kind with photographs, and I thought he was going to cry. Then he got all excited, and dashed into the back room, and came back with… this."

And Trent removed a small black and white photograph from his jacket pocket and placed it carefully on the table. "I had to promise to bring it back to him. It's the only one he has. But he says it shows all of them—well, except for him, since he's behind the camera—not long after the company opened."

Scott picked up the small rectangle by its edges, took a good look, and passed it to Granville.

Who looked even more closely at the three men captured on film. "Who are they, do you know?"

Trent nodded. "The one on the left works in the packing room along with George. The one on the right is responsible for which parcels get sent where. And for keeping the books. And the one in the middle is the owner."

"Abernathy?"

"That's what George says."

Granville stared from the photograph to Trent and back again. Could it be this easy? Somehow he doubted it. "Do you believe him?"

Trent shrugged. "I believe he believes it."

Granville considered the photo. The man in the center was middle height, neither fat nor thin. His hair looked to be a light brown, as was his neatly trimmed beard. His was a bland face, with regular features and no particular expression. Easy to forget. And to underestimate.

He didn't recognize him. Did Abernathy exist after all? Or could this be the puppet master?

"Why would Abernathy, if this is indeed he, take such a risk? He seems to have buried everything else that could identify him very carefully. Why pose for a photograph?" Granville said.

He was half thinking aloud, but Trent answered him anyway. "George says it was a personal memento. When Abernathy handed him the camera, he was afraid it wouldn't turn out. So he took two identical shots and when the photographs came back they were both good. George kept the second one for himself. Abernathy doesn't even know it exists."

It was plausible. Maybe. "I still don't entirely believe Abernathy would take the risk of being photographed at Vancouver Box. Especially if he's the puppet master himself," Granville said. "But whoever these men are, they're connected to the puppet master.

We need to verify their names, and find out everything we can about their connections. Who do they know, who have they worked with? Somewhere in that web of connections will be the puppet master."

"But how are we going to ask about them?" Trent asked. "We can't use the photograph, 'cause there's only one, and it's pretty small."

"It's a sharp likeness of all three," Granville said. "And it takes us a lot closer to the puppet master than we've been. Well done, Trent."

"May I see?" Miss Kent asked, as Trent beamed at the praise.

Granville handed it to her, watched as she studied it closely.

"I think I can do several sketches from this, and you could use those to ask about these men," she said after a moment.

"Clear enough for people to identify them?" he asked.

"Yes, I think so."

"Can you do individual head and shoulders sketches, rather than showing all three of them as the photograph does?" Carver asked her.

Miss Kent looked startled, then thoughtful. "Yes. In fact, that would be easier. And faster. But why?"

"If it comes to it, the individual sketches would stand up better in court," the lawyer said. "And seen in a group like this," and he tapped the photograph. "It's pretty obvious you're looking into Vancouver Box."

Miss Kent looked thoughtful again. "I can do the sketches on small individual sheets," she said. "So you can ask about just one of them, or all three. Depending who you're talking to."

"That's much better," Carver said.

"Might help keep the rumors down, too," Scott said. "We want to find the puppet master, not spook him."

"True," Granville said. Though he had a feeling that whoever the puppet master was, he was firmly rooted in Vancouver. Fleeing might not be an option for him. "Thank you, Miss Kent."

He turned to the others. "Scott and I didn't get very far with finding facts on the smuggling today," he said. "We did visit Clark & Company, and they appear legitimate on the surface. No one we met admitted to having met Abernathy or knowing much about him. We'll just need to keep digging."

He looked across the table. "Mac? What about the four of you?"

Mac shrugged. "We have more figures, which all suggest there's something illegal going on somewhere. They're all pieces of the same puzzle, but we've still got nothing solid enough to suit Randall or Carver." He grinned at the two lawyers, who smiled back.

"So nothing that would stand up in court?" Granville asked.

"I'm afraid not," Randall said. "And there's nothing to identify your puppet master, either."

"Could Abernathy be an alias for the puppet master?" Granville asked.

"Probably not, even if the photograph is real," Carver said. "And there's another problem."

"What's that?" Scott asked.

"Abernathy's name is all over these documents, some of which are legally questionable when taken together," Carver said. "It seems too obvious, given how difficult you've found it to find any information at all about this puppet master so far."

Granville nodded. He'd been expecting as much.

"So my big lead won't lead anywhere?" Trent said, leaning forward.

"Not necessarily," Granville said. "The photograph should help us find Abernathy. Who could lead us to the puppet master."

As Trent sat back, looking mollified, Granville passed the photo around the table. "Does anyone recognize this fellow?"

No one did.

"Emily, do you want to brief everyone about our meeting with Trans Pacific Trading?"

His fiancée looked across the table at her friend. "Clara?"

"You go ahead," that exceedingly well-dressed young lady said calmly.

He knew that look in Emily's eye. Unless he missed his guess, Clara would be the one reporting in at their next meeting.

"Well, it was enlightening," Emily said, looking around the table. "I can see why the owners might be interested in selling. They're very disorganized, and I suspect they aren't making much of a profit."

"How does that help us find the puppet master?" Trent asked.

"I'm not sure it will, unfortunately," she said. "Not directly, anyway. But if the opportunity for Mr. Bray to buy the company is real, then he may be in contact with the puppet master."

"And from everything we've learned about Mr. Bray," Clara added tartly, aiming her words at Trent. "He thinks enough of himself that he wouldn't hesitate to keep pestering this puppet master. And he's just stupid enough to lead us to him."

Hiding his smile at this byplay, Granville looked around the table. "Anyone have anything else?"

When no one did, he adjourned the meeting. They seemed to be gaining a little momentum on this case, though every step felt like wading through the knee-deep mud of a melting creek bed. He just hoped they weren't all chasing fool's gold.

3 O

Tuesday, September 25, 1900

T he next morning, Emily woke early with one thought on her mind. She needed to talk to her mother about Mr. Bray and his engagement to her sister Jane. She'd been dreading this meeting, but it had to be done. If she could find a private moment with Mama, that is.

These days, Mama was always enmeshed in Jane's seemingly endless wedding planning. Emily had been trying to have a quiet word with her since Saturday. Surely Mama didn't need to spend every waking moment on Jane's wedding?

Or perhaps Mama was avoiding a conversation she expected to find as difficult as Emily did? Could that mean Mama was as worried about Mr. Bray and the engagement as Emily had become?

And wasn't that an unsettling thought.

She had to wait until after they had all eaten, which seemed to take longer and be more boring than usual. And as soon as the last poached egg and slice of toast was finished, Mama excused herself with a vague murmur. Gritting her teeth, Emily followed her as she flitted from the parlor to the kitchen to have a word with cook to the pantry to inspect their stocks of cake and pastry flour and finally to the empty sewing room, where she managed to corner that lady in the angle between the bookcase and the sofa.

"Mama. We need to talk," she said.

"Not now, Emily," Mama began, attempting to edge her way past her youngest daughter. "Jane and I are working on the embroidery for her trousseau, and it's such delicate work, it will take forever. We need to get an early start."

"This will just take a moment," Emily said, continuing to block her mother's exit.

"I'm sure it isn't more important than your sister's trousseau," Mama said, moving close enough so that her wide skirts touched Emily's.

"Yes it is," Emily said. "If I'm right, you won't want to be embroidering anything with their combined initials."

"What?" gasped her mother.

Mama was doing her best shocked look, Emily thought with an inward grin. And it was impressive. But she'd been working with Granville too long now to be taken in by just facial expression and exclamations. It was all about watching the eyes, and her mother's eyes were not shocked. In fact, she'd call them almost hopeful as they searched her own.

"I have a few concerns about Mr. Bray," she said.

"Concerns? About your sister's fiancé? Why Emily, whatever do you mean?"

Now Mama sounded like she was indulging in one of her own mother's dramatic turns. Which was no more like Mama than the flitting she'd been doing earlier. It was all playacting.

So Mama did know. She'd been right about that, after all.

Unless this really was about the stress of wedding planning, which Mama appeared to take far too seriously. Could she be wrong?

No. She had to trust her instincts here. Taking in a breath for courage, Emily faced her mother.

"You can stop now," she said. "I know about the company Mr. Bray is interested in buying. And that he's been working hard to get

Papa to invest. And I'm pretty sure he's a confidence artist, and that Papa would lose most of his money. And Gra... I mean, Mr. Granville agrees with me," she said, determined to get it all out before Mama intervened.

Instead she watched her mother's face soften and her eyes brighten.

"Oh, thank goodness," that lady said. "I didn't trust the man from the moment I met him. And as for this 'investment' your Papa is considering?" She shook her head. "Sheer nonsense. Though he still won't hear a word against it."

"Why didn't you just tell me?" Emily asked. "It would have been much simpler. I was afraid of offending you."

Her mother gave her a sharp look, and smiled. "I couldn't very well criticize my eldest daughters' choice of a mate to another of my daughters, now could I? But I wasn't about to let her marry a bounder, either. If that's what he turned out to be."

Emily watched the lines of her mother's face shuffle into something harder. "Nor would I stand by and see the money our family depends on stolen by a smooth-talking crook," Mama said bluntly.

It was fascinating, Emily thought. She'd never seen the iron in Mama's spine so clearly before.

"I feel the same way," she said. She stepped a little closer to Mama, and lowered her voice. "We need a plan."

"I hoped you would have thought of one by now."

Was that a twinkle in Mama's eye? How... unexpected. "Well, I have," Emily said. "I'm just not sure how you'll feel about it. You see, it's about the ball."

"Try me," Mama said.

"And you'll have to find a way to stall Papa. He can't promise any money to Mr. Bray. Not before the ball."

"That man will never see any of our money," Mama vowed. "Not so much as a worn dollar, let alone Jane's dowry. Or the thousands he's trying to get your Papa to 'invest'."

The scorn in Mama's voice had Emily's lips quirking up. Mr. Bray had really got her dander up. "You really don't like him, do you? And yet you never let any sign of that slip."

"This is the man my daughter thinks she wants to marry," Mama said briskly. "What kind of mother would I be if she thought I didn't like her choice?"

Emily blinked. The Mama she thought she knew would never hesitate to tell any of them where they were going wrong. On anything.

"Besides, Jane is stubborn. Like as not, if she thought I didn't like the man, she'd cling to him harder than ever," Mama added.

Now that sounded more like her mother. Though she'd never heard her mention Jane's stubborn nature before, no matter how much Emily herself complained about it.

Leaving Emily wondering what Mama really thought of her own flaws. And of her engagement to Granville.

"As it is…," Mama continued, then glanced at Emily and stopped abruptly, as if just remembering who she was talking to. "Well, never mind. Now, how does this plan of yours include our ball?"

Emily leaned forward and dropped her voice. "Before we discuss the ball…" She hesitated, feeling awkward.

"You want to talk about your Papa?"

"Yes," she said, relieved she didn't have to say it. "He was going to talk to Gr… Mr. Granville about investing with Mr. Bray, wasn't he? If we'd come to dinner on Sunday?"

"I'm afraid he might have been," Mama said. "In fact, I suspect they were both planning to."

"Then, well…forgive me, but I need to know how you're planning to get Papa to stall on this investment that he seems so fired up about," she said in a rush.

Mama gave Emily a knowing look that made her blush. "When you've been married to your Mr. Granville for a few years, you won't need to ask that question. Just trust me that he won't move forward on it before the ball."

"Oh. Ummm," Emily said, suddenly feeling very uncomfortable and far too young to be marrying anyone.

"Now, about that ball. What exactly are you planning?"

"Well, we think Mr. Bray has made a few unfortunate friends.

And the Black and White Ball will give us the perfect opportunity to find out."

"And what role do you need me to play?" Mama asked.

"Between us we need to keep an eye on Papa. And see whom Mr. Bray introduces him to. And if they look like potential investors, we need to interrupt that conversation somehow."

Mama gave her another sharp-eyed look. "You'll want to know as much as possible about the ones who are not potential investors, then. Am I right?"

Emily suddenly wondered if a talent for investigating could be inherited. "You are. We need to know who Mr. Bray is working with. You're good at this."

A small smile curved her mother's lips. "Your Papa is likely to spend half the evening in the card room," was all she said. "Mr. Granville will have to keep an eye on him there."

But Granville needed to be free to search for the puppet master. Not to be stuck looking after her father and ensuring he didn't do something rash. She felt embarrassed for Papa, hating the idea of even having to talk to Granville about it.

"Can't you do something to keep Mr. Bray in the ballroom for most of the evening?" Emily asked, feeling a tad desperate. "He and Jane are newly engaged, after all. And since there hasn't been an engagement party yet, most of your friends likely haven't been introduced to them as a couple."

Mama gave her a sideways glance, but didn't say whatever she was thinking. Much to Emily's relief.

"I believe an approach like that might work," she said. "And I agree that your Papa should be in the ballroom under these circumstances. Leave it to me."

Emily was happy to do so.

"Meanwhile, what are you and your fiancé planning for that evening?" Mama asked.

That question Emily wasn't quite so happy about.

IT WAS STILL EARLY when Emily got to the office, but Miss Rizzo confirmed that Granville was already in. Giving a quick tap on his office door, she slipped inside. As she arranged her sweeping skirts and sank into the chair opposite his desk, she smiled at him. "I spoke with Mama earlier about the Black and White Ball, and it's all arranged."

"That's good to hear," he said, returning the smile. "Did the two of you talk about Bray?"

"We did. Finally."

"So? How did that conversation go?"

"Surprisingly well," she said, and told him everything.

"I'm glad to hear your mother shares your concerns about Bray," he said. "That will make things easier."

"It's a relief," she confessed. "As is Mama's promise that she'll make sure Papa doesn't agree to any business deals with Mr. Bray. Hopefully if Papa hasn't yet signed a contract, he won't encourage anyone else to do so, either. That should buy us a bit of time to expose my would-be brother-in-law as a fraud."

"That's good. It could be embarrassing for your father, otherwise."

"I know," she said. "As if the engagement isn't bad enough."

And she made a face that had him laughing, which made her feel better.

"Maybe you can come up with a way for Jane to repudiate him in front of others," he suggested with a grin. "Leaving your sister looking like a heroine and Bray like the bounder he is."

She knew he wasn't serious, but as Emily considered his words, she began to smile. It might not be a bad idea. Bray deserved for people to see him as he really was. And she had the first glimmerings of how to make that happen.

Granville looked a little uneasy, though. He was coming to know her very well indeed, if he could spot her planning like that.

She decided not to share it with him, though. Not yet. It was too early to discuss such an amorphous idea. And she didn't want to be distracted from today's purpose.

She tucked the idea away, and gave him a speculative look.

He shook his head at her. "Now what?" he asked.

"I've been wondering about the puppet master," she said.

"Go on."

"He's made it almost impossible to find him, because he's built all these layers to hide behind. So why does he need them?"

He stared at her as he considered the question. "He's likely making a great deal of money illegally."

"So is Mr. Benton. Everyone knows who he is."

"That's true. And if a criminal makes enough money, there are still key members of the local police force who can be bribed to look the other way."

"Despite the Police Commission's best efforts to root out that element," she said.

He grinned at that. "Despite them. Unfortunately,"

"Which suggests to me that if the puppet master is a successful career criminal, he has no reason to go to such lengths to hide his identity," she said. "He must have another reason for remaining anonymous. Like protecting his reputation."

"In which case, he'd have to have a reputation to lose," Granville said. "You think our puppet master has a legitimate identity?"

It pleased her that he'd so quickly gone to the same conclusion she'd reached. She must be on the right track.

"I think it's a possibility," Emily said. "And so do you, or you wouldn't have brought in Mr. Draper. Or asked him to look at people who attended Mr. Randall's trial. The ones who didn't seem to have a reason to be there."

"True enough."

"But if the puppet master has non-criminal identity, and he's protecting his own reputation? Then everything we've learned so far seems to fit," she said. "Doesn't it? Even Mr. Benton doesn't seem to know who the puppet master really is. And if he was hiding amongst the other criminals, Mr. Benton would know, wouldn't he?"

"You'd think so," he said. "Though with Benton, nothing is ever really certain. He makes it a point of pride."

Emily nodded, but ignored it. She was more interested in the puppet master than the gangster. "And that legitimate identity—it must be worth protecting. He has to be someone we'd know, or have heard of. Or why would he bother?"

Granville gave her a considering look. "I think you might be right," he said. "And I think we need to bring the team into this discussion, because it's going to turn our planning on its head."

Emily grinned at the validation. She'd been right about how important this was! "I think so too. And that sounds like a Klondike expression," was all she said.

"Guilty," he said. "I'll ask Miss Rizzo to set up the meeting. And to include Carver and Randall if they're available. If we set the meeting for nine, that might help. Neither lawyer should need to be in court before ten."

"Isn't it too soon to involve both lawyers?"

"Not if you're right about the puppet master, and I think you are," he said. "Both lawyers have connections and information we don't. And we'll want to move quickly on this."

"Yes, we do. It's too bad we're meeting so early, or I'd include Clara too."

"We could try to move the meeting later, if you think it's important she be here too?"

"No, Clara isn't at her best in the morning. I can brief her later. The sooner the team is part of this discussion, the better."

3 1

Miss Rizzo was able to arrange the meeting for nine. Which left Granville just enough time to review his notes and revise his strategy.

His mind was still working through the implications of Emily's simple question, as the loose threads of the investigation, the ones that had been nagging at him for days, fell into place. She had an uncanny knack of asking just the right question, seemingly out of nowhere.

Once everyone was in the conference room, Granville glanced around the table. He wasn't sure "better" was quite the right word to describe this, he thought as he considered the familiar faces. It was likely to be an explosive meeting.

"I suspect you've all become as frustrated with this case as I have," he said, meeting each pair of eyes. "And as of this morning, I think I know why. We've been going about this investigation all wrong. It's no wonder we weren't making real progress."

Scott frowned. "What do you mean? We're making progress. It'll all come together, just like always."

Granville shook his head. "No. We're chasing too many facts in too many directions. And despite everything we've done, the puppet master remains more of a ghost than the assassin we named the ghost."

"But what else can we do? We need more facts if we're going to find the puppet master," Mac said.

"Yes. And no." Granville said. "We need to focus on the puppet master first. Not the facts."

He looked around the table, saw frowns and confusion. Meeting Emily's expectant look, he winked. She smiled at him, but said nothing.

"The question we need to be asking ourselves, is why has it been so hard to find him?" he said.

"Because he's very, very well-hidden," Miss Kent said into the sudden silence. "Behind a conspiracy of silence, behind companies, even behind fake names, if we're right about Abernathy."

"He hid behind the assassin, too," Trent put in. "No one talked about him because they were afraid of being murdered."

"Even his assassin was a ghost," Scott said. "There were rumors of disappearances, but no bodies. And if they did find a body—no one would talk about the killer."

"Taken together, he's running a very elaborate series of schemes. So what does he want out of it?" Granville asked. "It clearly isn't fame, or notoriety."

"That's easy. Money," Trent said immediately. "He wants money."

"I think that's a fair assumption," Granville said.

"How much money are we talking here?" Trent asked.

Mac and Miss Kent, aware everyone was looking at them, exchanged glances. Mac shook his head. "It's hard to know."

"Big money? Or huge money?" Trent wanted to know.

Mac grinned at the lad's categories. "If he's smuggling opium, using all these side ventures that otherwise make no sense, then he has to be making enough money to do almost anything," the accountant said. "For that kind of money, he could be running a criminal empire."

"Like Benton," Scott muttered.

Mac nodded. "Yes. Or supporting an extravagant lifestyle: a mansion with servants, a stable of horses and a carriage or two."

"Huge money, then," Trent said with some awe.

Mac nodded. "To make money like that? If he wasn't a criminal, he'd need to run a very large, very successful business. Or have a private income."

"Which takes me to my next point. How does he get that money?" Granville asked. At Mac's confused frown, he elaborated. "How does the money from the sale of the smuggled opium flow back to the puppet master?"

Mac and Miss Kent exchanged glances. Shook their heads.

"I have no idea," Mac said. "We haven't been able to trace the sales, let alone follow the drug money, if that's what it is, back to the puppet master."

"This whole scheme seems much too elaborate for most criminal organizations," Granville said. "Especially ones that thrive on intimidating both their victims and their competition. And Emily asked me an excellent question earlier this morning."

Which had changed everything, he thought, and paused for impact.

"She pointed out that the puppet master has built all these layers to hide behind. Why does he need them?" He smiled at her as he said it.

"The puppet master isn't Benton, whom no one would name a gangster to his face, but everyone knows what he is," Granville continued. "This fellow has put a great deal of effort into remaining hidden. And he's ruthless in protecting that."

"As if he's someone with a great deal to lose if he were ever identified," Emily said.

"A man who lives a double life?" Randall said. "Whoever he is, he must need the money, but given his willingness to kill, he must be equally desperate to hide its source."

"Exactly that," Granville said. "And desperate is a good word for him. But why would he be so desperate?"

He paused to let his words sink in. He could tell from the expressions on their faces that everyone present was considering that question. A question which turned all the facts they'd gathered so far upside down.

"What if this puppet master is someone very well-known; a man whose name we'd all recognize?" he added, and watched the question resonate around the table.

"He could be a respected businessman, like Mr. Bray is pretending to be," Emily said. "Only someone much smarter, and a far better planner than my would-be brother-in law."

He grinned at the expression on Emily's face. She hadn't said much, but he'd seen the tension in her lately whenever she mentioned her family. And she really didn't like Bray at all.

"In fact, I'm beginning to wonder if the puppet master is a gentleman, possibly even titled," he said.

"How'd you get there?" Scott demanded.

"For one thing, because of the elaborate, and very well thought out screens the puppet master is hiding behind," Granville said. "No matter how hard we've searched, he remains invisible. Keeping up appearances must be very important to him."

"So he's a gent?" Trent said. "Like you?" Then he realized what he'd said and flushed.

"Not exactly," Granville said dryly. "But yes, he could be a younger son sent here to make something of himself."

"And you think he's killing people to protect appearances?" Randall said in disgust.

"Something like that. Because the only other thing we know about the puppet master is that his schemes have to be bringing in a great deal of money. And yet there's no sign of where all this money is going. It remains invisible too."

Carver leaned forward, his eyes intent. "As if the money from those schemes was needed for something. The expenses were already there, so there would be no unexpected outlay of cash."

Trent grinned, quick to recover from his earlier faux pas. "You mean like those carriages and horses?"

Granville nodded. "Exactly like that. Which fits in with him being a gentleman. Or at least someone determined to maintain a particular style of living."

"And seemingly he'll stop at nothing to protect that lifestyle," Carver said.

"Exactly."

"Wait a minute. If he's a gentleman, and lives here, why didn't you recognize him in the photograph?" Trent asked.

"Because Abernathy isn't the puppet master," Scott said.

"No amount of digging gets us any more information on Abernathy," Carver said, nodding. "And no one can hide an identity so thoroughly, I don't care how sneaky they are. I agree with Miss Kent that he's a paper front."

"You mean Abernathy really doesn't exist?" Trent asked.

"Probably not," Granville said. "He's just another layer for the puppet master to hide behind. Which makes the photograph a stroke of genius on the puppet master's part."

"But…" Trent began, then stared at him, his eyes narrowed. "You mean he'd hire someone to play Abernathy—who doesn't really exist—in order to confuse anyone doing the kind of investigation we are."

Granville nodded. And waited for the lad to move to the next step.

Which didn't take long. Trent's face grew red and he practically stuttered out the words. "So… the photograph, and George who was so helpful because I asked the right questions… That was a setup?"

"Probably."

"He was helpful so we'd waste time chasing some nobody who wouldn't know anything?" Trent's voice rose.

"It almost worked, too."

"So who's that in my photograph?" Trent said.

"That's a good question," Granville said. "Possibly he's just someone hired to play Abernathy when the need arises."

"You mean he's a fake?"

"Most likely," Granville said. "But identifying him will still get us closer to the puppet master. Someone had to hire the fellow to impersonate Abernathy, after all."

"They played me," Trent said, clenching his fists on the table and half-rising. "We have to get this guy."

"We will," Granville said. "He's been playing all of us."

"So how are we supposed to find him?" Scott asked. "Since none of our leads are good for much."

"We look for someone with a spotless reputation, who lives very well," Granville said. "Someone who seems to have no need of money, but who has actually lost access to the money they were living on. Perhaps investments failed, or a family business went bankrupt, or they were cut out of a will."

"An Englishman?" Carver asked.

"Or a an American or Canadian with family money. Likely someone from out East," Scott said.

"It doesn't sound like you need me to do sketches from the photograph," Miss Kent said.

"I doubt it would be a good use of your time," Granville said. "Even if we found the fellow, he isn't likely to know much."

She nodded. "Then I propose that Mac and I follow up on the money. There has to be a trail somewhere."

"That is very good thinking, Miss Kent," Granville said. "See where that takes you. Meanwhile, Scott, Trent and I will begin digging into anyone in town who appears to have the right kind of wealth. And yet might be as desperate for money as the puppet master is."

"And Clara and I will keep digging into the background of my would-be brother-in-law," Emily said with a wicked smile. "If we can find the right incentive, he might tell us all about our puppet master. Or grow careless and meet with him."

He knew that look. Bray wasn't going to see this one coming.

"And what do you want me to do?" Carver asked.

"Your role, and Randall's, will come later," Granville said. "Once we have the puppet master identified."

It wasn't legal expertise they needed now. This was pure detective work.

Carver's eyes glittered. "In that case I'll keep my ears open for the latest gossip. It's surprising how often a key piece of information is generally known, but seems irrelevant."

Granville considered the statement, decided Carver was likely right. "Any and all relevant gossip will be greatly appreciated," he said.

And grinned when Emily rolled her eyes. Apparently despite his fiancée's new regard for the value of gossip, her current investigations with Clara had already used up her tolerance for the subject.

———

CARVER AND RANDALL were the first to depart, followed by Mac and Miss Kent, who were already discussing strategies for unearthing the needed financial details. Satisfied that everything was in hand, Emily went off to call Clara about their arrangements for the day.

As the door of the meeting room closed behind them, Trent looked from Granville to Scott and back. "So what do we do now?" he asked.

"Carver might have a point about the value of gossip," Granville said. "Especially given our current speculations. I think I'll take lunch at the Vancouver Club."

If the puppet master was wealthy enough, the odds were good that the members there would know him. Making it one of the best places in town to pick up any rumors that might connect to him.

"Isn't it too early to be thinking about lunch? It's barely after ten," Trent said. "And what are Scott and me supposed to do?"

"Scott and I," Granville said, at which Trent gave him a confused look. "Never mind. Why don't the two of you start by paying Bertie a visit."

"I'd love to. But I don't get it," Trent said. "If finding the puppet master is so urgent, why d'you want us to waste time talking to Bertie?"

"We're looking for someone with 'huge' wealth who suddenly didn't have money," Granville said. "Since the puppet master only seems to have been in business for a few years, that gives us a possible time frame for when his financial troubles, whatever they were, occurred."

He stopped, realizing what he'd just said, and looked at Scott. "I'm an idiot."

"I won't argue with that," his partner said with a grin. "Any particular reason?"

"Yes. We have a major lead right in front of us. And I didn't even see it."

"And I still have no idea what you're talking about," Scott said.

Granville ignored him. "I need to talk to Miss Kent again."

He strode into the main office, with Scott and Trent behind him. No Miss Kent. Nodding to Miss Rizzo, he headed for Mac's office, and wasn't surprised to find Miss Kent there poring over a ledger. There was no sign of Mac, though. Presumably he'd gone out to gather more of the information they needed.

"Miss Kent, I have one more question," Granville said. "When you first looked into Clark & Company, you mentioned that Abernathy had registered the company a few years ago."

"Yes, that's right," she said. "I think it was about two years ago, but I could look up when exactly if that would be helpful."

"It would indeed. But first, do you recall if Vancouver Box also recently changed hands?"

"I think they might have," Miss Kent said. "But I'm not certain exactly when. I could find out."

"Yes, I'd appreciate that," he said. "How long do you expect it would take you?"

"Less than half an hour. Do you want me to do that now?"

"If you would," Granville said. "It could give us a timeframe for when the puppet master's financial troubles began. It would also be helpful to know if the puppet master, using the Abernathy name, owns both places outright, or if he has investors or partners."

"I'll get back to you as soon as possible," she said, her pencil flying over her steno pad. "You'll be in your office?"

"Thank you. And yes." Granville glanced at Scott, who nodded. "The three of us will be in my office."

It took Miss Kent twenty of the thirty minutes she'd promised to come back to them with the information.

"You were right," she said, slightly breathlessly. "Both companies changed hands within three months of each other, nearly three years ago.

I still can't find out the exact ownership of the stores Barnabas Jones manages. The owner of record for the first two is Abernathy, who has a controlling interest. The rest of the money seems to come from a group of investors. And it's a different group in each case."

Interesting. And just how had the puppet master persuaded so many to invest in his projects, Granville wondered. Especially if everything was done in Abernathy's name.

Either the fellow had sold them on a good story, or the payouts had to be substantial enough to entice them. He was betting on the latter. "Where are the investors located?"

"England."

Which made sense. A lot of English investors were looking to the colonies these days as a better place to grow their capital. It was even possible that if the puppet master was in any way related to the aristocracy, an English investor could comfortably invest with him, since he came from a "good family". And never find out that the firms he was investing in were registered under another name.

"Do you have names for these investors?" he asked.

"Yes. Those were easily available." She handed him a list, and he scanned it quickly.

He recognized most of the names, but didn't know any of them well. Writing to each of them and waiting for a reply from England would take weeks. And sending a telegram risked one of the investors alerting the puppet master—since he couldn't explain this mess in a telegram.

And none of the men listed had any reason to trust Granville without an explanation. In the future, perhaps his detective agency might become well enough known to have earned that trust. It wasn't yet.

But Pinkerton's was.

He'd need more information, though.

"None of these firms is making a great deal of profit?" he asked Miss Kent. Who was looking a little nervous at the silence that had fallen since her last answer.

"No. Not on paper, anyway," she said quickly.

"What about the payouts to investors? Are they in line with the profits? As well as with other similar firms?"

"I don't know. I could check, but it would take me some time. Though it would go faster with Mac's help."

She was looking nervous again. He smiled at her. "Please do so. The more detail you can provide me, the better. And let me know as soon as you have something."

"We'll do what we can. Is that everything?" she asked.

"One last thing. Can you tell me exactly when each of the firms changed hands?" he asked.

She consulted her steno pad. "Thirty-five months ago for Clark & Company. Thirty-two months ago for Vancouver Box."

Granville made a note of the dates, considered them for a moment.

"I wonder how that fits with his financial situation?" he said, half thinking aloud. "This scheme must have taken some time to set up. And yet the puppet master had enough money left to keep a controlling share of these companies? How does that fit?"

"Perhaps he began to run into his financial problems not too long before that purchase?" Miss Kent said tentatively.

"Talk to Mac about it, will you? And see what the two of you can come up with."

She nodded, and turned to go.

"And Miss Kent?" She turned to look back at him. "Thank you. You may have just given us the key to solve this investigation."

"I'm glad," she said, giving him a half smile as she left the office.

He turned back to Scott and Trent. "So, just over three years ago, our puppet master began his criminal empire. Which probably wasn't too long after his financial troubles began. Let's assume for now it was six months or so after."

"Makes sense," Scott said.

"And it gives us a timeline. We're looking for the source of those financial troubles."

"Which should lead us to the puppet master," Scott finished his thought for him.

"Yes, exactly."

"So why are we talking to Bertie?" Trent asked.

"The puppet master's connections to Chinatown," Granville said. "Whoever he dealt with three years ago on the opium, might know him by his true name."

"So, not Abernathy."

"Definitely not Abernathy."

"You really think Bertie would know any of that?" Trent said.

"No, but Bertie has connections in Chinatown that we don't. And I think his uncle might know. I'm not so certain he'd be willing to tell us. But he might tell his nephew."

"Oh."

"We'll follow up on whatever we find out," Scott said, hiding a grin at Trent's crestfallen expression. "And meet you back here later this afternoon."

SCOTT AND TRENT had already departed, the new timeline in hand, but Granville was standing at the window, watching the bustle of carts and delivery wagons on the street directly below. He disregarded the clanging of the trolley bell up the block as he turned the information Miss Kent had given him over in his mind.

They were searching for some kind of financial event from three and a half years ago. It wouldn't be easy.

There was a quick rap at the door, then Emily's bright head appeared, followed by the rest of her. "I'm off to meet Clara," she said. "But before I go, I had a couple of thoughts after our meeting."

"Go on," he said.

"It struck me that the puppet master sounds like just the kind of man who will be present at the upcoming Black and White Ball. Isn't it lucky we have tickets to attend?" she said, giving him a smug look.

He laughed, as she'd meant him to. But she was right. This ball could prove an interesting place to continue their hunt for the puppet master.

"I thought I'd get a copy of the guest list for the ball from Mama," she added. "It might be interesting to compare it to Mr.

Draper's list. You know, of the men who attended Mr. Randall's trial."

"It's worth a look," he said.

"I don't really expect it to be very helpful, since there are so many people coming to the ball. But it could rule out a name or two for us."

"That's one of the challenges of detecting," he said with a grin. "Most of what we do is a complete waste of time. Until it isn't."

Emily smiled at that, then cocked her head to one side. "How is Mr. Draper getting on with this case? When Clara and I talked to him and Tim about Trans Pacific Trading, he didn't talk about the puppet master. But when we mentioned a possible link between the puppet master and imports from the Far East, he was quick to jot that down. Has he made any progress since?"

"All I have at the moment is his list from last week," he said, returning the smile. Appreciating how fresh she looked in her blue and white striped suit, despite the growing heat of the day.

"I'm planning to follow up with Draper today. Especially in light of our earlier conversation. Who better to know all the financial rumors than a business reporter?" he said.

"Indeed," she said, copying his favorite remark with a cheeky grin.

He winked at her, then his smile faded. "I'm an idiot," he said.

"Mr. Bray is an idiot," she said. "You're a detective."

He laughed at that. "I'm a poor detective, then. It isn't a reporter I need to be talking to. It's a banker. Specifically our banker."

"You've said all along that this case is all about money," she said.

"And someone's desperate need for it. I should have listened to myself. William Wardle knows more about how money flows here than anyone else in town."

"What a good thing he's our banker, then," Emily said.

"Why don't you join me?"

"Your Mr. Wardle would be shocked."

"I doubt it. I suspect it would take a great deal more than this to shock him. But if he is shocked, then the experience will be good for him."

"I wish I could join you. But I don't want to lose this opportunity to learn more about Trans Pacific. I'm too close to exposing Mr. Bray, I can just feel it."

"Then we'll have to compare notes after our respective meetings."

"And plan our strategy for the Ball," she said. "I think the evening will prove to be a fascinating one."

He knew that demure look of hers. It didn't bode well for the puppet master.

"I'm suddenly looking forward to dancing with you for entirely different reasons," he said.

She winked at him. "This should be fun," Emily said, and left his office as abruptly as she'd entered.

Leaving him wondering exactly which aspect of the upcoming ball she expected to enjoy the most. And how much he should worry about it.

As THE DOOR closed behind Emily, Granville glanced at his watch, and mentally rearranged his day. The Vancouver Club was still a good source for information, but it was too early for many of the members to be stopping in for luncheon. And it was much too early for the bar, which would actually be a better bet for his purposes.

The same would hold true for the Terminal City Club. And no banker worth his salt would accept a luncheon engagement at this hour. Or on such short notice.

But it was a perfect time to invite a reporter for lunch. And he had two reporters already working on aspects of this case. He could trust both of them not to spring this story too early, at the expense of his case.

He spent a moment contemplating whether O'Hearn or Andrew Draper would be the more helpful source. They'd each bring a different perspective. And both were good company. In fact, it might be entertaining, as well as enlightening, to invite both of them. Which decided him.

Emily had arranged to meet Clara early so they had time for a stroll before their appointment with Granville's new decorator. "It's a lovely day," she'd told her friend. "There's a crispness in the air this morning, and the leaves are just beginning to turn along the boulevards. We might as well enjoy the day before it gets too hot."

Which was all true, but not her real reason for setting it up. Since her conversation with Granville, Emily hadn't been able to stop thinking about his joking reference to making her sister Jane the "heroine of the hour."

It was torn straight out of a Penny Dreadful, which was what made it funny. That, and the fact that Jane was the most unlikely heroine anyone could ever imagine. Plus her straitlaced sister would never agree to such a role.

But it would be justice.

And if Mr. Bray was humiliated, and Jane was seen to have recognized his villainy for what it was, and paid him back in kind... Well, that might go a long way towards healing her sister's pain. Jane was too proud to hold on to a love bought with humiliation.

Or at least Emily thought she was. Sometimes she wondered if she knew her sister at all. And just what Jane was really hiding behind that starchy front of hers.

It couldn't be easy, being the eldest daughter, the one who carefully followed all of societies rules, and yet was still unmarried because those rules weren't what was really important. Watching her with Mr. Bray, Emily had wondered if Jane loved the man, or just the idea of being his wife. If it were the latter, it wouldn't be her heart that was broken. It would be her hopes for the future.

Which might be worse, if only because she could never really admit it. For a woman, marrying for money had always been an unspoken but acceptable plan. Being married for your own money or your social connections? Was not.

Which was an odd mindset, now that she thought about it. Not that she'd ever applied either to herself, even when she'd thought about marrying someday. Then she'd met Granville, and money and social standing were irrelevant.

Which was a good thing, since he was penniless at the time. Though he had always carried himself with the unconscious confidence of one born and raised a gentleman.

She wondered for a moment if that held true of the puppet master. It certainly didn't hold true for Mr. Bray, no matter how much he pretended. Perhaps that was what grated so—oh, not that the fellow wasn't a gentleman. She'd never quite understood all the fuss about social standing, much to Mama's dismay.

But there was a falseness about Mr. Bray. He wasn't who he seemed to be, and neither his stated motives nor his actions felt honest to her.

Clara's flurried arrival into the over decorated front parlor where Emily was waiting startled her out of her thoughts. "Are you ready?" she asked quickly, to cover that fact.

"Just let me find my bag... ah, there it is," Clara said, grabbing the straw bag that matched her hat. "Let's go."

Once they'd reached the sidewalk, well out of earshot of any eavesdroppers, Clara slid her a sideways glance. "So why are we *really* strolling?" she asked.

That figured. Emily should have expected Clara to see through her. "It was something Granville said this morning," she said. And proceeded to tell Clara what she'd been thinking.

"And Jane would save the day? Your sister Jane?" Clara said opening her blue eyes wide. "No one would believe it."

"Don't try to fool me with that look of yours. I know you too well," Emily said. "We shall just have to make them believe it."

"How?"

"I have no idea. Not yet," she said. "But if the two of us put our minds to it, I know we can work something out."

"You surely can't think your sister would go along with this."

"Of course not. We'll just have to work around that," Emily said firmly.

"And still make her the heroine of the piece? Emily, you can't be serious. Are you feeling well?"

"I'm fine. But Jane won't be, not once we expose Mr. Bray. Think about what society would make of that."

Clara's golden brows drew together, just a little. It was an artful pose, one that was likely to snare her suitors left and right. She'd likely practiced it, Emily thought, watching her friend, until it had become second nature. She probably didn't even realize she was doing it.

For Clara, that was what shock looked like.

"She'd be… cast out. Ridiculed. And she's nearly twenty-three, isn't she? Her chance of marrying after this would be nil."

"I know. That's why we have to do something," Emily said. "How hard can it be, to turn society's own rules against them?"

Clara just stared at her for a moment, then the corners of her mouth tipped up. Her eyes began to gleam with that mischievous glint that Emily saw so seldom these days, but which had been the reason they had first become friends, back when they were both nine. Before Clara had discovered boys. Or fashion.

"We'd need a large social event for this to work," Clara said. "What do we know about?"

"There's the Black and White Ball on Friday," Emily said.

Clara nodded slowly. "Yes, that always draws the right people. And the venue is perfect for a very public exposure of Mr. Bray."

"But I suspect that's too soon for us to come up with a workable plan," Emily said. "Or a way to get Jane to play her role."

"Most likely," Clara said. "But let's keep it in mind. What else?"

"The Smythe's are holding their annual dinner dance two weeks from now."

"Not important enough," Clara said.

Emily grinned at her friend's dismissive tone. Even Emily knew that Mrs. Smythe would be horrified to hear her social aspirations so thoroughly dismissed.

"The Harvest Ball for the Opera Association? Though that isn't until next month."

"Can you wait that long?" Clara asked.

Emily shook her head. "Mr. Bray is making too many plans. I think we might have to work with the Black and White Ball."

"I think you're right."

Emily bit her lip. "That doesn't give us much time. How are we going to do this?"

"We need to plan. And we're going to be sneaky," her friend said. "No one will ever suspect we had a hand in it. Not if we do it right."

"And we will," Emily said. "We have to."

Clara drew out the little leather covered notebook with its silver embossed pencil that she usually used for deciding on additions to her wardrobe. And they set to planning.

They hadn't been discussing options for very long when Clara looked up at her. "You do know we'll need to include your Mama in this planning?"

"Oh dear," Emily said.

THE SHORT WALK from the Miles's home to Granville's new home took them far too little time for Emily's taste. As they walked up the steps, she took a deep breath and let their upcoming meeting with the decorator from Trans Pacific Trading drive all thought of her plans for Jane's role as a heroine out of her head.

Granville had insisted on giving her a key to the house on the day he received the set from the realtor. "It will be as much your home as it is mine," he'd said, over her protests. "I want you to feel that from the start."

Emily still felt a little like she was invading his privacy when she used the key, but when she and Clara had begun working on the updates and decoration of the house, she'd been glad to have it. And today, it made it easy to meet Mr. Tremblay here.

Clara had already shooed the builders out of the dining room, and closed the double doors behind them. It wasn't exactly quiet in here now, but at least they could hear each other, which was a decided improvement. Clara rolled her eyes at the noise level, and Emily grinned at her.

"You didn't really expect quiet, did you? On a Tuesday?"

"We should have given them the day off, like I suggested," Clara retorted.

"And have Granville paying for all those lost hours of work? I think not," Emily said firmly. Then cringed a little. "Sorry, I think that was Mama's tone, wasn't it? I definitely recognized her words."

Clara was laughing. "They say we imitate whatever we're most familiar with. You just proved it."

"They also say we all turn into our mothers," Emily said. "I didn't believe that before, and I don't believe it now. We become whoever we want most to be."

"You keep thinking that," Clara said, but she looked thoughtful for a moment. "For now, we should probably wait in the hall for our decorator. We'll never hear him in here. Not over all this noise the builders are making."

"I keep thinking about when we looked at this house in the summer. It looked perfect then," Emily said as she followed Clara towards the front door. "I find it hard to believe it really needed this much work."

"It's just paint, Emily," Clara said.

Emily pointed towards the hole in the wall they were passing, and her friend laughed....

"Well, with a bit of work on the lighting. And a few other things. You must admit that the parlor had one wall too many."

That was true.

"It will all be worth it, you'll see."

"I just hope Granville thinks so," Emily said.

There was no point worrying about it now, so she forced herself to think about the questions she wanted answers to about Trans Pacific Trading.

She and Clara met the over-eager young man in the future dining room of Granville's new home. Ten minutes later the three of them were standing in the dining room, trying to ignore the floral wallpaper half pulled from the walls, the sawhorses with slabs of plywood making up rough worktables in the center of the room, and several holes in the ceiling. Mr. Tremblay was squinting a little as he looked around the room, as if trying to picture how the room would look furnished.

"But this is going to be beautiful," he said to Clara. "I can see why you were considering a chinoiserie theme. Together with the furniture we discussed the other day, it will go beautifully in here. And with that subtle gold-toned paint on the walls, it will be stunning. Just stunning."

Clara smiled and nodded. "My thoughts exactly."

Emily squinted a little to see if that would help, but she couldn't quite picture it. She was better with blueprints and the shape of rooms than she was with how color and furniture would work together. And at the moment, she was more interested in anything that might help her bring down her detestable would-be brother-in-law. But how best to approach it?

"Have you all the furniture this room would require in stock?" she asked. "Or would we need to order some of it?"

"We have quite a remarkable variety for our size," he was quick to say. "And yes, I think we have most of what this room needs."

"How long would it take to order anything that isn't in stock?" Emily asked.

"That depends on whether it is a custom order and would need to be made by hand. Which would of course, take substantially longer."

"Of course," Clara agreed.

"Let's assume it isn't a custom item," Emily said. "How long might we be waiting?"

"We receive goods from the Far East every month," Mr. Tremblay said. "The steamships are remarkably fast. And an urgent order could be sent by telegram, and expected within six weeks at the longest."

This was more like it. "You have deliveries every month?" Emily said. "That is amazing. Do you use the *Empress* liners? Are all of your shipments of the same size, then?"

The decorator smiled. "Yes, we have regular deliveries on the *Empresses*. In fact, we reserve space for several containers on every sailing. We also ship, as needed, on other liners at times when demand is high, or when a special-order is required."

Emily nodded. "I see. That makes sense. Though I understood that the Empresses are much faster than other lines, are they not?"

"Very true."

"So a custom order would be slower than a regular one?"

"If you disregard the time needed to manufacture the item, then yes, that is true."

"I see," Emily said, trying to sound disappointed.

Mr. Tremblay correctly read his cue. "However, a custom order on a tight timeline could be shipped on an *Empress* liner. There would be an extra charge, of course," he said, looking a little embarrassed to be discussing such a thing.

"Of course," Emily said, exchanging glances with Clara. "That is good to know."

"Would the regular shipments be displaced, in those instances?" Clara asked.

"Sometimes. Though often we can simply purchase extra space in the ship. Though the price then rises for us, and must be passed on to the customer. You understand?"

Emily understood better than he could imagine. Whatever they were smuggling would go through, no matter what. Which made it perfect for Mr. Bray if he succeeded in purchasing the company. And for the puppet master, if they were right about his potential involvement. Now, how to turn that information to their advantage?

She missed several minutes of the conversation between Clara and Mr. Tremblay while she pondered that question. When she began to pay attention to them again, she realized they were discussing ornaments for the mantel and the sideboard in the room.

"Two tall, narrow lamps on the sideboard, I thought," Clara was saying. "And perhaps a vase or two?"

"The lamps will work well. You have a good eye. For the vases, I would suggest we start by choosing two large Chinese vases for the mantelpiece," Mr. Tremblay said.

Like the ones she'd purchased while she was pursuing the murder case in Victoria last month? "I have several large vases that might be perfect in here," Emily said.

Clara turned and gave her a stunned look. As if what was left of the wallpaper had suddenly developed a voice, Emily thought in amusement. "You have?" she said.

"What colors are in the vases?" Mr. Tremblay asked.

"Blue and white. A traditional pattern," she said.

Clara and Mr. Tremblay exchanged glances.

"That *could* work here," Clara said, half doubtfully as she glanced around the room.

"We'd have to see them," Mr. Tremblay said.

"Of course, they might suit better in the parlor," Clara said, and hurried out of the room, with the decorator right behind her, and Emily trailing them, no longer trying to suppress her laughter.

She'd just thought of a few more questions for Mr. Tremblay.

33

B y quarter past eleven, the two reporters had joined Granville at a small table at the Terminal City Club. He was interested to note that while Draper had more years of experience, O'Hearn had gained considerable confidence since he'd first met him. The younger reporter seemed more focused, no longer so boyishly eager.

Granville hadn't known many reporters in either of his previous lives: not as a failed gold-miner in the Klondike nor as a disappointing fourth son in England. But one thing he'd learned quickly—there wasn't a reporter out there who'd pass up the chance of a free meal. Or maybe it was the lure of a good story.

Whatever the reason, he was pleased to see both of them.

After reminding them they were sworn to secrecy, he updated them on the direction the hunt for the puppet master was taking.

"So which one of us gets this story?" Tim asked.

"Whoever gets me the best lead," Granville said, then waited as they both glared, first at each other, then at him. He grinned. "Actually, I think there might be two stories. Since this one involves at least one murder, as well as smuggling and fraud." And he explained about the dockworker.

"Now there's an intriguing business angle," Draper said. "Depending who the puppet master is, I could play this up big."

"And a solid crime story," Tim said. "Front page stuff."

"But who gets the scoop?" Draper said.

"Both of you. I'm sure your publishers will see the value in it."

"We can talk 'em around. Especially after it worked so well on the last scoop you gave us," Tim said as Draper nodded slowly.

They fell silent as the soup was served. As soon as the waiter was gone, Tim leaned towards Granville. "I'm in. Draper?"

"Likewise. But you mentioned fraud. Which companies are involved?"

"This has to stay confidential, and may only be a partial list," Granville warned them, and the two reporters nodded agreement. He named the companies, and Draper took quick notes.

"So what do you need from us?" Tim asked.

"I suspect that the puppet master is someone well- connected socially, who has a lifestyle to maintain and is prepared to do whatever it takes to protect that," Granville said. "My guess is that he's either English himself, or well-connected enough there to attract English investors."

"You aren't saying you think this is one of Vancouver's movers and shakers?" Draper said.

"Yes, I that is exactly what I'm saying."

Draper's pen stopped and he stared at Granville. "Any idea who?"

"None, unfortunately. That's where I'm hoping you two can help."

"How? I certainly don't move in those circles," Tim said bluntly.

"I believe the puppet master had a devastating change in his financial circumstances, likely three to three and a half years ago, which he managed to hide from almost everyone. To do so, he created a complex criminal web that likely allows him to maintain his former standard of living," Granville said. "A change that big had to leave a record somewhere. With a little luck, that record will lead us to the puppet master."

Draper was eying him with a quizzical look on his face. "You're no ordinary detective."

Granville smiled. "Can you help?"

"I suppose you have no idea what kind of financial devastation this might have been."

"None whatsoever."

"Hmmm."

"So it could be criminal," Tim said. "A major theft, something like that."

"Keep in mind this would need to be the loss of a recurring income," Granville said. "Loss of an inheritance, too many investments gone bad, possibly arson if there were income producing properties involved, something of that nature."

"You realize this is an almost impossible task," Draper said. "We'd need to look into the recent history of practically every member of the Vancouver Club."

"It's why you'll get an exclusive," Granville said.

"It won't be that bad," Tim said to Draper. "Don't you see? We're not looking at the individuals, we're looking at the news."

"That's a lot of digging," Draper said.

"Anything big enough to set a toff to smuggling and murder is going to be news in its own right. Front page stuff," Tim said. "And the timeframe's not so bad. Three and a half years, give or take."

"A news story isn't going to give us this puppet master," Draper said.

"If we can't connect a story like that to the right guy, we aren't worth the salary our papers pay us," Tim said.

"Hear, hear," Granville said, raising his wineglass. "And I believe those are our steaks coming this way."

Several hours later, Granville sat in the expensively stodgy office of William Wardle, his banker. Wardle had smiled to see him, and was happy to accommodate his unexpected visit. For all his mild exterior and humble approach, Wardle was one of the canniest and most successful bankers in town. And, Granville had always suspected, one of the sneakiest.

When he'd met the fellow on a previous case, it had taken a little time to see past his unassuming demeanor and realize just how capable the man really was. But he'd never have hired him as the company's banker, had he not realized that he and Wardle both valued honor above all else. Something the puppet master definitely did not. Which made Wardle the perfect ally.

He explained the case to Wardle in some detail before going into their evolving theory about the nature and likely position of the puppet master.

"I believe this fellow had a devastating change in his financial circumstances—most likely some three and a half years ago—which he managed to hide from almost everyone. To do so, he created a complex criminal web that likely allows him to maintain his former standard of living," Granville said. "A financial change that big had to leave a record somewhere. With a little luck, that record will lead us to the puppet master."

Then he sat back. And waited.

"You know, even if your firm was not going to make me a lot of money, I think you would be one of my favorite clients," Wardle said after a moment during which the banker had seemingly stared at the ceiling. "You always present such interesting problems."

And he smiled. A shark's smile.

Granville had to laugh. "I'm glad I'm entertaining. Can you help?"

"Oh, I think so," Wardle said. "From what you've deduced already, this puppet master fellow is probably someone I have dealt with often."

The banker steepled his fingers on his desk, contemplated them. "We all have facades, you know. Some are better than others. And this fellow's must be a particularly good one, since no one name springs to my mind as a possible culprit. But even the most circumspect of us has cracks in our facades. And money tends to be the most effective way of breaking those cracks open."

He nodded sagely at Granville. "Mark my words. In a case as

closely tied to money—and the loss of it—as this one seems? Applying the right pressure in just the right spot should crack it wide open."

Which was the conclusion Granville had come to earlier. Along with the realization that Wardle was probably the best, if not the only, candidate for helping him do just that.

"Where do we start?" he asked.

"We need to start by examining your assumptions about the timeline for all of this. A criminal scheme that brings in the kind of money you're theorizing, and allows the master criminal—your puppet master—to stay hidden? Such a scheme would take time to build and mature. It wouldn't just all come together one day.

Plus how did he learn his trade, let alone make the connections he'd need? Your puppet master had to have money from somewhere, and some idea what he's doing."

"You don't think three and a half years is long enough for all of that to develop?"

"It's possible, I suppose. But less likely if you look at the historic and economic context." Wardle smiled at the expression of distaste Granville couldn't quite suppress.

"Which isn't quite as boring as you might suspect," the banker said. "It's probably not dissimilar to the one that sent you to the Klondike, caught up in the madness of a rich gold strike."

Granville had a sudden flash of Edward's slack face, and the pool of blood he lay in, his life ebbing. All over a gambling debt. He hadn't been able to save his friend. But he couldn't stomach the life he'd been living any longer.

He'd had his own reasons for fleeing England. Reasons that had nothing to do with economic history.

Wardle had been watching him with compassionate eyes. How much did he know?

"There are often forces we don't consider, hiding behind the events that drive us," Wardle said quietly. "A world-wide recession in the early part of the last decade saw markets and businesses collapse. By the time word got out of the gold strike up in Dawson, people were desperate for any way out. The Klondike rush seemed a golden ticket."

He'd certainly been desperate enough, Granville remembered. But if there had been challenges other than gambling available to the fourth son of a relatively wealthy Baron—perhaps business opportunities of some kind—might he have chosen to spend time there, instead?

"How does all this relate to our puppet master?" he asked.

"At the time, Vancouver was in the midst of a real estate boom," Wardle said. "One that had lasted more than half a decade. No matter what kind of property you bought, and where it was located, you could expect to see your investment double or even triple in a very short time. Until the fall of 1893."

"That world-wide recession you mentioned?"

Wardle nodded. "Yes. That is when it hit North America. Trade slowed, even stopped. There were no markets for goods. Vancouver's real estate market collapsed, and more than forty real estate firms just vanished."

"In a town this size?" Granville said. "How could it sustain so many?"

"It couldn't," Wardle said. "It was a bubble, and like so many before it, when it burst, it hurt a lot of people, and took a lot of companies down with it. Even the tram lines nearly went bankrupt, because people couldn't afford the fares."

It didn't seem possible, not when he thought about the thriving city he'd found here a year ago. "But properties seem to get more expensive every day," he said, thinking of the house he'd just purchased. Which, as promised, was now worth quite a bit more than he'd paid.

"By its very nature, this city is founded on growth and expansion," Wardle said. "And those of us who call it home have a great deal of faith that growth will always return, and that real estate values will always rise."

"Boom and bust," Granville said slowly. He'd heard the phrase, but he hadn't really thought about what it meant. "And our puppet master would have found himself caught in the midst of that bust."

"That would be my guess," Wardle said. "So if he had family money, and it was invested in British funds—those funds could have taken a hit. Perhaps his income was reduced or cut. By late 1893 or early '94 your puppet master's source of income could have dried up."

"He didn't set up his own businesses until late in 1897," Granville said. "So what was he doing in the meantime?"

"Panicking, probably," Wardle said. "And scrambling to build some kind of replacement. He may even have speculated in real estate—properties were available for a song at tax sales as businesses failed. A lot of people bought these "bargain" properties, not realizing how deep the recession would be, or how long it would last."

"That eternal optimism of the boom returning that you mentioned," Granville said.

Thinking about how convinced he'd been that the next section of creek they panned would be the one that would make them rich. Until the crushing realization that it might not ever do so, as eventually even his belief began to wear thin.

And he'd been feeding only himself. What if he'd had a family dependent on him? And on that gold panning out.

Or real estate, in this case. Or whatever it had been that the puppet master was counting on.

He couldn't feel sorry for the fellow. Not with everything he'd since done, and become. But he had some glimmering of fellow feeling.

And the beginning of an understanding of how the puppet master had ended up making the decisions he'd made.

It was amazing what finding the right person and asking the right questions could do for an investigation. People's various skills, their approach to the world, could provide an unexpected shift in perspective, and hold the key to the case. As Wardle had just done.

Wardle saw the likelihood of the same character traits in the puppet master that Granville did. But he knew the players in town in a way that Granville hadn't had time to learn. And he knew the intricate games that could be played with money in a way that Granville never would.

Together they reviewed the case again, with Wardle asking for clarification on a few key points. The banker asked several questions Granville would never have thought of, some of which sent his own thoughts down different pathways.

Throughout, the banker nodded and made notes at Granville's answers. When they were done, Wardle looked thoughtfully at his notes, then considered Granville's face.

"I see several avenues here I'll be pursuing," he said, waving off Granville's questions. "Once I have something, I'll call you."

"There is some urgency..." Granville began, struggling to stay courteous. Wardle was helping him after all, and the older man deserved his respect.

Wardle waved him off again. "Yes, yes, I understand. For now, only I can safely ask these questions. I'll telephone you as soon as I have something."

"Just be careful," Granville said. "The puppet master, whoever he is, uses murder to solve his problems."

"As a banker, I've made a lifetime study of acting cautiously," Wardle said with a rare grin.

As he left the banker's office, Granville felt much better about the direction the case was taking. And his ability to take down the puppet master before anyone else could be endangered. Especially not Emily. Or his team.

But he still wanted to punch someone. Preferably the puppet master.

AFTER HE LEFT Wardle's office, Granville returned to the Terminal City Club bar, nearly deserted at this hour. With a mug of ale in front of him, he considered his next move. Summarizing the case for Wardle and the two reporters—all of whom knew very little of how the investigation had unfolded in the last week—had given him a new perspective. He was beginning to get a sense of the puppet master, something that had eluded him since this case began.

On some level he understood the fellow. They most likely came from a similar background, had faced some of the same choices. But the puppet master was coldly ruthless in a way he'd never understand.

Yet if he was going to catch him, Granville needed to predict his actions. How?

He thought about what he knew of the puppet master—the things he'd done, how elusive he was. In his mind, he pictured some giant African cat, trapped behind bars, snapping at anyone who came close. That was how he saw the fellow—all teeth and claws, attacking anything that threatened his position.

Ruthless. Deadly. Without remorse or even a shard of humanity.

And all that fierceness was hidden behind a facade so benign that neither Wardle, with all his contacts and years of experience, nor Draper, the experienced business reporter, could name a single person he suspected might be the puppet master.

That was the man he needed to find. Leaving his ale unfinished, Granville strode purposefully from the bar.

3 4

It was much later than she'd expected when Emily finally made it back to the office. She and Clara had ended up taking Mr. Tremblay on a tour of the entire house. Emily still wasn't sure about the man's so-called vision for the house, but Clara was enthused. She and Mr. Tremblay had agreed on color schemes and everything from furniture to draperies for each room.

Clara then revisited what she insisted on calling the "substance" of every room on their short walk back to her house, and was still talking about what the finished decorating project could look like when they paused at the top of the drive.

Emily couldn't quite picture it, and she was even less sure what Granville would think of it. Luckily, Mr. Tremblay was equally as enthusiastic about the project as Clara. He'd offered to draw up some plans for furniture placement in each room, and do a few drawings of what the various rooms might look like, as well. That might help.

Granville could always veto everything he didn't like, once he'd seen the drawings. And once Emily had seen the plans, she'd have a better sense for how the rooms would actually work to live in. Then the two of them could make whatever decisions were necessary, together.

Even more luckily, Mr. Tremblay had answered all of her questions about Trans Pacific Trading without either hesitation or guile. Emily suspected he hadn't even realized how much he'd told her about how the company was run. Or how unhappy the owners would be if they ever found out that she now knew how close their company was to utter ruin.

No wonder Mr. Bray was interested in buying the business. He could likely buy it for next to nothing, and use it for his schemes. Furnishings and home decor items were not going to save this company. It would take something far more lucrative.

Like opium?

She couldn't wait to discuss everything with Granville.

Though perhaps she wouldn't mention the beginnings of the plan that she and Clara had come up with. The one where they discredited Bray, in public, in such a way as to turn Jane into a heroine. The details were still very rough. And probably a bit too risky, yet. They'd need to work on it a bit more before she was ready to discuss it with anyone other than Clara.

That decision made, Emily smiled to herself and walked a little faster. She wanted to hear how Granville had made out with his banker, and what he might now know about the puppet master.

———

It was nearly five, but Granville was still in his office. He looked up with a smile when Emily burst into the room. "Do you have a few minutes?" she asked, smiling at him.

"For you? Always," he said, closing the file in front of him and using the pen-wipe to swipe the excess ink from the nib. "How did you make out with the decorator?"

"Honestly? I'm not sure," she said. "He and Clara had a marvelous time looking at most of the main rooms."

"I thought it was only the dining room he was hired for?"

"It was," Emily said. "But Clara liked his ideas so much she took him on a tour of the rest of the house. And now they have plans for all of it."

"That can't be good."

"I'm not sure if it is or not. Clara is very enthusiastic," she said, and smiled at his exaggerated wince. "And her ideas are mostly good. But I'm still not sure if she understands the kind of home you and I will want."

She watched his expression carefully, knowing he'd try to avoid hurting her feelings by criticizing her friend. But he showed no sign of worry at all. In fact, he looked pleased. Why?

"Mr. Tremblay is going to draw up plans and make drawings of what several of the rooms might look like," she said, still watching him closely. "I thought that you and I could spend a bit of time discussing them before we decided. I know the timing is bad, with the puppet master and all..."

She broke off, staring at him. He looked even more pleased.

"Just what is going on?" she demanded. "Why do you look pleased at the notion of taking time away from this case to talk about home decor, of all things. I thought you hated living in all the mess of this project?"

"I do," he said. "But we aren't talking about home decor. We're planning the home we're going to make together, the home we'll live in once we're married. That is never a waste of time."

"Oh," she said, and could feel herself blushing, just a little. "It wasn't actually a waste anyway, because Mr. Tremblay told me quite a bit about Trans Pacific Trading. Probably more than he realized."

He grinned at that, but followed her lead without further comment. "And?"

"And they're in financial trouble," she said. "From everything Mr. Tremblay said, I suspect they're no more than a month or two away from bankruptcy."

"Which explains Bray's interest. The fellow would only have to pay for the shell of a company. Which is all he'd need if he's using it as a front for smuggling."

"That's exactly what I thought," she said, pleased. "But tell me, how did you make out with your banker? Are we any closer to the puppet master, do you think?"

"It went well," he said, and filled her in. "I think we're getting closer to the puppet master—he's starting to feel real to me."

"Instead of a shadowy figure that dissolves whenever you look in his direction?" Emily said.

"Something like that. How did you know?" he asked.

"Looking for the killer on my last case felt a little like that," she said, not really wanting to talk about it. He nodded, and to her relief, didn't press her.

"I also spoke with O'Hearn and Draper," he said. "Though I had to call both after my meeting with Wardle, and tell them we may need to look as far back as seven years ago for the financial cata-strophe that set the puppet master on this path."

"You think it was the depression of '93 that caused the puppet master's financial troubles?" Emily asked.

"Wardle thinks it's a strong possibility. But how do you know about the depression?" he asked. "You couldn't have been more than what? Twelve?"

She smiled. "I was eleven, actually. And Papa occasionally discusses business over the dinner table, much to Mama's chagrin. But I was always fascinated. So I started reading the newspapers before they were thrown out."

"You read the newspapers when you were eleven?"

"I did. Much to Papa's displeasure. In fact, I'm still reading them. And Papa is still annoyed every time he catches me at it."

"You're unique," he said, and smiled at her. The glint in his eye made her feel uncomfortably warm.

"Not really," she said. "Even at eleven I couldn't miss the suffer-ing. Our local grocer had to go out of business. So did Mama's favorite stationer, and the place we got our shoes made. The trams nearly stopped running because so many people couldn't afford to ride them. I just wanted to know what was happening around me."

"You still do," he said.

He was right. "I know. Some people find it irritating. I'm glad you don't."

"Hardly. When I look at the breakfast room, I imagine us sitting with our coffee, reading the morning papers together."

His words were so evocative Emily could almost taste the coffee. She couldn't bear to wait four *years*—or even two—for his vision to be a reality. But other than to expose Mr. Bray, she didn't know what she was going to do about it. And she wasn't quite ready to talk to Granville about that yet, either.

Which gave her a momentary pang of worry. Was it usual to keep so much from one's fiancé?

"I hope the plans for the dining room will match what you're seeing," she said lightly. "At one point they were back to discussing red walls in there."

He grinned. "That won't be happening," he said, and winked at her.

And she started to laugh. "Then you get to tell Clara."

"How about I take you out for dinner instead?"

Dinner with him, or avoiding a discussion she'd end up having anyway with her friend? She was no fool. "Done."

35

Wednesday, September 26, 1900

The following morning Granville woke abruptly from a restless sleep. This case had too many details, and no answers. When it came to the puppet master, they were teasing away layer after layer, with no clear answers. He needed to be doing something. Something that would make a difference now.

He needed a plan.

He found Scott and Trent in Scott's office, and pulling up a chair, quickly brought them up to speed. "There's something we're missing on this case. And we aren't going to find it chasing after dusty financial ledgers."

"Then where?" Scott said.

"I'm not sure yet," Granville said. "We're still missing something key, though. How did you two make out yesterday?"

"Bertie didn't want to help, but when I told him we were looking for a connection to the puppet master, then he was happy to," Trent said.

He exchanged a wry look with Scott, who grimaced. "Did Bertie take you to see his uncle?"

"No," Trent scowled. "He said his uncle would only talk to you. He went by himself instead. And made me do his chores to cover for him."

Granville bit back a laugh. "I see. How long was Bertie gone?"

"Two whole hours."

"And did you do chores too?" Granville asked Scott with a grin.

"Hardly," Scott said.

Trent forgot his own woes. "He's too big. They'd trip over him in that kitchen," he said, grinning at the idea. "I collected him from the pub later."

Of course he had. "And did Bertie learn anything in Chinatown?"

"Yes. His uncle said to tell you that the puppet master hasn't replaced his hired killer yet. The rumor is he's having some trouble finding someone willing to work for him."

Interesting. What was the fellow doing when he needed muscle, then? "Was that all he said?"

"No. His uncle also said you need to speak to the man who runs the opium factory at Number 11 1/2 Dupont. But only you. He won't talk to anyone else," Trent said.

That factory had been on their list to visit on Saturday. Now he was kicking himself for not pursuing it then. That decision had lost them time he couldn't afford to lose.

"Then let's see what Wong Sun's man can tell us," he said. "Maybe that will give us the lead we're missing."

"I'm going with you," Scott was saying. "I'll hang back if you want, but I'm not leaving you in Chinatown with no one watching your back."

He knew that tone in his partner's voice. There was no point arguing with Scott when he sounded like that. "Fine. Trent ..."

"I've got a few leads of my own to follow up," their apprentice was quick to say. "I'll see you later."

"Fair enough. I'll have Miss Rizzo set up a team meeting for five. Watch your back today, though. We're still being followed."

"You watch yours. I'm not the one in danger," Trent said.

THEY WERE HALFWAY to Chinatown when Scott nudged Granville with an elbow. "We're being followed."

"Again? How many this time?"

"I only spotted the one," Scott said.

"You think he's the puppet master's man?"

"Too far away to tell. But probably."

"How long has he been behind us?"

"Since we got off the streetcar, at least. I caught a glimpse of him then."

"So he could have followed us from the office. But why now?"

"Something must've stirred the puppet master up. Maybe the questions we're asking?"

"Could be." Granville considered their surroundings. They were just on the fringes of Chinatown. That would work. "Might be a chance to get more information. We'd best deal with it now."

"Ambush?"

"It will have to be," Granville said, pausing in front of a barber shop and risking a quick look back. "Tall, muscled, cheap navy suit, straw hat, pale hair?"

"Yeah, that's him."

"He's hanging well back, so he's not looking for a fight. Especially not outnumbered like he is." He grinned at Scott. "You wait here. They'll have a back entrance off the alley. I'll see if I can come up behind this fellow."

"You think he'll fall for that?"

"Not if he's any good. But he shouldn't be expecting the move."

"I would," Scott said.

"You're good."

"Gee, thanks. That why I have to stand out here?"

"Just try to look bored and impatient."

Scott gave him a look, then propped himself against the doorway. "That won't be hard. This is probably a waste of time," he muttered.

Just loud enough for Granville to hear as he sauntered into the barbershop, announced by the cheery clang of the bell over the door. It was the work of a moment to tip his hat to the barber and slip out the back door.

The alley ran straight behind the shops, which he'd expected. And it was drier and less rank than he'd feared. By the time he made his way back out to the street he'd retraced their steps by a block and a half.

He could see their pursuer, who had paused to stare intently into a window a block up. Scott was another half block ahead of that. Perfect.

Granville sauntered up the street, balancing his weight evenly with each step so he could lash out with either fist if needed. And tapped their pursuer on the shoulder from behind.

The fellow froze for an instant, started to swing around, then caught a glimpse of Granville over his shoulder. He froze again.

"Smart," Granville said, showing the fellow the hilt of the knife he carried at his hip. Seconds later Scott appeared behind their quarry. "We just want to talk. Walk on."

"About what?" their pursuer asked as he walked on, flanked by Granville and Scott.

"Your current boss," Scott said as they steered him towards a deserted alley. "Who do you work for?"

"That's need to know," the fellow replied, then winced as Granville's grip tightened on his arm.

"Wait a minute," Scott said suddenly, startling both Granville and the thug himself. "I know you. You were one of Jackson's men."

"I was."

Jackson had been one of Benton's lieutenants, and solving his murder had been Granville's first case. He hadn't thought much about the fellow—or his men—since. And he certainly hadn't expected to find one of them following him now.

It would be interesting to know if this fellow was still part of Benton's gang. And if so, how the puppet master had got to him. Because this had to be the puppet master's doing, somehow.

Scott was still staring at the man. "Parvo, isn't it?"

"It is."

"I'm assuming there's a reason you're following us, Parvo?" Granville asked their captive.

No answer.

"I'll take that for a yes," he said. "You still work for Benton?"

Their captive grunted a little as Scott let him feel the tip of the knife he'd pulled out once they were deep enough in the alley that they couldn't be seen from the street. "Sometimes," he said.

"I'm guessing Benton doesn't know about this particular job, though," Granville said to Scott. "He'd have no reason to have us followed."

"Makes sense," his partner said. "I doubt he'd be at all happy to learn what this guy's been up to."

"Probably not," Granville said. "So, you ready to answer a question or two yet?"

Another grunt. "Ask," Parvo said.

"What do you know about the fellow who hired you to follow us?" Granville asked.

"He pays well. And he always gets what he wants."

Granville scrutinized his face. Not quite expressionless. There was something here. "How did he threaten you, that you'd go against Benton?"

Parvo glanced at him. "You didn't hear it from me."

"Fine."

"He had my boss killed," the gangster said.

"One of Benton's men?" Granville asked. Had to be, to be an effective threat with this fellow.

"Yeah. Another of his lieutenants."

One of his key men, then. Benton must have been livid. And yet he'd never mentioned it. Which figured. "And what did the fellow hire you to do?"

Silence. Scott tightened his grip on his knife, and their captive's eyes followed the motion. "Keep eyes on you. Report back."

"Nothing more?" Granville asked.

"Me? Against both of you? What else d'you figure I could do?"

Interesting. "And what else does he get you to do?"

"Various things."

From Parvo's height and build, and the scars he bore, he'd likely been hired mainly as muscle. Though his grey eyes were sharp. Benton wouldn't tolerate a fool. "This fellow have a name?"

"Not one I know. Our interactions are usually arranged through a post office box."

"Usually," Granville repeated. "But not always?"

"A couple times, when time was short, he sent someone with instructions. A thin, Chinese guy, moved so silent it was creepy."

The ghost. Who was now gone. "What about for today's assignment?" Granville said.

"Someone else met with me."

"Where?"

"A bar down on Alexander Street. This morning."

"Describe him," Granville said.

"Middle height, middle weight. Brown hair, blue eyes. Pleasant face."

Distinctly unmemorable, by the sounds of him. Just like the fellow who'd posed as Abernathy. Which couldn't be coincidence. "How old?"

"Early thirties, I'd guess, but it was hard to tell because he kept looking down, looking away. Not much memorable about him."

Again, just like Abernathy. Who didn't exist. How many layers of subterfuge was the puppet master hiding behind? "Anything else that struck you about him?"

Parvo started to shake his head, then stopped. "Yeah, one thing. He had something in his pocket that he'd finger now and again. Like it was a habit."

A tell. One that no one had mentioned in Abernathy. And wasn't that interesting. "You see it?" Granville asked.

"No, but when he was leaving he started to pull it out, then caught me watching and shoved it back. From the way he was holding it and the glimpse I caught, it looked like a pocket watch. His clothes weren't expensive, but that watch was gold. And it was good, heavy gold. With that gleam, you know."

He did know. It was a nice detail, one a detective could draw some really useful conclusions from. Could it be this was the puppet master himself? Would he have taken that risk? Or was this yet another stand-in for him?

The question didn't sit right. All the instincts that served

Granville so well in a high stake poker game went on high alert. Maybe it didn't matter which it was. This had the feel of a double bluff.

"You think he expected us to spot you?" he asked.

Their captive compressed his lips and didn't answer.

"Or maybe we were meant to do so," Granville said.

Scott grimaced. "He playing with us now?"

"Someone is. I don't think it's Parvo here, though."

"No? Why not?" Parvo asked in a deliberately belligerent voice.

Granville laughed, loosened his grip on their captive's shoulder, and stepped back. "Nice try. Tell your employer it didn't work. He'll have to come up with something better."

Parvo didn't say a word, just winked at Granville, tipped his hat to both of them, and strolled off down the alley.

"What was all that about?" Scott said.

"The game is on," Granville said. "And it's getting interesting now."

"Great," Scott said with feeling. "Can't we just shoot this guy and put him out of our misery?"

"We have to find him first."

"We haven't done so well up to now. What did you have in mind?"

Granville smiled. He was beginning to get a feel for the puppet master. Finally.

No wonder the fellow had been so hard to find. He excelled at seeming something he was not. And probably played different roles with different people with ease.

He still didn't have a name for him, but that would come. What he did have was the first hint of a plan. It glimmered at the edge of his mind like the puppet master's watch. Which was going to prove deadly for the fellow, if he had anything to say about it. Two could play at this game.

"I thought we'd go and tell Benton he has a traitor in his midst. See what he thinks of that," Granville said with a grin as he watched Scott's eyes narrow.

"You thought what?"

"I have a plan," he said. And as he laid it out for his partner, he watched Scott's grin widen.

This should be fun.

"You know, I've been thinking about the Black and White Ball," Emily said to Clara, carefully putting down her rose-flowered teacup on the matching saucer.

When she was much younger, she'd once left a tiny watermark on the over-polished surface of one of a pair of the mahogany end tables. She'd never forgotten the commotion that arose, and for a time she'd thought Clara's mother might never forgive her. Eventually Clara had been allowed to invite her back, but since then, Emily had never felt easy about drinking tea at the Miles's.

"I should think so," Clara said, casually putting down her own teacup. "Since it's only three days away. Have you decided what to wear?"

"It doesn't matter," Emily said. "My green silk will do. But I've been thinking it could be the perfect opportunity to trap Mr. Bray after all…"

That was as far as she got before Clara let out a pained shriek. Emily instinctively glanced around, but the Miles's front parlor was as quiet as ever. "Are you ill?"

"Are you mad? You can't wear the same gown you wore at the

New Year's ball. And especially not when it isn't even white," Clara said fiercely.

Emily rolled her eyes. "It doesn't matter what color my gown is."

Clara shuddered. "You cannot wear a green gown to a Black and White ball."

"Fine. I'll wear a black one."

"You will not." Clara glared at her. "If you wear anything other than a white gown, you'll embarrass your fiancé."

"He isn't that shallow."

"Perhaps not. But your mother is."

"I told you, I don't care," Emily said calmly. "All that matters is exposing Mr. Bray for the confidence man he is. And I think we can do that on Friday."

"How?" Clara demanded.

"We'll need to work fast to pull it off. And there's no time to worry about my wardrobe."

Clara's her eyes narrowed. "Whatever you've got in mind, you'll never pull it off without the help of one of the organizers. Like your mother."

Emily scowled. "There must be a way."

"Be realistic. There's no time," Clara said. "Unless you'd rather talk to one of the other organizers?"

Emily pictured the half dozen others who were responsible for pulling together the annual ball, and made a face. "What about your mother?"

"You can't be serious. Don't even consider it," Clara said. "No, you need your mother's help if you're going to expose Mr. Bray. And you know it."

"Fine. I'll talk to her."

"And she won't even consider playing any role if you think you can get away with wearing a gown in any color except white."

Knowing Clara was right didn't help. "It's impossible. I have nothing that fits. And there's no time to order something made."

Clara smiled. "Nothing is impossible. But first, we have to speak with your mother. Is she at home?"

Much to Emily's regret, her Mama was indeed home. And the moment Clara mentioned Emily's lack of a suitable dress for the upcoming Ball, Mama tore herself away from a discussion about Jane's future trousseau—leaving Jane and their middle sister Miriam to argue over the virtues of yellow versus pink for a going away outfit suitable for the honeymoon journey to New York. Without a backward look, Mama lead the way to the morning room at the other end of the house.

"The ball is in three days, Emily," she said once the three of them were comfortably seated. "How can you not have a suitable dress?"

"I thought my green silk," Emily said, knowing Mama would be even less impressed than Clara had been.

Which she was.

"For a Black and White Ball?" Mama exclaimed, exchanging glances with Clara. Then they both turned disapproving looks on Emily.

"The truth is, I didn't think about it," Emily said before they could launch into more of the same. "I was too busy trying to solve the problem of Jane's would-be fiancé."

Mama's gaze dropped, as did her voice. "I should have checked on your choice of gown sooner," she admitted. "Especially when I had to remind you about the ball in the first place. If I hadn't been so worried about Mr. Bray's suitability…"

"Or lack thereof," Emily muttered.

Which her mother ignored, continuing, "And if I hadn't been trying not to let Jane see even a hint of my doubts, this would never have happened."

Emily stared at her mother. It was the last thing she'd expected.

"Regardless of how it came about," Mama said. "You can't go in your green silk. It simply wouldn't do. And there's no time to have something suitable made up now. You'll have to miss the ball this year. I'm sure that won't worry you too much."

"But I can't miss it," Emily said. "This is our best opportunity to show up Mr. Bray for the bounder he is."

"I don't see how we could pull either of those things off," Mama said. "Your gown, or exposing Mr. Bray."

"Leave the gown to me," Clara said. "My modiste will accommodate us."

"Even at this late hour?"

"Yes," Clara said. "And she'll do an exceptional job, I guarantee it. But it won't come cheap."

Mama turned to Emily. "And you're sure the Ball is the time to expose Mr. Bray? And without ruining Jane's future prospects?"

"With your help, I believe we can expose him, and do so in a way that even improves her prospects," Emily said.

"If that's true, then I don't care how much your gown costs," Mama said firmly. "I'll explain it to your Papa if the housekeeping money won't cover it. Just charge it to my account."

Clara nodded. "Good. Then we'll go now. Emily needs a fitting, and we still have to choose the fabric."

Emily rolled her eyes, but Mama nodded, looking satisfied. "I'm trusting you with this," she said to Clara.

Who smiled. "You can," Clara said with utter confidence.

Mama nodded and turned to Emily. "And I'm trusting that you can expose Mr. Bray for the fraud he is. And that you'll fill me in when you can. But the gown comes first."

"I know," Emily said. "And I'll tell you later. Because we'll need your help with the planning, too."

"You have it," Mama said. "Whatever you need."

And she didn't look the least bit concerned that she'd just handed Emily *carte blanche* on solving this mess. She must be far more worried about Jane's engagement than she had ever let on, Emily realized.

Which suddenly made her more nervous than she had been already.

TWO HOURS LATER, the Emily and Clara were seated in comfortably upholstered chairs in one of the back rooms of Clara's favorite dressmaker. They had been advised that Madame would be with them as soon as her current customer was finished, and offered tea or sherry. They had asked for tea, which was served with small sweet biscuits.

"It's far too early for sherry," Emily said quietly to Clara when they were alone.

"You'd be surprised," Clara said. "We're going to be here for hours yet. But never mind that. We need to talk about your dress, and how it needs to fit into your plan."

"Wait. I, or rather we, need to be back to the office for a meeting at five."

"You didn't mention the meeting earlier," Clara said.

"It's hours away. I didn't think I had to," Emily said. "But just in case..."

"You can miss one meeting," Clara said, overriding her.

"Not this one," Emily said. "There's too much information coming together now—we all need to be there."

"But you need the gown for your plan to work," Clara said. "That has to come first."

"If I miss this meeting, there will be no plan," Emily said firmly. "So I won't need the gown after all."

"You're just trying to get out of this fitting," Clara said. "You've always hated them."

"True. But this time it's for a purpose. One that I care about." She gave her friend a persuasive look. "We still have hours, yet. And all day tomorrow and most of Friday. Surely your amazing modiste can pull something off? The gown doesn't have to be elaborate."

Clara just shook her head at that. "You really don't understand, do you? Simplicity done well takes more work than the most over-frilled gown does. But never mind. It's a good thing your Mama agreed to pay whatever this costs."

She cast a critical eye over Emily. "And given these new time constraints, it's even more essential that we know exactly what kind of gown will best work with your plan. We'll need to decide now. *Before* Madame arrives."

"I don't understand," Emily said, lowering her voice. "My dress needs to be suitable for attending the ball. It has nothing to do with Mr... I mean, our plan."

She could hear the murmur of voices from at least one other fitting room. Even though she couldn't make out actual words, Emily wasn't taking any chances of being overheard. Even one stray word in the wrong ear could end their chances of exposing Mr. Bray.

And she made a shushing noise towards her friend and cupped her own ear to indicate that they needed to be quiet.

Clara sighed noisily.

"Emily, you're impossible," she said, but she lowered her own voice. "Your gown is all-important."

Emily said nothing, though she didn't agree. Apparently she wasn't as subtle about it as she'd thought, because Clara frowned at her.

"Think about what my Grandmama told us, about how we all play a role in society," Clara said. "Your gown is your costume. It helps give you the impact you need for your plan to work."

Emily frowned at her. "I don't quite see..."

Clara shook her head at her, and put down her teacup and the biscuit she'd been nibbling on. She motioned for Emily to stand up, then led the way to the standing mirror off to one side, and positioned Emily in front of it.

"Think of it this way," Clara said. "If you want to be noticed by a potential suitor, you might wear something frothy that takes up space, but subtly clings in all the right places. Since you are engaged, you could wear something more daring, that would make your Mr. Granville proud."

"He doesn't need dresses to think well of me," Emily protested, looking at Clara instead of the mirror. Though she rather liked the thought of showing off a little for Granville. "And I don't see how any of this helps with our plan."

"If your plan involves being noticed by our... quarry, then you want a fancier gown, to draw all eyes to you. If you want the focus to be on your sister, then you want simplicity. Elegant, of course, but without the lines that draw the eye to you."

"Oh, I see," Emily said, feeling suddenly more interested in this outing of Clara's. "That's actually quite fascinating. How do you know all of this?"

Clara just smiled at her. "So, which is it to be?"

"The latter," Emily said decidedly. "Or at least, mostly that."

"Good. Since that is your natural style anyway," Clara said.

"It is?"

"Have you learned nothing from me?" Clara asked, an assessing look in her eye that made Emily nervous.

It reminded her too much of a look Mama got sometimes. Which usually meant she'd be poked and prodded and end up wearing something she felt uncomfortable in.

Luckily Clara had better taste. Didn't she?

"What did you mean by mostly?" Clara asked.

Emily gave Clara a wary look. "I think my sister needs to be the one to actually denounce him. Loudly and clearly. So she is the one we need people to focus on," she said. "And with a little help from you and Mama, I know just how to feed her that information in a way that will create that effect."

"But before that, I need my sister and our quarry to pay attention to me. So that I can set them up. I need to be somewhat noticeable for that. Maybe we could add just a little froth?"

Clara just shook her head.

"You need to impress people, not amuse them," she said tartly. "No, between Madame's genius with design and your natural elegance, you will draw plenty of attention. Especially when you arrive on Mr. Granville's arm."

Clara thought she had natural elegance? Emily considered her image in the mirror for a moment. It wasn't how she'd ever thought of herself, and she still couldn't see it. But in the right gown, perhaps…?

When she married Granville, an elegant appearance might be a useful quality from time to time.

Dismissing the thought, she focused on what really mattered. For this little play of theirs to work, every detail had to be perfect.

"What about my sister's gown?" Emily said. "She won't have

time to make one up, and if it doesn't have the right impact, then it won't matter what my gown looks like, will it?"

As she heard her own words, she realized with an inward smile what an odd conversation this was for her to be having.

"You mother will have taken care of it," Clara said confidently. "She understands your sisters very well, even if she's never quite figured you out. Your eldest sister is finally engaged, and her dress will both make a statement and celebrate that fact. In the best of taste, of course."

"Of course," Emily said, trying not to laugh. She was picturing the extravagancies Jane would likely have chosen for such an occasion, if left to herself.

"But even with the right dress, I'm concerned that this plan of yours..." Clara began.

Then the modiste arrived with two assistants bustling with fabrics, measuring tapes and pins, and the moment was lost.

When Granville and Scott arrived at his office unannounced, Benton didn't look at all pleased to see them. But he didn't keep them waiting, either, Granville noted. Which meant he was more interested in whatever information they brought than he'd admit.

"You have a traitor in your ranks," Granville said, and helped himself to one of Benton's cigars.

From behind his massive desk, Benton gave Granville a look that should have slayed him where he stood. "Leave. Now," he gritted out.

Luckily he was made of sterner stuff, Granville thought as he lit the cigar, inhaled deeply and lounged back in the guest chair. "You're the one who hired me, remember? Something about a puppet master who was interfering with your business dealings, I believe?"

"You're not half as funny as you think you are," the gangster said.

Granville blew a plume of smoke in Benton's direction. "Good thing you're not paying me for my sense of humor, then. But I thought you wanted this fellow dealt with? Didn't he?" he asked

Scott."

"He did. Paid us'n all," Scott said with a straight face.

"By any means necessary, as I recall," Granville said as he reached for a second cigar and passed it to Scott.

"Those were the words, all right," Scott said, then bent his head to light the cigar.

Benton scowled from one to the other of them. "Fine. Cut the comedy act. What did you find out?"

"You know a fellow named Parvo? Used to work for Jackson?" Scott said.

"What of him?"

"The puppet master sent him after us," Granville said. "It doesn't take much brain to figure he's working for him, now. And if he's still working for you…"

"That makes him a traitor," Scott finished.

Benton sat back and slowly lit a cigar of his own. Then he puffed a cloud of smoke between them. "Say I believe you. What would Parvo get out of it?"

"Funny thing. That's what we came to ask you," Granville said, sending more smoke Benton's way. "And we haven't all day to waste on it. We have a puppet master to catch."

"Ha, ha. What went so wrong the two of you have decided you're a couple of comedians?" the gangster said.

"We're simply tired of playing your games," Granville said. "Thought you might appreciate a taste of ours."

"Well, I don't."

Granville exchanged glances with Scott. "Do we care?"

The big man shook his head. "Nope," he said with a broad smile.

Granville leaned forward. "Look, Benton. This has gone on long enough. First the puppet master threatened my team, and sent his pet assassin after Scott and I. We got the assassin run out of town, so now the puppet master is trying again with one of your flunkies."

"Not mine," Benton said. "Jackson's."

"Jackson's more than a year dead. Can't see he's got much say in the matter."

"Then why are you here with this latest wild speculation?"

Benton said. "I hired you to deal with the puppet master, as you pointed out. You haven't done that yet."

Granville watched Benton like one wolf watches another, waiting for that betraying twitch. And seeing a sharp smile instead.

The gangster wasn't reacting with the bitter anger he'd half expected. Nor did he seem to be treating this like the game he so often played with Granville. What was he hiding?

"I hear the puppet master ordered one of your men killed," Granville said slowly, his eyes on Benton as he dropped this bomb. "You'd never allow that to go unavenged."

Benton's grin vanished. "Your theories are always interesting," he bit out.

"Based on what I've learned so far," Granville said, rapidly rearranging the facts he held. "I'd say the puppet master decided to expand his operations into an area you do care about. Which changed the game."

Benton showed no reaction.

"Then he had one of your key men killed to undermine your operations, and the game wasn't so amusing any longer. So you hired us. Which sent a message to the puppet master," Granville continued, watching the gangster's expression closely. "And turned us into targets."

"That sounds inventive of me," Benton said blandly.

"Does it?" Granville said.

"Which is why we need to know if Parvo still works for you," Scott said. "Or not?"

"He does," Granville said abruptly, his gaze still fixed on the gangster. "Part-time, anyway. Doesn't he, Benton? Which is why Parvo now also works for the puppet master."

"Wait a minute. He's your spy?" Scott said, staring at Benton. "And you've been keeping it from us? After you hired us? Oh, that's rich."

"I prefer to keep my men alive, whenever possible," Benton said, calmly.

"And you didn't trust us to keep your secret?" Scott demanded.

His partner seemed to have gained every bit of heat Benton had lost, Granville noted, and intervened before Scott said something unforgivable. Or Benton did so.

"What have you learned about the puppet master?" he asked Benton.

"Much too little."

"For our purposes, even the smallest detail could help," Granville said.

Benton gave him an assessing look, then nodded. "Ask your questions. But stick to what's relevant."

At the gangster's words, Scott blew out a thick cloud of cigar smoke.

Which made Granville smile. "That is easier said than done, when none of us know what's actually relevant, and what is simply a smoke screen," he said.

"Try," was Benton's response.

Which figured. "We know the puppet master needs the money to maintain a lifestyle. He may have lost money in the '93 depression— or his family did so—and he turned to crime a few years ago as a way to fund his lifestyle. Which limits our suspect pool."

Benton raised an eyebrow. "I'm not hearing a question."

"Do you know who he is?"

"I know him as Abernathy."

Scott gave a disbelieving snort. "Abernathy."

"You really don't know his name?" Granville asked, distracting Benton from Scott's antagonism.

"No. I don't."

Which didn't seem like Benton's style. He was too fond of control. "You must have known Abernathy wasn't his real identity," Granville said.

"I did."

"So why get involved with him?"

"He sold me some property," Benton said.

"You bought property from a seller you couldn't identify? Why would you do that?" Scott asked.

Benton gave him a hard look. "The price was excellent. He sold at a substantial loss."

"And when was this?" Granville asked.

"Nearly four years ago, more or less," Benton said.

"So we're right about the timeline," Granville said.

"Should I be impressed?" Benton said.

He ignored the sarcasm. "It means we're getting somewhere. And then?"

"What makes you think there's more?" Benton asked.

Granville puffed on the cigar—which was truly excellent—and waited.

"He did some work for me."

Wardle had been right about that, too. "What kind of work?" he asked.

"Importing," Benton said.

Which probably meant smuggling. Was that where the puppet master got his start? "From the Far East?" he asked.

"Mostly."

Definitely smuggling.

"He had some contacts I found useful," the gangster added.

"What kind of contacts?" Granville asked.

"Shipping," Benton said.

"And you still didn't know his real name?"

"No."

Granville gave him a skeptical look. "And from there?" he said.

"Abernathy's business grew," Benton said. "He still did work for me occasionally. I found him useful from time to time."

"Until he betrayed you."

"He'll regret it," Benton said evenly. And ruthlessly stubbed out his half-finished cigar in the heavy crystal ashtray.

"I'm sure he will," Granville said. It was rare to see the gangster display his temper so openly. Benton must want the puppet master dealt with as badly as he did.

"What has Parvo learned while working for this fellow?" Granville asked.

"The puppet master's keeping a close watch on you. And your firm," Benton said.

He'd assumed the puppet master was watching him, but the

team? He felt a slow burn of anger hearing that. He'd have to make sure that the team resumed their safety precautions. Emily especially, since she was inclined to like taking risks. As was Trent.

"Anything else?" he asked.

"Just a few minor details that don't matter," Benton said, inhaling deeply and blowing out a cloud of fragrant smoke.

Granville exchanged glances with Scott. Benton was still holding back.

"We're beginning to suspect the puppet master is part of what passes for high society here," he said. "Does that make any of those 'minor details' more relevant?"

Benton's expression shifted momentarily, too fast for Granville to read anything other than some kind of shock before the gangster resumed his usual poker face.

So that information meant something to him. What? And why was he working so hard to hide it?

No matter. Granville had the scent of his quarry, and he wasn't losing it now. With or without Benton's cooperation, he was taking the puppet master down.

"GRANVILLE. SLOW DOWN," Scott said from behind him as they strode away from Benton's office. "The bar isn't going anywhere."

"What bar?" Granville asked. Glancing at his watch, he kept up his pace. It was a good thing they hadn't made an appointment at the opium factory—their meeting with Benton had taken longer than he'd anticipated.

"Whichever bar you're headed for now. After that little chat with Benton, I could use several whiskeys."

"I'm headed for Chinatown," Granville said. "We have a factory manager to talk to, remember?"

"You're just going on with the investigation? Why aren't you too angry with Benton to see straight?"

"Like you are?" He glanced at his partner. "Benton isn't worth it. And frankly, he gave us more information than I'd expected."

"You got a lead? Out of that… that…" Scott sputtered for a moment, then shook his head. "I can't think of anything vile enough at the moment. What lead?"

"Benton had the puppet master working for him nearly four years ago. And he just verified every theory we'd come up with."

"All of which he could have told us two weeks ago. And we'd be that much farther ahead. And my sister thinks that lunkhead…" Scott muttered another curse. "He's an arrogant son-of-a-gun, that one. Thinks he's better than everyone else."

"He's Benton. As you've pointed out to me more than once."

Scott growled at him, and Granville laughed. "I thought you wanted this case over, so we don't have to deal with Benton as a client."

"I do."

"Then why are we still standing here talking about it?" Granville said with a grin. "Let's see what Wong Sun's man can tell us."

FIFTEEN MINUTES LATER, Granville was pulling open the heavy metal door—bearing only a small metal sign lettered in Chinese characters —of the opium factory at Number 11 1/2 Dupont Street.

Scott took up his post by the door, standing with his arms crossed and a vigilant look on his face. As Granville walked up to the heavy wooden counter that ran across a third of the room, the manager came forward to greet them. He was a short, slight man, dressed in traditional Chinese silk robes with his queue wrapped tidily around his head. "How can I help you, sir?" he asked in confident English.

"I'm hoping you might be able to provide us with some information," Granville said, slightly exaggerating his own Oxbridge accent.

"I see. And what information might that be?" the fellow asked with a note of caution in his tone.

"A friend of mine recommended I invest in a local company. Said I'd make a tidy profit, as the owner is pretty savvy. Trouble is, I can't remember either the name of the company or the fellow who owns it. And my friend is on his way to India now, and I can't reach him.

Only thing I'm sure of is that this new company was buying opium locally and selling it elsewhere. And making a fortune in the process."

"And why did you think of our firm, sir?"

"Wong Sun suggested I speak with you. I'm looking for a man who began buying large quantities of opium some three years ago, and he suggested I talk with you about the fellow."

"Wong Sun?" The tone hadn't changed, but the fellow's eyes were even more wary now. "He told you to talk to me?"

"Yes. He did," Granville said. "Do you know this man?"

"The man who was asking is not a customer here," the factory manager said carefully.

Interesting distinction. "But you do know who he is?"

"I know of such a man," the manager said. "Though I do not know if he is the one you seek."

"Any possible names would help, if only to jog my cursed memory," Granville said. Then waited silently while the fellow considered just how much he was willing to say.

Wong Sun's name was clearly a powerful one here, and Granville hoped it would be enough.

Just as the silence had stretched long enough that he'd begun to think this would end in another dead end, the fellow spoke. "He called himself Jones. I suspect it may not be his real name."

"Ah, that is familiar. I remember now. Was it Barnabas Jones?"

"Yes.

Their second invisible player. How convenient. "Thank you," he said. "And he came here to ask questions about opium?"

"Yes. He came maybe three, four year ago. He asked about buying opium, shipping opium. Even prices."

"But he never bought opium from you?"

"No. Never. Though he came several times with questions, I have never seen him since."

That fit with Granville's theory that the puppet master's opium came from Victoria. Whoever the puppet master was, he covered his tracks well. "Did anyone ever accompany Mr. Jones?"

"No. Always only him."

So he'd been discreet even here. "And could you describe the man you know as Jones?"

"He is tall, but not like you." The manager raised his hand several inches about his own head to indicate the height. "Hair, lighter than yours. Eyes same, but lighter. Dressed like you."

So about five foot nine or ten, with medium brown hair and light blue eyes. Wearing a decent suit. And sounding very like the fellow Parvo had met with.

Unfortunately nothing in either description distinguished him from half a dozen men he could think of.

Was this, finally, the puppet master himself? Given the name he'd used, it was a distinct possibility.

It was equally likely to be another double bluff. Yet another layer of confusion the puppet master was hiding behind.

Granville was beginning to look forward to the Black and White ball. He'd like nothing better than to make his next encounter with the puppet master face to face.

As they exited onto Cambie Street, Granville clapped Scott on the shoulder. "Time for that whiskey of yours."

His partner grinned. "Past time, you ask me."

A brisk several blocks took them to the Carlton, which was nearly empty this time of day Two minutes later, they were sitting at a back table with whiskeys in front of them.

"What's on your mind?" Scott asked.

"Well, thanks to Parvo and our friend in Chinatown, we know a few things about the puppet master that we never knew before."

"Like what?"

Granville considered him for a moment "Like what he might look like," he said. "And I'm finally getting a sense of who he is."

Scott frowned at him. "I get the bit about what he looks like. If you're assuming he's kind of nondescript."

"I think that's a good working assumption," Granville said. "And I'd take it one further, and speculate that he's either disguising himself, or hiring others that share his general physical characteristics."

"To confuse us?"

"Of course."

"Y'know, I'm starting to really hate this puppet master of yours."

"Hardly mine," Granville said. "But I know what you mean."

"I don't get how we know more about who he is? We still don't even have a name for him."

"We've known from the first that this fellow stayed invisible, and operated from behind the scenes," Granville said.

"Yeah. So?"

"He's running this elaborate scheme, which is almost as invisible as he is. And every layer we uncover has another layer behind it."

"He's good at being sneaky," Scott said, and took a hefty swallow of whiskey.

"I think he enjoys it. Maybe even needs it," Granville said. Then downed a little of his own drink. "You know, I'd been thinking of the puppet master as a large predator—like one of the big cats—sleek, stealthy, and deadly. But trapped by the circumstances he found himself in.

Now I think I was wrong about him. He's more like a black tailed weasel in winter. Quick, agile, and smart. Almost looks cute until you get a look at its eyes. That's where you see the viciousness."

"A weasel? You're not thinking this guy might be your old pal Gipson, are you?"

"No, Gipson's just a regular weasel. The puppet master is an ermine. Bigger, more impressive to look at. And more vicious."

"In winter?"

"When its fur turns white, to match the snow. You can't see him at all, unless he moves. And even then your eye has trouble following him. By the time you're really sure you saw him, he's vanished again."

Scott nodded. "Yeah, I see that. He blends into his background, and what's inside doesn't show unless he wants it to."

"We named him right."

"Because?"

"He really is a puppet master," Granville said. "He's trying to make us dance to his tune."

Scott grinned. "Fat chance."

"It nearly worked. We've been chasing his illusions."

"Some of it's real. And Mac and Miss Kent will likely have more to tell us about his financial dealings."

"Maybe. That's not what will catch him, though."

"No?"

Granville shook his head. "This fellow is too wily for that. No, we're going to have to trap him on his own ground."

"And where is that?"

"In the society where he makes himself most at home. The place he'll kill to protect."

"And he has," Scott said. "But how?"

"I'm taking a leaf out of Emily's book," Granville said with a grim smile. "She's been wanting to attend this ball on Friday to keep tabs on her would-be brother-in-law. Which is smart."

"A ball?"

He nodded. "It's a benefit for the hospital. One of the grandest events of the year, I understand. Penguin suit and all."

"So you both have to attend?"

"Yes. And not just us. You're going too."

His partner scowled. "Me? You're joking, right? I don't belong at a ball."

"The puppet master wouldn't miss an event like this," Granville said. "I need you to have my back. And Emily's."

Scott didn't look happy, but he didn't argue any further. "So what do you plan we do until Friday?" he asked instead.

"We're going to dig into every bit of information the team gathers, and we're going to identify our main suspects. Then you and I are going hunting."

Granville paused, gave Scott a considering look. "And you, my friend, are going to spend some time with a barber. And be fitted for a tuxedo."

"Wait. What?"

3 8

Several hours later, Emily looked at the faces of the team gathered around the meeting table and smiled. It was a good thing she'd been adamant that she be here on time. After endless discussions of just what her gown should look like, and hours of being poked at and prodded by Clara's modiste or one or the other of her assistants, it was a relief to be back in the office. It was beginning to feel more like home to her than her parent's home did.

For a second she wondered if that would change once she was married and living in her own home, and hoped it would. Perhaps she could mention it to Clara—no. Heaven only knew what her friend would decide had to change in the decorating to make it more "home-like." Besides, it was the people who mattered, not the furniture.

Though it did help if the furniture was comfortable to live with. And perhaps if the decoration was not over-fussy.

She stopped that thought, horrified. Was she turning into Clara? Or worse, Mama? Was that what being married would do to her?

She looked at the familiar faces gathered around the table, with notes and files everywhere. They were here because they had a case to solve. And the dress she'd just spent hours thinking about was part of that case. Which actually had made it more interesting than usual, somewhat to her surprise.

If she told Clara that, her friend would just roll her eyes. Mama would be horrified, though. So that was all right. She was still herself, pending marriage or no.

"Is Trent not back yet?" Granville asked just then.

"He said he had something to look into, and might be a little late," Miss Rizzo said, coming in with as stack of folders and several typewritten pages and handing them to Laura.

She hadn't seen Trent today, Emily realized. And Granville had obviously expected him back sooner. What was he up to now?

"We'll start without him, then," Granville was saying. "Thank you, Miss Rizzo. Please ask him to join us as soon as he arrives."

Marie nodded, brought in the tea things and left quietly. As the door closed behind her, Granville looked across the table at Mac and Laura.

"Why don't you start by telling us what you learned today," he said.

"We weren't getting very far on any of the avenues we tried," Laura said. "So we went back to looking at the financial information on Vancouver Box and Clark & Company, looking for patterns."

"Both operate on relatively small profit margins," Mac said. "The make a reasonable profit in some areas, but anywhere they are shipping small items, they are making little or no profit."

"Particularly on those items going to the United States," Laura said.

She took the mimeographed pages Miss Rizzo had brought in and passed copies around the table. "As you can see in these summary sheets."

Emily smiled as the familiar pale purple ink, limp feel and sharp smell of the duplicated copies reminded her of her typewriting classes. She recalled so clearly her own amazement at how much easier even this finicky process was than re-typing all those copies.

Then she lost the smile as she considered the information on the pages. Laid out like this, the patterns seemed clear. But they didn't seem to make any sense. Was she missing something?

"Some of these operations don't make any financial sense," Granville said.

Apparently not.

"That's because they're barely breaking even. No company can carry those kinds of margins for long," Mac said. "It's been three years. These operations should have been discontinued."

Granville was still looking at the figures. "These companies have shareholders. How is he getting away with this?"

"It's all in the presentation," Mac said. "On the surface, the companies look good. In fact, they look very good. It took us quite a bit of work to break out the figures like this. And… didn't you say the shareholders are British?"

"Yes," Granville said.

"They could be receiving a different set of figures," Mac said. "From Britain, it would be difficult for them to check them for accuracy, and most wouldn't bother."

Emily nodded. That made sense. And Granville's expression said that was his suspicion as well.

"These smaller transactions still only make sense if they are using these shipments to conceal something they're smuggling," Laura said. "And then money from the illegal sales is coming back in some other way."

"And ending up in the puppet master's pocket," Mac said. "If we knew who he was, we could likely trace those payments, possibly even all the way back to the smuggling."

"We might be a little closer to identifying the fellow," Granville said, and explained what he and Scott had learned earlier that day from Parvo and Benton.

"Do you trust those sources?" Mac asked.

"Benton's henchman and the opium seller?" Granville asked. "Of course not. Still, they gave essentially the same description, which gives them more credibility."

"I'd be more worried that this is another misdirection on the puppet master's part," Emily said. "And that the real puppet master looks exactly the opposite of these descriptions."

"That's a definite possibility," Granville said. "Unfortunately, it's also possible that this is a double bluff."

"I like that idea," Laura said. "Especially when this particular build and coloring are so common here. And it's the same description as we have for Mr. Abernathy. A description which the photograph matches."

"But we know the photograph is staged," Mac said. "Could mean this new guy is fake too."

"Not if the puppet master has chosen to hide in plain sight," Laura said. "And is counting on his reputation to avoid suspicion. Given three men of a similar looks—who would ever expect a wealthy gentleman to be a smuggler?"

"And a killer, don't forget," Mac said. "But it's a risky move."

"If I'm right about this fellow," Granville said. "He probably enjoys that aspect. And he'd see himself as more intelligent and cleverer than anyone trying to catch him, anyway."

Mac nodded. "I've had clients like that. Oh, not killers, but ones who were cooking the books. Figured no one would ever question them, and if they did, their clever strategies would fool everyone."

"So let's make a note of the suspects who fit the general description," Granville said. "That's who we'll focus on for now. But we'll keep the ones who don't fit on a separate list for now. In case the puppet master assumes that we'll suspect a double bluff."

Emily grinned at that. "A triple bluff?" she asked. "I wonder if our puppet master knows you're a poker player."

"It didn't take him long to find out we were looking into him," Granville said. "So we have to assume he does know that. Which is why we're keeping both lists. At this point, trying to outwit the puppet master is a dangerous strategy. We still know too little about him."

Laura was nodding. "That explains why I can't quite see the patterns in everything we've uncovered so far," she said. "It's as if I'm following his footsteps, but he keeps doubling back, and crossing over his own path, so the trail isn't clear."

Scott met Granville's eyes across the table. "Just like an ermine," he said. "Fast and tricky."

Emily rolled her eyes. "We are not calling this suspect an ermine. He started off as the big fish. Then it was the puppet master. Now he's an ermine? Forget it."

Granville laughed. "No, we'll stick with the puppet master."

"Good," she said, with a pretended grumpiness that had Laura giggling, then looking appalled at herself.

Emily kept her face straight with an effort. "The list of those who match the description might prove very useful on Friday night."

And she explained to the others about the Black and White Ball, and what she, Granville and Scott were planning.

"If we're right about the puppet master having a position in society to maintain, he'll be there," she said. "As will Mr. Bray. We're hoping to play the two of them off against each other."

"But we still don't have *any* idea who the puppet master is?" Laura said.

"Not yet, I'm afraid," Granville said. "We're not even sure about the description we have. That's where the work we're all doing on our lists is so important."

"How many people will be at this ball?" Laura asked.

"Well over a hundred, I understand," Emily said. "My mother is one of the organizers, and she tells me they expect quite the crush."

"More than fifty of them men," Laura said.

Emily nodded. "Yes. So you can see where even a vague description can be useful."

It amused her to see Laura bristle, as if preparing to argue further. Something about the information must be setting off warning bells for her. She was pleased to see her friend truly stepping into her new role.

"*If* the information can be trusted," Granville said before Laura could speak. "It came from Benton and his pet spy, remember. Not the most trustworthy sources. Laura is quite right to be uneasy about it."

"But Benton's the one who hired us," Trent protested. "Why would he lie about this?"

"Benton plays a long game. And he never really trusts anyone.," Scott said. "It's safest to assume everything he tells us is a lie."

Granville nodded. "Which means verifying everything. And I'm concerned about how easy it would be to mislead us in this case, since we have so little information. And it's almost impossible to verify the little we do have."

"We can verify the financial data," Mac said.

"Yes, eventually," Granville said. "But…"

Just then, the door was flung open and Trent raced into the room. His eyes touched on each of them, and he acknowledged them with a wide grin. Then his gaze focused on Granville. "You'll never guess what I found out."

———

"You know who the puppet master is?" Granville said dryly.

"Well, it's not quite that good," Trent said. "But nearly."

He closed the door and flung himself into a chair at the head of the table, looked at Granville again. "After you and Scott left yesterday, I decided to do some digging on my own. People my pop used to know."

Mostly petty thugs, from what Emily had heard.

"Learn anything?" Granville was asking

"Nah. They think too small," Trent said.

Emily wasn't sure if that observation was a good thing or a bad one, coming from Trent. Sometimes she thought he had it in him to end up a master of crime himself, if he ever decided to go that route. She smiled to herself at the thought.

Not with Granville as his mentor, he wouldn't.

"So then what?" Scott was asking Trent.

"I made a list of people I know that think bigger," Trent said. "And this morning I went to see Miss Frances."

Trent growing up fast, Emily realized. And this move suggested he had an ability to read people that most boys his age couldn't manage. They'd see the exotic fan dancer, not the woman who did exactly as she chose, had built a comfortable life for herself, and managed to keep Benton intrigued while she did so.

She wondered for a moment if it was a skill he'd been born with, or if it had grown from necessity out of the difficult and often uncertain life he'd lived with his wastrel father.

"Turns out she knows quite a bit about who has money and who doesn't," Trent was saying, oblivious to what she was thinking. "Miss Frances came up with a few names of well-known men who'd lost money or had something awful happen during the downturn. And she was taking tea with her sister, and her sister had heard about a few more. Course, we were careful not to ask how Miss Lizzie had heard about them."

Emily noted Scott glancing at Granville and rolling his eyes at Trent's statement. Granville hid a grin, which amused her.

No one ever alluded to Lizzie's brief history as a prostitute, nor the opium addiction that had resulted from it. Except Trent. Who apparently didn't see any value in discretion. She wondered for a moment what Granville was going to do about that.

"Then Miss Frances said I needed to talk to Benton about the names," Trent added. "So I did."

"Please tell me you didn't go to Benton's office alone," Granville said.

"Of course not. Miss Frances went with me. In a carriage."

Granville looked pained. "And what did Benton say to your unexpected arrival?" he asked.

"He was really interested, especially in the list Miss Frances brought."

Watching the byplay, Emily wondered if Trent was really as oblivious as he sometimes seemed. Now and again she spotted a glint in his eye that suggested he might not be. Which intrigued her.

"So did he have anything helpful to add?" Granville asked.

Trent grinned broadly. "He crossed a couple names off. Said he knew where their money had come from."

"Probably Benton himself," Granville said.

"Wonder who he managed to buy off?" Scott muttered.

"And?" Granville asked Trent.

"And I have five names," Trent said, and slapped a list of names written in Frances's flowing hand in front of him.

Granville quickly skimmed the list. Only three of them were on Draper's list, which meant they had two new names.

"This is an excellent start, Trent," he said. "Five names gives all of us something to work with."

"I'll work with Laura to create a new master list of suspects," Emily said. "Then ask Miss Rizzo to make copies of that list for all of us."

"That would help immensely," Granville said.

39

Thursday, September 27, 1900

Despite his feeling they were finally making progress on finding the puppet master—or perhaps because of it—Granville didn't sleep well that night. Scott found him at his desk the next morning just after seven.

He stared from the files stacked on both sides of Granville to the coffee steaming in front of him.

"How long have you been here?"

"Sunrise, or thereabouts," Granville said absently. After a glance at his partner, he'd gone back to flipping through his notebook. "There's coffee if you want it."

"You made coffee?" Scott said, and disappeared into the other room, coming back with his own cup. "You look like you're making progress," he said.

Granville looked up at that. "I think we have most of the pieces. And I can almost see the puppet master now. But not how to find him."

Scott settled back in the leather armchair opposite Granville's desk, coffee in hand, and stuck his feet on the desktop. "Tell me."

By the time the others had arrived in the office, Granville and Scott had argued their way through their respective notes from the investigation and most of the files on Granville's desk. Miss Kent took one look at them, and asked Miss Rizzo to make a pot of tea. "And perhaps a plate of biscuits. Can you bring them with the notes I gave you yesterday and the relevant files into the meeting room for us, please?" she added. "I suspect we'll all be unavailable today except for emergencies."

As Miss Rizzo nodded, Granville wondered where this new more assertive Miss Kent had come from, and how much it was due to her release from the reception position that Miss Rizzo now occupied.

Whatever the reason, he was pleased to see it. She'd proved herself a most capable member of their little team, and it was good to see her growing confidence in that role.

Though he noticed her quick glance at Emily, as if for confirmation of her actions. A little reinforcement might be in order. "The meeting room is a good idea," Granville told Miss Kent.

"We'll also need the latest version of our list of the possible suspects," he said to Miss Rizzo. "And the list of shipping and ground transport from Benton's files. Copies for all of us, please. And if Mr. Draper or Mr. O'Hearn ring, I'll take the call."

He noted that Miss Rizzo made quick notes with a pleasant smile, then began to gather the documents Miss Kent had requested. She too was taking on her new position with alacrity.

He glanced at Emily to see if she'd noticed and found her watching him. The glint in her eye and the grin she gave him confirmed that of course she had. He grinned back, and gestured for her to precede him into the meeting room.

———

WHEN EVERYONE WAS SEATED around the long table, with cups of tea and small plates with scones and butter jostling for space with the various papers in front of them, Granville began.

"We have a challenge in front of us," he said with a smile. "And it won't be easy. Between now and tomorrow night, we need to use our collective knowledge to create a final working list of the most likely suspects for our puppet master."

"How?" Trent asked.

"Miss Rizzo has made duplicates of the latest version of the current list," Granville said, picking up his copy and running his eyes down the list. "Let's see if we can eliminate anyone, shall we?"

"Good idea," Miss Kent said briskly, then flushed a little.

He could see Emily hiding a grin.

"Any of these fellows show up in Benton's files on international shipping?" he asked.

Miss Kent scanned the two lists Miss Rizzo had provided, then flipped through her notebook. "No, I don't see any connections."

"It must be there, for Benton to have collected this information," he said. "We're missing something. Anyone have any ideas?"

"Benton said something yesterday about the puppet master being anonymous from the beginning, but having useful shipping contacts even early on," Scott said. "What if someone knows the puppet master from back then?"

"It fits," Granville said. "Especially if he's originally from a family with money. Those could be family connections in the business. We'll look into that. Anyone have anything else?"

No one did.

"So we'll put the shipping list aside for now," he said. "Next, the suspect's height and coloring. We need to review the revised list and identify those we know who match the description."

Miss Kent handed around a mimeographed page. "These are the names on the combined lists from yesterday."

"Excellent." Granville said, scanning it quickly. "I recognize Fairfield and Knox. Both are the right height and coloring."

"I know Allsop by sight," Mac said. "He doesn't fit the description."

"Anyone know the others?" Granville said.

No one did.

"So now what?" Trent said.

"We need to look into those possible shipping contacts for the puppet master. Can you find out which of the international ships are in port, and who their officers are?"

"Course I can," Trent said.

"Good. Once you have the names, we'll see about talking to them."

"I can do that," Trent said.

"No, we don't want to alert the puppet master if we're getting close. For now, just bring the names back here. Then I'd like you to help Mac and Miss Kent check those names for any connections to the companies we're looking at."

Trent grimaced, but made a note.

"Miss Kent and Mac, in addition to cross-checking the shipping information when Trent brings it back, can you two go back through the financial information you've amassed and look for any connections to our suspects?"

"We can do that," Miss Kent said.

"Anything more we can discover about the puppet master or his businesses will help," Granville said. "And if you start to see patterns…"

"We'll let you know," she said.

"Emily?" he said, meeting her eyes.

She smiled. "I'll keep working with Clara on unmasking what Mr. Bray is up to. Unless Laura and Mac need my help?"

She looked to Miss Kent, seated beside her. Who shook her head. "We're fine for now."

"Scott and I will work on finding out what the remaining three on our original list look like," Granville said. "And dig into all of them, especially the ones that end up on our primary list. Starting by meeting with the two reporters and both lawyers, as well as our banker.

"Then can we go back to the docks and start asking questions?" Trent asked.

"That depends what we find," Granville said. "We need answers. If we can't find them directly, we're all going to be combing through dusty documents."

Trent scowled and opened his mouth. A frown from Scott had him closing it again.

"Then we have a plan," Granville said. "And a villain to catch."

4 0

Since the Terminal City Club was central for all of them, Granville had asked both reporters and both lawyers to meet with him and Scott there. It was still early enough that the bar was deserted, and the seven of them pulled up chairs around one of the larger round tables. As he'd requested earlier, one of the waiters from the dining room brought in cups, several pots of coffee with creamers and sugar bowls, and then departed.

When the six of them had the room to themselves, Granville thanked them for joining him on such short notice. "I have an update, and looking for your input. My hope is that collectively we can create a workable list of potential suspects."

He handed around the copies of the revised list Miss Rizzo had prepared for this meeting. "This is our best information to date, derived from various sources. The information is highly speculative, and very confidential. I'm looking for your comments, and your additions to this list."

"You do realize you only brought this element of the investigation to us two days ago?" Draper said as he rapidly scanned the names.

Granville nodded. "Yes. And I made clear how short our working timeline was."

"Hmmpf," Draper said. "Well, I've made progress. In addition to a number of phone calls, I spent far too much time in our newspaper archives."

Better the reporter than himself. "You have names, then?" Granville asked.

"Of course," Draper said. "Three of them are already on your list, two of whom were at Randall's trial. One is new."

And he gave them the four names, and a brief summary of what had happened to each. The financial catastrophes ranged from bad stock investments to failing harvests on family estates to one fellow who'd been cut off from family funds entirely.

Granville made quick notes on his copy, adding checkmarks to the names that were already there, and writing in the new name. The list now numbered seven.

It rather surprised him how unstable the lives of the truly wealthy could be. Though as someone who had in the past been too fond of gambling, it probably shouldn't.

Risks always seemed reasonable. Until they weren't.

"I have two names, but only one of them is not on this list," O'Hearn said, and gave the same level of detail that Draper had.

Granville's list now had eight names on it. He looked across the table. "Randall, Carver, can you add anything to this list?"

"I have no additional names to add, I'm afraid," Carver said. "But my list had these four men on it." And he pointed them out.

Interestingly, Randall's list agreed with Carver's.

Now Granville's list had three names with three checkmarks, two names with one, one name with two checkmarks, two names with one and one with none.

"Interesting," he said, passing it around the table. Each man looked at it without comment, then passed it on.

When the list reached him again, Granville glanced at it, then looked around the table. "Let's see if we can narrow this list down a little," he said. "Draper, can you describe your four? I'm looking for height, build and coloring."

"You have a description?" Draper demanded. "Why didn't you tell us that before?"

"I have a possible description, from two sources, neither of them entirely trustworthy. I'm not certain this is actually our man. I didn't have either description when we last spoke."

"So?" Carver said.

"I'd like to hear your descriptions first," Granville said.

"I suppose that avoids bias," Draper said. "Very well." And gave him brief summaries that sounded like police reports.

As Granville made notes on his list, he wondered if Draper had covered the crime beat at some point. He'd certainly developed solid investigative skills somewhere.

"So. Do they match your 'possible' description?" Draper asked, putting a sarcastic edge on the final words.

"Let's hear from the other two first. If possible, I'd like brief descriptions of all these men."

"I'm next," O'Hearn said, and gave them two more descriptions.

All eyes turned to Carver. Who gave them a tight smile, and fixing his gaze on Granville, described the last three men. "Now it's your turn. What do you know?"

He grinned, then summarized what they'd learned since he'd last talked with them.

"So," Draper said, "One of mine is too tall. Another too short."

Granville consulted his notes, and crossed off several names. "I believe we're down to three possible names, then. James Fairfield, George Knox, and Seth Roberts. All of them have at least two checkmarks."

He passed the list around the table again. "Which gives us a working list of suspects."

"If your description actually fits the right man," Draper said.

"Of course," Granville said. "Which is why we'll maintain a copy of the entire list. Just in case."

"So what happens now?" Carver asked.

"We keep digging into these three men. I'm planning to attend the benefit for the hospital tomorrow evening," Granville said. "I expect our three prime suspects will also attend, which should give me a chance to talk to each one."

"You're attending the Black and White Ball?" Draper said. "Those tickets are expensive."

Of course the business reporter would know that.

"It's a business expense," he said smoothly.

"You aren't planning to confront these three men who could be the puppet master at the ball, are you?" Carver asked before Granville could reply.

"Of course not," he said. "This will be merely a conversation."

"Especially since I assume you'll be escorting your fiancée," Draper said. "Her presence should keep him out of trouble."

He held back his grin and carefully didn't meet Scott's eyes, since in reality the reverse was likely to be true.

"As my business partner, Scott will also be attending the ball as well," he said. "Which doubles our ability to make use of the setting."

From the expression on their faces, this statement completely undermined Granville's explanation of how civilized his interactions with the suspected puppet master would be.

No matter. Their opinions weren't going to change his plans anyway.

***

WILLIAM WARDLE WAS AS PLEASED to see Scott and Granville as Trent had been dismayed to stay behind and update Mac and Miss Kent on the list of names. If he hadn't been so aware of the hours counting down to the ball, Granville would have been amused at their assistant's creative reasons as to why he needed to accompany them. Not today.

"Please excuse our lack of an appointment," Granville began, but Wardle waved it off.

"As it happens, I was just going to call you," the banker said.

"You've made progress, then?" Granville said, glancing around. Wardle's large office was as neat as the proverbial pin, despite the amount of paperwork on display. Everything was ordered in even stacks, each carefully aligned with the edges of his heavy desk.

"I'm quite pleased with it. See what you think," Wardle said, extracting a page from one of the stacks and sliding it across to Granville.

Accepting it with a nod, Granville accepted the list, written in a narrow stately hand. He scanned the four names written there in a matter of seconds, and passed the page to Scott.

Three of those names were on their short list. One was entirely new.

"We've been compiling a list also, from a variety of sources," Granville said, and passed his list to Wardle. "You'll note it includes all but one of your picks. We've obviously missed something."

Wardle placed a narrow pair of gold spectacles on his nose and considered their list. "All of these names make sense from one perspective or another. Though I think you'll find the men I've noted are a better fit for the puppet master you seek," he said. "Why are some of these names crossed out?"

Granville quickly explained their suspicions about the puppet master's appearance.

Wardle nodded, and handed the list back. "Then Jasper Cooper, the man who appears on my list but not yours is worth taking a hard look at. And I wouldn't write off Albert Heywood, either—he's taller than the subject described, but the way he carries himself? I have observed him, on occasion, and seen him hunching somewhat. Enabling him to present himself as being shorter than he is."

It sounded like something the puppet master would do. Yet another lie to hide behind. Granville made a note and added both names to the short list.

Five names now.

Knox. Heywood. Fairfield. Roberts. Cooper.

One of them was likely the puppet master.

But which one?

"Thank you," he said, looking up from the list and meeting Wardle's eyes. "I, we," and he indicated Scott and himself, "Truly value the time you've taken here."

"Nonsense. What are bankers for?" Wardle said with a straight face. "You will let me know when you catch this killer, won't you?"

"Of course."

"And will you be attending the ball tomorrow night?"

"I plan to be there, with my fiancée, Emily Turner. In fact, I hope to talk to all five of our suspects then. We'll see if I can make someone a little nervous."

"Indeed?" Wardle said, looking thoughtful. "Well, I'd been considering not attending this year. But I wouldn't want to miss seeing you and your lovely fiancée in action," the usually understated banker added with barely subdued glee.

"I look forward to it," Granville said, catching a glimpse of Scott's broad grin out of the corner of his eye.

"Don't say a word. I don't want to hear it," he told his partner as they exited.

Why did the mental picture of Emily at tomorrow night's ball, dressed in her finest gown, her eyes alive, make him suddenly nervous?

As soon Granville and Scott were back in the office, they gathered the team in the meeting room—except for Emily, who was off somewhere with Clara. He and Scott briefed the others on the meeting with the reporters and the lawyers, as well as the one with Wardle, and the subsequent changes to their suspect list.

"We went from three names back to five?" Trent said. "How is that an improvement? Are you sure that this banker knows what he's talking about?"

Granville laughed. Trent could always be counted on to break the formality of any meeting. "Yes, I'm sure. William Wardle is a big part of the reason we solved the Sinclair case, remember?"

"That was different," their incorrigible assistant said.

"At the core, both cases are about money—who has it and who wants it," Scott said. "And Wardle knows money."

"Oh," Trent said.

"I trust you were equally successful with the list of ships in port?"

"Of course," Trent said in what he probably imagined was a condescending tone, and handed across a scrawled list of names.

The lad's penmanship could use some improvement, Granville noted as he scanned the list. "This is thorough work. Thank you."

Trent shrugged as if it was nothing. "Welcome."

Hiding his own amusement, Granville turned to Mac "How are you making out with the names you had?"

Mac and Miss Kent exchanged glances. "We're still digging," Mac said. "But we'll get started on the new names, too. With a little luck we can get you and Scott some information before the ball tomorrow night."

"We'd appreciate it," Granville said. "Any information would help, though we intend to talk to all five men tomorrow night. You never know what a few leading questions might uncover."

"Just be careful," Miss Kent said unexpectedly. "I know Emily would never forgive you if you set yourself up as bait for this killer."

Which was exactly his plan, and from the look she gave him, Miss Kent knew that. Which meant Emily likely knew it too.

He winced a little at the reminder, and the not so subtle threat.

He'd have to rethink his original plan. From what he'd learned of the puppet master, the fellow wasn't given to hasty action. He'd keep an eye out for an opportunity to challenge the fellow in such a way that he'd take time to plan a response.

"Understood," he said with a grin. "And Scott has my back."

He pushed back his chair and stood up. "Let's get to it."

BACK IN HIS OWN OFFICE, Granville shut the door behind Scott.

Who turned and scowled at him. "So we're back to those dusty old ledgers, are we?"

"Ledgers?" Granville said with a grin, and holding up the list Trent had given him. "Now that we know which ships are in port, I was thinking we needed to check them out, myself. And I hear their captains are the thirsty sort."

Scott grinned at that. "Ship captains? Now you're talking good company. Might almost make up for that ball you're making me attend," he said.

"You mean the one Emily is making both of us attend?"

"You're really going to blame your fiancée?"

"Would it work?"

"No."

"Well then. Grab your coat and let's get out of here."

E mily spent most of Thursday afternoon at Clara's, briefing her friend on what was happening, and gleefully plotting Mr. Bray's downfall. But nothing had prepared her for the family dinner that evening.

When Mama had mentioned that morning that Mr. Bray would be joining them for dinner that night, Emily hadn't placed much importance on it. He'd been dining with them at least one evening a week since the engagement, and often two. This would be another such—a dull evening, but unavoidable. She'd given it no more thought than to resolve to interrupt any chance he might find to get Papa alone to talk business.

The reality was something different.

Dashing home from Clara's barely in time for the dinner bell, she hadn't even considered changing for dinner. It was a shock to find Jane wearing her most elaborate pink gown, and Mr. Bray in formal black and white. For a family dinner?

What was going on?

No-one explained anything, or even seemed to notice anything unusual. Instead, she sat silent through a tedious meal with Papa and Mr. Bray making inane conversation and praising each other. It felt like she'd swallowed lead, and every bite tasted like ash. This wasn't going to end well.

After dinner, Mr. Bray stood up and stated proudly that he had the support he needed to buy Trans Pacific Trading. And he brought out champagne, for them all to celebrate as Papa signed the papers that bought him a quarter ownership in the newly renamed company, which Mr. Bray proposed calling Pacific Gateway Trading.

"Subtle," Emily thought. Apparently Mr. Bray had been reading too many real estate listings. Did he really think a potential buyer would trust a company with a named pulled straight from the most blatant of the advertisements?

She wished madly that Granville were there so she could share the thought with him. But he was off tracking down shipping officers—and they were running out of time before the ball.

She knew he'd appreciate the humor of it all, despite the gravity of the situation Bray had created. And he wouldn't betray her with even the lightest twitch of a smile, either.

But he wasn't there. All she could do was to exchange panicked glances with Mama.

She hadn't expected Mr. Bray to act this fast. Mama was supposed to keep the two of them from even discussing business. How had the bounder managed it?

Not that it mattered now. It was too late to do more than watch helplessly as Papa signed the wretched thing. Then beamed as Mr. Bray opened the champagne with a loud pop and handed around glasses. Papa even looked proudly around the table as Jane's fiancé saluted what he termed "the grandest, most daring venture ever to hit these shores."

Which was probably how the fool saw his own undertakings, as he merrily pulled the wool over everyone's eyes, and conned them out of their life savings.

It took an effort of will to keep from rolling her eyes.

And an even bigger one to keep the desperation from showing on her face, as with one sweep of her father's pen, all her plans fell apart.

The only thing she'd been able to manage was a hurried word

with Mama about Papa holding onto the signed documents for a few days to 'review' them. Which was a stop gap at best, with Papa and Mr. Bray clapping each other on the back and calling each other partner.

How could she expose Bray for a conman who intended to use other people's money to set up a criminal company, when her own father was participating in the fraud?

There might be no hope for Jane, now.

4 2

With Trent's list of the ships running international routes that were currently in port—and the names of their senior officers—in hand, Granville and Scott strolled along the waterfront. Several of the ships listed might prove interesting sources of information. The challenge would be in finding a few officers who could be persuaded to talk.

They started at the Docksider, the grimy cafe that Officer Daniels had introduced them to. The location was good, since it was close to the Union Pacific wharves, where most of the overseas freighters docked. To be honest, though, it was the memory of those spicy flavors that had drawn Granville back.

He was hungry, and the food was good enough here to give them a perfect reason to be here. Besides, they might as well combine dinner with their information gathering.

Scott didn't complain much, either, he noted with a grin as huge bowls of some spicy shrimp and noodle dish he couldn't identify were set in front of them. At least he knew the shrimp would likely be local. And the fresh, sweet flavor of those shrimp, which contrasted nicely with a fiery sauce that nearly took his head off, confirmed that assumption.

He surveyed the other patrons. Most looked like seamen, which wasn't surprising. Sailors usually knew where to find the best food in any port. And working the international routes out of Vancouver, most of them had likely developed a taste for these spicy flavors on their Eastern runs.

There was a table of older men, captains by their uniforms, seated near the grimy window. He pointed them out to Scott.

"Recognize anyone?" he yelled in Scott's ear.

"Not yet. You?" Scott hollered back, and Granville barely heard him over the din.

"No. If neither of us sees anyone we know by the time we finish our food, I suggest we buy them a round."

"It's a plan," Scott said, and dug into his meal with single-minded determination.

Which wasn't quite what Granville had intended. But the food was, if anything, even better than the last time they'd been here.

Less than half an hour later, his offer to buy a round of whiskies for that table generated a careful scrutiny from four sets of eyes used to rapidly evaluating the individual merits of a very diverse crew. Acceptance and an invitation to join them quickly followed.

"You're Granville, aren't you? And Scott?" a swarthy fellow with a slight Spanish accent asked as soon as they sat down. "I'm Perez. Captain of the *Flores*, out of San Francisco."

"I am, and pleased to meet you," Granville said. "But I don't recognize you?"

"No reason to," Captain Perez said. "I like to know who the players are in all our ports. And Pinkerton's mentioned your firm as being the go to if I run into certain kinds of difficulty."

"That's good to hear," Granville said, surprised. He'd known their reputation was growing, but hadn't realized it extended beyond the city. Though that was one of the reasons he'd wanted to build an affiliation with Pinkerton's, after all. "And we're at your service, should you need us."

"Glad to hear it," Perez said. "But I doubt you're here tonight to look for new customers."

"Not exactly," he said with a grin. "We were hoping one of you might be able to help us out on an existing case."

"Be happy to," Perez said after a quick, searching glance around the table, and he introduced his fellow captains, with ships out of Singapore, Hong Kong and Australia—the last one being the *Aarongi*, to Granville's amusement. "Now, how can we help?"

"Have any of you dealt with Clark & Company, the importers? Or Arbuthnot, the fellow that runs the place?" Granville asked.

None of them had.

"The companies were founded under a pseudonym three or four years ago by someone I believe has ties to a family owned shipping firm."

"Out of Vancouver?" the Australian captain asked.

"Most likely out of England, and with ties to the Far East," Granville said. "The firm may have encountered a financial setback around that time."

"Also, there may be an East Coast connection," Scott added, with a sideways look at Granville.

"Three years ago, you say?" Perez said.

"Probably closer to four," Granville said.

"That's a pretty broad net you're casting there," the captain from Hong Kong said. "Quite a few firms lost money in the downturn."

"But wasn't there one that nearly went under?" the Australian captain said. "A London firm, if I'm not mistaken."

"You mean Quigley's?" Perez said. "And what a story that was. But I've never heard they had a connection here."

"Tell me," Granville said.

The story was a simple one—an old family firm, a few speculative investments combined with several ships lost to a bad year for storms, coupled with the market downturn in North America. They'd had to retrench, sell more than half their merchant fleet. And they'd still nearly gone under.

"You must have heard?" Perez said to him.

"Only a mention in passing," Granville said, remembering the round of clubs and gaming hells, interspersed with the occasional ball or society affair that had been his life then. "You said the firm was Quigley's?"

Perez laughed. "I did. It was a nickname, though. Old Lord Broadville was known by that in his younger days, when he sailed with his ships. Long time ago—most have forgotten. M'father told me."

"Broadville? That's the Baylor family, isn't it?" Granville said, trying to recollect which branches belonged to that family tree.

"It is."

Granville was picturing their revised suspect list. There were no obvious links to the Baylors, but it wasn't a family he knew well. He'd need to do some research. But this was the first real lead they'd had.

"From what I recall, the Arbuthnot's are a minor relation of the Baylors," the Australian captain added.

And there it was. Had the puppet master actually been arrogant enough to use a family name, no matter how obscure? Or this was another misdirection, aimed at pointing everyone in entirely the wrong direction? Still, even that could prove valuable, with the help of some diligent research.

"You ever hear of any relations of that family living out here?"

"In Vancouver?" the captain from Singapore said. "You're joking."

"No, I'm not. Why?"

"They're too top-lofty to live with colonials."

"From what I heard, that family's got a few black sheep," the Australian captain added. "They'd think nothing of banishing them to the colonies."

"And probably, having done so, would happily cut them loose the minute their financial problems hit," the captain from Hong Kong said.

That fit, and all too well. Which worried Granville. Either he really had hit the motherlode of gossip. Or this was yet another series of smoke screens the puppet master was hiding behind.

Either way, he needed to follow it up.

"Any of you know the names of these black sheep?" he asked. "Or anyone in town with trade connections to the family?"

"I never heard more than the rumors," the Australian captain said. "Once the economy recovered, so did the Baylors. And even without money, that family held some power in the shipping world."

"As I recall, there were a lot of rumors," Perez added.

"True. But once the economy turned around, the family rebuilt their business pretty damn fast. No one was going to say too much against them. The Far Eastern route is a pretty closed one—everyone knows everyone."

"Yet you don't have even one name for me?" Granville said. "I find that odd. Don't you, Scott?"

"Very odd," Scott said, scowling. "And after we bought the last few rounds, too."

"It isn't like we'll be discussing this with anyone," Granville said. "We are detectives, you know. You said yourself that Pinkerton's vouched for us."

Perez held up his hands, laughing. "Very well, I concede. I might have heard a name or two."

"Oh?"

"Fellow named Knox occasionally does some work with them. And I think Heywood does, too. Knox might even be a connection. But you need to understand. These are just rumors."

Both Knox and Heywood were on their final list. They were closing in on the puppet master, whoever he might be.

"Fair enough," Granville said calmly, jotting down the names. "Another round?"

"I wouldn't say no," Perez said.

Granville signaled to the bartender, then turned back to the table. "While we wait, what can you tell me about Heywood and Knox?"

"You'll have to be more specific," Perez said.

Granville shrugged. "What's the relationship between the two?"

"No idea," Perez said.

The Australian captain shook his head.

"It could be quite distant," the captain from Hong Kong said. "Neither one has direct dealings with the family firm, obviously."

"Are either of them involved in the import business, then?" Granville asked.

There was a quick exchange of glances around the table, followed by nods.

"Both of them?" Granville asked.

"Yes," Perez said. "But they're both small time."

"They working together?" Scott asked.

"No," the Australian captain said.

"Or seemingly not," Perez added.

"Meaning?" Granville asked.

Perez lifted on shoulder a little and let it fall. "None of the paperwork ever has both names on it. But it seems to me I've seen bills of lading where both of them have cargo on the same ship."

Interesting. Granville made a mental not to see if that bit of information led anywhere. "And what kinds of cargo do they import?"

"A little of everything, but you'd have to ask my cargo master if you care about details. Only from the Far East, though," the Australian captain said.

Granville made a note of that, just as the next round of whiskeys was delivered and quickly passed around. "My thanks for the information," he said, raising a glass. "Cheers."

<hr>

IT WAS several hours later that Granville and Scott left the Docksider. Despite a great deal of talk and several more rounds of whiskey, they hadn't learned much more that would help them find their quarry.

"What do you make of that?" Scott asked him as they made their way along Alexander Street. "It sounds like either Heywood or Knox is our puppet master."

"I don't trust it," Granville said. "It's almost too easy."

"Easy? It's taken us weeks to get to this point."

"True. But the puppet master? He's slippery," Granville said. "If he belongs to that family at all—which I'm inclined to doubt—he's the one no one remembers."

"So how are we supposed to find him if he's hidden behind so many layers of intrigue?"

"The way we solve any case. We just keep peeling away one layer at a time."

"More paperwork?"

"It's probably worth another call to Pinkerton's. And if I can lay my hands on a copy, I'll be spending some time with Burke's Peerage."

Scott cursed. "More dusty research that'll take forever. And then putting on a penguin suit and going to a ball. I need another drink."

"Good thing we still need to check out a few more bars, then, isn't it?" he said.

His partner scowled. "We keep buying all these rounds, we aren't charging Benton enough to make any money."

"Since we're essentially paying for information, it counts as an expense," Granville said. "Which Benton pays on top of our fee."

Scott's expression changed instantly. "Well, in that case, bring it on," he said, and quickened his stride.

43

Friday, September 28, 1900

The morning of the ball, Emily woke with her stomach fluttering as if full of butterflies. Which had less to do with the ball than it did with the utter destruction of all her plans for Bray's downfall. And for saving her sister.

How was she supposed to save Jane, now?

By the time Emily had eaten a hasty breakfast and drunk several cups of tea, though, she had the beginnings of a plan and was feeling a little more hopeful. Luckily she was to collect Clara in less than an hour, for a final fitting of her new ballgown with Madame. She didn't need the fitting—the measurements the modiste had taken would be fine. So she and Clara would have all day to devise a new plan for dealing with Mr. Bray.

Perhaps not surprisingly, Clara didn't see it like that. No matter how much Emily explained what had happened.

"Emily, this is your final fitting. For the ball gown you'll wear tonight. For your plan to work, your gown has to be perfect."

"Haven't you been listening? That plan has already been

destroyed. And if we can't come up with something else that will work in time, there's no point in my even going to the ball."

"And you're planning on telling your mother that?" Clara asked.

It was a low blow. They both knew that as one of the event's organizers, Mama would be embarrassed if all three of her daughters didn't attend.

"Fine. I'll go to the ball," Emily said. "But we need time to plan. And I've already done so many fittings. I'm sure Madame has enough measurements already to finish my gown. In any case, there's no time to do another now. Not if we're to come up with another plan by tonight."

"There's no time not to have that fitting," Clara said firmly. "You can't expose Mr. Bray if you don't have a dress for the ball."

"And if we don't have a workable plan, there's no need for me to go to the ball at all," Emily said. "This isn't something we can make up as we go, and you know it, Clara."

"I know, I know. But we can talk all day if we have to, Emily. The modiste was only able to squeeze in your fitting at nine-thirty this morning. And only because it is such an unfashionable hour," Clara said. "Really, you have to be there."

She paused, and stared at her friend. "I know that look. Emily, what are you plotting now?"

"Never mind, Clara," Emily said, seizing her friend's arm. "Grab your wrap and your bag, or we'll be late."

"I don't trust that look, Emily. You aren't going to try to change the dress or something at this late moment, are you?"

Ignoring Clara's questions, Emily dragged her towards the carriage. "Come along, Clara. We don't want to be late, do we?"

***

THE FITTING WAS every bit as painful as Emily had expected. She did feel a little twinge of awe at seeing how she looked in Madame's creation, though she'd never admit it. Who would ever have thought she could look like that?

And really, it had been worth it. Not only would she be finely enough dressed at this annoying ball to please the harshest of critics, one of the seamstresses had been unexpectedly helpful with her other dilemma. Not that she knew it, of course. But whenever the young brunette thought her employer was out of earshot, she complained about Madame's constant requests to make adjustments and little changes 'on the fly,' as she phrased it.

"She is good with a needle, but she won't last long," Clara whispered to Emily at one point. "Madame has ears like a bat, and she'll never put up with an assistant who is so critical of her genius."

"Mmmm," said Emily, too caught up in the idea the assistant's choice of phrase had triggered to pay much attention. They couldn't expose Mr. Bray outright, as she'd anticipated so eagerly. But by signing those papers, he'd now committed himself to fraud. Even if no one else knew it was fraud. Yet.

Mr. Bray couldn't pretend he had no intention of taking over the company now. Those papers might have given them a way to expose him after all. And without making either Jane or Papa look like a fool.

The minute their appointment was done, Emily turned to her friend. "Clara, after that ordeal I think I need a cup of tea. Shall we have a luncheon at Stroh's?"

It was ridiculously early, and Clara gave her an odd look, but she didn't challenge her. As Emily had expected, the lure of the Stroh's pastry cart was too strong for her friend to resist. Likely Clara knew exactly what Emily was up to, but neither of them cared.

<hr>

BY THE TIME EVENING CAME, Emily was bathed and standing in front of the cheval mirror in her room in her thin lawn shift, holding her breath as Hannah, their maid, tightened her corset. Emily cheated as she always did by drawing in a deep breath first, so that the laces could never be fully tightened. She intended to dance tonight. And she liked being able to be able to breathe while she did so.

Besides, in this new job of hers, she never knew when she might be required to chase after a suspect. Or even run from one, as she'd had to do last month. She could never do that in a tightly laced corset.

Hannah surely knew what she was up to. Especially since she also helped Emily's sisters dress. Jane and Susan would never deliberately leave their corsets a little loose, and would be shocked to know that Emily did so.

But the maid had never said a word. Nor had she attempted to draw Emily's laces tighter, or even let on that she knew. Which was a blessing.

Emily gave the girl a little half-smile along with her thanks, and received a slight nod of the head in return. And was that a wink? It left her with a warm feeling, along with an odd worry about how she'd manage once she and Granville were wed.

As Hannah lifted the deceptively simple creamy white gown over Emily's head and let it slide down her body, then began to do up the tiny buttons running down the back, Emily avoided looking in the mirror and followed the thought.

Surely she wouldn't need a maid just to help her tighten her corsets once she was wed? And their house wasn't big enough for more than a housekeeper cum cook. Yet she couldn't imagine Granville—John—doing the task for her. She flushed at the intimacy of the thought. Perhaps someone would invent corsets that a woman could tighten herself. Then she wouldn't have to worry about such nonsense.

Though really, she was just nervous and excited about her new gown. Was it too much? She couldn't bear to look. And the ball. There was so much riding on it.

Could she and Clara pull off their new plan? Would Granville be able to identify the puppet master?

"Oh, miss," Hannah was saying. "It's lovely on you."

And it was. It really was.

Clara and her modiste had outdone themselves.

Emily just hoped it would be enough.

44

At nine o'clock that evening, Vancouver's grandest citizens turned out dressed in their finest attire for the Fifth Annual Black and White Ball in honor of St. Paul's hospital. It made Granville smile. The formality, the orchestra playing softly, the glittering jewels—all of it reminded him of some of London's finest balls.

The contrast between the two cities couldn't have been greater. There was sophisticated London, with its centuries of history. Here was colonial Vancouver, which hadn't seen two decades yet, and was perched on a rocky inlet between a wilderness and the vast ocean. Yet he felt at home here in a way he never had in London.

With Emily on his arm, Granville had even arrived early for this event, breaking a long-term habit of being late to every ball he'd ever attended. Tonight, he wanted to watch his suspects before he sought an introduction. All five were here tonight. And he planned to spend as much time as he could with each of them.

If one of the five men was his quarry, the odds were that the puppet master wouldn't cause any trouble tonight.

Everything Granville had learned about the fellow suggested he was a strategist, and meticulous with the details. He'd know how important Granville's fiancée had become to him.

Granville wanted Emily safe even more than he wanted to take the puppet master down. And he wanted the fellow caught so badly he could taste it at the back of his throat—lodged there, nearly choking him.

With any luck, the puppet master wasn't even paying attention to Emily yet. But this evening was Granville's opportunity to finally get some answers. Or at very least get the fellow focused on him.

He smiled, though it was little more than a baring of teeth.

"You're looking a bit savage, there," Scott said from beside him, as Emily's hand tightened on his arm. "Unless you're planning on attacking one of the guests, you might want to back off."

Granville didn't respond, but he stopped smiling.

Instead, he watched the couples taking to the dance floor as the band struck up the first dance. One of the men here tonight was likely the puppet master. No matter how careful he was, one of these days the fellow was going to make a slip. And Granville planned to be there to catch him.

This might just be that day.

For now, he'd be content to stay in the ballroom and watch the interactions. No one would be in the card room yet anyway. In any case, he'd have to stay in the ballroom at least long enough to dance several times with Emily before he could disappear.

Which was never a hardship. And in the gown she wore tonight, she looked simply stunning. Someone had outdone themselves.

STANDING beside Granville on the edge of the dance floor, Emily could feel the tension humming through him as he scanned the faces present. He was looking, she knew, for the five men on their list of suspects. Glancing up, she could practically see the fierce concentration he was bringing to his examination of every male there who might fit their criteria for the puppet master.

She put a hand on the smooth fabric of his sleeve just as Scott bent down to say something to him, and she could feel Granville's tension decrease a little. Though his focus didn't change.

The evening had begun with the usual socializing. Once everyone had shed their wraps—necessary now that the evenings had turned cooler—they gathered in small groups to socialize and comment on each other's attire.

Emily's own gown attracted more attention than she'd anticipated. She shared a victorious glance with Clara when Mrs. Smythe's jaw dropped at her first sight of Emily's new look. That alone suddenly made all those fittings she'd had to endure seem worthwhile.

Then came the first dance. The ball opened with a waltz, led off by the ladies who had organized the event, and their partners. Despite her frustration with Papa, Emily had to admire the figure her parents cut as he and Mama move slowly and gracefully around the dance floor.

As other dancers began to crowd onto the floor, Granville looked down at her. "Shall we?" he said.

She nodded, and he led her onto the floor.

Emily kept forgetting how much she enjoyed the twirling and the dipping of the waltz, at least the way Granville danced it. He was a wonderful partner, and she'd never felt as graceful dancing as she did with him. As the room whirled past, she caught sight of Jane and Mr. Bray across the floor, and her heart thumped in her chest.

It was nearly time.

Her sister's fiancé looked slightly uncomfortable in his formal attire, which Emily hadn't noticed before. She wondered if he were less accustomed to formal events that he had been pretending. What exactly was his background? She really still didn't have an answer to that.

Perhaps that was an avenue worth following up.

Jane too seemed less comfortable and less graceful dancing with her fiancé then she had with previous partners Emily had noticed her with. Everything seemed to confirm that her sister didn't belong with this man. She had to save her from a marriage she'd regret forever.

Yet her heart thumped even harder in her chest as she considered her new plan. Would it even work?

When she'd told Clara her plan earlier in the day, everything she had in mind had seemed so reasonable. But actually being here in this elaborate ballroom, with everyone looking so formal, it no longer felt that way. She risked a huge creating a huge scandal, perhaps without even accomplishing her goal of unmasking Mr. Bray as the charlatan he was.

Was it really worth the risk?

Then she took a hard look at Jane's uncomfortable face. The alternative might see her sister wed to this horrible man for life. It didn't bear thinking of.

And even without considering Jane, Mr. Bray had to be stopped. He was defrauding Papa, and others, through his schemes. And he might also give them the lead they needed to unmask Granville's puppet master. Unwittingly, of course.

Any one of those things would be worth the risk of a little social embarrassment. Wouldn't they?

It didn't matter anyway. She had to try. She couldn't live with herself if she didn't.

She glanced around for Clara, and found her waltzing with yet another gentleman she suspected had aspirations for her friend's hand in marriage. Clara's face wore what Emily thought of as her polite look. Which wasn't a good sign for her dance partner's hopes.

Perhaps it was time to track down Tim O'Hearn again. Clara always look much happier when she was around him. Whether she was prepared to admit that or not. After all the help Clara had given her, Emily wanted at least do something to return the favor.

Even if Clara didn't much appreciate her efforts, and kept telling her not to interfere. But she'd seen the way Clara looked at him, when she thought no one was noticing.

When the music ended, Emily tucked her hand back into Granville's arm and pointed out a small group forming off to one side of the ballroom. It included Mr. Bray and her sister, her parents, Clara and Clara's current partner. Perfect.

"That looks an interesting group. Let's join them," she said. Granville grinned down at her, then led her across the floor to join the others.

"Is there anyone you need to talk to?" she whispered to him as they walked.

"I think most of those discussions will happen later, in the rooms set aside for the card players," he said. "But we need to pay attention to the actions of everyone on our lists. If the opportunity presents itself, we should join their groups. And you?"

"If Mr. Bray happens to be part of one of those groups..." she said, giving him a meaningful look.

He covered her hand where it rested on his arm for a moment. "Of course," was all he said. But there was an entire conversation in those few words.

As she and Granville danced, Emily paid more attention to how other couples were dancing than to how she was. It was a good thing Granville was such a strong dancer. After a few dances, she began to recognize the shifting patterns they made on the floor, and as they moved around the edges of the room, socializing.

It reminded her of the colorful, ever-shifting patterns she'd seen in the kaleidoscope she'd loved as a child. Only this was much more intriguing.

She kept a particular watch for Mr. Bray, and for those of the suspects she recognized. Several of them she recognized, like Mr. Fairfield and Mr. Knox. For some of the others, she knew the wife but didn't recognize the husband, so she was reduced to guessing.

After several more dances, Emily spotted Mr. Bray and Jane making their way towards a group of dancers that included at least one of their suspects. She recognized Mr. and Mrs. Fairfield, who were always part of any large social gathering. She also recognized

Mrs. Heywood as part of the group, though she didn't know if the gentleman escorting her was her husband.

She gently squeezed Granville's arm. He followed her glance, then gave her a quick smile and smoothly changed direction.

They joined the group, and after a nudge from Jane, Mr. Bray introduced them to those they hadn't met. He looked a little annoyed to be doing so, Emily thought, and wondered why that might be. She glanced quickly from face to face, but the others simply wore what she called their 'social faces'. Which was frustrating, because it told her nothing.

The conversation was light, and mostly centered around the great success this ball was proving to be. Mrs. Knox was on the organizing committee with Mama, so she was particularly proud and pleased to discuss the success of the ball.

As their wives chatted, the men said little. Emily wished they'd be a little more forthcoming. Though she did note an exchange of glances between Mr. Fairfield and Mr. Knox. And Mr. Bray seemed to be trying to catch both those gentlemen's eye.

They seemed to be ignoring him, though. And Jane had a firm hand on his arm.

It was frustrating to realize that the meaningful conversations between the men would likely happen in the card rooms over the next hour or two. And women were most definitely not welcome there.

But still. Men discounted what Emily was beginning to think of as women's secret power. The constant exchange of information, with an emphasis on seemingly mundane details. In other words, gossip.

Which was available to her.

And which she was planning to use to its fullest extent.

WHEN THE LAST notes of the waltz ended, Granville led Emily off the dance floor and back to where her mother, her sisters, and Clara now stood.

"It's warm in here," she said, opening the ivory spokes of her painted fan and fanning herself. "And I've lost sight of our suspects. Well, the ones I recognize, at least."

"I suspect the migration to the card room has begun. And that I'll be abandoning you shortly," he said with a grin.

"I don't mind. I have my own plan to unleash," she said, and glanced at Clara, who was deep in conversation with Jane.

"Bray?" he said.

"Of course," she said. "Though there's no sign of him now, which is a little concerning. Perhaps he's gone to fetch Jane a glass of punch."

"I was hoping to see him in the card rooms," he said.

"If you do, watch him carefully. I doubt he'll be there for long. Not when they are so newly engaged," Emily said. "Clara advises me it sends entirely the wrong message. My sister would never forgive him."

"And they're not married yet," Granville said, completing the thought for her.

"Exactly. He won't risk that." She smiled, slowly, as she said it.

"You do know that's a lethal-looking smile?" Granville said to her. And she made it believable, which wasn't easy. Since she'd joined the agency, Emily was rapidly growing into a force to be reckoned with.

"What a good thing it isn't directed at you, then," she answered with a sideways glance that had a hint of mischief in it.

He had to agree. "Looks like Bray is in deep trouble now."

"I hope so," she said. Then endeared herself to him by looking suddenly uncertain. "This has to work."

"It will," he said. "He won't be expecting to get his comeuppance from his fiancée's younger sister."

"Thank you," she said. "Then he should pay really closer attention, shouldn't he?"

"He should indeed," he said with a chuckle. "Since I'll be headed for the card room shortly, I should request the pleasure of your company for the supper dance now."

"So formal," she said. "You don't need to ask, you know. And besides, it's the perfect chance to compare notes."

"My thoughts exactly," he said.

Just then, William Wardle tapped him on the shoulder. "Come along, my boy. There are several people you should meet."

"First let me introduce you to my fiancée," he said, and turned to do so.

4 5

Wardle ushered Granville into a back room that was serving as the bar and card room, and was already pungent with the cigar smoke. There he introduced him to Heywood, who was talking intently with Fairfield. Granville noted Knox off to one side was chatting with Bray, and wished he could overhear what the two of them were discussing so intently. Especially if Emily was right that Bray would need to get back to his fiancée before long.

Granville shook hands with Heywood and Fairfield and was soon chatting easily with them. He was relieved to see Scott following them in, and joining a different group. Not that he expected an ambush here, but they had each other's backs for a reason.

Before he knew it Roberts and Cooper had joined the conversation, followed in short order by Knox and Bray. Granville glanced at Wardle. This was far too dangerous. What was the wily banker up to now?

When two other men who were on the original list of suspects joined the group, Granville recognized a social pattern he'd seen many times before, in the card rooms set aside for gentlemen at various glittering events. Though for him it had happened more often in London than here or in the Klondike.

These were all men who shared a certain position in society, and the card room was a normal gathering place for them. Of course they'd know each other. Their backgrounds were different—some English, some American and several Canadian from back east, but judging by their accents, all had attended either Oxford or Cambridge. And they had all suffered recent financial hardships, whether they knew that about each other or not. Likely they did. That shared background and experience would naturally draw them together.

Except for Bray. He didn't fit in, and Granville wondered if that was further proof that the puppet master was just using the fellow. It seemed even more likely when Bray quickly excused himself and returned to the ballroom. Which of these seven men had Bray come here to talk with?

Knox was the obvious choice, but obvious choices made him uneasy.

Granville fought to keep his expression neutral when he suddenly recognized that, unlike Bray, he did fit in with these men. He too came from a privileged background, including a degree from Oxford. He too was used to operating at a certain level of society. And at a certain level of wealth. He too had lost all of that—if mostly through his own choice—then fought his way back. And Wardle knew it.

It was an unsettling realization. He had a great deal in common with these men. With the puppet master.

Which didn't mean they were anything alike—they weren't. Any more than the rest of the men on his list were like the fellow. There was only one puppet master.

But it did mean that Granville was uniquely qualified to find and unmask him. And to see the puppet master pay for his crimes. He'd do it, too. With the attempts on his team's life firmly in mind, he was determined to take the puppet master down.

Whoever he was.

As the conversation ebbed and flowed, Granville was surprised to find himself enjoying the company. At first the group seemed all too similar—they even looked alike. Medium brown hair in the shorter cut that was popular now, light blue eyes—though Cooper's were a light greenish hazel that changed according to the light. All were clean shaven, and of medium height. Except for Heywood, who was taller, but slouching enough that his extra height wasn't easily apparent. All seven would easily fit the physical description he had for the puppet master.

Physically, at least, Granville didn't fit, since he was darker and taller than the others, his eyes a darker blue. It was the one difference between him and them, and he was unexpectedly pleased by it.

He did wonder how such strikingly similar men had become a group, and if the puppet master was behind that, as well. Collectively, they provided a very effective background for him to blend into.

Gradually, though, the different personalities of the men around him began to emerge. Heywood had a sly wit. Roberts was a practical man at heart, though he tried to cover it with trivialities. Fairfield was a gentleman to his fingertips, and seemed a little out of place beside the very business-like Knox.

And Cooper was a poker player, a man Granville had played against in several backroom dens without ever knowing his name. Too far away to speak privately, Granville raised his glass in a silent toast, and they exchanged smiles acknowledging their previous encounters.

Whatever else the fellow might be, Cooper was not the puppet master. His gambling style made that clear—he wasn't a calculating enough poker player.

Which left four men. Or possibly six. He wasn't ready to abandon the original list of suspects quite yet.

He looked from face to face. It told him nothing. Which wasn't a surprise.

Everything he knew or had guessed about the puppet master said that the fellow had worked hard to keep his criminal side invisible. He'd done so effectively, too. After two weeks of investigating, they still couldn't track exactly how he was profiting from his crimes. Much less prove anything.

They didn't even know who he really was.

The puppet master was playing all of them. And winning. It was insulting, is what it was.

As he nodded and chatted, Granville was watching the other men carefully, noting how they interacted, the subtle mannerisms that betrayed them. He absorbed impressions of each of them, evaluating them as he would have done had they sat at a poker table. He didn't expect this to be easy. This was the puppet master's game, after all.

For now.

And Granville's entire focus was on taking that game away from him.

When Emily saw Mr. Bray reappear in the ballroom and hurry to Jane's side, she had to take a breath to bolster her own courage. The time had come. And she knew what to do, after all.

She considered the newly engaged couple. Mr. Bray looked smug about something. Had he connected with the puppet master? If so, she hoped Granville had seen them.

Her attention switched to her sister. Despite the proprietary grip Jane had on her fiancé's sleeve, her sister looked a little annoyed with him. Perfect.

"Emily?" Clara's voice came from just behind her. "Is it time?"

"I think so," she said. "Are you ready?"

"Emily, I am feeling a little faint," her friend said. "And nauseous."

"Well, the lemonade here is a little insipid," Emily said. "Not to mention warm. Perhaps that is the problem?"

"Emily!" Clara said, concealing her desire to glare at her rather well, Emily thought. "I need your company in the retiring room. Now."

"Oh, very well," Emily said. She knew she shouldn't, this was serious, and they had to play it exactly right if it was going to work. But for some reason she felt better for teasing Clara. And she thought her friend did too.

Besides, it would be Clara's turn to tease her very soon. And Clara would have a chance to get more than even. Which she'd probably enjoy immensely. Even if Emily wouldn't.

Maybe because of it.

The retiring room was empty, and Clara was quick to splash some water on her handkerchief and apply it to her brow.

"You're right, I do feel better. Though do you think I'm pale?" Clara asked as she peered at herself in one of the mirrors above the marble counters holding the two sinks on the far wall. She patted her cheeks a little, at watched the color in them deepen.

"There, that's better," she said, then cocked a head a little to one side. It was their signal.

Emily heard it too—the rustle of silks and laces in the corridor outside the room.

"But Emily, I don't understand how you could not have heard the news about your sister's fiancé," Clara was saying. "Surely she must tell you everything."

"I simply can't believe what you were told is true," Emily said, pretending to keep her voice down, but in reality pitching it so it would carry. "Tell me again what you heard?"

"I heard that Jane's fiancé has found the investors he needed and bought out the company he has been working for."

"I don't understand. That is good news," Emily said. "Jane will be thrilled."

"No, she won't," Clara said flatly. "Because that is not the whole story."

"Then what is?"

"He's been lying to his investors. He has no money of his own to put into the company. He had to borrow it."

Emily laughed. "Men borrow money for their businesses all the time."

"From criminals?" Clara sounded horrified.

"He wouldn't borrow money from a criminal," Emily said.

"It only makes sense that he would," Clara said. "Since he is intending to run the business as a criminal enterprise."

"Jane would never agree to marry such a man."

"Well, she has."

"How can you say such a thing," Emily exclaimed. "Have you proof?"

"Well, not proof exactly," Clara said. "Though I hear Jane does."

"My sister has proof that her own fiancé is a con man and a criminal?" Emily said. "How can that be?"

Clara gave an elaborate shrug, seemingly unaware of the eyes peering in at them around the edge of the door. "She may have made an error in accepting his proposal. But she is more than making up for it now. You know, I've come to admire your sister Jane."

"Jane?" Emily said. "Really?"

"Indeed," Clara said. "She seems to have acted fast, and with great fortitude. Why, I think she might even be called a heroine."

"Jane, a heroine? You're talking about my sister Jane?"

"Yes, of course. Don't you think so?"

"I think I need to talk to her. And this fiancé of hers."

Clara smiled, and patted her shoulder consolingly. "That's probably a good idea. Why, from what I heard, she's planning to confront the villain soon with the proof she's been collecting. I'm expecting fireworks."

Emily could just hear a very low murmur coming from the hall. It was exactly the noise she'd been hoping for—the sweet sound of gossip, taking hold.

"Fireworks? Surely you're wrong. I need to find Jane immediately," Emily said, pitching her voice just loudly enough to give the eavesdroppers in the hall fair warning. And was rewarded by the soft sounds of ladies scrambling to get back to the ballroom before they were discovered.

It was working.

Now they needed to return to the ballroom and see if Jane had continued to unintentionally play along. That would be the trick.

Taking Clara's arm, Emily allowed herself a small grin. She felt much better now that her plan was underway.

And if Jane didn't manage to do what she needed to? Emily knew just the right buttons to push. Jane had always had a temper that she didn't hide as well as she thought she did.

An hour passed, and then two. The whiskey flowed, and the air grew ever heavier with cigar smoke. Wardle joined another group after a time, as did several of the other fellows. The core group —Knox, Fairfield, Cooper, Roberts, and Heywood—remained, as did two of the suspects on Granville's longer list. He'd thought of suggesting they all adjourn to the card room, but was reluctant to do so. They'd all moved to a round table that made conversation easier. And he was learning more here than he'd expected.

Watching the seven men interact with each other and with him, it was clear they knew each other well socially. They probably they did business together as well. Deals were made in surroundings like this.

He kept waiting for a leader to emerge for the group, but it didn't happen.

On the surface, this appeared to be a group of equals. There was no sign of anyone jockeying for position, no good-natured joshing that spelled out an underlying hierarchy. He didn't believe it.

And he should know. He'd fled to the Klondike to escape England's rigid social hierarchy with its petrified expectations of class and privilege. Only to find other hierarchies emerging in the goldfields. The only difference was that hierarchies on the diggings were based on gold rather than class, survival skills rather than social ones. Though the ability to tell a good tale was welcome anywhere.

So he knew there was a hierarchy at work here, real or imagined. Probably with the puppet master sitting at the top. The others would each have a place in that hierarchy, and a role to play. He just couldn't see it.

It was time to stir things up.

He maneuvered the conversation around to his recent journey to the opium factory. Cooper, who was now sitting beside him, looked intrigued. "You're a smoker then?"

"Only occasionally," Granville said. And looked pointedly at the thick cigar Cooper was holding.

The fellow grinned and offered him one. Which he accepted with pleasure—Cuban cigars were something he hadn't indulged in since he was last in London.

"And only of these," Granville added as he lit up and drew in a satisfying breath of the rich tobacco.

"Then why an opium factory?" Knox asked from across the table.

Granville smiled slightly. "It's part of a case I'm working on at the moment. I can't give any details, I'm afraid."

"Now that's hardly sporting of you," Heywood said from beside Cooper. "Tell us more. We don't need to know names."

"Yes we do," Knox said.

The two exchanged a look, which Granville couldn't read. Were they allies, or was Knox subtly challenging Heywood?

"The story will be enough," Heywood said, finality in his tone.

Knox finished his drink in one swallow and signaled for another round.

Interesting. Granville glanced around the table and found all eyes on him. Apparently they all wanted to hear the story.

So he told them a carefully scrubbed version of the truth. Their trek through Chinatown. Questioning the manager in the opium factory. What he'd learned of opium importing. He simply avoided anything other than a carefully coded version of why he was there. And he left out any mention of Scott or Trent.

If he was painting a target on his own chest, he wasn't going to endanger them, too. But if his actions kept the puppet master's attention away from Emily and the rest of the team, any risk he took was well worth it.

"So what was it like? At the opium sellers, I mean. And the factory?" Knox asked.

"Both establishments were remarkably clean and orderly," he said. "Aside from a strong smell of slightly scorched peanut butter at the factory, and an overabundance of gilt at the store, it could have been anywhere," he said.

"What about the danger?" Fairfield asked.

"There was none," Granville said. "Not a thug in sight."

"Don't you find Chinatown dangerous?" Roberts asked. "Menacing, even?"

"Hardly. I was there as a customer, remember. No, it's the garden variety criminal type I'm after who is dangerous," Granville said.

"Though not nearly as dangerous as he seems to think himself," he added, as if to himself.

If Granville was reading the puppet master right, the fellow would hear that comment as a direct challenge. Something he'd have to answer in person. How could he resist?

And Granville suspected he couldn't. Or at least he hoped he wouldn't.

He drained his whiskey, and glanced at the avid faces around the table. "But that's all I can tell you, I'm afraid. Everything else is confidential."

And he held to that, despite the repeated demands from the gentlemen—and at least one criminal—gathered around the table.

The talk soon turned to other matters, most notably a discussion of the local political climate. Granville only half-listened as he watched the players around the table. If he were wagering, he'd be betting that Knox was the puppet master.

Or possibly Heywood.

Wardle had been right about Heywood. The way he carried himself was deceptive. For a man nearly as tall as Granville, he managed to leave the impression that he was as short as the other men around the table.

So, Heywood.

Or Knox.

Though he wasn't quite ready to cross out Fairfield. Something about the man, and the way he interacted with the others struck Granville as odd. He didn't stand out, and yet, somehow he kept ending up at the center of the group, the one all six men revolved around.

And now that he'd noticed it, that pattern grew clearer. They were all interacting with Fairfield or Knox, more than with each other.

Granville covertly watched his three primary suspects. Their looks were similar enough, he could almost believe they were related. And yet generic enough that there were four other men who looked very similar.

The puppet master was a wily one. Had he even chosen acquaintances who could serve as yet another smoke screen? Or had they gravitated together because they had similar backgrounds?

Heywood had stayed mostly silent, while Knox had been badgering him with questions. Either action would be in character. As was Fairfield's near-invisible control of the group's interactions.

None of them was giving anything away now.

That was when he noticed Fairfield was fingering something in his waistcoat pocket. A quick glance told him that while the pocket watch was concealed, the watch chain had the rich gleam of high-quality gold. Like the one Parvo had described.

It was hardly a unique item in this group. Likely all the men present had a pocket watch of some kind, most of them made of heavy gold. But Fairfax was the first one he'd noticed make that particular gesture.

Could Fairfield be their puppet master?

It was still impossible to know.

Well, he'd set the hook. Now it was up to the puppet master. Would he bite?

                                  4 8

───────────────

When Granville rejoined her just as the supper dance was
about to begin, Emily was relieved. Not that she doubted
he'd return, exactly. Just that she'd already learned that investigations seldom proceeded the way one expected them to. And certainly
not to a predefined timeline.

What if he'd been caught up in a conversation he couldn't leave?

Then she'd have been left partnerless and embarrassed, not just
for the dance, but for the supper following it. And to her surprise,
her new gown made her very noticeable indeed. Which had been
very helpful in laying a trap from Mr. Bray.

And would have been very *un*helpful if Granville had been
delayed.

Besides, there was so much she wanted to discuss with him. The
whole evening had been rife with small clues that, taken together,
might give them a direction on this annoying case of theirs.

To say nothing of the Bray problem. For so she'd begun to think
of it.

She thought her plan had worked. Clara thought it had worked.
And Clara, of anyone, would know if their story was spreading as
they'd hoped.

Still, she'd found herself wanting to talk to Granville, to tell him about it and hear his perspective. As well as to hear what he'd learned in the card room.

Which, as it turned out, had been a great deal, she decided, as he told her in a low voice what he'd learned of their suspects as they whirled around the room in time to a Strauss waltz.

"So you think Mr. Knox is the puppet master?" she asked, pitching her voice so no one but he would hear it. "But that's wonderful."

"He seems the most likely," Granville said. "But it still feels too easy."

"Even after all this time?"

"Even then," he said, and whirled her into a turn that had the room tilting around her. "He seems… too obvious a choice."

"And our puppet master is anything but obvious."

"Exactly. I'm not ready to discount the other two."

"Still, we are down to three suspects," Emily said, watching him closely. It wasn't like Granville not to have a plan already in place. There was something he wasn't telling her. Which meant either he was protecting her, or she wasn't going to like whatever he'd already set in motion. She suspected the latter.

But the middle of a waltz was hardly the time to be digging into it.

"Three potential suspects," he said. "Pinkerton's came through with some information this afternoon, and Heywood looks almost as strong a candidate as Knox. Which we can talk about over supper. But tell me about your plan for exposing Bray."

She gave him a skeptical look, but accepted his change of topic. For now.

"I think it worked," she said, feeling again the glow of success when she had begun to hear snippets of the story she and Clara had spread being discussed in little pockets of conversations. Which stopped the moment anyone noticed that she was within earshot.

"People are already talking, though I can't tell yet whether they'll believe he is who he really is," she said. "But they're watching him and Jane. And noticing."

"Which is exactly what you planned," Granville said. "Well done."

"I hope so," she said. "We won't know for a few days yet."

"It might be telling who chooses to speak with him now," Granville said as the final notes of the waltz played. He guided her through a last turn, then offered his arm. "Supper, milady?"

She smiled and placed her hand on his arm. "I'm famished," she said with a private smile. "All this intrigue, you understand."

AFTER THE LIGHT supper they were served, Granville returned to the card room. It was nearly one a.m. when he rejoined Emily in the ballroom for the last waltz of the evening. She was tired, and yet exhilarated. It had been the most exciting dance of her life, and perhaps the most exciting evening.

She suddenly wished they were going home together, just the two of them, to the house she'd helped choose. Where he now lived alone. Then Scott joined them and the moment was lost.

After saying their goodbyes, and slowly making their way through the crowds to the front doors, the three of them left the ball. When the carriage Granville had hired for the evening stopped in front of her parent's house, he escorted her to her front door. Scott waited in the carriage.

Emily turned towards him, and looked up. "You two will be discussing the ball after this, won't you?"

"Probably."

"I wish I could join you. There was so much going on tonight, and very little chance to talk about it without being overheard. It feels I could talk for hours, just to understand what all happened."

"That's because we're nearing the end of the case," he said. "Instead of having too little information, we almost have too much. Enough that it's hard to tell what is relevant and what isn't," he said.

"Well, I find it frustrating," she said.

"As do I," he said. "Especially when you look as lovely as you do tonight. That ball gown is truly spectacular on you, by the way."

She felt the heat rising in her cheeks. "Thank you. Clara was right about it. It did give me more confidence, knowing that I looked the part."

"Looked the part?" he repeated with a grin. "Were you playing a role, then?"

"In a way," she said, smiling back. And explained what Clara's Grandmama had told her. "For my plan to expose Mr. Bray to work, I needed people to pay attention to me. And in this gown—this costume, if you will—they did."

"From my point of view, that costume had side benefits, you know," he said. And bent down to kiss her.

At which moment her parent's carriage rolled up, and the moment was lost.

In the ensuing hubbub of greetings and goodnights, there was no chance for further conversation with Granville. After a hurried goodnight—without even a kiss—and his promise that they'd talk in the morning, Emily slipped inside.

It hurt her heart to know that she was being left out of a conversation she wanted very much to be part of. While Granville and Scott could talk half the night if they wanted.

All because of society's rules about acceptable behavior for young, unmarried ladies. Even the engaged ones. Which was ridiculous.

4 9

As they drove away from the Turner's, Granville pictured Emily's piquant face just as he was about to kiss her. And her disappointment about not having more time to discuss the case.

It was hard to say goodnight to her.

If she had succeeded in engineering Bray's downfall tonight, and thereby ending her poor sister's engagement, perhaps it was time to reopen the discussion of moving their wedding date forward. The house would be finished soon, or so he hoped. And ready for his bride.

On that optimistic thought, he nearly invited Scott back to the house for a drink. But the mental picture of the mess the workers had made was enough to kill that idea. He gave the driver the office address instead. When they arrived, he paid the driver off.

"I need a drink," he told Scott. "You?"

His partner nodded. Without the need for further discussion, Granville turned his steps toward the waterfront and Scott fell into step beside him.

Granville's mind was still spinning with all the information he'd picked up this evening. He could use a drink with someone who wasn't a potential killer, in a much less formal location. Even if they'd both be seriously overdressed.

Appearing at the Docksider in their tuxedos drew a mocking wolf whistle or two, but the ale was cold and they found a spot with some elbow room at the far end of the long bar.

"So, how did you make out?" he asked Scott as soon as they'd placed their orders.

"Can't say I much care for fancy balls," Scott said. "But I managed to find a few people to talk to, so it wasn't a complete waste."

And Scott had never lost sight of him, either, for which Granville was grateful. "Learn anything new?"

"Nothing that helps us find the puppet master," Scott said. "I heard a few things that might come in handy sometime, though."

But he just grinned and shook his head when Granville pushed for details. "Let's focus on this case for now," was all his partner would say.

Since this case was so close to breaking open, he could only agree. The timely arrival of their ales, which the surly bartender plunked in front of them with a grimace, ended the topic.

"What about you? You spot our puppet master yet?" Scott was quick to ask as soon as the fellow was out of earshot.

"I've got two contenders. Perhaps three," Granville said, lowering his voice.

"Three out of five? That's an improvement."

"It's a start." Especially if the puppet master took the bait he'd dangled, and made a move that would expose him. He just hoped the fellow would do it soon.

Scott glanced over at him. "You'd hoped for more."

"I want him behind bars."

Scott nodded. "You're not alone," his partner said, and took a long swallow of ale. "D'you think our five are the right ones to have been looking at?"

Granville had been thinking about that. "They are seven, now. And they're a lot alike," he said, and shared his realization about the similarities between the seven men. Though he kept the part about his own role to himself.

He was still chewing on that one, as Scott would put it. And the more he thought about it, the harder it was to escape the feeling that he should have recognized what kind of man the puppet master was on sight. The fact he still couldn't decide between Heywood, Knox and Fairfield annoyed him. And he couldn't shake the sense that he was missing something—that he already knew everything he needed to solve this case.

Which wasn't helpful.

"Maybe they're all in it together," Scott said, only half joking.

Granville shook his head. "Like calls to like? Not when the puppet master has gone to such lengths to hide what he is."

"He's hiding that he's a criminal, so he'd never hang around with criminals?"

"That's it."

"Then how's he doing such a good job of convincing his good buddies that he isn't one?"

Granville considered that for a moment. There was something about Scott's question that pulled on his sense that he was missing something.

"He knows their world. Probably comes from the same background they do. Went to the same kinds of schools, learned ancient Greek and Latin."

"Just like you," Scott said, not missing a beat. "But this guy doesn't flinch at killing anyone who gets in his way. You can't tell me they taught that along with the Greek and Latin."

"Hardly."

"So where'd he learn it?"

"Pardon?"

"Guys I hung with in Chicago—they weren't all on the up-and-up. But the ones that weren't started small, same as the guys that were legit. They all worked their way up to the bigger jobs. Look at Benton. He didn't start off as a big noise in this town."

"So how did this fellow start out a gentleman and end up a puppet master?" Granville said slowly. Scott had just nailed the piece he'd been missing. "We've been looking at what happened three or four years ago, when this particular scam got set up. But if you're right, the odds are good that he didn't start there."

"It doesn't make sense he's suddenly this big criminal," Scott said. "Out of nowhere."

No, it didn't. "Benton, in the little he did tell us, led us to assume the fellow had served a kind of apprenticeship with him."

"It wouldn't be enough," Scott said. "Not for someone from a background like yours was before you got to the Klondike."

Granville had a sudden vivid flash of how green he'd been when he began that climb up that steep snowy pass. How little he'd understood hardship before he got to the goldfields. He'd never been tested like that—not before or even since.

Where had the puppet master's testing ground been? Because Scott was right, he must have had one.

"He'll have a past," Granville said, thinking about what he knew about the puppet master, and the men he'd met that night. "And a taste for making big money fast, without much concern about legality."

"So he might have a record somewhere?"

"I doubt it. Or at least not under any name that's likely to be connected to him."

"You think he's used fake names before, too?"

"Yes. He's much too good at concealing his real identity for someone who's never done it before. Which I should have seen earlier."

Scott shrugged, and signaled the bartender for another round. "We all should've seen it earlier. This guy has been ahead of us every step of the way. Which is gettin' downright annoying. I'm starting to suspect he's been ahead of Benton, too. No matter what he told us."

Granville had to laugh. "I still can't imagine Benton not knowing who the puppet master is."

"Yeah, that's how he wants you to think."

"And the real man doesn't move in Benton's world," Granville said thoughtfully. "Only his aliases do that."

"Yeah. This guy is good."

"We're better." Granville raised his mug. "To solving this one."

Scott thumped his mug against Granville's. "I still think all the suspects might be in on it. They all had money problems, right? And now they all have big money again? How's that possible?"

"Easy. They're playing for big stakes," Granville said. "Your earlier point holds there, too. It's possible if they've all made and lost money on this scale before. And this is the kind of town that makes that possible."

"Huh," Scott said, raising his mug and taking a deep swallow. "Yeah, okay. So that's how we find him, then. The puppet master, I mean. We look at where that big money of his came from."

"Which is what we've been trying to do for the last week and more," Granville pointed out. "And failing, I might add. If we're right and the money is from illegal sources, those sources have been well-hidden. They might take months to track down. If we could find them at all."

"Huh," Scott drank deeply, wiped his mouth. "So we're back where we started."

"Not quite," Granville said. "Not if our puppet master has been involved in illegal activities before. And probably in murder, too. He may think he's invisible, but there's a pattern to his actions. That's what we look for. Somewhere along the line he'll have made a mistake."

"Cause when you're learning, you make mistakes," Scott said with a broad grin.

"Exactly," Granville said. "We'll meet with everyone in the morning, focus on this angle. See if we can't find the mistake that will crack this one open."

"Try not to get killed in the meantime," Scott said, and drained his ale.

So Scott did know he'd set himself up as bait. Dammit. He'd hoped to slide that past his partner.

It would be simpler all around if the puppet master took his bait. And Granville would finally get his shot at the fellow.

50

Saturday, September 29, 1900

Despite their late night—or perhaps because of it—Granville didn't sleep well. The following morning he again woke early, feeling sluggish after a night of broken dreams, none of which he could remember. His first thought was for Emily.

His second thought was of the men he'd met the night before. Particularly Heywood, Knox and Fairfield. His gut told him one of them had to be the puppet master? But which one?

And had he taken the bait?

Granville made a point of following his usual routine, including breakfast at Mary's. Might as well give the fellow every chance to track him down. But in his impatience, their always excellent eggs tasted like cardboard and the toast seemed dry. Even the coffee smelled wrong.

Less than an hour later he was in his shadowy office, digging into the copy of Burke's Peerage that Miss Rizzo had somehow tracked down for him. Then he sat and thought about the men he'd met the previous evening, and began updating his notes by the thin light of his desk lamp.

He'd based of his current theories on *when* the puppet master had built his hidden empire. Seemingly out of nowhere. He'd assumed that, forced into it by a financial crisis, the fellow had somehow learned his trade here. But Scott's words of the night before changed all that.

He needed to rethink every one of those theories, based on the assumption that they'd all been wrong. Again.

What would it mean if the puppet master's seeming ability to build an empire from nothing was only possible because he'd done the same thing somewhere else first? Somewhere that had seen a similar increase in crime.

It felt like he was finally on the right track. Of course, so had his last theory. This time, though, his gut said it was different.

But he wasn't going to rely just on theories any more.

When the team got in, they needed to take a fresh look at everything they knew, and everything they didn't. And start working on the missing connections that might help them catch their prey.

While he needed to spend as much time as possible being bait. Which meant being out of the office. It would only take one false move from the puppet master, and he'd have him.

THE SUN WAS WELL up when Granville heard booted footsteps coming down the hall. Scott and Trent. He recognized their steps—neither of them was trying to hide their approach. Both walked straight into his office, and Trent carefully placed a covered mug of hot coffee on the desk in front of Granville before pulling up a chair beside Scott.

"We missed you at the cafe," Scott said.

"I was up early."

"Couldn't sleep?"

"Not well. You?"

"So-so," Scott said, looking at the thick tome lying on Granville's desk. "That doesn't look like fun. Find anything interesting?"

"I did indeed. I can't find any connection between the Baylor family and either Fairfield or Heywood, but Knox looks to be a remote connection. As is Arbuthnot. Which makes Knox and Arbuthnot distant cousins, several times removed."

Scott stared at him. "Arbuthnot? But he…"

"Doesn't exist. I know," he said. "My guess? The puppet master chose the name to taunt us, if we ever got this close to him. He's proving, yet again, that we can't keep up with him."

"This puppet master of yours is getting annoying," Scott said.

Trent glanced from one to the other and rolled his eyes. "So what happened last night?"

Granville filled him in on what how their evening had gone.

"And is one of these guys the puppet master?"

"After last night I've narrowed it down to three primary suspects. Heywood. Knox. And Fairfield. All of whom were on our list. But they're only three of the seven men I want to know more about."

"You've expanded the list?" Trent said.

Granville explained the dynamics he'd seen among the group the previous evening.

"So how'd you choose those three? Your primary suspects?" Trent asked.

How to explain? "I know these men," he said. "I grew up with them."

"You didn't tell us that," the kid said.

Granville restrained himself from rolling his eyes by sheer force of will.

Scott didn't bother. "He doesn't mean literally."

"Oh," Trent said, looking bewildered and annoyed, all at once.

"But I came from a similar background to theirs, learned the same values," Granville said. "I understand how they think."

"You learned the same values as a killer?" Trent asked.

"I did," Granville said.

"Like what?"

"Like Honor. Integrity. Loyalty. And I believe in those values. The puppet master doesn't."

"But he learned them," Trent said. "So he can mimic them?"

It was a solid bit of reasoning. The lad was showing promise as investigator. Some of the time, anyway.

Scott saw it too. "That's it," his partner said approvingly.

"And there are three of them?" Trent asked Granville.

"Not three puppet masters," he said. "But at least three men who probably don't believe in those values."

"They could be working together," Scott said, and Trent nodded.

"It's possible," Granville said. "But the puppet master has gone to a great deal of trouble to separate his real identity from his criminal ones. I doubt he would trust anyone with the secret of the identities he hides behind."

"So how do we find out which one he is?"

"We'll start looking for his prior patterns. If Scott is right about him, this won't be the first time he's done this."

Trent thought about that for a minute. "I stayed last night to help Mac and Miss Kent," he said. "We didn't come up with much. But I think I just heard them come in, and we should include them in this discussion. They're the pattern people, after all—particularly Miss Kent. You wanted them to hear this, right?"

"Good idea," Granville said, exchanging a grin with Scott. "Though I think we'll wait until Emily is here as well. I've ordered a hack for her and she shouldn't be long."

While they waited for the rest of the team, Granville drank the coffee Trent had brought him, idly wondering how Trent had talked Mary into sending one of her precious coffee mugs along with him. And why the mug had a lid.

He considered it for a moment. The lid had a peaked shape, with a vent hole for the steam. It was made of plain white ceramic, and matched the cup, though there was something vaguely oriental in the shape. As if Mary had seen a chinoiserie version, and had someone make copies for her cafe. It was an excellent idea, actually. Perhaps Emily would enjoy having something similar for their breakfast china?

Oddly enough, the coffee now smelled good and tasted even better. He'd have to remember to thank the lad.

GRANVILLE HAD FINISHED his coffee by the time Trent returned with Emily, Mac and Miss Kent in tow. The six of them moved to the meeting room and settled around the long table to consider the problem of how to find the puppet master's previous crimes.

After he, Emily and Scott gave them all a thorough briefing of the events of the previous evening, Miss Kent tipped her head to one side and stared into space for a moment. Granville waited. He'd seen this response from her before, and it usually preceded an insightful observation.

"I don't think any of the seven you mention have been in town more than four years, so if there's a pattern of behavior, it must have started somewhere else," she said. "For now, it would be easiest to focus on the three you've identified as primary suspects. Then if we somehow prove it couldn't be any of them, we can look at the others."

As she finished, she gave him an odd sideways look, as if she expected him to disagree.

"Good plan," he said with a smile. "What do we know about where Heywood, Knox and Fairfield came from before Vancouver?"

"Not very much," Mac said.

"Do we know how long they've been in town?" Granville asked.

Mac looked at Miss Kent, who consulted her notes. "Between four and five years," she said.

"All three of them?"

She nodded. "Yes. Fairfield moved here just over four years ago. Knox a month or so later. For Heywood, it has been nearly four and a half years."

Which didn't move their search forward. Though it did support their theory that the puppet master had a criminal background. Somewhere.

"Fairfield has a British accent, one that suggests somewhere like Liverpool to me, though he's polished it enough that I can't be sure," he said. "Knox I think might be another Brit, but there's something mixed with that. And Heywood is clearly American, though I don't recognize the accent. Scott?"

"Eastern Seaboard for Heywood, I'd say. But some of his words sound like you."

"Cambridge," Granville said, deciding not to be offended. "And Knox?"

"I think he's from back east," Emily said. "Toronto, most likely. He might even have been born there, then educated in England."

"Have you dug out anything on where any of them are originally from?" he asked Miss Kent.

"I haven't been able to find anything," she said.

"What about any of their more recent activities or locations?"

"Nothing, I'm afraid."

"We need to find out more," Granville asked.

"How do we do that?" Trent promptly asked.

"I need to have another chat with one of the Pinkerton's fellows regarding what they might know about Fairfield. And I'd like them to dig a little deeper on Heywood."

"Why Heywood?" Mac asked.

"Just a feeling I got from him and Fairfield," Granville said. There had been something between them, and he wanted to know what it was. "It's worth a call."

Granville looked around the table. "A word of warning. The puppet master was after us before," he said. "But now we're bringing the fight to him. So he'll have something to prove. And I can't guess whom he'll target."

"No. But you're counting on it being you," Scott said. "Even puppet masters get riled when you start setting their safely hidden world on fire."

Damn. He'd hoped that overnight Scott had forgotten that he'd set himself up as bait. Apparently not. It had been a feeble hope, anyway.

The comment naturally prompted the peppering of questions Granville had hoped to avoid, while Scott sat back with a smug look on his face. And he couldn't read Emily's expression at all, which wasn't a good sign.

He attempted to reassure everyone, which didn't work out too well. Especially when he also delivered a warning to each of them to be careful.

To his relief, Scott agreed with him. "The puppet master is sneaky," his partner told them all. "We can't make assumptions about what he might do. Or not do."

Granville nodded. But from the look she gave him, he'd need to have a long talk with Emily when he got back. For now, his first priority was drawing out the puppet master.

"We're done, then. Unless anyone has anything else?" he asked, glancing around the table. "No? Let's go, then. Scott?"

"Right behind you," his partner said.

"We need to start by updating our banker and the two reporters and setting them loose on the latest suspect list," he said as they headed back to their respective offices.

"Try to do it without irritating them," Scott said.

"That's an easy one. I'll just make sure to leave you here," he said with an easy grin.

"Not a chance," Scott said harshly. "If the puppet master is going to try killing you, it's going to cost him."

One look at Scott's iron jaw told him there was no point in arguing.

51

As the meeting ended, Emily stopped to have a quick word with Laura, who wanted to hear all about her ballgown, and the success of her plan with Mr. Bray. Which was still far from assured.

Then she tracked Granville to his office, and closed the door behind her. He looked up with a smile, and stood up to fold her into an embrace. After a long kiss, which made her feel somewhat better, she deliberately moved to put the desk between them and settled into an armchair.

"Emily," he said. "What has put that look on your face? Is it the threat from the puppet master?"

"How can you ask that? You've set yourself up as bait for him."

"I have," he said, and sat back at the desk. "He's wily. It may be the only way to draw him out."

She laced her fingers in her lap and fought back her fear for him. "Why now?" she asked. "He's been a threat to all of us from the moment you started investigating him, and you know it."

"True," he said. "The rumor is that he's negotiating with another assassin. He needs to be dealt with before he hires one. Yet we still don't know who he is, or have any evidence against him. So I challenged him last night."

"But why?"

"To raise the stakes enough that the fellow would come after me personally."

"The man's a coward. He's likely to shoot you in the back," she said. "From the shadows, so no one can identify him."

"I hope not," Granville said. "I think he's too arrogant to see me as a true challenge. To him, I'm more like a fly to be swatted."

"You think so?"

"I do." He paused and considered her for a moment. "But I'm not prepared to risk anyone's life on that belief."

"Except yours," she said.

He shrugged. "I doubt it's much of a risk. And I had to do something. So far the puppet master has only been predictable in hindsight."

She smiled a little at the truth of that. "As you said earlier, he's wily."

"Which is why I've asked everyone else to stay here today."

"Except you."

"And Scott," he said wryly. "Who seems to feel much as you do."

"Good."

He ignored that. "Can you work from the office today?"

"I need to see Clara."

"Can she not come here?"

"While you're out being the obvious target, I suppose."

"It may just be for today. I don't have much patience left for this game the puppet master's been playing with us. And I suspect he may not, either."

She wasn't going to be able to talk him out of it. "I don't want to see you shot."

"I'll be careful."

Not likely. "Why is it acceptable for you to risk your life, and not for me?"

He looked about to say something furious, and she had to give him credit for stopping to think before he answered. "It probably isn't," he said. "Though it's not how I was raised. But I have training and experience in dangerous situations that you lack."

She wanted to continue arguing, because how was she to gain that experience if she never did anything dangerous? But she could see how hard it was for him to know that she was being threatened because of his actions. And at the moment, she didn't have the experience with dangerous situations that he did. At least he hadn't argued with her.

"For today, I can ask Clara to come here," she said. "As long as you promise not to take foolish risks."

"I promise," he said with a half-smile. "And Scott will have my back."

"Good," she said. "And tomorrow, we'll have this discussion again."

"If the puppet master isn't behind bars by then," he said.

Which wasn't exactly reassuring.

WHEN GRANVILLE LEFT HER OFFICE, Emily was left with her own thoughts. By the time Clara arrived, she was tempted to unload all of her fear and her worries about Granville on her friend. But talking about it would only make it worse. There was nothing either of them could actually do to make it better.

Or was there?

"Clara, I've been thinking about Mr. Bray," she said, as soon as she had her friend seated across from her.

"You must be feeling pretty pleased with yourself," Clara said.

Emily stared blankly at her for a moment. This felt like one of the worst moments of her life. "What do you mean?"

"Well, after your success last night."

"What success?" Emily said.

"Surely you've heard?" Clara said.

"No, I haven't heard. Some of us have work, you know. Heard what?"

"Emily! What is wrong with you?"

"Nothing is wrong! Except that Granville is close to identifying the puppet master, and has set himself up as a target to draw him out," she said in a rush. Then flushed hotly and felt the prickle of tears. She hadn't meant to say any of that.

"Oh, Emily." And Clara put down her own tea and rushed to her side.

Emily gave her an unfortunately watery smile. "Don't mind me. I'm furious about the whole thing, and he's going to insist on putting himself in danger and there's nothing I can do, except that I thought of Mr. Bray and…"

"Drink some tea, Emily," Clara said, patting her hand. "And don't worry, we'll think of something."

Emily drew in a shaky breath, and then another, and tried another smile. This one was better. "Of course we will," she said.

Then had to bite the inside of her cheek to stop the shiver that shook her. "But I can't bear it if he gets himself killed."

Clara gave her a hug "We'll just have to make sure he doesn't. What plan were you coming up with? You said you thought of Mr. Bray?"

"Well, I still think he's probably been in touch with the puppet master. Even if he doesn't know who he is, maybe he knows how to contact him. And if we could somehow draw him out, the puppet master, that is…"

"Then he won't need to kill Granville, because he'll have killed you instead," Clara said tartly. "Oh, Emily. That's a terrible idea."

"I don't mean him to know we've identified him," Emily said. "We don't have to confront him, after all. We just need to know which of three men he is. All we'd have to do is to follow Mr. Bray…"

"But that's what I was talking about earlier," Clara said. "Hadn't you heard? Mr. Bray has left town."

"What?"

Clara nodded. "He fled. Sometime in the night. Packed his bags and left. After the gossip we started spread through the ballroom last night, growing worse with every telling? Well, I guess he couldn't take it."

"He fled?" Emily said. "And the fraud he was planning? The companies? What will happen to them?"

And to Papa, she thought but didn't—couldn't—say.

"From what I heard this morning, nothing will happen. He's left a few people holding empty promises, but he hadn't managed to get his hands on anyone's money yet."

And if he'd fled early this morning, Papa would still have all the copies of the document he had signed, Emily realized. And his money. So he would be fine. "Oh, that's a relief."

"And as for your sister's reputation? Jane was wonderful, putting on that brave face. Everyone is talking about what he was up to, and what a heroine she is. However did you convince her to play her part so well?"

Emily managed a smile. "That was the easy part. That isn't Jane's brave face. That's her stoic look when she's embarrassed and refusing to admit that anything is wrong. I knew I could count on that expression if she heard even a little of the gossip last night."

Clara let out a peal of laughter. "Well, whatever it was, it worked beautifully. Everyone is praising her to the skies, and more than willing to believe Mr. Bray capable of everything we suspect him of and more. You must be thrilled. Your plan worked."

"And Mr. Bray has been tried and charged in the court of public opinion," she said. Why didn't it feel more satisfying?

"Just as you planned," Clara said with satisfaction. "I told you gossip could be a potent weapon."

Actually it was Clara's Grandmama that had told both of them that. But Emily was too grateful to quibble. "Just as *we* planned," she said. "I couldn't have done it without you."

"So you'll come with me to 'at-homes' in future?" Clara said.

"Some of them," Emily said. The ones that would help her with investigations, anyway.

Clara shook her head, knowing exactly what Emily hadn't said. "At least that's better than the 'no' you usually give me," she said.

Emily smiled a little. "I do wish our plan hadn't been quite so quickly effective. Especially just when I need Mr. Bray in town so he can help us unmask the puppet master."

Clara just shook her head. "I think you can leave that to Mr. Granville," she said. "He's more than capable of handling it."

"Yes. By setting himself up as a target," she said bitterly.

"So you don't think he's capable of defending himself?" Clara asked.

"Of course he is!" Emily said.

"Oh. Then the puppet master is smarter than he is?"

"No!"

"More capable then?"

"Hardly," Emily said, but she'd begun to grin. She should have known Clara wouldn't leave her to wallow in her own fears.

"You've taken Mr. Bray out of the picture, and foiled what was probably one of the puppet master's long-term schemes in the process," her friend added. "That had to frustrate him. Which can only help Mr. Granville in his plans to expose that monster."

"But…" Emily said.

"No buts," Clara said. "Just be happy you have done your part. *And* rescued your sister from a terribly unhappy marriage."

She gave Emily a sideways glance. "Now you're free to marry Mr. Granville again. Whenever you want," she said with a sly smile

Emily swallowed hard. That had made an excellent goal. It was an unsettling reality.

5 2

Tim O'Hearn was first on Granville's list of those he wanted to talk to. It was the puppet master's past criminal behavior they were looking into now, not any financial shenanigans. Which, frankly, he'd rather be doing in any case. Let Mac handle looking into the financial end.

And O'Hearn was increasingly becoming known for his reporting of the crime beat.

The redheaded reporter didn't look at all surprised to see them. The newsroom was as crowded and noisy as ever, but the minute O'Hearn spotted Granville and Scott striding down the narrow aisle between the desks, he grabbed his coat and hat and came to meet them.

"There's news?" he said. "We can talk outside."

The day was clear and mild, the leaves of a few sad looking maples in the front of the building already turning red. A fresh breeze was coming off the ocean to the west, and Granville turned his steps in that direction and strode briskly towards the docks. Scott matched him stride for stride, but O'Hearn, caught off guard, rushed to catch up.

"Hey, wait up."

He grinned. "I have an assignment for you. Might be a front pager. We don't want to be overheard," Granville said over his shoulder.

Just in case O'Hearn needed some incentive.

He didn't.

"I thought this whole business with this puppet master was supposed to be a front pager," O'Hearn said. "And where is Draper, anyhow? Weren't we supposed to be working on this one together?"

As they strode south and west towards the ocean and Stanley Park, Granville drew in deep lungfuls of the salty air. "We have a new angle," he said. "And this part of it is a better fit for you than for Draper."

"If that means that I won't be digging through financial reports, then I'm all ears," O'Hearn said with a wide smile. "Give."

"Having met Heywood, Knox and Fairfield, I think I underestimated how long this puppet master has been making his money through crime. He's also much too comfortable with killing people for that to be new behavior," Granville said, and filled him in on what they had learned at the ball.

O'Hearn paled enough that his freckles stood out. "So this guy is probably a hardened criminal. Wait a minute. Didn't we just look for guys that had recently lost their money? How does that fit?"

"That's a question I'll be asking Draper and Wardle to look into," Granville said. "Though we do know that the three fellows who are my prime suspects each moved to town a little more than four years ago."

"A lot of people did so. That's why we're in the beginning of a new real estate boom," O'Hearn retorted.

"And why would someone running a successful criminal empire suddenly move on and set up somewhere else?" Granville asked.

"He's expanding?" the reporter said. But he looked thoughtful.

"Or something went wrong with his previous endeavor, and he had to leave town," Granville said.

"Ahead of the law? That's an interesting thought," O'Hearn said.

"It could explain how he was able to set up his empire here relatively quickly," Granville said. "He's done this before."

"He still could have been expanding here," O'Hearn said, his jaw set.

Scott laughed. When Granville looked at him inquiringly, he shook his head. "Listen to you two. Not a fact between you."

"Touché," he said, and O'Hearn looked sheepish.

"I guess I'll be looking into what the three of them, Heywood, Knox and Fairfield, were up to before they got here?" the reporter said.

"That would be most helpful," Granville said, copying his elder brother's stodgiest tone and hiding his grin.

O'Hearn made a face. "At least it's about crime," he said.

"And whatever sent the puppet master here, it's likely to have been reported on, at very least," Granville said. "But we don't have much time."

"Of course not," O'Hearn said. Then he looked sideways at Granville. In a different tone, he said, "You're concerned about Emily?"

Granville nodded.

"I'll do my best," O'Hearn said. "Once I have some idea where these three guys are from, I'll make some calls. If whatever's in their background was messy, it shouldn't take that long."

"Good enough. And I'm asking everyone to a meeting at our office this afternoon. I think we need to pool information. Half past four?"

"I'll be there."

"Appreciate it, O'Hearn," Granville said. And the three men turned their steps back towards town.

Granville repeated the meeting with Draper and with Wardle, though on a more businesslike footing than he'd done with O'Hearn.

Tim was a friend. The rules were different.

Both Draper and Wardle agreed to continue looking into where the money was going, but to factor the new information into their search. And both promised to attend the meeting that afternoon.

"So now what?" Scott asked him as they walked back towards their offices.

It was a very good question. So far, there had been no sign of the puppet master or any of his henchmen. Neither of them had any sense of being followed. It seemed the puppet master hadn't taken the bait.

"I can't just sit behind a desk today," he told Scott. Who nodded.

He hadn't talked to Randall or Carver yet. "Let's go talk to a lawyer or two. And then maybe the police," he said, and abruptly changed direction.

IT WAS after two when Granville and Scott returned to the office. The front office was empty except for Miss Rizzo, who started when the door opened and stared at Granville, wide-eyed.

Maybe she hadn't expected him to return? If the puppet master had gone after him, he could have ended up in hospital, at best. Or he could have killed the fellow.

But nothing had happened.

Or so he'd thought. Until Miss Rizzo swallowed hard, and handed him a note addressed to him. And he discovered the puppet master had responded to his dare. Just not in the way he'd expected.

Written in flowing script on good quality paper, it had been delivered with the afternoon post while Granville had been out. The unsigned note was a brief one. It read:

"I had heard your most interesting fiancée was back in town from an extended visit to Victoria. It was a pleasure to see her last night in her stunning gown. You are to be complimented on your acquisition.

I wonder. Did she feel safer being far away from you while you poke into matters that don't concern you? No matter, her safety is a delusion in any case, whether she is here or there."

He was wordlessly furious. Threatening him was one matter, but straight out threatening Emily? No.

That went beyond all acceptable bounds, no matter what game the puppet master was playing. He'd known the fellow was ruthless, but this was utterly cold. And cowardly.

The puppet master was still hiding. Rather than attack him

directly, the coward would send someone after Emily. Or go after her himself. And he was going to regret that until the day he died.

Granville clenched his fist around the note until his knuckles gleamed white. He would not give up until the puppet master was behind bars. Or six feet under. Either was fine.

None of the others would give up, either, if he knew his team.

"Granville?" Scott said sharply. "What's wrong?"

He looked up to realize he was still standing in front of the reception desk, the note clutched in his hand. He didn't know what his own face looked like, but Scott's face told him it was bad. Miss Rizzo looked frozen where she sat.

"Is Emily here?" he asked Miss Rizzo, keeping his voice even with an effort.

She nodded. "Yes. She and her friend are still in her office."

Thank God. "Has she seen this?"

"Granville? What's wrong?" Scott said.

He passed the note to Scott and turned back to Miss Rizzo. "Has anyone else seen this?"

She shook her head. "No. I thought it best to wait… until you returned." Her voice shook on the last words. "Was I wrong?"

"No. You did well."

"Granville, this is monstrous," Scott said harshly.

"I know."

"We need to meet with the team," Scott said.

Granville nodded. "We need everyone we've been working with, too. As quickly as possible. Can you set that up? I need to talk to Emily."

53

Emily and Clara were seated on either side of her desk, discussing how the news of Mr. Bray's perfidy had spread. After Clara had introduced the topic of weddings, and specifically Emily's wedding, Emily had quickly returned to the topic of Mr. Bray's abrupt departure for parts unknown, and exactly how their plan had played out. And what the rapid spread of the gossip they'd started might mean for any future planning. Clara seemed much more interested in the topic than she had been before last night's success.

They both looked up when there was a sharp knock on the door. Before Emily could say anything, the door opened and Granville stepped in. She took one look at his tightly drawn face, and leapt to her feet. "Granville? What's wrong? Is it the puppet master? Are you injured?"

"No, I'm fine," he said, moving quickly towards her. "He didn't come after me. Instead, the scoundrel is threatening you."

"Threatening me? How?"

"This was just delivered," he said, passing her the note. "I hate that you have to see it. And I'll make sure you're protected."

"Of course I have to see it. I'm glad you didn't hesitate to show it to me," Emily said, reading it quickly, then more slowly. "He's playing with you."

"He is. Which doesn't mean he won't act. The fellow has no morals, and with this note, he's no longer even pretending to be a gentleman."

"I don't think he'll come after me," Emily said, passing the note to Clara. The barely reined in violence in Granville's every move worried her.

"I doubt he values women much, or considers me in the least consequential," Emily said. "This is aimed at you. He's trying to rile you up enough to do something rash."

She glared at him. "The stupid man doesn't realize you're already doing so by making yourself a target for him."

"Probably." Granville gave her a tight smile. "He must know that if he harmed you, it would devastate me. Though he wouldn't live long enough to enjoy it."

Clara, looking stricken, handed the note back to Emily. Who glanced at it again. "He certainly knows you were setting yourself up as a target."

"I'm afraid that may be what triggered his threat against you," he said.

"The note, perhaps," she said tartly. "Not the threat."

"I'd intended to raise the stakes enough to make the fellow angry enough that he'd deal with me personally," Granville said.

"I always said he was a coward," Emily said. "He sees me as weaker, and will use your feelings for me to get even if he can."

"He'll try," he said, frowning heavily. "And I'll make sure he never gets the chance to get near you."

Clara looked from Granville's strained face to Emily. "I think a cup of tea is called for. I'll go and fetch a tray."

And she slipped out of the room, leaving Emily and Granville staring at each other.

"It will be fine," Emily said. "Truly. I'll be careful, and I won't take any risks. Well, at least no more than you are."

He gave her a wry smile. "Which, as you've just pointed out, is hardly reassuring."

"Well, no. But then it wasn't meant to be," she said. "Granville, there has to be a way to get to the puppet master. Without getting either of us killed."

"That's my plan," he said. "He needs to be arrested and convicted. And I'm making it my personal mission to see that he is."

"I thought so," Emily said with satisfaction. "Like you did on Randall's case. It's what I was trying to do with Mr. Bray."

"I'd say you succeeded there," he said. "Since I've heard that the fellow left town in the middle of the night."

"You could say he was tried and charged in the court of public opinion," she said. "But it doesn't feel very satisfying. It feels like I cheated."

"Because he didn't end up in court?"

She nodded.

"You didn't have much choice."

"But why not?"

"Unlike the puppet master, Bray hadn't actually done anything yet. He'd planned it. Put all the details in place. But he hadn't yet done anything illegal."

"So I should have waited," she said, trying to picture it in her mind's eye.

She could almost see Mr. Randall standing in front of the judge, with Mr. Bray on the stand. Called to account for everything he'd planned, every nefarious scheme he'd launch. All the damage he would have caused. And slowly wilting under Mr. Randall's relentless cross-examination. Until everyone in the room could clearly see just what a villain he was. It was a very satisfying picture.

Granville laughed. "You're picturing it, aren't you?"

"Yes," she said. "And taking great pleasure in thinking about him, with his villainy exposed. Does that make me a bad person?"

"Not at all. Just one with a strong sense of justice."

She nodded. That felt right. "I should have waited until we had enough to prove what he was. Like you're doing with the puppet master."

"The two situations are very different," he said.

"Are they really? As far as I can tell, the only difference is I knew who Mr. Bray was. You still don't know who the puppet master is. Their crimes are very similar."

"Mr. Bray has not hired an assassin."

"Not yet," she said darkly. "Not here, anyway."

"True enough. You're still forgetting one very key difference."

"Am I? What difference?"

"In order to arrest Bray, he needs to have broken the law. And then the prosecutor has to be able to prove it."

"But he did. The minute Papa signed his papers, Mr. Bray broke the law."

"Is your Papa the only one who has signed those papers?"

"Yes, so far," she said. "Though I believe Papa is still planning to talk to some of his friends about the opportunity."

Then she felt the blood drain from her face. "Oh," she said. "In a court of law, Papa would look like a fool, wouldn't he?"

Granville nodded. "At best. He might even have a hard time proving he isn't an accomplice. Or if Bray is as devious as I suspect he might be, he may have set up your father to look like the real villain in the case."

"Oh," she said again, as she pictured that awful scenario unfolding before her. "Oh, poor Papa. But surely he wouldn't have fallen for that…?"

She looked to Granville for reassurance, and saw compassion on his face instead. And swallowed hard. "He wanted so badly to see Jane wed to a man he could respect," she said instead.

"And Bray had fooled half the town," he said. "Your mother has better instincts, however. And she trusted you to get your father free of the mess."

Emily hadn't thought of it like that. Mama had sought her help, hadn't she? In a typically convoluted fashion, of course. But still…

"Which you have done," Granville added.

"Well, he's left town, anyway," Emily said. "And Papa still has the only copies of the papers he signed, thanks to Mama."

"Thanks to your planning," Granville said. "And Jane's reputation is clear. Also thanks to your planning."

"Oh," Emily said, feeling a little shaky. "Yes. Well. I suppose you could look at it like that."

"In fact, you have dealt with a tricky situation beautifully, in a case where getting proof was either impossible or would only have made things worse. Congratulations."

Emily smiled slowly She really liked his perspective on the matter.

And he was right. Mr. Bray was gone, Papa hadn't lost any money, and Jane was even more marriageable than before.

"Thank you," she said. Then she gave him an impish grin. "Now, what can we do about this puppet master problem of yours?"

He laughed at that, and the worry that had lurked behind his eyes since he showed her the stupid note lessened a little.

It was time to push a little harder.

"We need to tie the puppet master to his crimes in order to get him arrested," she said. "How do we do that?"

"We need to catch him in the act." Granville said.

"He's too wily for that. Which is why you're trying to anger him into coming after you, isn't it?" Emily said.

"It is. And even that might not work."

Emily looked at the note she still held. "Unless we can turn this against him."

"I like the way you think," he said. "Though at times it terrifies me. How? And don't say by turning you into bait."

"I wasn't going to," she said. "Though that would be the simplest. And he'd never expect it."

"No," he said flatly.

She grinned at him. "No. He's expecting you to panic, and come after him, isn't he?"

"Yes. You were right to call it an insult. A very deliberate one"

She nodded. "You said it yourself. This isn't the act of a gentleman."

"Which is what makes it insulting."

"To another so-called gentleman. Which he thinks you are."

His eyes laughed at her. "Did you just insult me?"

"I think it's a compliment," she said, pretending to consider it. "You're better than most who call themselves gentlemen even pretend to be. Those values formed who you are, but you're more than the rigid rules. Maybe the hardships you faced on the goldfields changed you?"

He looked a little embarrassed, she thought with glee. But it was true. He gave most so-called gentlemen a bad name.

And he had no problems following her off-center logic, either.

"So he'll expect me to be insulted and furious and do something useless and very old-fashioned," Granville said. "Like call him out."

"What if you did?"

"Did what? Challenge him to pistols at dawn?"

"Demand he meet with you and explain himself," she said.

He grinned. "It would be the gentlemanly thing to do. And unexpected. Unfortunately, we still don't know which of the three he is."

"And if we did?"

"If I sent a note to the puppet master's home, demanding he meet with me the following day?" He gave her an appreciative look. "It would be a slap in the face, combined with the threat of exposure. Pretty much guaranteed to force him to act. I like it."

"The puppet master wouldn't be able to resist, would he?"

"No, I don't think he would. And he'd want to attack me before the meeting. Take me off guard."

"Then I guess we'll need to identify him, don't we?" she said.

"Which is why I've just called a meeting to do so."

Emily nodded. Of course he had. "Good. Let's get to it, then."

5 4

Less than an hour later, Emily and Clara accompanied Granville to the meeting room. Where the rest of the team, plus two lawyers, a banker, two reporters and a police officer were gathered around the long table, waiting for them.

Granville looked at each of them as he said, "We are going to take the puppet master down. Tonight. We need to share what information we have, and work together to uncover who he is and what he's done. If we do our job right, the facts will see him hang."

He paused. "He sent this earlier," he said, and passed the note around the table. Saw the shock on the face of each person who read it.

He noted that Trent had hastily begun scribbling in his notebook, and that Miss Kent was staring at the table, and wondered what his own expression looked like. He was still beyond angry, and it probably showed.

It didn't matter. Not now.

When everyone had seen the note, he looked around the table. "Last night I took the game to the puppet master, essentially challenged him to take me on in front of everyone. And this," he flicked the note disparagingly. "Is his response.

He may be an exceptional strategist—would have to be, to pull off some of what he's done without being uncovered. And we know he's utterly ruthless. But he's a coward at heart.

And that will be his downfall."

"We'll make sure of it," Trent said firmly. Then spoiled it with his next words. "But how?"

"He's going to betray himself," Granville said. "In fact, he's just done so. And probably not for the first time."

"Huh?" Trent said.

Granville smiled. "We know the puppet master is brilliant at protecting his real identity. What he's just shown us," and he tapped the note that threatened Emily. "Is that his real motive is cowardice. He works in the shadows, hides behind layers of lies. Never puts himself at risk."

"You've said yourself the man is brilliant at it," Carver said. "Why should he put himself at risk?"

"He's a criminal," Daniels said. "Crime is a risky business. Always has been, always will be."

"So he's better at it than most," Carver said. "How is that betraying himself?"

"If his decisions are made from cowardice, too many of them will be wrong. He'll end up sabotaging himself," Granville said.

"He seems to be doing pretty well so far," Carver said.

Granville couldn't tell if the lawyer was playing devil's advocate or not. It didn't matter. The questions were useful. "But for how long?" he said. "Did anyone uncover exactly where Heywood, Knox and Fairfield are from?"

"From what I can tell, Fairfield comes from a minor branch of a family in Liverpool, who made their money in importing," Wardle said. "He has money flowing from London, which I assume is family money, though I haven't been able to confirm it."

Knox is Canadian, hails from Toronto. His money came from there at one time, though he's mostly living on goodwill these days, from what I can find.

Finally, I couldn't confirm Heywood's background. Though he

has banking connections in the Northeast, especially Boston and Philadelphia," the banker added.

"Which might provide some answers as to where the proceeds from the smuggling go," Granville said. "O'Hearn, did you find anything interesting in their history?"

"I sure did," O'Hearn said. "Before Fairfield moved here, he lived in Toronto, seemed to be active in society, welcomed everywhere. The same as he is here."

"And Heywood?" he asked.

"Similar story, but in Boston."

"What about Knox?"

"Fairfield's connections in Toronto were Knox's connections first. And they came west around the same time."

Interesting. Could they be related? "And did you find any financial or criminal scandals in either city around the time any of them left town?" Granville asked.

O'Hearn nodded. "In Boston, there was an investment firm that collapsed amid allegations they'd been running a pyramid scheme. Investors lost a lot of money, but they couldn't find the man behind it. No arrests were made."

So Heywood was the puppet master? Somehow, that answer didn't sit right with Granville. What was he missing? "What about Toronto?"

O'Hearn grinned. "It gets better. In Toronto, there was a string of murders in a short period of time, which suddenly ceased when a smuggling ring was broken."

"What were they smuggling?"

"Opium," O'Hearn said. "They were hiding it in furniture and smuggling into the United States. A few people were arrested, but they never caught whoever was behind it. And the murders stopped."

Wardle looked fascinated, and Miss Kent was nodding to herself as she drew something into her notepad.

"So either Fairfield or Knox would seem to be the logical choice to be our puppet master," Granville said. His instincts said it was

Fairfield. There was more to the fellow than he showed. "Were you able to trace any of the men back further?"

"Once I got this far, I enlisted Draper," O'Hearn said, nodding to the other reporter.

"I did some digging on Heywood," Draper said. "He lived in Boston for three years, but before that, I can't find any trace of him, anywhere."

"You think he changed identities," Wardle said.

"I do."

"Which doesn't fit what we believe to be the puppet master's pattern," Granville said. "What about Knox and Fairfield?"

"Knox was born in Ottawa, sent to England for his schooling, then moved to Toronto until he came west," O'Hearn said. "He lived well until the crash."

Granville nodded. "Not a fit for the puppet master then, though he could still be an accomplice. And Fairfield?"

"Fairfield was in Hong Kong for four years before he came to Canada," O'Hearn said. "He appears to have been living very well."

"And what happened just before he left?"

"A series of murders," O'Hearn said. "Still unsolved."

"And the breakup of a ring that was selling counterfeit Chinese antiques into the export market," Draper said. "The ring was shut down and there were low level arrests made, but they never found whoever was behind it."

"And there's the pattern," Granville said.

"If this *is* Fairfield, he relies on violence, makes money by smuggling, hides his identity, and runs when there is any threat of exposure," Miss Kent said, ticking off each point in her notepad. "Just as the puppet master does."

"A coward, making cowardly decisions," Scott said.

Carver laughed. "I concede," he said. "It seems that in each case, Fairfield left a profitable, and still viable, business and ran thousands of miles away. And he wasn't even under threat."

"That we know of," Officer Daniels said. "The investigation may have been pointing towards him. Or them, if Knox is involved. But they must have lacked proof."

"Which is why we'll make sure we have sufficient proof this time," Granville said. "Anyone have anything else to add?"

"I do," Trent said, speaking directly to him. "It's only rumors, but you said that sometimes rumors are more accurate that what people perceive to be facts, right?"

"That depends on the source of the rumor," Granville said.

"Well, one of mine is that clerk at Vancouver Box," Trent said. "I've been thinking about my last chat with him, and I don't believe he lied to me on purpose."

"He showed you photos of Abernathy," Scott said. "Who doesn't exist."

"Well, yeah. But what if he doesn't know Abernathy isn't real?" Trent said. "He's young, and he's pretty gullible. He knows I work for you, but he thinks I'm on the take, looking for fast ways to make a buck, same as him. He seemed to be trying to impress me. And I'm pretty sure that's genuine."

Which was amusing, because Trent was pretty young and gullible himself, Granville thought with amusement. But the hard life the lad had led with his father had pounded some practical savvy into him that at times belied his age. Was this one of those times?

They couldn't afford to ignore the possibility that it was. "So what are the rumors?"

"There's rumors of a shipment coming in soon, down at the docks," Trent said.

"If this clerk is that gullible, why would they tell him about the smuggling run?" O'Hearn asked.

"They didn't," Trent said smugly. "He was complaining about having to work late tonight, and the number of boxes he'd had to order in because they were going to be so busy."

"Still," O'Hearn said. "That could be anything."

"Yeah, it could. But if it's real? You could set a trap for them."

If it was real, they could use the information to set several traps. "If it's real," Granville said.

Trent grinned. "Isn't it worth the risk? Also, this same guy heard that puppet master doesn't have a new enforcer yet. But the rumor is that he's in talks with somebody. And the guy didn't even want to speculate about who. Turned pale when I pushed a little. So I backed off," Trent said with a certain pride.

"Well played," Granville said, and the lad beamed. "Would you be willing to start a rumor of your own?"

"Course I would," Trent said. "To this guy?"

"Yes. I need to you leak word that Scott and I will be down on the docks tonight after dark, watching the harbor for shipments coming in. Think he'll fall for that?"

Trent's eyes brightened. "You bet he will!"

"Then you head there as soon as we're done," Granville said. "But first, are we agreed that Fairfield is our best bet to be the man we're looking for? The Puppet Master?"

Everyone nodded.

"Then if we assume Fairfield is the puppet master, does that leave any doubts or questions we can't answer?"

"It all seems to fit," Mac said.

Wardle nodded thoughtfully. "To be honest, he seems so bland, he wouldn't even have been on my list. Except for his financial reversals. If that was family money, why did it diminish, then increase? And if his income is not family money, it doesn't have an obvious source."

"We still don't have solid proof of any of this," Carver said. "Not that would stand up in court, anyway."

Granville exchanged glances with Randall, but neither said anything. Their strategy, if they ended up needing it, would be best not discussed ahead of time.

"We also don't have a legitimate reason to arrest him," Daniels added.

"Not yet," Granville said. "But at least we have a suspect. So it's time to force the puppet master to make a mistake."

Scott looked across the table at him, and grinned. "A big one," he said with satisfaction.

"What do you have in mind?" Randall asked quietly.

"I'm going to leave my card at Fairfield's home, along with a note inviting him to meet with me tomorrow to explain himself," Granville said.

Most of those around the table stared at him. Wardle chuckled quietly from his corner. Beside him, Emily exchanged a satisfied smile with Clara. And reached for his hand under the table.

"You're raising the stakes," Randall said. "Telling him you know exactly who he is, and expecting him to meet with you like a good little gentleman."

"Which he isn't," Trent burst out. "He's a cowardly villain, and now that he knows you know, he'll likely shoot you in the back."

"Exactly," Granville said.

Randall nodded. "It's brilliant."

"If it's him," Carver said. "If it isn't, you're still nowhere."

"Even if it isn't Fairfield, I'm gambling the puppet master will hear that we'll be at the docks tonight. I'm betting he'll come after us. We're getting too close."

"But… he'll shoot you," Trent said.

"He can try," Scott said fiercely as Emily gripped his hand more tightly.

"I'm assuming you'd like an undercover police officer or two down on the docks tonight," Daniels said.

"Only if you can trust them," Granville said. "Otherwise, just you will be fine."

It was a dark, clear night. The stars seemed nearly close enough to touch. Granville stood back to back with Scott, watching a ship docking at the far end of the docks. It was risky bringing them in at night. He wondered why they'd done so.

He hated waiting.

After the team meeting, he'd had his calling card delivered to Fairfield's residence along with his regards. And a request that they meet the following morning. With that simple gesture, he'd taken the war into the enemy's camp.

I know who you are. I know where you live.

Now it was up to Fairfield to respond.

And after meeting the fellow, he was willing to bet that there was no way Fairfield would let that kind of provocation go unanswered. Not if he was the puppet master.

And if he'd been wrong, and Fairfield wasn't the puppet master?

He hated the thought, and the fact he still couldn't be certain who it was. But even so, the odds were good that the puppet master would take the bait and try to kill him from the shadows tonight.

Granville had to laugh at his own thoughts. It wasn't so much that the fellow had been trying to kill him—he'd grown rather used to people doing that. But he'd been using underlings to do so. If he had a grudge, the fellow needed to come after Granville himself. It was only sporting.

Though expecting a killer to be sporting was a form of insanity. And a reminder of the more useless nature of some of his own schooling. Though the puppet master had the same education. Would that make a difference?

No.

For someone like the puppet master, everything was pretense for the sake of deception. Including fair fights. And honor.

As he thought, Granville's eyes were constantly scanning the shadowed wharf, alert for any sign or sound of movement. A faint clatter from somewhere along the wooden walkway on the rise behind them had him listening hard. Was that…?

It was followed by silence.

He wasn't fooled. He nudged Scott, who shifted his weight slightly from one foot to the other. Readying himself.

More silence.

A faint creaking. Again from the walkway a good ten feet above them. Someone standing in that spot would be looking nearly straight down at them. And the puppet master was a coward. If that was him, was there any chance he could see well enough to shoot them?

Nudging Scott again, Granville ghosted back away from the lantern that dimly lit the pier, and farther into the shadows. Scott followed him on silent feet.

Their new location was nearly underneath the walkway, in the shadow of the steepest part of the bank. Which would make for a nearly impossible shot, even in daylight.

Good.

That thought led to another, and he cursed under his breath. Before he set up this ambush, he should have found out if Fairfield— or the other two, just to be on the safe side—was a marksman. He doubted any of them were hunters. Not of game, anyway.

But shooting as a pastime was considered an acceptable leisure sport for gentlemen. One the puppet master would undoubtedly find useful in his particular line of work. And if he had a rifle? For a good shot, it might just be doable.

Both he and Scott held their own pistols ready. The plan called for Fairfield to attempt to murder them. Getting shot, even killed, was not supposed to be more than a slight risk.

Somehow he sensed Scott's amusement even in the thick shadows. He suspected Scott had already found out about Fairfield.

"He's a marksman?" he asked, pitching his voice soft and low. The rush and slide of the waves against the pebbled shore would cover his words.

"Oh, yeah," Scott said just as softly.

Granville cursed again. "Why didn't you say something?"

"Why? Your plan's still a good one."

"Not if it gets you shot."

Very faintly Granville heard the sound of footfalls on the walkway about them. He froze, listening hard. Just what was the puppet master up to now?

He'd be looking for anything that gave him an edge. Had he found something?

A sudden thud. Followed immediately by the crash of a rifle and a burning, then an icy numbness along his arm was his answer. The puppet master had found a convenient knothole in the walkway.

Convenient for him, anyway. Granville stared up at the walkway for a moment, wondering how the fellow had spotted that weakness in the poor light. He was in shock, he realized, as Scott dragged him further back against the bank.

"Hey, there's people down here," he called out as soon as he figured they were out of range.

There was another bang, and the whistle of a bullet.

"You hit?" he asked his partner.

"Nope," Scott said, still softly. Then more loudly, and pitched to be heard. "This guy's a lousy shot."

"Not that bad," Granville said quietly, leaning more heavily against the packed earth behind him.

In fact, the blighter was a remarkably good shot. And it was now abundantly clear he was aiming for them.

"Can you see who it is?" he asked. "Is it Fairfield?"

His voice was swallowed by loud cursing and a barrage of shots from overhead. Then a metallic click and more cursing.

Followed by Officer Daniels calm voice. "Drop the gun. Now! You're out of ammunition. And you're under arrest."

And Scott's increasingly urgent voice. "Granville?"

"What? I'm fine."

"You're bleeding."

It couldn't be serious. His arm burned and stung a little, but he'd had worse. And he had a few things to say to Fairfield.

"It will keep," he said. And took the stairs two at a time back up to the walkway.

Where he came face to face with the puppet master, standing in handcuffs in front of Officer Daniels and two armed policemen. One of the policemen was carefully holding an engraved rifle, the expensive detailing clear under the street lamp.

A grin split his face, and he felt a deep sense of satisfaction. "Evening, Fairfield. What a surprise to see you again. Nice rifle."

Fairfield glowered at him, but his voice held the tones of a cultured English gentleman. "I don't know what this is about, but it is all a mistake."

"Attempted murder is such a nice, useful charge," Granville said. "We thought we'd start there and see what else you've been up to."

Fairfield sputtered something about not even knowing anyone was down on the docks as he was led away. Granville was aware Scott had come up behind him, but he watched until the police wagon was out of sight.

"Satisfying?" Scott asked him.

"Immensely."

"You think there's enough to keep him locked up?"

"I intend to make sure of it," Granville said, and turned towards Scott.

Who looked at his arm, now clearly visible in the lamplight. "You're still bleeding. And heavily. Granville? Granville!"

5 6

—————

Sunday, September 30, 1900

On Sunday morning, Granville's heavily bandaged upper arm ached and burned as if the bullet were still lodged in the muscle. He was grateful that visibility had been so poor last night, and Fairfield's angle so bad. The shot had deflected just enough going through the knothole to lose some of its momentum before it hit him.

"Another quarter-inch and it would have either hit an artery or been lodged in the bone," the doctor on duty had told him cheerfully as he fished around in his arm with a pair of long-nosed forceps. "That would have meant surgery, and your odds of surviving this go way down."

"Good to know," Granville had said through gritted teeth. He'd refused painkillers, and he was regretting it. He preferred whiskey to any other painkiller, but even the good Scotch from his hip flask wasn't helping much at the moment.

But at least they'd caught Fairfield. Now they needed to make sure he paid for his crimes.

As soon as the clock struck nine-thirty, Granville headed for the police station, with Scott beside him. Daniels would be working this morning. And Fairfield would still be in jail. He intended to better the odds that the fellow stayed there.

Then he talked to Daniels.

"We can keep Fairfield locked up until Monday," Daniels explained. "But once he gets hold of his lawyer, we probably don't have enough evidence to hold him. He'll be released on bail."

"He tried to murder me," Granville said, fighting to keep his tone civil. This wasn't Daniels' fault.

"Fairfield says it was an accident. A most unfortunate, but entirely accidental discharge of his pistol, is how he puts it," Daniels said.

That sounded like Fairfield. He'd been saying the same thing last night. But Granville had been too busy bleeding to pay much attention.

"And he says it to anyone who will listen," Daniels added.

"He's a killer. And I've got the note to prove it."

"You're going to have to help me there," the police officer said frankly. "Can you prove it's his writing?"

"Probably not," Granville said, disgusted with himself for not seeing it sooner.

Knowing what he did about the puppet master? The fellow would undoubtedly have disguised his handwriting.

Daniels nodded. "With the few facts we have now, a half-way competent lawyer will have him out by tomorrow."

Much as he hated to admit it, Daniels was right. They couldn't tie Fairfield to anything, not to the smuggling or even a single murder.

The police hadn't even been able to keep the ghost in jail, and he had killed at least two men, and likely quite a few more. All on Fairfield's orders.

Even worse, with the ghost gone, so was any chance of linking Fairfield to those murders.

And if they couldn't tie the threatening note to Fairfield, they couldn't prove he'd meant to injure Granville. Much less murder him. At best the incident would probably result in some kind of improper use of firearms charge.

Which—given the fellow's sterling reputation—would likely earn him no more than a figurative slap on the wrist. It was beyond frustrating. It was a total miscarriage of justice.

And the only one who would even listen to him was Daniels, whose hands were tied.

"Then we'll find you the proof you need," Granville told Daniels.

"We're going to what?" Scott said from beside him. "And just how are we planning on doing that?"

"Let me talk to Fairfield," Granville said to Daniels.

Who gave him a skeptical look. "Why would he talk to you?"

"Because he's the puppet master," he said. "He thinks this is all a game, and he's winning. He won't be able to resist crowing over me."

"That's because he is winning," Scott put in. "Or hadn't you noticed?"

Both men ignored him.

"And how will that help you prove anything against Fairchild?" Daniels asked.

"He's careful, but he's arrogant, too," Granville said. "And in his mind, I'm the reason he lost his assassin. He won't intentionally tell me anything, but he won't be able to resist taking cryptic jabs at me."

Daniels looked like he wanted to argue, but instead just shook his head and disappeared through a heavy door at the back of the room. Several minutes later he was back, looking irritated.

"Our prisoner says he won't talk to anyone until he sees his lawyer, so don't waste his time," Daniels said to Granville. "Oh, and he's planning to sue the police for false imprisonment, and he said to tell you he's going to sue you for libel and bearing false witness."

Granville's mind stopped as he stared at Daniels, then it began to race. The police might not have enough to charge Fairfield, but there was nothing to stop Granville from suing him, personally. For reckless endangerment, or some such charge. With Randall as his lawyer.

And wouldn't that be an interesting case.

He started to grin. "What a good idea," he said.

Daniels and Scott both stared at him.

"He's been shot," Scott explained to Daniels. "Lost a lot of blood. The doctor said he was fine, but…"

"I am fine," Granville said. "And I was right. Fairfield's arrogance just got the better of him. You'll hear from us, Daniels. Let's go, Scott."

Without another word, Scott opened the door for him, then followed him out of the building.

"You don't sound fine to me. How can you call being sued a good idea?" Scott demanded as they descended the granite steps outside the police station. The church bells had rung an hour before, so the street was deserted, leaving them in no danger of being overheard.

"If Fairfield sues us, we can countersue," Granville said.

"And that helps us how?" Scott asked.

"Nothing short of a murder charge is going to put the puppet master in jail permanently," Granville said.

"So?"

"So everything we have is circumstantial. We don't have enough proof that he had the assassin commit murder for him."

"You just told Daniels we were going to find it for him," Scott said. "Just what are you planning on finding?"

"There's another problem, too," Granville said, ignoring the question. "Even if Fairfield has slipped up somewhere, and that proof exists? If we get too close to finding it, he'll probably skip town. He's done it before."

His partner scowled. "That's your argument? There is no proof?"

"Sure is," Granville said with another, broader grin. "Look, we know they can't keep Fairfield in jail on the evidence we have. And Fairfield has covered his tracks too well. The only hope we might have is at trial, and then only if Randall is the lawyer that Fairfield and his counsel have to argue against."

"But Randall's a defense attorney," Scott said. "Murder's a Crown case, even if it's attempted murder. And the current Crown

Prosecutor is an ass. Randall could argue circles around him. In his sleep."

"Exactly," Granville said as they headed towards Emily's church.

Scott stopped in the middle of the deserted sidewalk and stared at him. "But if Fairfield sues you for… what was it? Libel?"

"And bearing false witness," Granville said with a nod.

"Won't the judge throw it out?" Scott asked.

"Probably. But it gets us all into court. Especially if I counter sue."

"For what?"

"Something equally nonsensical, and therefore non-threatening. Most likely reckless endangerment. Or maybe defamation of character."

"And Randall would represent you. I get it," Scott said. "No wonder you were grinning."

"It should prove an interesting case."

"Unless the puppet master is too wily to trip up at trial. He's smarter than most of Randall's previous victims."

"He is. Until that arrogance of his gets in the way," Granville said.

"Yeah. Suing you is not his brightest move," Scott said. "Not with Randall behind you."

"Besides, I have a plan," Granville said. "And we're going to need to get the team together to pull it off."

"Another meeting?"

He grinned. "Right after we take Emily to lunch. And you get to explain to her how you let me get shot."

Scott groaned. "This day goes from bad to worse."

J ust after one that afternoon, Emily looked around the table at the familiar faces gathered in the office meeting room and took a calming breath. Everyone who had been involved with the puppet master case was here. This was their chance to deal with the fellow, once and for all. Judging by their expressions, they all knew it.

And these were the people who could do it, too. They'd teach the puppet master not to mess with them. Or shoot at Granville.

She swallowed back the surge of emotion that thought brought along with it. Granville had called her just after breakfast to say he was fine, and to apologize for not escorting her to church that morning.

"What happened last night?" Emily had asked. She'd barely slept the night before, worrying about the trap he'd set for the puppet master. "Did he show up? Was it who you expected?"

"Yes, and yes," he'd said, a laugh in his voice. "Daniels arrested him, so I'm off to the police station this morning to make sure our puppet master stays put."

"Good," she said, letting out a breath she hadn't even realized she was holding. "I'm so glad."

Then she'd realized what he hadn't said.

"You're fine?" she repeated. "What does that mean? Was someone injured?"

"It's just a flesh wound," he said quickly. "It only needed bandaging."

"He shot you?" It was the nightmare she'd been running from all night long. "How? I thought you were going to stay out of range."

"Pure bad luck. He didn't have a clean shot, but the bullet deflected. Which took most of the bullet's energy, so it did very little damage."

"What about Scott? And how did…"

"Why don't I take you for lunch, and fill you in," he interrupted before she could finish the thought. "Scott and I will meet you at the church, at the end of the service, if you like?"

"Yes," she had said decidedly. She needed to see for herself just how badly he'd been hurt.

Not too badly, as it turned out, though she thought he was pretending to be less affected than he was. Partly for her sake, and partly because he was so determined that now was the time to take the puppet master down that he had every resource he had focused on that.

She was equally determined to help him do so.

As were those gathered around the table. There were questions about Granville's bandaged arm, but he waved them off. Then between them, he and Scott filled everyone in on the events of the previous evening. And what Daniels had said that morning.

"So Fairfield is still in jail?" Trent asked gleefully.

"For now," Granville said. "He can't do much about it on a Sunday. But you can bet his lawyer will be asking for bail tomorrow."

"So what's the plan?" Mr. Randall asked. "Since you know as well as I do that Fairfield will likely be released tomorrow."

They all knew the puppet master was lethal. And from what Granville and Scott had said about Saturday night, vengeful. He'd not hesitate to have Granville killed. Or anyone important to him.

There was really only one choice, and all of them knew it.

"We need to make sure Fairfield doesn't get a chance to attack any of us," Granville said. "And that he gets what he deserves."

"We're going to shoot him?" Trent said. He sounded pleased, Emily thought with amusement, as she noted the resigned glances Scott and Granville exchanged.

"Not quite," Granville said. "We have a great deal of information about what the fellow has been up to in the last few years. Buried in that is the thing or things that will convict him in any court. We are going to find that thing, and put together the pieces to ensure Fairfield has to answer in court for what he's done. See how he likes spending the rest of his life behind bars."

Emily approved. It wasn't frontier justice, but it was equally effective.

"You don't think he'll jump bail and leave town?" O'Hearn asked.

"If he thinks he's in danger, I think he'll do exactly that," Granville said. "But he thinks he's won this round. He'll be focused on his own lawsuits, and how much damage he can do to us and the police by suing us. He's too arrogant to believe we could ever prove anything against him. Don't you agree?"

Both Tim and Mr. Draper nodded.

"You keep saying we're going to get proof," Trent said. "But we still aren't getting anywhere."

"On Saturday we didn't know who the puppet master was. Today he's in jail," Granville said. "I'd call that pretty decent progress. Wouldn't you?"

Trent nodded, looking a little sheepish.

"So what do we have, and what do we need?" Granville asked the others.

"I'm still trying to find out if Fairfield is wanted anywhere for previous crimes," Tim said. "Even if there are no outstanding warrants, there might be enough similarity in the criminal activity to help put him away here."

"I'll help him," Mr. Draper said.

"Excellent idea. I'll call Pinkerton's and get them to dig deeper on him," Granville said.

"Miss Kent and I will go back through the financial details and see if we've missed something, now we know who we're dealing with," Mac said.

"I have a feeling we did miss something," Laura said. "It's as if I saw something out of the corner of my eye, but..." She shrugged, spread her hands wide. "I'm sorry. I can't explain it. But maybe if I can find what triggered that feeling, I can see the pattern that I missed."

"I might be able to help," Emily said. "Since I haven't been working directly with you on this, just the act of explaining it to me might trigger something for you."

"Fresh eyes," Laura said, brightening. "Yes, that might help."

"Carver, can you work with them from the legal perspective?" Granville said. "What we're looking for is proof of anything illegal or criminal Fairfield has done or been a party to."

Carver nodded. "My pleasure."

"Wait a minute," Trent said. "Talking about missing something... When I was out yesterday, I heard whispers about there being another murder on the puppet master's account. But I figured it couldn't be true, 'cause we hadn't heard anything before. But what if it is true? Want me to go ask more questions?"

"Good idea. With Fairfield in jail, others might be willing to talk about the earlier killings," Granville said.

"Might be worth exploring," Scott said.

"Scott and I will come with you," Granville said over Trent's protests that he could handle it himself. "We'll leave once I've talked to Pinkerton's."

Emily was watching him closely. There was something he hadn't said, and she wanted to know what it was.

As they all stood up to begin their assigned tasks, Granville looked over everyone's heads. "Randall? If you have a moment, I'd like to have a word," he said.

EMILY WAITED until Randall had left Granville's office, closing the door behind him. He looked... shocked, she thought. And maybe a bit intrigued. What could Granville have told him?

And why was he doing so behind closed doors?

With only a brief tap on the door, and without waiting for a response, she burst into the office.

"The bullet hole in your arm is bad enough," she said. "I'm trying very hard to be a grownup about it, but now you're having secret meetings with your lawyer? Please tell me you're not updating your will."

"I'm not updating my will," he said. "Though that would probably be a good idea."

She could feel the blood leaving her face, and planted her feet more firmly.

"That is not helpful," she said, and glared at him.

"Sorry," he said. "I'm not planning on dying any time soon."

"Or being in danger?" she asked, narrowing her eyes at him.

"Not any more danger than we are all of us already in because of Fairfield's threats," he said.

She could hear the honesty in his words.

"Oh," she said, and sat down across the desk from him. "Then why the talk about your will? And the secret meeting with your lawyer? If it's about the case, why aren't you talking to the team about it?"

He held up a hand, and smiled at her. Emily was relieved to notice it was his injured arm, and he seemed to be moving it easily. She relaxed a little.

"I haven't updated my will since I bought the house," he said. "And I need to update it. That's all. And I'd rather do it now, since I plan to leave the house to you. Along with my share of the business."

Emily blinked at him. She hadn't expected that, and it took her breath away. But it distracted her only for a moment, then she glared at him again. "What are you hiding?"

He grinned, and explained about the countersuit he was planning, and why. "I've asked Randall to file my suit as soon as Fairfield files his. And to consider what strategy he'll use against the puppet master."

That explained the lawyer's odd expression.

After a stunned second of her own, Emily burst out laughing. "I can't help it," she said between bursts of laughter. "It's too perfect. But why not tell the team?"

"Because I want them focused on finding proof of Fairfield's illegal acts. Proof that will stand up in court," he added. "If they find something, we'll let the police deal with our puppet master. If all we find are unsubstantiated whispers and hints, then we'll use the countersuit and let Randall work his magic in court."

"Surely you didn't tell your lawyer that?"

"Yes, I did."

She wondered what Mr. Randall had thought of that. "You really think he can bring the puppet master down?"

"If we provide enough information for him?" He grinned at her. "You've seen Randall in court. What do you think?"

"I think I want to be in that courtroom," she said, returning his grin. "Like you said—I think he's magic, too."

5 8

The call to Pinkerton's researchers didn't take Granville long. He gave the fellow who answered Fairfield's name, asking for any information they had on him. He also asked for anything that might connect Heywood to Fairfield, then emphasized the urgent nature of the request.

"It will take at least a couple of hours," the researcher said. "I'll get back to you." And he ended the call.

As Granville replaced the handset, he wondered how important his search would be to someone he'd never met in Pinkerton's New York office.

"Looks like we have a couple of hours before we hear anything back," he told Scott. "We might as well collect Trent and see if there is anything behind those rumors he heard."

"It beats waitin' around," Scott said.

Half an hour later, Trent led Granville and Scott to a beat-up restaurant down by the docks which bore a strong resemblance to a fishing shack.

"I found this place the other week," their apprentice said. "Food's not quite as good as that place in Steveston, but it's still pretty decent. The fish is really fresh. And I'm hungry."

"You're always hungry," Scott said. "It was even worse when he was running around in the cannery," he muttered to Granville. Who grinned in reply.

"Please tell me it's also a good source for gossip," Granville told Trent.

"Of course. Would I waste your time with anything else?" Trent said righteously.

Which earned him an eye roll.

The small restaurant was packed and noisy, the air thick with heat and the smell of frying fish. And judging by the crowded tables, it was a local favorite.

"Wait till you try their potato fries," Trent said. "With deep fried fresh fish and lots of ketchup. Mmmm."

Breakfast had been early, and he and Emily had eaten an early, light lunch. The rough and ready meal sounded good. "Any chance of a malt vinegar instead of the ketchup?" Granville said, knowing it was likely a vain hope.

"Course," Trent said. "You aren't the only Brit in these parts, y'know. All you English insist on that brown vinegar with your fish and chips, for some reason." And he made a face.

Their conversation was enough to engage the attention of the wiry fellow behind the counter. "This place'd close in a week without the malt vinegar," he said, running an assessing eye over the three of them in their suits. "What brings the likes of you down here?"

"A small matter of business," Granville said. "I hear this is the place to come if you want to know what's going on around these parts."

"Could be. What're you hopin' to find out?"

"I'm interested in a fellow lost his pet assassin a week or so back. I'm wondering if he's replaced him."

"Assassin, is it, then? Why's a toff like you care?"

"I'm concerned about a certain lady. There might have been threats made," Granville said.

"Threats? Against your lady?"

"Yes."

"Now, that's not done, not in these here parts." He glanced around. "Hey, Karl. What d'you hear about a new killer on the streets?"

Karl, a heavyset blond fellow who topped six feet, said, "You mean since the Garroter vanished? A whisper or two that someone nameless is looking to hire. No takers, so far's I know."

The first fellow looked back at Granville, "That's what I heard, too. If there was a new killer on the street, b'lieve me, we'd all know about it. Now, you going to get yourself some of this fish? Or stand around blathering?"

"Fish it is," Granville said with a grin.

"Cod or halibut?"

"Halibut."

"You want mushy peas with that?"

"Not this time," he said diplomatically. He'd never developed a taste for the mushy, brownish-green plodge that many of his countrymen insisted on eating with their fish and chips.

A shrug and a steaming plate of crisply fried fish and rough-cut potato wedges was handed across. "Malt's on th' table."

Granville stretched out his hand. "Many thanks." His mouth watered as he made his way to a table near the door that had a few seats free. Sliding onto the rough pine bench, he nodded to the grizzled man in a fisherman's heavy cotton clothing who'd just slid into the seat on his right, and grabbed the promised bottle of vinegar. As he seasoned his food, the sharpness of the malt cut through the heavy smell of frying oil that hung in the air. It smelled of home, and for a moment he missed England with an equally sharp ache.

He looked up to see Trent and Scott making their way across the room to join him. Before they were half-way across the room, the fisherman leaned a little towards him. "I see you know how to eat fish n' chips," he said in a deep voice that slid underneath the clamoring noise around them.

"Is there any other way?"

"Not for me," the fellow said. "Course, we're surrounded by philistines," and he glanced at the oversize bottle of ketchup on the table. "You're missing a good bit of the truth, y'know?"

"Oh? How's that?"

"Couldn't help but overhear. You were asking about a hired killer?"

"I was. Was the information wrong?"

"Not wrong, exactly. Incomplete."

Granville helped himself to a tender morsel of perfectly cooked halibut and considered his neighbor. "What am I not hearing?"

"There was another murder."

Trent had been right. "So he did hire another assassin," Granville said, his mind working quickly.

"Better," the fellow beside him said, a sly look sitting incongruously on his broad face. "He had to do the deed himself."

The puppet master himself had killed someone? If this information was real, it was enough to see the fellow hang.

But who had Fairfield killed? And could they prove it?

"How do you know?" Granville asked. "And why are you willing to tell me about it?"

"You're that investigator fellow, aren't you?" his companion said. "Granville?"

"I am."

That earned him a nod. "The word around town is that you set yourself up as a target for this guy. And that you're why the Garroter —his previous assassin—left town."

Whoever this was, he was well-informed. "You hear a lot of words," Granville said, aware that Scott and Trent had slid into the seats across from him, but focusing on his new acquaintance. "How is that?"

Another sly grin. "You might say it's my business. Same as it's yours."

"You're an investigator?" He certainly didn't look like one. But it took all kinds. And if the fellow's current attire was a disguise, it was certainly more effective for gaining information in this place than Granville's formal suit.

"Not exactly. And only if it's worth my while, if y'know what I mean?"

A paid informant then? "Who do you work for?"

"Myself. And anyone who makes it worth my while. Like yourself, maybe?"

He needed information on the puppet master. If this fellow really had what he said he did… "It's a possibility. I'm willing to discuss terms. If your information is good."

That earned him a nod. "They said you were a savvy one. Glad to see it's true."

The fellow's gaze went to Scott and Trent, who were clearly listening while slowly eating their fish. "I can prove what I say. But not now. Meet me at the Beaver Tavern at seven this evening if you're interested."

And without another word he turned back to his own meal and devoured what was left of it. Then the fellow stood up and left without another glance at Granville.

As soon as he'd gone, Scott grabbed up his tray of food and slid around the table and into the spot beside Granville. "What was that all about?" he asked, pitching his voice so that only Granville could hear it above the noise.

"How much did you hear?"

"Not a thing."

So the informant had mastered the art of making sure he wasn't overheard, even in this crowd. That was good to know.

"According to him, there was another murder," Granville said. "Trent was right. But this time it was the puppet master himself who did the killing."

Scott sat back and stared. "What?"

"That's what he said."

"Sounds too good to be true. You get any details on that?"

Granville quickly explained the informant's terms, hiding a grin when Scott's face registered the same skepticism he himself was feeling.

"He could be lying about all of it. And seven o'clock at the Beaver Tavern? You do know it sounds the perfect setup for an ambush, right?" his partner said.

"It's a risk I'm willing to take," Granville said. If the puppet master didn't hesitate to kill, it made him even more dangerous than he'd feared.

Scott looked at him with narrowed eyes. "You're taking too many risks on this one."

He shrugged. "I'm tired of the puppet master. I want it over with."

"Right."

Granville poured a bit more vinegar on his chips, forked one up.

Scott just shook his head. "If you're determined to go through with this meeting, then Trent and I are going with you. And in the meantime, we might as well keep digging. Someone else has to know about this murder."

"They would also need to be willing to talk to us about it," Granville said dryly. "That part might prove a little more challenging."

THE THREE OF them had just returned and were gathered in Granville's office when the phone rang.

"I'm not sure how much use this is," the Pinkerton's researcher said. "We have no file at all on Fairfield. If he's crooked, he's managed to hide it from law enforcement everywhere."

"What about Heywood and Fairfield?" he asked.

"As we told you before, we do have quite a bit on Heywood. But no obvious links between him and Fairfield."

"Thanks," Granville said. "I appreciate the information."

"Welcome," the fellow said.

Granville hung up the handset and exchanged glances with Scott.

"They got nothing, huh?" Trent said, sitting forward on the edge of his chair.

"Not on Fairfield."

"At least the fellow's still in jail," Scott said.

"For now. The trick is keeping him there, and we're running out of sources," Granville said. "Hopefully this informant will have something useful."

"If you don't get yourself killed," Scott retorted.

"It's still worth a shot," he said. "Meanwhile, I'll pass this information to the rest of the team."

His partner still looked annoyed.

"If things get too dull, we could always go and annoy Fairfield in jail," he said, hiding a grin at Scott's glare and Trent's gleeful look. "That should liven up our afternoon. He might even tell us something useful."

At seven o'clock that evening, the Beaver Tavern still half-empty, but loud with the raucous voices of men who'd been drinking all day. The place was thick with smoke and reeked of stale beer and greasy food. Empty peanut shells crunched underfoot.

Granville peered through the murk and spotted his informant at the bar. He didn't acknowledge him, but strode towards an empty table in the back corner nearest the door. He always liked to know where his exit was, especially in a place like this.

Scott headed for the bar, and came back with two foaming mugs. He handed one to Granville, then without a word sat down at a nearby table. This time they'd left Trent behind, despite his protests. No matter how seasoned the kid thought he was, this evening's work was too dicey to include him.

When their informant—still dressed as a fisherman—slid into the seat beside him a minute later, Granville did waste any time. "So you say you know something about another murder? One the assassin, the fellow you call the Garroter, didn't do."

"Yeah, I do. You got the money?"

Granville slid an envelope across to him.

The fellow thumbed through it, nodded, and tucked it away. "What d'you want to know?" he asked.

"When was this murder you saw?"

"Friday before last."

Which made it the weekend before Benton hired him and Scott to deal the puppet master 'in any way they chose'. That couldn't be a coincidence.

"Who died?" Granville asked.

"You seem to know Benton pretty well, from what I hear," the fellow said with a knowing wink. "Why don't you ask him?"

One of Benton's men, then. The 'lieutenant' Parvo said he had reported to, perhaps? The one Benton had never actually admitted he'd lost.

But he was paying for information, not insinuations.

"Why would I ask Benton?" Granville asked. Two could play at this game.

"Because he's the one that lost someone."

Definitely not a coincidence. "I need a name."

"It'll cost you."

"You're already costing me," Granville said. "The name."

The informant's eyes flickered to where Scott sat at the far end of the bar, out of earshot but definitely within reach. And he probably already knew how fast Scott could move, despite his size. When properly motivated.

"Donati. He'd been with Benton awhile."

Granville didn't recognize the name, but Scott might. Or Parvo could confirm it, even if Benton wouldn't. He could find out if the informant was lying easily enough. And the fellow knew it, too. "First name?"

"He went by Fingers."

Interesting. "So you're telling me the fellow who hired the assassin—let's call him the puppet master—is the one who killed this Donati."

"The puppet master, eh?" The informant grinned at that. "I like it. And that's exactly what I'm telling you."

"Why would the puppet master do so? According to you, this

was before the assassin left town. And before the assassin's last killing, too."

"The last killing that you know of."

Granville scowled. "There was another?"

"It'll cost you."

Of course it would. He shook his head at the nerve of this fellow. "Never mind the Garroter's killings for now," he said. "Why would the puppet master go after Donati himself?"

"Seems Donati was in the wrong place at the wrong time," the informant said. "Maybe Benton had Donati following someone?"

"Someone like the puppet master, you mean?" Granville asked.

The informant gave him a sly look. "Maybe."

That sounded like Benton. "Go on."

"And maybe Donati got caught."

"By the puppet master?" It was plausible enough. "So how would you know about this? Assuming it happened at all."

"Oh, it happened."

"And?"

A shrug. "Maybe I was following Donati."

That figured. This fellow seemed to make his living selling information, and didn't much care to whom. Or how he got it. "So you actually saw Donati killed?"

"Maybe I did."

He'd take that as a yes. For now. "And you saw who did it?"

"Maybe so."

"So where did this killing happen?"

"Just off Water Street. Not far from the Ironworkers docks."

"What time of day was this?"

"Early evening."

"Some of those alleys are pretty narrow and dark. How'd you see well enough to identify him?"

"This alley had an open space partway down. It was nearly twilight, but the light was still good," the informant said. "This puppet master faked Donati out. He waited till the guy was out in the open, then confronted him. They had words. And the puppet master shot him."

"I need a name."

"Don't have one. Other than 'the Toff', which is what I've been calling him."

"Why that name?"

"Because he thinks highly of himself, that one. You can tell by the way he carries himself."

Which fit his own conclusions about Fairfield. And gave some veracity to the informant's words. "You saw him clearly then?"

"Clear enough."

Right. "Clearly enough to identify him in court?" Granville asked.

"If he's there."

"And to testify to what you saw?"

The informant put up his hands. "Whoa, there. I never said nothing about testifying."

"And is that a problem?"

"I'm allergic, like."

He probably had a warrant or three out for him. "I'm sure I can arrange immunity for you."

"I'd have no business left, if I did that."

That was probably true. But they needed a witness. "You're sure you saw him clearly enough to recognize him again?" Granville asked.

"Yeah."

"And you're sure he's the puppet master? The fellow who hired the assassin?"

"Yeah," the informant said.

"The puppet master is smart. And wary. And he'd just killed this Donati for following him, according to you," Granville said. "So how did you get close enough to identify him?"

"After he killed Donati? I kept following him. But you can bet I kept well back."

"Go on."

"He kept in the shadows for a few blocks, then he ducked into another alley. Met up with the Garroter. They were standing by the backdoor of some bar, cause the alley stunk of stale beer and puke. It was still light enough to see, and there was some light coming from a back window, too. I saw 'em clear enough."

Granville tried to picture it. "How did you know it was the assassin?"

"Him I knew by sight. It looked like a report back, and the Garroter got new orders."

The ghost said he'd never met the puppet master. Someone was lying here.

Or both of them were.

"How did you know which of them was giving the order?" Granville asked.

The informant gave him a crooked grin. "You're an investigator. You really need to ask?"

No. It would have been clear in how the two men interacted. This fellow paid attention. "So then what?"

"I followed the Toff, of course."

"And?"

"He lost me. And that's not an easy thing to do."

No, it probably wasn't. "How? And where?"

"Dunno exactly how. He was there, and then he wasn't. But I can show you where I lost him."

Granville took a last swallow of his beer and stood up. "Lead on, then."

The informant drained his own mug and thunked it down on the bar, then led the way out into the night.

WITH SCOTT IN TOW, they walked briskly west on Alexander. To Granville's surprise, the informant took a left up Carrall, then several blocks later he suddenly turned right into the shadowy depths of Blood Alley.

Granville reacted fast, turning into the alley right behind their informant. For a moment he didn't see the fellow. He paused, and Scott, right on his heels, nearly crashed into him.

The alley was an eerie place, named after its bloody history. For a moment, rising above the reek of rotting food and spilled whiskey, he could swear he smelled the blood that had seeped into the cobblestones over the years. Though the scent wasn't strong enough to be fresh. Or even recent. Then cursed at himself for having an overactive imagination.

There was a chuckle from somewhere behind him, and the informant emerged from the shadows behind a stack of moldering boxes. He had ducked into a narrow passage between two brick buildings.

"This is where he lost me," he said. "Still don't know how. It's a blind alley, and this passage doesn't go anywhere. I wasn't even half a minute behind him, I swear. I searched hard. And I know this alley as well as anyone."

Granville didn't doubt it. But despite the moniker he'd given him, the informant likely didn't suspect 'the Toff' of having the kind of society connections Granville now knew he had.

During the day, a stagecoach line kept the alley busy, but at night, the place took on a new character. Blood Alley was home to several sleazy nightclubs, popular with the fast set, as well as a run-down bar or two. He and Scott would need to come back later and see which crowd the puppet master might have slipped into, mixing easily with the celebrants to be found there late in the evening. Even on a Sunday, the understaffed police force never managed to shut this place down for long.

"Thanks," Granville said. "A few more questions, then we'll take it from here. For now. What time of day did all this happen?"

"Must have been past ten by the time I followed him here."

"Describe this man you followed."

"Dark suit and hat—quite well dressed, I'd say, though I didn't see him clearly enough to swear to it."

That fit. "What else?"

"Medium height, medium build. Probably darkish hair and light eyes. Forgettable features."

All of which fit the puppet master. And half his acquaintances. "Doesn't sound like enough to identify him," Granville said.

"Not by itself," their informant said. "But I told you there was something in the way he moved. I'd know him again."

"If you saw him move?"

"Exactly. You find him, I'll identify him."

It wouldn't put them much further ahead in a courtroom. No wonder the fellow didn't want to testify.

"Describe that something," Granville said anyway.

The fellow shrugged. "Like I told you before. He's got a kind of arrogance about him. And he's strung tight, but it's mixed with eagerness. This guy likes danger. And he liked killing."

Which meant the puppet master would be likely to kill again. Especially now Granville and Scott were getting closer.

All of which put Emily and the team at even more risk.

It wasn't information Granville was happy to have. He needed to find someone who willing to testify that Fairfield had been in the area last night.

60

Monday, October 1, 1900

It was nearly half past one the following morning when Granville made it home from Blood Alley. He and Scott hadn't begun their circuit of the clubs bordering the alley until nearly ten. Then they'd made slow progress from one whiskey-soaked dive to another.

As the hour grew later, each club grew louder, smokier and more crowded than the previous one. Just moving from the door to the bar was a challenge. Limp bodies draped against each other in a parody of dancing, or stood in small, unsteady groups laughing uproariously over nothing.

Men and women draped across chairs, even tables, calling for more drinks, and yet more. The noise level went from loud to deafening.

It was soon evident this was a lost cause. By the time Fairfield would have done his vanishing act, most of the club-goers would have been too drunk to recognize their best friends. Much less remember if they'd seen Fairfield on a particular day several weeks before. But Granville refused to give up too early.

All they needed was one good witness.

He did hear a few vague rumors about Fairfield floating around the clubs—mostly that he liked to party more than he let on, but that he preferred private parties. Questions about those parties drew a half-shrug and a wave of the hand, or a smothered giggle if he was talking to a woman. A couple of people thought they might have seen Fairfield in the area several weeks ago, but that was as definite as they got.

The only potential witness they could find was even worse than their informant. The fellow was a tall, skeletally thin young Londoner, shipped to the colonies just ahead of the scandals. A known drunk and doper, he had a fondness for opium that was likely to kill him before long.

The fellow was adamant he'd seen Fairfield saunter into the club through a back door on the night in question. He was also adamant that Fairfield had been followed by a large giraffe, wearing a bowler hat. Or maybe it had been a gorilla.

Fairfield's lawyer, no matter who he was, would turn this witness into confetti in a courtroom. If they were foolish enough to call him there.

It was nearly one in the morning by the time Granville had had enough. Enough of the hot, crowded rooms, enough of the raucous laughter and high-pitched giggles, enough of the vacuous stares and inane replies to questions he desperately needed answered. This line of investigation wasn't going to get them anywhere.

Glancing at Scott looming behind him, he'd nodded towards the door. There was nothing for them here. They needed to talk to Benton. And Randall.

Especially Randall.

He needed to let the lawyer know about the murder Fairfield had committed. And about the witness who wouldn't testify.

They were going to need a new strategy. Today.

EIGHT O'CLOCK FOUND Granville at Mary's diner, coffee in hand, waiting for his partner, and his breakfast. Not necessarily in that order.

His day had started much too early with a cacophony of hammering, followed by yelling, followed by more hammering. Which was particularly hard to take after too many whiskeys in too many clubs off of Blood Alley. And he'd come away with nothing.

Except a head that pounded in time with the hammering, and a mouth as dry as the sawdust he could smell from somewhere. Likely they'd start sawing again soon. He groaned.

He'd wanted nothing so much as to pull the bedclothes over his head for a few extra hours of sleep. He knew better. His morning chaos wasn't going to let up until the renovation of his house was completed. Whenever that might be.

And nothing but coffee—and maybe a shot of whiskey—would help his aching head. Mary's could provide both. And Scott could meet him there, help him plan Fairfield's comeuppance.

As soon as they'd eaten, he and Scott would head for Randall's office.

"HE'S WAITING FOR YOU," Randall's clerk said as soon as they entered the outer office. He showed them into their lawyer's well-organized office, and closed the door behind them.

"Scott. And Granville. Good to see you both," Randall said, standing and coming around his desk to shake hands. "Please, have a seat."

As soon as they were settled in the deep leather chairs opposite his desk, Randall leaned forward. "I don't have good news, I'm afraid," he said. "Fairfield is out of jail. As you suspected, the prosecutor didn't find any of the charges substantial enough, and essentially refused to prosecute."

That figured.

Fairfield was well-known and liked, and presented an impeccable front as a gentleman of gentility and honor. Granville was still a newcomer, and as an investigator—albeit a blue-blooded one—considered a bit questionable. Even Randall's persuasive skills weren't going to change that.

"And Fairfield has indeed filed suit against you," his lawyer said.

Good. He'd hoped the fellow wouldn't think better of it overnight.

"On what grounds?" he asked.

"Bearing false witness. And he—or his lawyer—added defamation of character, just for good measure."

"Not very creative of them, is it?" Granville said.

Randall chuckled. "Did you expect it to be? It's a nuisance suit. I've already filed the countersuit. And I upgraded the charges."

"To?"

"Attempted murder plus assault and bodily injury."

Granville laughed. "Good. That should make him pay attention."

"You're sure you want to go ahead with this?"

"It's worth it," Granville said. "Any chance of an early court date? Given the circumstances? It would help if my arm is still bandaged when I testify. I don't like the idea of him being out of jail, either. Not while he's still an active threat."

"We're scheduled to appear on Thursday morning."

He nodded. "That will work. Well done. And Scott and I have some new information for you that may have a bearing on how you present this case."

"Tell me," Randall said, picking up his fountain pen.

It didn't take them long to fill Randall in on their meeting with the informant, and what they'd found out about the puppet master.

Randall didn't seem surprised, just thoughtful. "And this witness of yours won't testify?" he asked.

"No," Granville said. "He won't."

"Not a chance," Scott said.

"But you believe he's telling the truth?" Randall said.

"Most of it," Granville answered. "At least about Fairfield."

"Then we still don't have enough evidence for the prosecutor to move forward," Randall said. "Three unreliable witnesses, one of whom won't testify. It's Fairfield's word against yours as to what happened the night he shot you."

"And mine," Scott said.

Randall shook his head. "I'm afraid you'll be seen as a prejudiced witness. Also, you can't testify to what Fairfield was doing, because you couldn't see him."

"Yeah," Scott muttered. "But I know what he was up to."

"Our problem is that Fairfield is considered an upstanding citizen, with friends in very high places, whose business helps fill the town coffers. I'm not surprised the prosecutor won't take a chance on us," Granville said, and grinned at Randall. "It's a good think we have an alternate plan. And an early trial date. Now all we have to do is make sure nothing shifts the puppet master's focus away from suing me."

Randall nodded. "As to that, I have a few thoughts," he said.

And the three men bent over the chart the lawyer laid out on his wide desk.

6 1

Thursday, October 4, 1900

As the courtroom slowly filled, Emily kept turning from her place in the front row to scan the faces behind her. She knew many of them, and suspected she'd recognize more than half the spectators by the time the trial began. Granville suing another prominent member of their closed little circle had been the talk of the 'at-homes' all week.

The fresh gossip had quickly eclipsed the speculation about Mr. Bray and his antics, and even about her sister Jane and what she'd do now.

Had this been just a business matter, there might have been a little gossip. But this was attempted murder, between two well-regarded members of society's upper strata. People couldn't get enough.

Especially with Mr. Fairfield saying that the whole thing had been a mistake. That Granville's accusations were just a malicious attempt to discredit him.

And Granville saying that Fairfield had shot him deliberately. Had, in fact, tried to murder him.

When Granville and his lawyer strode in and took their seat at the plaintiff's table, the murmuring increased as they noted the bulky bandage still visible on Granville's arm, despite his well-cut suit.

Every time she sat beside him, Emily was very conscious of not jostling that injured arm, despite his assurances that it was nothing, and that he was healing. It hadn't been just a flesh wound, no matter what he said. She'd had to fight back tears when she found out they'd had to dig the bullet out.

Then she was furious with him. It was only by luck that the puppet master's bullet had deflected just enough to miss anything critical.

Sandwiched between Scott on the aisle side of her and Clara on her other side, with the rest of the team arranged on the same bench or the one behind her, Emily was very aware that her fiancé was still taking every precaution to make sure that she and the team were safe from the puppet master and his hired assassin. Even now, with Fairfield about to appear before the judge and jury.

The murmuring escalated as Mr. Fairfield and his lawyer made their way up the side aisle to the defendants table. Emily was very glad that Scott's bulk was between her and the puppet master. Not that she expected him to try anything in court. Not really. But in her opinion, he was capable of anything.

"Do you think he's worried?" Clara asked from beside her.

Emily watched Mr. Fairfield unhurriedly seat himself at the defense table and glance at the sea of faces avidly watching his every move. Calmly, he turned to say something to his lawyer, Mr. Lloyd.

"I doubt it," Emily said. "He seems pretty cool."

"Though from everything you've told me, he's good at playing a role," Clara said.

"True." Emily considered Mr. Fairfield.

The puppet master wasn't impressive to look at, despite the expensive suit he wore. Which she suspected was deliberate. At the ball, amongst the people he'd consider his peers, Mr. Fairfield hadn't stood out, exactly, but he'd had a presence. Here he seemed—forgettable. And hardly threatening.

Which wasn't going to help Granville make his case.

Then came the call to order, and they all rose as Judge Knight entered the courtroom. The judge was a man of Papa's age, but he had a reputation for being unpredictable, depending on the state of his health. On his good days, he was a stickler for the facts of each case, and was in general a very fair man.

But on those days when his stomach betrayed him, his temper was short and he became irritable and somewhat arbitrary.

Granville had told her that since both lawsuits turned on the same facts, and his was the more serious accusation, the judge had decided to hear his case first. Apparently they had Mr. Randall to thank for that little piece of legal maneuvering. She hoped it wouldn't backfire on them.

Given the judge's current pallor and the small lines of pain around his mouth and creasing his forehead, Emily thought they might be in trouble. Both lawyers evidently thought the same—they kept their opening statements short and to the point. Which was one good thing, at least.

Mr. Randall's first witness was Officer Daniels. After he was called to the stand and sworn in, the lawyer thanked him for joining them that day, then began his questions with the night Granville was attacked.

"You and another officer were patrolling near the docks the night of Saturday last, when the incident in question occurred," Mr. Randall said. "Is that correct?"

The policeman drew out his police notebook and consulted it. "It is. Officer Jasper and I had that patrol on Saturday night."

"Would you tell the court what you heard and saw on the docks that night?"

"Mr. Fairfield was standing on the plank walkway that runs along a small rise above the pier on the Commission Merchants' docks," Officer Daniels said. "I observed him draw his gun. He appeared to take aim as he moved to several different spots along the walkway. And Mr. Fairfield sighted carefully each time."

"In your opinion, what was he aiming for?"

"He seemed to be sighting down towards the pier below him. Or possibly towards the water beyond the edge of the pier."

"And could you see what he was aiming at?" Mr. Randall asked.

"It was a dark night," the policeman said. "While the skies were clear, the moon hadn't risen yet, and away from the street lamps the shadows were deep. It was difficult to make out Mr. Fairfield's target, since the area beneath the walkway was in deep shadow. And the pier appeared, from my perspective—which was much further back towards Water Street than Mr. Fairfield's—to be deserted."

"So you didn't see either Mr. Granville or Mr. Scott."

"I did not."

"Or hear their voices?"

"I did not."

Emily glanced over at the defense table. Mr. Fairfield looked surprised at the direction that Mr. Randall's questioning had taken, and his lawyer looked pleased.

"Mr. Granville and his friend didn't call out to Mr. Fairfield during this time?" Mr. Randall asked.

"If they did, I didn't hear it," Officer Daniels said.

A murmur ran through the gallery, and Emily couldn't stop herself from looking back at the defense table. Now Mr. Fairfield was looking smug. She wanted to do something violent to knock that look off his face. Which wasn't like her at all.

"I see," Mr. Randall said, seemingly unaware that he was making Mr. Fairfield's case for him. "And what did you hear during that time?"

"Nothing except the wind," Officer Daniels said. "And the sound of three shots."

"*Three* shots? You're certain of the number?"

"I am. I know what I heard. And how many shell casings we found later."

Emily glanced at the puppet master. He was buffing his nails, as if this had nothing to do with him. But the smug look was gone. Good. She turned back, eager to see what Mr. Randall had up his sleeve next.

"I assume you found three casings?" the lawyer was saying.

"We did," Officer Daniels said.

"And what caliber were they?"

"The casings were Smith and Wesson .32's."

"I see," Mr. Randall said. "And what did Mr. Fairfield tell you had occurred that night, before you arrested him?"

"That he had intended to practice his shooting, using a log floating beside the dock as a target. And he said that the shot that hit Mr. Granville had accidentally misfired."

"I see," Mr. Randall said. "So that night, both parties agreed that Mr. Fairfield had fired the bullet that ended up in Mr. Granville's arm?"

"So they told me," Officer Daniels said.

"Did the gun confirm it?"

"It was a 32-caliber, recently fired. Which matches the shell casings we found."

"Was there other physical evidence?"

"We also found two bullets, buried in two of the wooden pillars that support the walkway," Officer Daniels said. "Both were found very near to the pool of blood marking where Mr. Granville was standing when he was shot."

"Could those bullets have been fired at an earlier time?" Mr. Randall asked.

"No. The bullet holes in the wood of the pillars were fresh, not weathered. And those bullets were .32's as well."

There was a collective gasp from the gallery.

"And the bullet that was removed from Mr. Granville's arm?" Mr. Randall asked.

"Also a .32."

"I see. So the gun would be a Smith and Wesson?" Mr. Randall asked.

"Not necessarily. There are a number of revolvers that use those particular bullets."

Emily watched in fascination as Mr. Randall nodded slowly, as if considering those facts. "As a serving police officer, you must be fairly familiar with guns," he said.

"I am."

"And have you ever known a gun to 'accidentally misfire' three times and yet hit so close to the same target?"

"No, I have not," Officer Daniels said decidedly. "In fact, I've seen men considered excellent shots with worse aim."

"Objection. Speculation," Mr. Fairfield's lawyer said.

The judge looked irritated. "Sustained. Ask another question."

"Of course." Mr. Randall paused, and gave the policeman on the stand a considering look.

Every eye in the room was on the two of them.

Emily was sitting forward on the hard wooden bench. Holding her breath. What would the lawyer ask next? And how was it going to play into Granville's plan?

"It was at this point you arrested the defendant, is that correct? Since you had already heard Mr. Granville's statement that Mr. Fairfield had attempted to kill him."

Another wave of hastily muffled sound ran through the gallery

"It is," Officer Daniels said. "Mr. Granville made that statement just before he collapsed from blood loss. Mr. Fairfield was then held until Monday morning, but no charges were brought by the prosecutor, so he was released."

"I see. And why were no charges brought?"

"After a conversation with Mr. Anthony Lloyd, acting as Mr. Fairfield's lawyer, it seems the prosecutor deemed the evidence we had collected to be insufficient for a conviction," Officer Daniels said.

Neither his face nor his voice conveyed any emotion, which impressed Emily. She was still fuming over the matter.

This whole farce of a civil suit should never have been necessary, if the prosecutor hadn't been, as Scott succinctly put it, 'a lily-livered coward'.

Mr. Lloyd sprang to his feet. "Objection. Hearsay," he said.

"Sustained," the judge said. "The jury will disregard the officer's answer."

They probably wouldn't, Emily thought, watching their fascinated faces. But would it be enough?

"I'll withdraw the question," Mr. Randall said to the judge, and turned back to Officer Daniels. "What did Mr. Fairfield say to you on learning he was being released?"

"That he was going to sue us for false arrest," the policeman said. "And he added that he was also going to sue Mr. Granville for libel. And bearing false witness."

"I see. Thank you." Mr. Randall turned to the judge. "I have no further questions, Your Honor. Though I may need to recall this witness at a later date."

The judge nodded, and looked to Mr. Lloyd. "Your witness. Do you wish to cross-examine?"

Mr. Lloyd stood to respond. "Not at this time, your honor," he said, and exchanged a look with his client. Both men looked pleased.

Emily sat back, feeling deflated. So far, Mr. Randall seemed to mostly have been making Mr. Fairfield's case for him. She just hoped his next witness would serve them better.

"I call Mr. John Granville," the lawyer said.

For a moment Emily was surprised he hadn't called Scott, then glanced at the man beside her. His blunt honesty might not play well with the strategy Randall seemed to be following. Plus she suspected that Granville would have refused to put any of the team on the stand, and risk making them a bigger target for the puppet master than they already were.

No, he'd take that risk on himself. He saw this as a showdown between himself and the puppet master. She suspected that the puppet master did so as well, judging by that note he'd sent.

Still, she wished Granville hadn't taken this particular risk. The puppet master was a dangerous opponent.

She sat forward again, her heart in her mouth, and watched as Granville took the stand and was sworn in.

6 2

W ith Granville on the stand, Mr. Randall wasted no time on preliminaries. "Can you tell the court why you brought this suit against the defendant?" he asked.

Granville smiled. "It's really quite simple. He shot me. Tried to kill me, in fact. And then he sued me for false arrest," he said. "This is my way of seeking justice."

"And yet the police haven't arrested Mr. Fairfield. Are you sure this upstanding citizen with his unblemished record attempted to murder you?"

Emily swallowed hard. Mr. Randall was still acting as if he was representing the defendant—Mr. Fairfield. And now he was treating Granville—his own client—as if he was a hostile witness. Mr. Fairfield was looking smug again.

Yet Granville looked unconcerned. "I'm sure," he said.

They were up to something, then, the two of them. Was this part of their plan? And for some reason Granville hadn't shared it with her, which hurt. Probably more than it should have.

Emily just hoped their strategy wouldn't end up helping the puppet master more than it hurt him.

She glanced at the jury. They were practically leaning forward in their seats. They weren't going to miss a word of this case. Which had to be good, didn't it?

"It seems there is no argument that it was a bullet from Mr. Fairfield's gun that ended up in your arm," Mr. Randall said, glancing across at the defendant's lawyer, who gave a slight nod.

Mr. Randall smiled, and turned back to Granville. "But there is quite a difference between an accident and attempted murder."

"I'm well aware of that," Granville said.

"The last witness testified that when the defendant began shooting, you did not call out to alert him of your presence on the dock below him. Is that true?"

"It is," Granville said.

"I see," Mr. Randall said. "And why did you not attempt to alert him?"

"Because he was trying to kill us. Me particularly. Calling out would only pinpoint our locations, and make his self-appointed task easier."

"I see," Mr. Randall said again. "What do you know about Mr. Fairfield that would lead you to believe he actively tried to murder you? And please remember you're under oath."

"Aside from the fact that Fairfield fired three times into the area of the dock in which my partner and I were standing?" Granville said. "Which was nowhere near the log he said he was using as a target."

The judge made a slight movement as if to protest. Mr. Randall glanced at him and said to Granville, "Yes, setting that aside. Please continue."

"And setting aside the threatening note he sent me, as well? Since he disguised his hand, which the prosecutor deemed made it impossible to prove the note came from him."

Judge Knight frowned, and Mr. Randall quickly said, "Yes, setting that aside as well."

"In addition to the threats Mr. Fairfield has made against my life and the lives of those I care about, including my fiancée,"—and here Granville paused to let the buzz of voices from the gallery die away under the bang of the judge's gavel, then continued. "And the knowledge of Mr. Fairfield's character I've gained through my investigations of his illegal business dealings..."

Here Granville again had to stop as the gallery erupted. This time the judge had to threaten to clear the courtroom to quiet them.

Emily had been watching the jury the entire time, trying to assess how they were taking Granville's testimony. Of the seven men, two looked uncomfortable. One looked like he wanted to turn to his neighbor and discuss everything that was happening. The other four were looking from Granville to Fairfield, with speculative looks on their faces.

She suddenly wondered if there were more rumors about Fairfield and his business methods. Ones their team hadn't been able unearth.

Granville had managed to get nearly everything they'd learned about the puppet master into a few sentences, leaving questions in the jury's mind that she hoped would be difficult for Fairfield and his lawyers to answer. After all, the puppet master was guilty of everything he'd told them.

Even if they didn't have any real proof of it. Nothing that the prosecutor would accept, anyway.

Which, come to think of it, was not so different from how she and Clara had used gossip to deal with Mr. Bray. How fascinating to see a courtroom serving the same purpose.

The defendant's lawyer was watching the jury as well. And seemed to have come to the same conclusion. The moment the courtroom quietened, Mr. Lloyd surged to his feet. "Objection," he said in a voice that carried. "This is hearsay."

Emily mouthed the words along with him, and Clara elbowed her in the ribs.

"Careful, or the judge will be throwing you out next," her friend hissed.

But Granville had been watching her too, and his laughing eyes sought hers. For a split second they shared a private joke. Which was worth being thrown out for, in Emily's opinion.

Luckily for her, though, the judge was frowning at Mr. Lloyd and paying no attention to the gallery.

Until Mr. Randall recaptured his attention. "Your Honor, my witness is testifying to the events that formed his knowledge of the defendant. And his assessment of the incident in question."

"I'll allow it. For now," the judge said. "But you're walking a fine line. Be careful, or I'll find you in contempt. Or worse. And Mr. Granville? Keep in mind that you are under oath."

Emily closed her eyes in despair for a second. How were they ever going to prove anything against the endlessly plotting puppet master with the judge stopping them all the time?

This was their best chance to take Fairfield down. And if they didn't succeed?

The puppet master wouldn't forgive Granville for this. And he'd focus all his complex schemes and resources towards getting his revenge.

She glanced over at Fairfield again. He was giving Granville a scornful and openly hostile stare. She looked from him to the judge, and shivered.

Could some of the proceeds from the puppet master's smuggling ventures now be lining the judge's pocket? Was that why he was being so difficult?

But that wasn't Judge Knight's reputation. And the man looked genuinely ill. Which made him unpredictable. It was just their bad luck that he wasn't ill enough to have cancelled court that day.

They'd have to find a way to outsmart the puppet master, even under these circumstances.

If only she were more confident it would work. She just hoped Granville wouldn't look her way and see her fears. She wanted to be confident for him, but for the first time she felt that confidence falter.

Not in him, not that. But in these circumstances? How could he— or he and Mr. Randall— possibly win?

"Thank you, Your Honor," Mr. Randall said, and nodded to Granville.

Who resumed speaking. "But none of these fully explain my conviction that last Saturday's incident was an attempt by Mr. Fairfield to murder me," Granville said.

"No?" Mr. Randall asked him. "Then what led you to believe that Mr. Fairfield would try to murder you?"

Emily held her breath. If she knew these two at all, this was the moment.

"I believe he's killed before," Granville said.

There was a collective gasp from the spectators, who had been watching avidly.

"And the witness to that murder told me that Fairfield enjoyed killing his poor victim," Granville added.

Emily's attention was fixed on the defendant as the smug look fell off his face. It was replaced with a flash of something dark and very angry, as Mr. Fairfield sneered at Granville. For a second she thought he was going to challenge Granville to prove it.

Instead he leaped to his feet. "That's a lie."

The judge looked pained. "Control your client," he snapped at Mr. Lloyd.

Who promptly stood up. "I object to this entire line of questioning. It is hearsay. All of it," he said.

Judge Knight glared from one lawyer to the other. "Mr. Randall?"

"My client is speaking to his own beliefs, and explaining why he holds them," Mr. Randall said. "Which is key to the case at hand, since this is a civil trial, and not a criminal one."

"You're treading a fine line. Watch yourself," the judge snapped. "And Mr. Granville? Need I remind you again that you are under oath?"

From his spot in front of the witness stand, Mr. Randall nodded. "My apologies, Your Honor," he said.

Emily could tell he was keeping one eye on the jury, while he waited for the until the noise from the gallery died down. It had to be clear to him that the jury was more forgiving than the judge at the moment.

When the courtroom was silent again, Mr. Randall looked back at Granville.

"That's a serious accusation," their lawyer said gravely. "I trust you have a serious reason for making it?"

"It is. And I do," Granville said.

"Go on," Mr. Randall said.

"You asked if I had reason to believe he's a murderer?" Granville reminded him. "I do. A man who witnessed Fairfield kill a business rival's employee recounted to me the details of that murder, in confidence. I have verified most of the details of that account, and I believe it to be true."

Mr. Lloyd was standing again. "Objection. This is still hearsay."

The judge was frowning at Mr. Lloyd. "I don't believe it is hearsay," Judge Knight said. "He's not repeating what he was told, he's relaying his own experience."

Judge Knight looked back at Granville. "That is what you're testifying to, is it not?"

"Yes, Your Honor. Exactly that."

The judge nodded. "Overruled. For now," he said. He looked from Mr. Lloyd to Mr. Randall, and then to Granville, looking increasingly irritated. "But you're all pushing the edge. I won't have it in my courtroom. Consider yourselves on notice."

"Yes, Your Honor," Mr. Randall said. "I'll abandon this line of questioning."

"Now, what of this man who saw this alleged killing?" the judge asked. "Why isn't he on your witness list? I'd like to hear from him."

"Because he doesn't exist," Fairfield said to his lawyer in a voice that carried to the back of the courtroom. Earning himself a glare and another warning from the judge.

But he couldn't very well throw the defendant out of court, could he? Emily wondered.

Granville waited for a moment, as if making sure that Fairfield wasn't about to interrupt again, before answering the judge. It was a nice touch, Emily thought, and she thought that the jury had taken note.

"The fellow fears for his life if he testifies against Mr. Fairfield," Granville said. "With good reason, in my judgement. He has declined to give his own name. And he flatly refuses to testify in a civil trial."

The judge frowned at that, and made a note on the legal pad in front of him. "Carry on," he said.

"I have three more questions for you," Mr. Randall said to Granville. "You were shot by Mr. Fairfield on Saturday night last. That fact is not in dispute. You have sworn that you believe he was attempting to murder you. Do you still stand by that?"

"Yes. I do."

Mr. Randall nodded. "Now, you are a very successful private investigator. I would assume that makes you very familiar with criminal behavior, up to and including murder, does it not?"

"It does," Granville said with a wry smile directed at the jury. "You might say it's my bread and butter."

There was a little ripple of laughter from the jury, though somehow that moment of levity only served to build the tension in the courtroom higher. Emily wondered if they'd worked this out beforehand, or if the two of them were just that good.

Mr. Randall paused only long enough to be sure everyone's full attention was back on his final question. "Given everything you have shared with this court about the defendant, including his alleged crooked practices and an alleged previous killing…" He paused, and looked from Granville to Fairfield and back, then glanced at the jury.

Emily was sitting on the edge of her seat, every muscle tense, as she waited to hear Mr. Randall's final question. She could tell that the jury was too. It was one of the reasons Mr. Randall was such an effective lawyer—he was a master at creating tension.

"Do you believe that Mr. Fairfield will attempt to kill you again?"

"Yes. I very strongly believe that," Granville said flatly.

Mr. Randall looked at Mr. Lloyd. "Your witness," he said, and strode back to his seat.

Mr. Lloyd considered Granville for a moment. Then he and his client exchanged glances. Finally the lawyer stood up to address the judge.

"I have no questions for this witness, since he clearly has no legal basis on which to base this fear he says he feels of my client," he said, sparking a little rustle of sound from the gallery.

The judge glared at them, and they quieted.

"Call your next witness," the judge told Mr. Randall.

"We rest our case, Your Honor," Mr. Randall said.

There were murmurs of surprise from the observers, and the judge banged his gavel hard until the room fell silent again.

"Mr. Lloyd?" the judge said. "Call your first witness."

———

FAIRFIELD'S LAWYER strode confidently to take his place in front of the judge. "I'd like to recall Officer Daniels," Mr. Lloyd said.

And then proceeded to grill the policeman on every detail of the shooting incident.

Emily found it at first tedious, and then unbearably boring, since Mr. Lloyd repeated every question Mr. Randall had asked. Since he didn't have Mr. Randall's sense of timing, it was a dull process, made worse by the extra questions he asked about the tiniest detail. She could tell by the juries wilted posture and wandering gazes that they weren't any more interested in this than she was.

Luckily for everyone, Mr. Randall declined to cross-examine this witness. But then Mr. Lloyd called Officer Jasper, the police officer who had been at the scene of the incident with Mr. Randall. And proceeded to ask him the same questions. In the same excruciating detail.

Emily half-expected to hear snoring from behind her when this farce was only half-way through. Especially since the heat had been slowly rising all morning, and by now the courtroom was unpleasantly warm.

The judge looked still more pained.

Again, Mr. Randall declined to cross-examine the witness. And the judge, mercifully, called for a half hour recess. There was a sigh of relief that seemed to come from everyone in the courtroom, and a stampede for the outer doors, and fresh air.

———

AFTER THE BREAK, Mr. Lloyd livened up the courtroom considerably by calling his own client to the stand. Emily could feel the surge of renewed interest flowing through the room. Every eye was on Mr.

Fairfield as he walked calmly up to the witness stand and took the oath.

Emily considered him with a critical eye. She'd met him before, of course, seen him at a number of parties and dances. But this was different. Especially now that she knew he was the puppet master.

And everyone in the court room knew he had to respond to Granville's testimony.

As she watched him, with every eye in the room on him and every person judging him, she could see the puppet master hiding behind the social mask. Now that she'd caught a glimpse of what hid behind that mask, she couldn't see anything else.

But she reluctantly gave him credit for how firmly he had that mask in place, even now. He sat quietly, waiting for his lawyer to begin. His expression was calm, even distant. He was very well groomed, but not someone you'd notice in a crowd. Everything about him appeared mild, unthreatening. Even humble.

A far cry from the furious anger she'd seen him display for that split second when Granville had pricked his vanity. She wondered if the jury had seen that moment. Probably not. Which was a shame.

And Mr. Lloyd would do everything in his power to cement that image of a tame gentleman who had been raised to the strictest standards, and had merely had an unfortunate incident with his gun.

Unfortunately for everyone in the room, Mr. Lloyd seemed to have a gift for making every question he asked unutterably dull. And tedious. He took his client through every detail of that incident on the docks, and Mr. Fairfield answered in equal depth. It made for a slow and painful process.

Emily wondered if the lawyer was just untalented, or if this was a deliberate strategy. Probably the latter, because Mr. Fairfield's responses, while affably delivered and seemingly genuine, lacked any trace of personality. They were almost as dull as his lawyer's questions.

Finally Mr. Lloyd reached the key question. "Did you shoot Mr. Granville on purpose?" he asked.

His tone made even that boring.

Emily frowned. That *had* to be deliberate. Fairfield could afford the best criminal lawyer in the city, and she suspected he'd accept nothing less. No lawyer had that kind of reputation if they couldn't grandstand with the best of them.

"As I have said all along, I absolutely did not shoot Mr. Granville on purpose," Mr. Fairfield said. "It was a misfire, as I have explained from the beginning."

He sounded slightly irritated and rather bored, as if this tedious process was simply not worth his time. Emily supposed that could be effective, if you were a gullible juror. She hoped none of them were.

"And do you wish Mr. Granville ill? Or worse, dead?" Mr. Lloyd asked.

"I do not," Mr. Fairfield said.

He was a good liar, she'd give him that. She couldn't read what the jury were thinking, though. They were still paying attention, though a couple of them looked like they were having difficulty staying awake. Though that might be the stuffy air and the building heat in the courtroom. Or sitting for so long on the hard wooden chairs that had been set up for them.

Finally the questioning ended, and there was a ripple of relieved sighs as Mr. Lloyd told the judge he had no further questions.

"Your witness," he said mockingly, looking across at Mr. Randall.

R andall stood up, and strode towards the witness stand. Watching his lawyer approach the puppet master, Granville let out the breath that it felt like he'd been holding since they first discussed this day. His plan had one major weakness—he couldn't be certain Lloyd would call his client as a witness.

But his gamble had paid off.

The puppet master watched Randall's approach with no expression at all. Watching him closely, Granville saw not the slightest flicker of anger. Fairfield had himself fully under control. But if anyone could expose the puppet master for what he really was, and do so in open court? It would be Randall.

And the lawyer didn't hesitate. "You testified a few minutes ago about the incident last Saturday, when you shot my client," Randall said.

"I did."

"Can you tell the court what kind of gun you were using at the time?" Randall asked. "I believe it was a 32-caliber?"

"Certainly. I was shooting the Forehand and Wadsworth hammerless revolver, with a double-action top-break. And it is indeed the 32-caliber model," Fairfield said easily.

"That model is one of their lighter guns, designed for concealed carry, is it not?"

"It is."

"And it is a seven-shot model?"

"It is."

"And have you owned that particular gun for long?"

"I have," Fairfield said blandly. If the lawyer's unusual approach worried him, there was no sign of it.

"Can you tell me when and where you bought that gun?" Randall asked.

"Certainly. I bought it from the manufacturer in Worcester, Massachusetts, perhaps four or five years ago. I was on a business trip to Boston at the time."

"Why did you buy the gun direct from the manufacturer? Worcester is not on any direct route to Boston."

"I object. Where my client chose to buy his pistol is hardly relevant to this lawsuit," Lloyd said.

Granville had the impression that Fairfield's lawyer was objecting more for form's sake than because he saw any real threat in Randall's line of questioning.

"The relevance will emerge if you allow me to continue, Your Honor," Randall said.

The judge looked between the two lawyers. He looked wilted in the heat, but his gaze was sharp. "Very well," he said to Randall. "Continue. But you'll need to prove relevance in short order. My patience is limited."

"Thank you, Your Honor," Randall said, and turned back towards the witness stand.

Fairfield answered without any prompting. "I am particular about my weapons, and I like Forehand and Wadsworth revolvers. Their factory made an interesting side trip."

"One that gave you a wide selection of choice from their various guns," Randall said. "And yet you chose the smaller, lighter model, that can be easily concealed. Why that one?"

"In my position, I occasionally require protection. The .32 is more than sufficient in those situations."

"Carrying a gun within city limits is illegal here," Randall pointed out. "Why did you choose to do so last Saturday?"

"I received, and have paid, the fine for my choice," Fairfield said.

"I am delighted to hear it," Randall said. "Please answer the question."

"Carrying my revolver for protection is a habit. And that part of town can be dangerous at night," Fairfield said.

Granville noted he still hadn't answered the question, but Randall didn't pursue it. The judge made another note.

"And why were you in that dangerous part of town that night?" Randall asked instead.

Fairfield shrugged. "I have a business trip planned shortly, to several coastal cities that do allow concealed carry. Places where I may need to use my revolver at night." He glanced at the jury and said—with a smile that expected to find agreement—"There are very few places hereabouts to practice one's shooting in the kind of low light, shadowy situations like that the deserted dock offered. I was taking advantage of that fact."

"I see," Randall said. "And it was simply unlucky that the docks were not deserted?"

"That's it," Fairfield said.

"So, to sum up, you shot my client by pure mischance," Randall said.

"Yes."

"You had no idea that my client was on the docks below you at the time?"

"None whatsoever."

"And you weren't aware that that my client and his partner planned to be there that Saturday night, watching the harbor for illegal shipments coming in."

"Now how would I know that?" Fairfield said.

"Please answer the question," Judge Knight said.

"No. I was not aware of that," Fairfield said, with painful politeness.

"No? Yet weren't those shipments your main reason for being there—and armed—that night?" Randall asked.

"I know nothing about shipments, illegal or otherwise," Fairfield said shortly. "My reasons for being there that night are personal, and private..." He stopped short, probably realizing he'd come close to contradicting his earlier testimony.

The judge scowled, and made another note. As Granville watched, several of the jury looked from the judge to Fairfield, then made notes of their own.

Fairfield was watching the lawyer carefully, and for a moment, Granville caught a glimpse of the puppet master glaring out.

It brought to mind a fencing match he'd once seen, with two equally skilled, highly trained opponents. Each slashing opening was met with a calculated defense. Sharp move followed by sharper counter-move as they took each other's measure. Randall and Fairfield reminded him of that match.

"I see," was all Randall said.

Leaving the jury thinking about the significance of the pistol Fairfield had carried. And what he'd really been doing on the docks that night.

Granville watched the seven faces, and thought the strategy had had an impact. But everything turned on how Randall handled the next bit.

Randall walked towards the jury stand, meeting the eyes of every juror as he did so. Then turned and faced Fairfield from there. "You say you've carried that gun for at least four years. Have you ever killed a man with that gun?" he asked.

The courtroom was utterly silent.

"Mr. Fairfield? Answer the question," the judge said. "And remember you're under oath."

"Twice," Fairfield said. "Both times in self-defense."

Granville watched the puppet master closely. Before he met the informant, he'd assumed Fairfield kept to the shadows, using other people as pawns to do his dirty work. Keeping his own hands clean.

The informant's story was the first inkling he'd had that Fairfield didn't avoid violence. Even liked it.

Now he was revising everything he'd assumed he knew about

the puppet master, and wondering just how many men the puppet master had really killed.

He had just admitted to killing two men. Which meant those deaths were on record, somewhere. And in Fairfield's name. He must have convincingly passed them off as self-defense, since Pinkerton's had no record of him.

Granville and Randall exchanged a quick glance. Randall had seen it too. But how was he going to take advantage of the moment?

"Did either of those shootings occur in Vancouver?" Randall asked, still standing in front of the jury box. Which forced Fairfield to face the jury as he answered.

"No. I told you, I travel on business, mostly to the States."

"And have you ever killed a man in Vancouver?" Randall asked.

"I have not," Fairfield said, talking straight to the jury now, his expression a nice mix of honesty and outrage.

The fellow was a good actor, Granville decided. Which was no surprise. He was the puppet master, after all.

And he'd just lied under oath. The jury might not have picked up on it, though several of them were giving Fairfield a wary look.

But the judge was frowning at Fairfield. He didn't look irritated any more. He looked intent, the look Granville's favorite dog had once worn when he caught the scent of rabbit.

Good.

"I have no further questions for this witness, Your Honor," Randall said.

———

As Fairfield stepped down from the witness box, his lawyer immediately recalled Officer Daniels to the stand. Which was a boneheaded move, though Lloyd had no way of knowing that, since his client probably hadn't been honest with him.

In fact, Lloyd was actually a better lawyer than he'd been giving him credit for, Granville decided. He might not have been in Randall's class, but then few were. But he didn't show any signs of the impact Randall's cross-exam must have had on his defense.

Instead, he launched into a grilling of the policeman designed, it seemed, to eradicate even the slightest question the jury might have about Fairfield. Unfortunately for him, Lloyd didn't know where the bombshells were hidden.

"So, Officer. When you arrested my client, what grounds did you have for charging him with attempted murder?" he was asking.

"The wound in Mr. Granville's arm. Mr. Scott's assertion that your client had been trying to kill them. The threatening note Mr. Granville had received. And the two other bullets found in the same exact area," Daniels said, ticking each one off on his fingers.

Granville nearly chuckled aloud as he noted the avid expression on several of the juror's faces. Lloyd also glanced their way, and from the way he rocked back on his heels, was beginning to realize his error.

"And yet this evidence was rejected by the prosecutor?" the defense lawyer asked, attempting to recover.

"Yes, as I testified earlier," Daniels said.

"Why did he reject your evidence?"

"I can't answer that, since I was not in that meeting," Daniels said. "I thought you were there?"

Lloyd's lips tightened as a stout juror laughed, hastily changing the sound to a muffled cough. "Were you told to drop the charges and release my client?"

"I was."

"Objection, asked and answered," Randall said. "And I object to this line of questioning, since it is surely clear, even to my learned colleague, that his client is not facing the Crown Prosecutor and a possible death sentence."

The judge frowned and made another note. "Sustained. Find another line of questioning."

Lloyd gave up. "Your witness," he told Randall.

Randall strode to the stand, and thanked Daniels for being there. "I do have several further questions," he said. "Though I'll try not to take us over the same ground we covered earlier."

The stout juror apparently found this amusing as well, but did a better job of stifling his laugh under a glare from the judge.

"Have you any unsolved murders on your books from the last four years, in which the deceased was killed with one shot from a thirty-two-caliber pistol?" Randall asked.

Officer Daniels looked surprised, but pulled out a battered notebook from his uniform pocket. "I can check. It will just take me a moment."

"Take your time," Randall said after glancing at the judge. Who nodded.

Daniels consulted the first few pages of his notebook, then flipped back and forth for a few moments.

He looked up to find every eye in the courtroom fixed on him, and blinked twice. Then said in a professional tone, "Yes. There are two unsolved murders where the weapon was a .32. In each case, the victim was killed with a single shot through the right eye," he said, and reeled off the dates and times.

"And what does that tell you?" Randall asked.

"That the shooter is an excellent shot. And he is likely to be left-handed. Because it's the more natural shot," Daniels explained.

Granville could feel the eyes of all six jurors on his injured right arm. Then they all looked at Fairfield. Who had just put down the pen he'd been using. And holding in his left hand.

Granville kept his face neutral with an effort.

"Are you aware of any solved murders over the last few years that fit this same pattern?" Randall asked, as if oblivious to the drama playing out around him.

"None. Most killers use a .38, or even a .44. And most take more than one shot, just to be sure their victim is dead."

"I see," Randall said. "Can you give us details of the two unsolved cases that you mentioned."

"Objection. He's fishing," Lloyd said.

"Overruled," Judge Knight said without even looking at him.

"In both cases, the victim was found dead in a deserted alley, not far from the docks. Both men had criminal pasts, and numerous enemies. We had no leads or obvious suspects in either case."

Which fit everything their informant had told him about the murder in Blood Alley, Granville thought with relief.

Randall thanked his witness. "I have no further questions," he said and strode back to take his place beside Granville.

Lloyd then called a series of character witnesses, most of them well-known businessmen who were also pillars of Vancouver society. Each of whom praised Fairfield's character and modesty while lauding his business vision and his contributions to local society.

None of whom had the least notion he was the puppet master.

It was dull watching, as each witness said virtually the same thing, and heartily denied Fairfield was capable of planning to kill someone. Lloyd's strategy was clear—create a glowing image of his client that would replace the accurate one Randall had presented to them.

Unfortunately for Lloyd, it wasn't working. The judge looked like he'd smelled something rotting. And the jurors?

Granville looked from face to face. Several were no longer even pretending to listen, others were frowning as they took notes. But the majority of them were fidgeting, and shifting uncomfortably on their upright wooden chairs.

As each witness finished testifying, Randall declined to cross-examine, to the visible relief of the jurors. Finally the defense rested, and Judge Knight called a half hour recess. "I'd like to see the lawyers in my chambers," he added.

Granville and Randall exchanged glances, and the lawyer shook his head. He didn't know what this was, either. And whether it was good or bad news for them.

As the courtroom emptied in a buzz of excited gossip, Granville collected Emily. If they hurried there was just time for a cup of tea.

"We need to be back in good time," she said. "I can't wait to find out what the judge is discussing with the lawyers."

6 4

As Emily and Granville paused on the courthouse steps, she slid a look at him. She couldn't tell if he were pleased or worried that the judge had summoned the two lawyers to a private conference.

"I haven't seen the judge demand to see both lawyers at this stage in a trial before," she said, keeping her voice low. "It this usual practice?"

"I don't believe so," Granville said. "Randall and I didn't have a chance to talk, and he's got the best poker face of anyone I know. But I was watching Lloyd, and he looked shaken for a fraction of a second."

"No wonder," Emily said. "He must be realizing now, if he didn't before, that he has a puppet master for a client. And that their case is in trouble."

He grinned at that. "I hope so. Now, would you care for a cup of tea?"

Tea sounded like heaven. "Have we time?"

He glanced at his pocket watch. "Only just. If you're up for a walk, Mary's will accommodate us."

After sitting still most of the morning, Emily could think of few things she'd like better. And so she told him. "But we need to be back in good time. I can't wait to find out what the judge is discussing with the lawyers."

He nodded. "I'll make sure of it."

"What do you think our odds are of winning?" she asked as they set out at a brisk pace. "Our strategy seems very much the stronger of the two, and Mr. Randall seemed confident to me. But then he always does."

"We still have closing arguments, and Randall excels there," Granville said. "It may depend on the judge, and how he chooses to advise the jury."

"And on what Judge Knight wants to discuss with the two lawyers," Emily said, smiling up at him as they reached the cafe.

"Which, judging by what we've seen from the judge so far, is likely to be explosive," Granville said.

EVEN GRANVILLE HADN'T EXPECTED the bombshell that awaited them when court reconvened.

"Did our strategy work?" he asked Randall in a hurried undertone as the two of them resumed their seats at the plaintiff's table.

"Better than we'd hoped. Judge Knight is insisting we call our informant," Randall told Granville in a hurried undertone.

"And Lloyd went along with it?"

"He didn't have much choice. His only other option was a mistrial. And the judge was clear that if he had to declare a mistrial, he'd insist the prosecutor arrest and try Fairfield for murder."

"How?"

"Knight is known to be a stickler for the letter of the law, and he has the bit between his teeth on this one," Randall said. "There aren't many lawyers in town who'll go against him then. Including our illustrious prosecutor."

"So what happens now?"

"We call our informant," Randall said. "Good thing you already have him on ice."

Granville pictured their informant, whom he'd paid to wait nearby, in case Granville needed him to "point out the killer" as the fellow put it.

"I need to stay anonymous, like," the fellow had said. "This is just confirmation that it's the right guy. But for what you're paying me, I'll hang around all day, if that's what it takes."

"He's going to refuse to testify," Granville said.

"Not in front of Judge Knight, he isn't. You don't dangle a murder witness in front of him, then say the fellow won't testify. Daniels has gone to collect our informant now. He'll arrest him if necessary."

"For what?"

"Obstruction of justice. Along with any other charge Judge Knight deems necessary to ensure he testifies."

"He'll just say I was mistaken. Or he was," Granville said. "Too dark, didn't see anything clearly, can't identify the killer, doesn't see him in the courtroom…"

"Leave that to me," Randall said with a dry smile.

THERE WAS a collective gasp from the courtroom when Randall called the informant to the stand. Granville smiled to see the jurors were sitting straight-backed and attentive, obviously determined not to miss a word.

There was some trouble getting the fellow sworn in, until he finally gave his name as Charlie Green, after further threat of incarceration from the judge. After one quick glance at the puppet master, Green was now sitting stony-faced on the witness stand.

Exactly the reaction Granville had feared. Green, more than anyone, knew what the puppet master was capable of.

He should have had more faith. Watching Randall cross-examine Green was like seeing a maestro at work.

"Can you tell the court what you witnessed on the evening of Friday, September 28 of this year?" Randall began.

"I can't rightly remember. It was some time ago," Green said, crossing his arms.

Judge Knight cleared his throat loudly, and Green gave him a wary look.

Had Green appeared before the judge in the past? Granville wondered. Probably so.

"Please remember you're under oath," Randall said. "You don't want your testimony contradicted by what others may testify regarding facts you may have told them. Not in this courtroom."

Green glanced at the judge again, then quickly away. A slight movement from the defense table had him looking at the puppet master. Sweat beaded on his upper forehead and his lips thinned.

Granville watched the interaction intently. Everything rode on this. Would Green's fear of the puppet master prove strong enough to trump his worry over whatever Judge Knight might do?

"It's a funny thing about a murder trial," Randall was saying thoughtfully. "It has all these repercussions, that don't seem obvious at first. Now, if someone happened to witness a murder, especially one where a killer who prefers to hide in the shadows is exposed for what he is? That killer loses much of his power. And the man who exposes him gains power in equal measure."

"Objection!" Lloyd sprang to his feet. "Counsel is testifying. And leading the witness."

"Sustained," the judge said with none of his usual irritation. "Ask a question, Mr. Randall."

"Yes, Your Honor," Randall said. Turning back to Green, he repeated his earlier question. "What can you tell us about that evening in Gastown?"

"Oh, that day," Green said. "Yeah, I do remember that day. I was thinking that was the Saturday."

"No, it was the Friday," Randall said. "What do you remember of that evening?"

Green straightened his back so he sat tall, and let his gaze sweep the packed courtroom.

Apparently he'd decided to embrace his new role, Granville thought with a spurt of amusement.

"I was out and about on my business. And I saw him,"—and he pointed straight at Fairfield—"murder a man. Shot him in cold blood."

Randall waited for the ensuing hubbub in the courtroom to die down before he asked if Green was sure. "It was that man? The defendant?"

"Sure, I'm sure. The light was just starting to fade. It was plenty bright. They were both out in the middle of the alley, no shadows or anything. And I'd been watching him for a while."

"And when you say the defendant shot the other man in cold blood? Could this have been self-defense?"

"Absolutely not."

"How can you be so sure?"

"Cause I'd been following him, the dead-guy-to-be that is, hadn't I?" Green said. "He was following the other guy—the defendant. Only the defendant spotted him and confronted him. They argued for a bit. The soon-to-be-dead guy was arguing, had his hands spread wide, when this guy—the defendant—pulls a gun from under his fancy suit-jacket and shoots him in the eye."

It took longer for the clamor of voices to die down this time. When it did, Randall hammered home the details. "What was the victim holding when he was shot?"

"Nothing. His hands were empty."

"You're sure? You could see him that clearly?" Randall asked, his eyes fixed on the witness.

"He had his arms spread wide, and his hands too," Green said. "You know the way these Italians do when they're arguing. The way this guy was waving his hands around, if he'd been holding anything, he'd have dropped it."

Several jurors were flipping back through their notes. Probably checking the dates from Officer Daniels' testimony, Granville thought. It wouldn't take them long to figure out that they matched.

"And did the killer hold the gun in his right hand? Or the left?" Randall asked.

Green squinted into the distance for a moment, as if he were picturing it. "The left," he said firmly after a moment.

"And the defendant shot the other man once through the eye, you say? Did it kill him?"

"What do you think?" Green said. Earning himself a glare from the judge.

"Yes, it killed him. Dead on the spot," the witness added.

"You're certain that just one shot killed him?" Randall said.

"Well, there was only one shot. And the guy wasn't moving after it. Or breathing," Green said. Apparently he was enjoying himself. "So yeah. I'm sure."

"Thank you, I have no further questions," Randall said. "Your witness."

Mr. Lloyd stood up, and strode towards the witness stand.

"He's trying to cow the witness," Randall muttered to Granville.

"Good luck with that," Granville said. "Green is all-in with turning this to his own advantage. Nicely done, by the way."

"Thanks," Randall said.

Lloyd hammered questions at Green, detail after detail, but couldn't manage to shake him on a single one. Finally he gave up, and Judge Knight thanked the witness, and excused him. He asked him to remain in the courtroom, however. Which, judging by Randall's expression, was unprecedented.

What was the judge up to now, Granville wondered.

After both lawyers had made impassioned closing arguments, he found out.

Judge Knight turned to Officer Daniels who was standing a little behind the defense table, and nodded. Daniels strode forward and clamped handcuffs on Fairfield. Ignoring Lloyd's protests, he told Fairfield he was under arrest for murder, and read him his rights in a voice that could be heard clearly by every person in the crowded courtroom.

With a nod the judge dismissed him, and Daniels resumed his stand against the wall.

The judge turned to the jury. "Members of the jury, you have heard both sides of this extraordinary case. Now it is up to you to reach a decision. In attempting to do so, I would ask you to ignore the unprecedented arrest of the defendant—he is accused of *a* murder, which has yet to be proven. A separate trial will determine his guilt or innocence.

However, that situation in no way implies that Mr. Fairfield attempted to murder Mr. Granville in the case we are trying here. I would ask you to take keep that in mind, and to focus solely on the facts as each side presented them when reaching your decision.

I will also ask you keep in mind that this is a civil case, and as such, does not require an unanimous verdict. A simple majority will allow you to decide either for the defendant, or for the plaintiff. You will also be asked to determine the monetary penalty, if any, that the losing party must pay. This penalty usually includes—but is not limited to—all court costs for both parties."

He went on at some length clarifying the jury's role and what was expected of them, before asking if they had questions. One hand went up.

"And if we find for the defendant?" the stout man asked. "Will that affect his upcoming trial?"

"It will not," the judge said. "That case will be decided on the facts as presented in that trial. Your job is to focus entirely on the facts presented in this one."

There were no further questions and the jury were removed to begin their deliberations.

Granville shook his head. "I don't envy them sorting this one out. How long d'you think they'll be out for?"

"With the information we managed to get to them?" Randall said. "Not long."

In fact, the judge was just about to clear the court when the guard came back and whispered in the judge's ear. Judge Knight looked surprised, then nodded. "Bring them back," he said.

EMILY WATCHED in fascination as the jurors filed back into the courtroom. She wasn't sure what she'd expected to see, especially after such a short absence. But she certainly hadn't expected the smug looks on all seven faces.

Behind her a clamor of voices rose, as the packed gallery reacted to this unexpected result.

She darted a quick glance at Granville, wondering what he made of it. But his face was inscrutable, even to her. Scott called it his poker face.

The jurors were quickly seated, and the bailiff called for silence. For a change, he was quickly obeyed. The court was deathly silent.

Emily found herself holding her breath as the judge considered the jury.

"Have you reached a verdict on all charges?" he asked them, his sharp eyes scanning the faces.

The one who'd been chosen as foreman—the thin one, she noted —stood up. "We have, your honor."

At these words, it felt to Emily as if the entire gallery drew in a breath.

"And on the charge of assault and bodily injury, what say you?"

"We are unanimous. We find the defendant guilty as charged, Your Honor."

Emily let out her breath in a rush, which seemed to echo throughout the courtroom. Though that could have been her own heartbeat, rushing in her ears.

They'd won. Granville had won. It was the lesser charge, but it was a start. And unanimous too. None of the jurors had believed the puppet master.

It meant there was a good chance he wouldn't be able to convince a jury at his murder trial, either.

It was only the furious beating of the judge's gavel that told her the noise she was hearing wasn't just her own excitement. The entire courtroom was in pandemonium.

And they hadn't heard even heard the verdict on the second charge yet. The judge hadn't forgotten though. He fixed the gallery with a gimlet eye until she couldn't hear so much as a rustle. It seemed the whole gallery was holding their breath as Judge Knight turned back to the jury foreman.

"And in the second charge, attempted murder? How do you find?"

"We find the defendant guilty as charged, Your Honor. And we are unanimous."

Emily couldn't believe what she was hearing. They were unanimous on attempted murder too? That was it. The puppet master was done for.

And from the grins on the jurors faces, they knew it too.

Unable to restrain herself, Emily stood up, and clasped her hands together. Only the sound of her mother's admonishing voice in her head kept her from clapping. It didn't stop half the gallery, though.

She'd been wrong to call it pandemonium before. This was pandemonium. The judge was banging his gavel, but she couldn't even hear the sound.

Eventually he gave up and sat back. He still didn't look well, but she thought he looked a little smug, too. Though not nearly as smug as the jurors.

She looked from them to Granville, who was shaking hands with Mr. Randall. Both of them were smiling. Somehow, they managed not to look smug, though she couldn't imagine how. As she was thinking that, Granville looked up. Catching her eye, he winked at her. So quickly that few would have seen it. It was just for her.

She looked across at the defendant's bench. Mr. Fairfield had seen it. He sat there in chains, exposed to the world for the blackguard he was. And she'd never seen such an open look of hate on anyone's face.

She swallowed hard, and looked away. Granville and Mr. Randall between them had succeeded in ripping away the puppet master's mask, showing him as the villain he truly was. He'd be spending the rest of his life in jail. And he knew it.

It was justice.

Finally.

"I still can't believe the verdict was unanimous," Emily said several hours later, taking a sip of the wine their waiter had just poured for her. "Granville won. And Fairfield has already been denied bail on the murder charge."

"I know," Laura said with a smile. "After all the dead ends we chased down. We were actually in the room to see the puppet master arrested and charged with murder."

From where she sat between Granville on her left and Laura on her right, Emily smiled at the familiar faces around the table. Each of them had a hand in this case.

And after the verdict had been handed down, Granville had invited them all for a celebratory dinner at Garrity's Steak House. He'd reserved the restaurant's back room before he'd even known how the trial would come out. It was the only space big enough to seat them all.

Emily glanced around the room. The entire team, plus a couple of reporters, a policeman and a lawyer, were clustered around a huge table, cut from long lengths of solid pine. The only one missing was Randall, who was still at the courthouse, but he hoped to join them later.

Even with so many people, the room didn't feel crowded—there was ample space to walk between the upholstered chairs and the wood paneled walls. Two multi-branched candlestick style chandeliers hung over the table, giving the big room some semblance of style.

They had already brought in baskets of freshly baked buns and little pots of just churned butter, filling the room with the smell of hot bread. And every time the door opened, Emily could smell steaks grilling. Her mouth was already watering.

Beside her, Laura took quick sip of wine, then drew in a shallow breath. Leaving Emily wondering what her friend was finding so hard to say?

And hoping she'd find the courage to say whatever it was.

"Is it selfish of me to wish that he'd been charged with smuggling and fraud, as well as murder?" Laura said at last, loudly enough for them all to hear. "Oh, I know it's the lesser charge. But we all worked so hard to prove just what the puppet master was up to. It's a shame to see it all go to waste."

She quickly looked down, as if embarrassed by the sound of her own voice.

"It wasn't wasted," Granville said. "Without all that work, without everyone following so many leads, we'd never have identified the puppet master. And it was only after we knew who he was that we found a way to get him put away. Hopefully for life, this time."

"Hear, hear," Scott said, and raised his glass. "A toast. To our team on this case, which is all of you here tonight. Without every single one of you, we'd never have pulled this off."

"Wait, wait," Emily said. "For this? We need champagne."

"Excellent idea," Granville said, waving over the waiter, who was standing at the serving station at the back of the room. Once two bottles of the finest had been uncorked and poured they all raised their glasses again.

Granville glanced at Scott. "To the team," they said in unison.

"The team," everyone said, their voices echoing in the nearly empty room.

Emily looked around her with satisfaction. They had done it. Against all the odds, they had not only found the puppet master, they'd put him in jail. On murder charges, which even a master plotter like him would have difficulty slipping out of. Wouldn't he?

She glanced at Granville beside her, and caught him looking at her, too. She smiled. "We did it!" she said.

"We certainly did," he said, and tipped his glass to her.

She clinked hers against his, and they both drank.

Emily savored the sharp-sweet flavor for a moment, wondering if it was the quality of the champagne that made it taste better than anything she'd ever tasted. Or if this victory was extra-special, and that was what gave the drink its extra zing.

"Do you think Mr. Fairfield will stay in jail this time?" she asked.

"I think he will," Granville said. "There's a fair bit of evidence that will stack up against him if they do a thorough investigation."

"You mean the evidence we found, don't you?" she asked.

"Yes. Daniels has already agreed to work with us to make sure that everything we've found ends up used against him."

"Good," she said. "Though murder might be enough to put him away for life, especially if they can prove he killed both of the men from the two unsolved cases. But I'd like people to know what he did. Who he really is."

"He'll hate that," Granville said.

"I know. That's the best part," she said.

"You're feeling bloodthirsty today."

"I really am. Do you think it's a flaw?" Emily asked.

She swallowed hard, lowered her voice, and confessed for his ears only, "As I watched the puppet master looking so smug in court, I wanted to shoot him myself. Putting him in jail didn't seem like enough."

"We have enough evidence to hang him," Granville said.

Emily nodded. "We do. And I fear I'm becoming bloodthirsty, because it comforts me to hear that."

"You aren't bloodthirsty at all. You simply have a strong sense of justice. And the more of the puppet master's machinations we uncovered, the clearer it was that he needs to pay for what he's done."

"Thank you," Emily said. "I needed to hear that."

At that moment, Clara tapped on her glass with her spoon. When she had everyone's attention, she raised her glass and said, "I have never had the pleasure of working with so many wonderful people. All of you deserve to savor this victory."

As everyone raised their glasses and drank, Clara blushed, which surprised Emily. Until she noticed that Tim's eyes were fixed intently on her friend. So there was still interest there, no matter how much Clara denied it. And wasn't that interesting?

"Well said," Mr. Draper said as soon as all the glasses were lowered. "A hearty well done is due to all of us."

"And especially to our leaders," Mac said. "To Granville and Scott."

And the glasses were raised again.

Then several waiters brought in their meals, piping hot and smelling like heaven, as far as Emily was concerned. They all ate well, and finished several more bottles of wine, and yet more champagne. By the end of the meal, everyone was sharing war stories of what they'd each been through, in trying to take down the puppet master.

Emily smiled, looking round the table again, and leaned a little closer to Granville. "You know what you've built here, don't you? You and Scott? This is a team that can take on any case, and win it for the good guys."

His eyes smiled at her and his lips quirked up, just a little. "You've been reading penny dreadfuls again, haven't you?"

She laughed, as he'd meant her to, and raised her nearly empty champagne glass. "To you," she said.

"And to you," he said, raising his own glass.

And in unison they drained their glasses.

LATER THAT EVENING, Granville walked Emily home through the dusk. She watched the lights along the pier glittering on the small waves as they made their way along the waterfront and sighed in content. "I can't believe it's really all over," she said. She tightened her fingers where they rested on his arm, and smiled up at him.

"And we both survived," she said.

"That we did," he said, smiling back. "Though it took what turned out to be an army to do so. Judging by the faces gathered around the table at dinner."

"The puppet master is in jail, and won't be getting out again. Mr. Bray has left town, and won't be back. So my sister is safe. The assassin, my third man, is also gone, and won't be back."

"Satisfactory all round, then," he said.

"Hmm." She slid him a sideways glance. "Except…"

He mock-rolled his eyes. "Now what?"

"Well, your poor house…"

"Our house, you mean?"

"Ummm, yes," she said, not about to touch that topic. "It has been neglected."

"Hardly. I have more workmen on the main floor of that house every morning than I did when the case began three weeks ago."

"Oh," Emily said. He hadn't mentioned that. "How very irritating that must be."

He just smiled at her.

"Never mind," she said. "Clara has finally found a decorator who understands her vision. Amazingly, he's someone both you and I like as well—which is probably statistically impossible, as Laura would point out."

He laughed, as she'd meant him to. "Your point?"

"Well, now things should go much faster on your renovations," Emily sat, and hid a grin as she watched his dawning consternation. It was satisfying to tease him, and see him speechless like this.

She should have known better.

"That's an excellent point," he said, after a moment. "The sooner the house is completed, the sooner we can be married. Now that your sister's marriage is no longer an issue, there should be no reason to delay our marriage. Should there?"

"Oh, but..." Emily began, caught left-footed by this sudden reversal. She'd been too busy—first in getting rid of Mr. Bray, and then in the hunt for the puppet master—to actually make any plans about their wedding.

"When are you planning to talk to your mother?" he asked with a sideways glance. "She shouldn't be able to protest too much, should she? After all, in dealing with Mr. Bray, you solved two pressing problems for her. Your sister's unfortunate engagement. And your Papa's equally unfortunate investment. Your mama is in your debt."

"Ummm," Emily said, taken aback by this view of events. "Well, I'm not sure Mama would see it that way..."

Though it might be possible to use this to her advantage. But it was all happening too fast. She'd not wanted to wait four *years* to wed Granville, but if he was expecting to wed as soon as the house was complete...

Her head spinning at the thought, Emily dragged Granville to a halt. "You can't mean it," she began. Then she saw the laughter in his eyes.

"Oh, you're teasing me," she said, and he grinned.

"Guilty."

She laughed, and gripped his arm tighter.

"We're both giddy," she said. "It's been a long, difficult few weeks. I'll be strangely glad to get back to normal."

"As will I," he said. "As long as normal isn't a wedding that is four years away?"

"I agree," she said. "And I will talk to Mama."

Soon, she promised herself. After they had both had a little time to recover from all of this.

"In the meantime, we both deserve a change," he said. "Perhaps we can take a day trip to Bowen Island on Saturday, and picnic on one of the beaches there, while the weather is still fine?" he suggested.

"I'd like that of all things," Emily said.

"It would be a perfect opportunity to discuss our wedding," he added.

"Oh, you," she said, feeling bold, stretched up to kiss him. It was one way to change the subject.

Though the picture of having coffee with him every morning in their own kitchen drifted through her mind. Maybe it really was time they wed.

If only to have at least a little time together that wasn't consumed by their next case. Whatever it might be.

AUTHOR'S NOTE

I hope you had as much fun reading this book as I did writing it! A note on the history:

The steamliner *Aorangi* was real and the British Royal Mail Service (RMS) ships served the run from Vancouver to the Far East for nearly two decades. The Canadian Pacific Railroad's *Empress* steamliners served the same routes, focusing on silk and tea, from the late 1880's to the 1930's, when the increasing use of the Panama Canal cut into their profitability and ended their run.

Smuggling heavily taxed or illegal goods to the United States was a favorite pastime on the west coast, from the opium smuggling that occurred in the first years of the twentieth century to the infamous rum runners of Prohibition days.

The depression of the early 1890's hit all of North America hard and Vancouver harder than most. The city has always had a boom and bust mentality in its real estate market, and that hasn't changed a bit. If anything, it's worse now that it was then. Hard to believe how little has changed in some areas, and how much in others

I'd like to thank the Vancouver Public Library Special Collections and the Vancouver Archives, the Royal British Columbia Museum and the Museum of Vancouver.

A number of historical works and on-line sites have also been invaluable to me—you'll find them listed on my website at: www.sharonrowse.com. And I'm always happy to hear from readers.

If you'd like to be the first to know when my next book is coming out, sign up for my newsletter (also on my website.)

www.ingramcontent.com/pod-product-compliance
Lightning Source LLC
Chambersburg PA
CBHW061341190726
48288CB00005B/1554